THE SECRETS OF THE FIVE RAYS OF LIGHT

Dino Diane's Adventures

The Secrets Of The Five Rays Of Light

A Quest To Find Joy

D. J. Kristoff

ISBN 978-0-578-90378-1

www.DinoDianesAdventures.com

"Falling in love with the Earth is one
of life's great adventures."
- Steve Van Matre

DEDICATION

To all those that I have loved along my
journey on this beautiful planet and have
shared the greatest adventure of all—*life!*

THE SECRETS OF THE FIVE RAYS OF LIGHT

FOREWORD

As an enrolled member of the Miami Tribe of Oklahoma (federally recognized), I was humbled and honored when DJ Kristoff invited me to review her manuscripts and the many references to several of the First Nations. She assured me she wanted precision and to show honor and respect to all Tribes while still allowing for fantasy when appropriate to her storyline. As a Faith Keeper, I was particularly careful in evaluating certain areas.

Diane's wonderful process of maturing in her own teacher preparation throughout the story adds dimension as valid as the truths revealed in the *"Five Rays of Light."* Often in Native ways, stories are and were the primary method of teaching, and this story is filled with intrigue and fascinating information for all ages.

As my own heart is touched by the severe abuse of our Mother Earth, the joy and hope offered here kept me eagerly enthralled and engaged in consuming page after page of beautiful verbal imagery.

I was deeply inspired by reading the book, "*I am the Fire Of Time*," by Jane B. Katz. I use this phrase regularly to describe myself when I speak or make presentations. I now pass this fire to Dino Diane. For I, as a First American Indian, pass the "fire" to all the new Native Americans born in this country, to care for Mother Earth's land, rivers, mountains, and wildlife.

Thank you, D. J. Kristoff, for this page-turning, spellbinding story filled with fact and wonder.

TERESA BRADSKEY
Faith Keeper, Miami Tribe of Oklahoma

PROLOGUE

O NCE UPON A TIME, before cell phones, before neon signs and endless lights, in a land where whirling winds carried red sands from arched canyon walls, dusting nearby juniper berries on their branches, Mother Earth stayed silent and watched. She watched as her Earth children grew and populated distant landscapes, filling her once-clear skies with dark, grimy soot, her rivers with chemicals and garbage, making war upon one another.

Always silent, ever still, she waited.

"Soon, Father Sun, soon. Our daughter is coming. I feel her presence once again upon the land," Mother Earth whispered solemnly, like a soft summer breeze.

"I feel her, too," he said, pondering. "How will we know her?"

"Her hair will be golden like your radiant orb, her eyes as green as the leaves on my trees, and her heart will be light with joy," she replied.

He smiled to himself, content with her response.

"Will she be open?" he asked, suddenly concerned. "Will she be ready?"

With a flutter of butterfly wings, Mother Earth shivered. "We shall have to wait…and see."

A dazzling summer sun reflected off the back and tail feathers of a soaring golden eagle as he circled high in a brilliantly blue sky—listening. The message received, he swooped down through ancient sandstone ledges and the rocky canyons of his ancestors to perch on a pine bough at the edge of a grassy meadow. His piercing, intelligent eyes glinted in the gleaming sunlight when, all at once, he was engulfed in a flash of tiny glittering lights that cascaded to the ground and disappeared.

Moments later an elderly man, slouched over with age, a long red shawl draped over his broad, gaunt shoulders, emerged from under the pine tree and walked briskly to his village, smiling slightly.

CHAPTER ONE

THE MYSTERIOUS MESSENGER

B illows of hot steam gushed forth from the tired train engine, anxiously anticipating another long journey. Misty white clouds tumbled hurriedly over each other as they flooded the platform, swallowing up all the dawdlers.

The train whistle blew its shrill announcement, as if saying, *Time to board!*

"I will *not* wear this stupid thing!" the girl roared defiantly, clenching her square jaw as she threw her bow-covered bonnet onto the dampened wooden planks. Grimacing, she stomped her resolve with her high-laced shoe, the latest fashion of the early 1890s. "I look so ridiculous in it, and I hate all these frills on this dress. Why can't I just wear my knickers to see Grandma and Grandpa in Phoenix?"

The girl cringed, regretting instantly that she had lost her temper as she watched her mother's eyes bulge and her thin lips quiver, mouthing words soundlessly. Her mother's hands began to tremble, and a slight twitch crept across her reddening face as she finally lost her patience and stormed off toward the terminal doors.

1

"Now, Diane," her father sighed, shaking his head. "You're twelve years old now, practically a young lady," he said, slowly picking up the bonnet and tucking it into his suit jacket. "Be patient with your mother. She just sees you a little differently than I do," he sighed again, gently gripping her shoulders.

"I know, Dad. I'm twelve and a half, nearly thirteen," Diane said breathlessly while she squirmed, awkwardly adjusting the frills on her dress. "I just want Mom to let me…be *me*. Why can't she understand that?" she pleaded, looking up into his compassionate brown eyes. "I'll never be her little girl who plays with dolls and loves to wear bows and frilly things." Her eyes brimmed with frustrated tears that she choked down and roughly swiped away.

Her father knelt on one knee and gave her a warm hug. Taking a handkerchief from his back pocket, he tenderly dried her eyes. He pressed the damp cotton cloth into her hand, gesturing for her to keep it.

"You know how proud I am of you—your grades in school and the way you can run a football." He chuckled at the fond memory of his daughter plowing through a defensive line of neighborhood boys. "But mostly, I appreciate your heart of gold. Remember, always do your best, and live each day to the fullest. If you can do that, you'll always be happy." He kissed her lovingly on the forehead.

"You know, your mother just wants what's best for you," he said, as he stood up and brushed the dust from his pants. "The world may not be so kind to a girl who can run through a bunch of boys and make a touchdown. People just aren't that understanding and accepting," he shrugged.

"Oh, Dad! Like you said, I'm almost an adult. I love my books now, so no more football for me. But I still dislike these frills," she said, smirking distastefully.

"My daughter, the bookworm," he said in disbelief. "It's important to have a little of both in your life. Balance, you know?" He then looked around them carefully and muttered from the slanted corner of his mouth, "If you don't tell your mother I said so, I think that stupid old bonnet looks pretty silly, too.

"Now, where's your brother? I'm counting on you to get along with him for few days. I've never seen two kids play so well together and then fight like cats and dogs," he chortled. "But in all seriousness, I *am* counting on you to watch out for him. He may be ten, but that's still young enough to get into heaps of trouble," he said, moisture glistening in his eyes. "Where is the little general? Benjamin!" he called out, concerned and clearly a bit annoyed. The Grand Central Station in Chicago was one of the largest in the world, and a young boy could easily get lost among its six train tracks and bustling passengers.

"General Nuisance!" Diane shouted, laughing at his nickname. "But Dad, really, he doesn't like to be called 'little,' and he *can* take care of himself."

"I suppose you're right; we are somewhat overprotective," he murmured. "But you two sure do have a way of getting into mischief." He stared at her with squinted, accusatory eyes and a raised eyebrow that revealed he knew who the ringleader was.

"All aboard!" squawked the tall, gangly conductor with the long neck as he hung by one arm from the train doorway. Dressed in his worn, black uniform with scuffed brass buttons, he looked a little like an ostrich with a protruding Adam's apple. His wiry brown mustache hid his quivering upper lip as he cawed out their departure.

He looks so odd, Diane sniggered, as she looked anxiously toward the terminal doors for her mother, still feeling the sting of regret. Hearing her father's shrill whistle, she turned and watched him gather their luggage under one arm, grasp a squirming Benji by the scruff of his neck with the other, and weave him along through a maze of chattering dawdlers scattered about the platform.

The scraping of heavy trunks dragged across the wooden planks and hauled clumsily up the metal stairs hurt Diane's ears. She clasped her white glove-covered hands to the sides of her head to shield them from the loud, scratchy noises. Her father nodded his head for her to join him as he made his way to the passenger car, where he set both a red-faced Benji and their luggage down on the first step of the doorway.

"Don't fret," he said, panting. "Your mother knows you love her," he added encouragingly, as if he were reading her thoughts.

Struggling to hold back her conflicting emotions, she slowly—reluctantly—climbed the stairs. Benji straggled behind her. Father followed with their two small suitcases as they made their way awkwardly down the crowded aisle to their compartment. Diane slid open the door, peered inside, and frowned. One bench was already occupied. Just as she was about to enter the cramped space, Benji darted up behind her, trying desperately to squirm past. They always fought over the window seat.

Diane doggedly stepped to the side, blocking him, and tossed her knapsack onto the bench in the corner under the sill, victoriously claiming possession of the prized seat. She grinned and patted a fuming Benji on the head, then took her place by the window, hoping to get a glimpse of her mother.

Her hot-tempered brother, being a tad short and scrawny for his age on account of the pneumonia that had nearly killed him when he was a toddler, plopped down beside her, deflated.

He glanced up at his sister, who was peering worriedly out of the window, and his expression turned from miffed to curious. With his fresh summer crew cut, his brown saucer eyes seemed huge and penetrating under his light eyebrows, which were furrowed with concern.

"She'll be fine," Father said in a hushed tone to Benji as he loaded their suitcases onto the overhead rack. He knew as much as Diane teased his young son, Benji was a very sensitive boy who adored his older sister and clearly saw the expression of regret and worry on her face.

Their train whistle blew for the last time, its pistons hissed, and the train jerked to life as their father gave them both a hurried hug and stepped out of the passenger car, its wheels slowly grinding and screeching on the metal rails.

At once, bursting from the decorative waiting room doors, Mother came running. The bun twisted on the top of her head, bounced in sync with the bustle of her dress as she scuttled across the platform. The coal-powered train strained and chugged, gaining speed as it started to pull away, sputtering and jilting down the tracks.

Running as fast as she could in her long, slender dress toward the escaping car, her mother saw Diane in the window frantically waving her hand. Diane removed her white glove and pressed her bare hand to the window as her mother, now panting and sweating, approached the car. On her mother's face, Diane read disappointment, yet in her soulful, brown eyes, she saw only deep love. Her mother removed her glove, too, then pressed her hand against the glass, covering Diane's.

With one last jerk, the train rocked the passenger car hard, and their hands fell away. Standing at the end of the long platform, Mother pressed her forefinger to her lips, and tenderly blew a loving kiss goodbye, then placed her trembling hand over her heart. A gust of wind suddenly swept her mother's loosened hair across her face, and she faded from sight, swallowed up in the billowy clouds of steam.

Diane pushed guilt and remorse down her throat as she swiped at the tears that had begun to dribble down her cheeks. She sighed, telling herself for the umpteenth time that she'd be more considerate when it came to her mother's sensitive feelings, and not allow her desire to be independent to have so much free rein. Still, as she sank back into the worn leather seat, her heart began to beat heavily with excitement for the days ahead.

She gazed out the window as the only world she knew flashed by. Reaching up, she released the locks and slid the window down, allowing the cool summer breeze to rush over her face. Even in these wee early morning hours, Chicago's narrow, cobblestone streets, lined with two-story bungalows, were filled with horses and buggies and the tired buzz of last night's gossip between passersby.

Sleepy-eyed farmhands driving horse-drawn carts full of fresh produce yawned and shouted, "Fresh vegetables here—tomatoes, cabbage, and cukes!"

She spied a milkman slowly trudging up the stairs to a neighborhood porch, his arms heavily laden with a metal container of glass milk bottles, while the knife sharpener pushed his rickety cart and called out, "Knives and scissors sharpened today!"

These familiar sights and sounds began to vanish away, replaced with open green fields and patches of woodland that stood as isolated islands among the cornfields of the Midwest.

"What's wrong, Di?" asked Benji, still frowning as he tugged on her lace-lined sleeve. A deep furrow creased his forehead.

"Nothing," she said moodily, her heart still aching with regret over how she had left things with her mother. Her brother knew her well and obviously sensed the turmoil beneath the surface.

Shaking her head, as if to clear her thoughts, she turned her focus to her immediate surroundings. The beautifully polished wood panels gleamed while the railings and brass fittings sparkled in her cramped compartment for four. Opposite her sat an elderly couple. The old, haggard woman sat deep in her cushion, crumpled over with age. Her rounded, plump face bore an ugly wart on the chin, while the rumpled buns of gray hair stacked on the top of her head reminded Diane of old, moldy doughnuts.

Ugh! she shuddered, dismissing any ideas of exchanging pleasantries with them.

"Let's go find the dining car," she whispered to her brother, reaching to yank him by the elbow just as he was about to say hello to the saggy old couple. Benji shot up, as if stung by a yellow jacket, to which he was highly allergic, and, nearly tripping over the old man's scuffed black shoes, dashed out of their car. Smirking, she watched him race to win the prized seat next to the window.

Diane made her way hastily through the crowded, chattering aisles from car to car until she found the dining car and plopped down into a worn, wooden bench next to a beaming Benji.

"I'm hungry," she said, licking her lips. Ignoring her brother's obvious satisfaction, she disdainfully flattened the disheveled ruffles on her dress. Feeling somewhat content, she whisked a few strands of hair behind her ear.

"Me too!" squealed Benji as he picked up one of the small paper menus on the table. "What should we have for breakfast?" he asked, as he scanned all the traditional breakfast items.

As the steward approached their table, Diane's eyes fell from the "Entrees" of bacon and eggs to the "Beverage List,"

7

and she immediately announced with a hint of grown-up sophistication, "I'll have a large chocolate malt, please."

"I'll have one too," chimed in Benji, grinning from ear to ear. He leaned in and mumbled, "Mom would have a fit, Di!"

With their frothy malts in front of them, Diane eagerly took a long, delicious sip.

"Mmm, mmm, MMM," she sighed, shutting her eyes in rapture.

Benji looked at his older sister quizzically. "Why do you do that?"

"It just tastes better somehow," she said, sighing again.

Benji was so tickled he could hardly sit still. He positively wriggled in his britches over his most unusual breakfast. Laughing, he snorted jerkily, causing foamy bubbles to emerge at the surface of his malt, making a brown froth that boiled over the rim of the tall fountain glass. Diane shook her head at his childish antics, but soon joined in on the new discovery. The two of them became gleefully consumed in chocolatey laughter and joy.

Their hearts lightened, they looked out the window and sighed audibly as a new feeling swept over them—the wondrous sensation of freedom.

With the last, lingering sips of their malts, they sank back into the bench, utterly content, with almost drunken smiles on their faces. In minutes, Benji dozed off, his head rolling slightly onto Diane's shoulder.

Annoyed, she fussed, "Hey!" as she bumped his head upward with her bony, hard shoulder. "I'm not your pillow." She stood up, and seeing only a few people still left in the dining car, muttered, "I'm going to find the ladies' room." With that, she headed briskly down the aisle.

As she walked past the double doors to the train's kitchen, she heard the haggard old woman from her compartment shouting shrilly at the chef, something about the lumps in the gravy and telling him how to fix it. The red, puffy-faced chef raised his rolling pin over his head and shook it violently at her, pointing his flour-coated, bony finger toward the doors.

"Get out of my kitchen!" he scowled angrily at the old woman as Diane scuttled by the doors. Chuckling to herself, she continued her search for the elusive ladies' room.

Upon her return to the dining car, Diane heard the old woman arguing once again, this time with the gangly conductor, about an extra pillow. Peering through the small window in the car door, she noticed Benji had fallen across the bench and was sleeping soundly on his arm, which hung straight into the aisle, obstructing the passengers' way. Diane hurriedly opened the door, and as she took a step inside, she saw the old hag lean over him. Grimacing, she watched in surprise as the wrinkled woman retrieved a small pillow from the rack above the bench. Then, along with another pillow offered by the nervous conductor, she tenderly placed them both beneath the sleeping boy's head. Gently moving his arm to his side, she patted Benji lightly, and slowly turned and smiled warmly at Diane.

A mysteriously radiant young woman in a forest-green dress with a bladed hem, like the serrated edge on a leaf, sat solemnly at the counter—watching. The woman's long, wind-swept hair reminded Diane of a field of dried grasses at the end of autumn; light yellow, dark gold, and muted shades of brown all woven together. Her soulful hazel eyes, crystalline facets of green flecked with golden caramel, glittered with wisdom beyond her years. She flashed a dazzling smile that swept through Diane like a soft summer's breeze and warmed her heart like the rays of the sun.

As if reading her mind, she said tenderly to Diane, "Don't

let looks deceive you, young lady. Look deep inside people to see who they *really* are, and have compassion. You'll discover wondrous things when you do."

Diane's slender face blushed beet red as she felt the woman's words touch deeply inside her. *How did she know what I was thinking?* Stunned, Diane knew the woman spoke the truth, and she felt ashamed for judging and dismissing this old, kind woman. *After all, she can't help the way she looks,* Diane pondered, her heart aching with embarrassment. Had she shown her just a little bit of kindness and respect, she would have discovered the old woman's warm nature.

"Thank you," Diane said faintly to the wise woman, who seemed to radiate an aura of soft green light around her.

"Life is rich with experiences and lessons to learn," the woman said softly. "You've just learned a very important one: *have compassion, and let kindness always be your first impulse.*"

Diane glanced at the old woman, and a warm feeling flooded her heart. When she turned to the beautiful woman again, she had vanished—a few tiny glittering lights flashed momentarily in her place, then faded away.

How strange, she said to herself, blinking her eyes in disbelief. Just then, she noticed a curled piece of parchment on the counter where the mysterious woman had sat. Diane slowly walked over to the counter and picked up the parchment. Her mouth fell open, and her eyes bulged. It had a written message addressed to her.

Diane, seek first the mysteries of the ancients, then the riches of Cibola will be laid before you. M.E.

Utterly bewildered, she gingerly rolled up the parchment and tucked it into her pocket. *How did she know my name?* Diane reflected.

Hurriedly, she woke a sleeping Benji and dragged him groggily to their cabin. "Whew! We're alone. Wake up, Benji, wake up!" she squealed, shaking him.

As he rubbed his tired eyes, Diane excitedly rummaged through her knapsack and pulled out a book she had packed for the long trip. Frantically, she flipped through the pages as an awakened and curious Benji scooted closer to her side, peering over her shoulder at the pages that quickly flashed by. She stopped at a page and stared down at the bold, black letters.

"Look, Benji," she said hushedly, running her fingers over the words as she read them quietly out loud, "Seven Lost Cities of Cibola."

Completely perplexed, Benji shrugged and closed the book to see the title, *Legends of the American West*, and then turned back to the page Diane held with her finger. His big brown eyes looked up into hers, questioning. She then slowly pulled out the rolled parchment from her pocket and told him the story of the mysterious woman who had vanished, leaving the message behind.

She handed the parchment to him. When he had finished reading the short message, he asked, "So, what's in Cibola, Di?"

"Gold," Diane said keenly, a glint of mischief in her eye.

CHAPTER TWO

STOP AT DURANGO

I t was dusk of the second day aboard the train when it slowed, chugged, and rumbled into Durango Station. An orange glow on the horizon deepened into midnight blue as a few stars began to twinkle overhead, lost suddenly in the misty, hot steam exploding from the engine. The day had started out quite uneventfully as Diane and Benji peered aimlessly out the train's window at the endless landscape.

Benji fiddled with the pocketknife he had tucked in his pocket, annoying his sister. They gazed at the neat rows of cornfields with their golden tassels blowing in the wind as they gradually gave way to dry grassy prairies, finally spreading outward into the expansive cattle ranches of Colorado.

But, as the landscape had changed, so had Diane's mood. Her face had lit up brightly, watching the prairie dog towns that dappled the open grasslands along the track. She'd pointed out to Benji a sentinel guard dog that stood tall on its mound, chirping a warning as a stalking hawk flew overhead. Alarmed by the sentinel's signal, dozens of dog-town members immediately scurried into their safe burrows underground, where they waited patiently until the sentinel chirped once again, signaling that the coast was clear for them to resume their daily routines. Diane had delighted in making her brother laugh.

The highlight of the day had been witnessing a mother cow give birth to a calf under the shade of a spreading oak tree. They just happened to see the last moments of the mother's final push to expel her young one into its new world. It was a fantastic sight to behold, something neither of them had ever experienced in the suburbs of Chicago. Here in Colorado, though, the world was all new, fresh, and terribly thrilling for the blossoming adventurers.

The sprawling cattle ranches had transformed once again into green foothills, and then into the rugged ridges of the Rocky Mountains, still capped with glistening white patches of snow that resisted the warming sun of early summer. Diane had never seen mountains before and was awestruck when she saw her first herd of elk in the emerald-green meadow below the railway. Clear mountain streams and twisting rivers rushed past the train as it chugged its way through the valleys between the towering peaks, and she was thrilled when she spotted a young deer taking a long drink before it scampered off into the bush, startled by the sound of the train's whistle.

Her heart was light and flooded with excitement, experiencing all this natural beauty. She had lived her whole life in the cobblestone world of crowded, brick bungalows. Now the world was myriad shades of green, filled with tall forest trees, wild animals, raging rivers, and mountains taller than any building she'd ever seen in Chicago's burgeoning skyline.

"Tell me about Cibola, Di," Benji pleaded as he turned his gaze from the window to the treasured book in her lap. The elderly couple had returned early the night before, interrupting their secret conversation. Retrieving their luggage from the overhead rack, they shuffled from the compartment to disembark in Durango.

Smiling kindly to the old woman as she shut the car door, Diane opened the book to the page with the folded corner and read in a haunting voice, "Spanish tales told by four shipwrecked survivors from the failed Narvaez expedition of 1527 rumored of legendary cities of gold scattered across the Southwest territories of the recently discovered New World. The survivors, including a Moroccan black slave named Estebanico, claimed to have heard stories from the native peoples they encountered of cities to the north with great wealth and untold riches.

"Having recently conquered the Aztec in Mexico, plundering their temples filled with gold, the Spanish lust for the precious metal prompted another expedition to the New World with a Franciscan monk, Marcos de Niza, as the leader and Estebanico as the guide. The black slave was regarded as an intelligent, educated man who presumably spoke several languages and had acquired an extensive knowledge of the wilderness and the ways of the native..."

Just then, the train's whistle blew shrilly, announcing their arrival as the brakes suddenly clamped down on the metal wheels, causing their car to rattle and rock. The train screeched to a final stop at a small station made entirely of hand-carved wooden planks.

"Golly gee!" Benji gulped as the gangly young conductor came into their compartment. Exasperated, Diane quickly closed the book and shoved it back into her knapsack.

Adjusting his bow tie, the conductor nervously waggled his finger across his mustache, and stiffly staring out the window, formally announced with a stuttered crack in his voice,

"F-folks, we have a two-hour b-b-break at this s-s-stop to load supplies and additional c-cargo. You're welcome to exit the t-train and explore this western t-town of Durango. You'll find great food and s-s-spirits at Jake's Saloon, just a short jaunt from the station. Be back promptly in two hours as the train will depart at 8 p.m. sh-sh-sharp."

He glanced sideways at Diane and Benji and raised his wiry eyebrow. "You two s-s-stay close to the train. Your f-father asked me to keep an eye on you," he said curtly. Then, seemingly noticing the pained expression of disappointment on Diane's face, he added, a glint in his beady eyes, "Oh, all right, have yourselves a sarsaparilla at Jake's and then come back pronto. No v-ven-venturing off."

"Come on, Benji," Diane said hurriedly, grabbing her knapsack. She flung it over her shoulder and pulled her brother by his shirt collar. "Let's go exploring!"

"What about Cibola?" Benji cried out, frustrated by the interruption—again.

Diane shrugged, and Benji gasped as they stepped off their train and into a strangely unfamiliar, yet wondrous world.

"Later," she murmured, glancing down at Benji.

Nestled in the heavily forested terrain of the San Juan Mountains, Durango was known for its timber, gold, and silver mines and got its name from its territorial governor A. C. Hunt, who had the notion that the region looked a lot like Durango, Mexico, which meant "well-watered place." A perfect spot for Jake's Saloon.

The streets were filled with large sweaty horses ridden by worn, ragged mountain men draped in deerskin pants and beaded overshirts lined with bear and fox fur. Raccoon-skin caps like Davy Crockett's completed their striking wilderness outfits.

Proud Indian men of the Ute tribe, wearing breechcloths and leather leggings made from dyed deer hides and bone-threaded breastplates over their buckskin shirts, sauntered in front of the women draped in long deerskin dresses fringed with beads, shells, and elk teeth. Some were barefoot, while others wore sandals made from yucca fibers. Most trudged along in buckskin moccasins with heavy wrapped bundles on their backs, heading to the town's trading post. Diane goggled for a brief moment at the unusual facial tattoos painted on the Ute warriors, then quickly turned her eyes away, blushing.

Gunslingers wearing long black dusters and ten-gallon hats with pistols holstered to their bullet-studded belts moseyed along on horseback. Rickety old wagons overloaded with supplies for digging rolled by as tales spread like wildfire of new finds in the mountains nearby that were filled with veins of silver and gold. Dirt-covered prospectors ambled along the creaking wooden boardwalks—everyone headed toward Jake's Saloon.

This was the Wild West that Diane and Benji only read about in their schoolbooks. They stood in the dirt street, transfixed at the sight of it all, their mouths gaping open in utter amazement. Diane adjusted her knapsack on her shoulder, brushed a few stray hairs from her face, and grasped a gawking Benji by the arm. Together, they blended in with the other passengers bustling through the crowded streets toward the popular watering hole.

As she took it all in, Diane noticed a lanky, brown-haired teen wearing reddish-brown deerskin pants, black boots, and a tan shirt with big billowy sleeves—like a pirate—leaning against the wall of the saloon. A beaded Indian necklace hung low on his chest, and he wore a raccoon-skin cap with a long, striped tail. He was staring with interest at two younger boys who were skulking along the side of the large fountain in the town square before them.

Diane watched as the two youngsters, who were both about Benji's age or perhaps a year younger, surreptitiously poured something into the fountain and then silently crept away. Immediately, the fountain exploded into foamy bubbles that rose to the rim and overflowed into the street, making soupy puddles of brown, foaming mud.

The older boy who had been watching fell on his back, laughing and stamping his boots, until a big, burly mountain man stomped flat-footed out of the saloon and growled something in a foreign language at the youth, who now lay cowering beneath him in the dirt, trembling. The big man kicked at the frightened youth before he yanked him up by his ear and dragged him through the street.

"Papa, *laissez-moi*! Let me go!" the boy screamed, squirming violently until he finally broke free from his father's drunken grip and dashed down the dark alley behind the saloon.

Diane watched as the angry man swayed and slowly staggered in the street toward a hitched horse. He clambered onto the worn saddle, slapped the reins hard to his horse's flanks, and rode off, dangerously listing to one side. She shuddered and yanked Benji by the arm. "Come on, let's go!" she said as she pulled him into the cluttered alleyway. There they found the boy huddled in the shadows, hugging his legs with his head buried in his arms.

"Hello," she said softly, "Are you alright?"

He lifted his head slowly, his cheeks blotched with tearstains as he peered out from beneath his coonskin cap, dabbing his brown-crystalline eyes with the sleeve of his shirt.

"*Ça va!*" he said in a voice that Diane did not expect. It wasn't the deep voice she had heard in the street, but to her surprise, a higher-pitched voice with a slight French accent. He, she suddenly realized...was a girl, just a few years older than she.

"Who are you?" Diane gasped, dumbfounded.

Regaining her composure, the girl quickly swiped away the moisture from beneath her eyes.

"*Je suis*...hmm ...I am Lee Planchet," she said, with great confidence and a smattering of flair. "Greatest fur trapper in all the West," she added as she jumped up and stood with her feet squarely planted, her head held high, fists thrust onto her hips. "Well, at least my papa is, anyway," she muttered.

"Why are you dressed like a boy?" Diane asked, perplexed.

"My papa has no sons, only three daughters. I'm the middle one and the *only* one brave enough to go with him on his trapping expeditions. *Ma mere* and my two sisters are still back home in New York," she sighed, tonelessly.

"So, why dress like a boy?" Diane repeated.

"My papa said that the West was too wild and dangerous for a young woman. He wanted to hide my identity to keep me safe," she replied, with a note of resentment.

"But he's so *mean* to you."

"Only when he drinks," Lee said bitterly, sighing. "Which seems to be all the time lately. He said it would toughen me up to face a harsh world. I've had enough of traveling. I miss my family, and I'm sick of killing these innocent animals." She sighed deeply again before leaning forward and asking, "Can I trust you with a secret?"

"Of course," Diane answered, intrigued. "I love secrets."

Lee lightly tapped her raccoon cap, and Diane saw something suddenly move among the fur. She could hardly believe her eyes. As the fur parted, a little black nose with two button eyes in a banded mask peered out at her, blinking.

"*Ça va!*" Lee said to the baby raccoon that climbed out of

the secret compartment and crawled onto Lee's extended hand. "This is Niki," she said. "She's what changed my mind about trapping." The baby raccoon made funny clicking sounds and sat up on its hind legs, looking curiously at Diane and Benji, pawing the air as if waving a greeting.

"Gee whiz," giggled Benji.

Diane listened as Lee told her the raccoon's story. Every morning, Lee checked her father's traps to see what they had caught overnight. When she came upon the trap around the tall pine tree, she heard the panicked chattering sounds of a very tired, very frightened animal. She immediately saw two scared, masked black eyes looking out from beneath the pine bough they had used to camouflage the trap. The eyes cried imploringly for mercy with such a pitiful look, they pierced Lee's soul. At that moment, she noticed five other pairs of smaller eyes staring at her. They had snared a mother raccoon with her young still clinging to her underbelly.

"I just couldn't kill her, knowing all those babies would die if left alone to fend for themselves," she recalled with a tone of sadness in her voice. Her brown, clear eyes grew warm as she sighed, "So, I let her go. At first, she stayed still, trembling, and wouldn't move. Then, she darted for the woods with her babies clinging on for dear life. This little one fell off and rolled under a bush," she said, sadly.

"She was still dazed when I picked her up. We've been best friends ever since. She lives under a flap I sewed into the top of my cap to keep her safe—and a secret. Today, Papa found out about her and gave me a day to get rid of her, but I just can't. She'd perish in the woods without me. She's still too young!"

"May I pet her?" Diane asked.

"*Bien sur!*" Lee responded. "Of course!"

Benji shifted, annoyed that his sister got to pet the baby

raccoon first, "I'm thirsty," he grumbled. "I'm going to drink me a sarsaparilla in the saloon. Is that all right with you, sis?" He asked, sarcastically.

"Sure," Diane said, scratching the tiny ears of the baby raccoon, ignoring Benji's sulky pout. "But keep an eye out for Lee's papa," she warned.

Benji strolled off, shuffling his feet, and disappeared around the corner in a cloud of yellow dust. Diane continued to talk with Lee and pet Niki, captivated by her cute antics and tiny little paws. A short time later, Benji came running around the corner of the saloon, his eyes wild with excitement.

CHAPTER THREE

SADDLEBAGS OF GOLD

D arting from around the corner of the saloon, Benji slid into the dusty alley, stumbled awkwardly, falling face-first in the dirt at Diane and Lee's feet, panting hard.

Just then, someone lit a lantern in the room behind them inside the saloon. Beams of dim light seeped into the shadowy darkness of the alley. Benji quickly got up, brushed the dust from his dungarees, and held a finger to his lips. Diane and Lee went silent as they heard muffled voices from the other side of the old, flimsy wall. The three of them pressed their ears against the cracks between the slats of wood, straining to listen.

"I tell you," a deep voice said gruffly, "there's easy gold waiting for us in those mountains just beyond the town."

"How'd ya know it's easy gold?" guffawed another voice stupidly. The tone was high-pitched, scratchy, and loud.

Diane held her hands over her ears, wincing at the sound of it. But only for a moment.

"Shhh!" warned the gruff voice sharply. A slap echoed in the musty room, followed by a thud and a sudden yelp of pain.

"I just had me an interesting conversation with a scruffy old prospector that wandered into town this afternoon. Cost me a bottle of Red Eye, but he was boiling about something and itching to tell, I reckon. He spouted off about finding a prospector's bony skeleton next to the moldy, rotted carcasses of three dead mules, up in a box canyon with saddlebags stuffed with gold nuggets still strapped to their decaying bones," he pounded the table, cackling. "The drunken old buzzard told me he gathered them up and hid them in an abandoned mine east of the Silverton mining camp," said the man in a snarly tone.

Benji excitedly nodded his head up and down, confirming the story. "I heard it all waiting for my sarsaparilla," he said, gasping for air.

"That's Ramus Thorn," muttered Lee. "He's the mean one, about ten years older than me."

"The old fool," grouched another man with a low, gravelly voice. "Did anyone else hear his tale?"

"That's Ramus' younger brother, Wadey," Lee spoke loud enough for Benji to hear, too. "Oh, is he nasty!"

"Just a kid, maybe, standing at the bar nearby," Ramus continued with a cocksure smirk. "Anyway, the old coot drank too much of that Coffin Varnish and suddenly dropped stone-cold dead on the saloon bar. It was quite an afearing sight. I moved away so quickly, I nearly fell over the kid, who high-tailed it out of the saloon."

Benji continued to nod his head, pointing to himself with satisfaction.

"The prospector turned all purplish, and his eyes bugged out. Then, his wrinkly, bald head turned blue with veins popping, all whilst he grasped wildly at his throat. Must a choked on a peanut shell," Ramus cackled. "The doc will know for sure once he takes a good hard look at him, that is before the gravedigger removes his body for the undertaker."

"So, we're free to get that gold for ourselves," Wadey grizzled.

"Yup, yup!" stammered the addled, scratchy voice.

"That's their pea-brained older brother, Duffy," Lee sniggered. "The Thorn brothers are known for all kinds of skullduggery in town. The folks around here don't much take a liking to them."

"Alright then, it's settled," said Ramus Thorn, who seemed to be the brains of the bumbling outfit. "We'll leave at sunrise and trudge up to the mountains to find the abandoned mine where the old buzzard hid the saddlebags, collect the gold, and be rich forever."

"How'll we know where to look?" mumbled slow-witted Duffy.

"Before he croaked, the old prospector rambled on about the mine's opening being beneath an overhang of granite outlined with black veins of muscovite. It's on the north side of the mountain about twenty-some miles from here," schooled Ramus. "We'll follow the Animas River into the San Juans and then trek along the ridge until we find it. It'll take us most of a day to get there, find the saddlebags, and load them up. We'll be back in town the next day—two days, tops, and we'll slug down some shots of Tarantula Juice to celebrate."

"Cool beans," said Lee tersely, as she jumped to her feet. "How would you like to be rich in two days? Richer than you ever dreamed of?"

Diane was stunned, excited, and perplexed, all at the same time. "We're s-supposed to be b-back on the train in an hour, headed to my grandparents in Phoenix," she stuttered, disappointment dripping from every word. But the thoughts of wealth, pretty things for her mother, and a nice home for her family, with her own library filled with books, were swimming crazily in her mind. She shook her head jerkily to clear away the tempting fog, "My parents would thrash me and skin me alive." She shuddered.

Lee looked at her pensively. "The prospector found the gold, and he's now dead. The original owner, probably a prospector, is long gone, by the way he described the bones and decay of the mules' carcasses," she argued, "most likely killed by a wild animal. Anyone else, a partner or a rival prospector, would have taken the gold," she surmised. "So, the gold now belongs to whoever finds it first," she beamed. "We've just got to get to it before they do. And, I *know* those mountains well. I've seen that mine opening and know a shortcut to getting there. We'll be safe, and it'll take only a day or two at the most!" Lee implored. "You can send a telegram to your grandparents and catch the next train to the Arizona territory."

"I don't know, Lee," Diane said, shaking her head. "Sounds reasonable enough," she murmured slowly, staring up at the sky, looking for answers in the stars. Then she paused, and sighed tonelessly. "I just can't. I'm responsible for Benji. My parents would never understand."

Benji nudged her, "Come on, Di, think of all the books you could buy," he said, rolling his eyes. "Anyway, I'm old enough. I don't need *you* to take care of me," he pleaded. "When do you ever turn down a chance for adventure?"

Lee and Benji both stared at her with wide, begging, puppy-like brown eyes and hopeful anticipation scrawled across their faces. "No, and that's final," she said hotly. "Benji, let's get back to the station. It's about that time."

Lee shrugged and walked them back to the train, her shoulders slouched—sulking—her eyes on the ground. All at once, a loud bang and raucous clatter filled the cool, summer night air. Lee looked up and grinned at the sight before her. Diane and Benji followed her gaze to the train station, where they saw several greasy and befuddled engineers working feverishly on the tired train's engine. All kinds of curious-looking parts and gears were strewn across the tracks.

The gangly conductor saw Diane and Benji as they approached and scuttled hurriedly to meet them. "I'm s-sorry to report," he gabbled, "b-but the engine has s-suffered a s-s-serious breakdown. We're making accommodations available for our p-passengers at the Durango Hotel, but not for fare, I'm a-fr-fraid," he sniffled apologetically. "The parts we need c-can't be delivered for a day or two, coming from San Francisco, you know, and then we have to reassemble the engine, reload our s-supplies, and round up and board the passengers," he said, panting. "So, we may be delayed by several days." His cheeks reddened and twitched as he nervously pulled on the corner of his mustache. "Did your father give you any traveling money for your trip?" he asked, concerned and clearly flustered. "I mean, any money for an emergency, for fare, I mean, food?"

"Yes, yes, some," Diane said offhandedly, her mind already reeling.

"Whew!" he exhaled and turned abruptly, scurrying to other passengers just arriving with looks of horror etched into their expressions.

Lee and Benji both looked at each other, and then stared at Diane with a glimmer of hope in their eyes. They both cocked their heads to the same side and shrugged their shoulders.

"Alright," she sighed with feigned exasperation, giving a mischievous wink to her brother. "We've been given a few days' delay, I guess," Diane said, poking Benji, who was beside himself with glee.

"Golly gee!" he exclaimed. "Here we go again!"

CHAPTER FOUR

BEST BE PREPARED

"**S**o, what's the plan?" Diane asked, her eyes getting bigger and brighter with every word.

"The first thing we have to do is get you both some riding clothes and supplies," Lee said, taking charge.

"Oh yes, please!" Diane said with a sigh of relief. "I hate this frilly dress my mother made me wear."

Their first stop was Wilcox's Mercantile & General Store, where Lee's papa had an account. Lee and her father had been trapping and selling their pelts to Mr. Wilcox for many years, and he knew Lee well and trusted him—or her, as it were. A tinkling bell rang somewhere in the depths of the shop as they stepped inside under a horseshoe nailed above the doorway. A wildly magnificent chandelier made of elk antlers hung from the low ceiling, and Diane had to duck to walk under it.

Store owners in the thriving mining town were used to prospectors and trappers knocking on their doors at all hours of the night, on a whim or a fancy, so they slept in a back room, or if they were fortunate enough, a second-floor apartment over the store. So, the enterprising owner gladly opened his store at this hour past closing and eagerly agreed to put all the supplies—food, matches, cookware, canteens, an ax, torches, rope, sleeping blankets, and such—on Lee's father's account.

"Aren't you worried how your papa will react when he finds out you've put all this on his account?" Diane asked, concerned.

"No," Lee answered curtly. "He owes me. There's a bundle of pelts back at our camp that we were going to deliver tomorrow. Half of those are mine, I figure. I've worked hard enough for them."

Understanding, Diane blurted, "But, we should help pay too! It's only right."

"You can pay me back later, okay?" Lee replied.

Somewhat convinced, Diane nodded agreement and turned to Benji with a brilliant smile. Gleefully, she picked out dungarees—labeled blue jeans—for herself, along with a lightweight collared shirt with long sleeves, which she liked to roll up. She loved the Western brown dusters coated with linseed oil for waterproofing. They smelled funny, but she picked out two of them, one for Benji, just in case.

Diane remembered seeing some storm clouds building up overhead when they had walked back to the train station. They reminded her of reading about Colorado's summer monsoon rains. This high mountain altitude was much colder in June than she was used to, for the summer nights in Chicago were frequently sweltering hot.

Best be prepared for any kind of weather, she reflected, as she wrapped the stiff, brown duster around her, soaking up its warmth.

Benji turned up his nose and reluctantly put his on. "Phew!" He winced, scrunching up his face in disgust.

She found a long, forest-green vest with lots of pockets and snickered at the ten-gallon hat that completely buried Benji beneath its broad rim. He finally picked out a black cowboy hat that was more suitable for his age and head size. Diane settled on a white hat with a flat top and a broad rim—unique but stylish to protect her from the sun and summer rains.

I think I'll wear this now, she decided, finding a leather ribbon to hold back her shoulder-length hair. A short ponytail protruded from under the back of the hat, and long, wispy strands of blonde hair framed her slender face.

They finished off their outfits with tan cowboy boots made of supple cowskin leather that came up to their knees—perfect for tucking in her new blue jeans.

Diane insisted on paying for their clothing from the emergency money Father had given them. *I guess this is an emergency,* she reasoned, thrilled and a little apprehensive about the adventure ahead.

When she stood at the counter with the store owner tallying up all their purchases, Benji approached. "Here, Di," he said, pulling out a few crumpled bills from his pocket. "It's from our lemonade stand and the 'Odds and Ends' sale we had last weekend." They were quite the enterprising youths, and Benji was a good saver.

"City slickers," Lee smothered a chuckle with Mr. Wilcox as she walked hastily through the store with the owner, ordering this, pointing to that, gathering the supplies for their journey.

At last, she asked the owner for a quill and parchment, and scratched a note to her father letting him know that she'd be back in a few days and to settle these charges from her share of the pelts they'd trapped. She folded it, sealed it with some wax the owner kindly offered, and handed it to him.

"See that he gets this note, Mr. Wilcox, whenever he finally makes his way back to town. You'll probably find him at the saloon later tomorrow," she said grudgingly. "He'll be around with your pelts, eventually," she shrugged. "Until then, I'm scouting a new area." Which was kind of the truth.

The next stop was the town's stable, where Lee bartered with the sleepy-eyed blacksmith, trading a promise of fur pelts for two smaller horses.

"Can you ride?" Lee asked Diane.

"Yes," she said fervidly. "And I ride with a Western saddle."

Lee raised a surprised eyebrow. The blacksmith scratched his head as he rummaged through his tack room and found two smaller saddles and a blanket for Benji, who was going to ride behind Diane.

Lee had left instructions with the owner at the general store to deliver their supplies to the stable that night, and the blacksmith agreed to pack up the horses for an early-morning departure the next day. He lazily waved goodbye to the adventurers as he dozed on the porch in his creaky rocking chair, awaiting the arrival of Mr. Wilcox and their supplies.

Their last stop was Western Union. They fortuitously caught the clerk locking up for the evening and sweet-talked him into sending just one more message before closing. Diane sent a telegram to her grandparents, letting them know that they were all right but would be delayed by several days. She explained the train's engine problem and instructed them to wait for another telegram, giving them the exact date and time of their arrival. She asked for them to let her parents know as well.

The sky was a dark purple when they agreed, over a late snack at Lulu Belle's Café, that they needed to keep a keen eye on the Thorn brothers.

"When should we leave?" Diane asked, feeling they were as prepared as they would ever be.

Lee explained that it was too dangerous to venture into the forest at night, with all the bears, wolves, and mountain lions on the prowl. She also didn't want the Thorn brothers coming across their fresh tracks and following them if they left before them. "Better to be following them out of town," Lee said with a serious tone. "Then, we'll take the shortcut I know."

So, the three of them sauntered back to Jake's Saloon before midnight and peered over the swinging doors to find the Thorn brothers passed out at a table, slumped deeply in their chairs, snoring. They had drunk too much, already celebrating their imagined riches.

Oh, this is going to be interesting, Diane mused, remembering the mysterious woman on the train and her words, "Life is rich with experiences and lessons to learn." *Life is indeed rich!* She chuckled to herself. *But what lessons do I need to learn?* she pondered deeply and shivered. Then the message came to mind, *"Seek first the mysteries of the ancients..."* and she stopped dead in her tracks. *What on earth does that mean?* She nervously swept a strand of loose hair behind her ear, swallowed hard, then with resolve, took a firm step forward to catch up with Benji and Lee, who were deep in conversation, plotting, and hadn't noticed that she had stopped. *I guess I'll just have to find out,* she thought as she fell into step with them.

They tiptoed quietly back through the alley to find a hiding place behind the saloon and slipped into a dark corner filled with discarded wooden crates. There, they would wait out the night.

CHAPTER FIVE

GLITTERING LIGHTS

P assing the time, Lee pulled out her antler-handled knife and started carving on one of the wooden crates.

"What are you writing?" Diane asked, looking curiously over her shoulder.

"Just my name," Lee murmured pensively.

"P-L-A-N-C-H-E-T," Diane mouthed each letter as Lee carved them into the thin wooden slat. She cocked her head to the side, looking bewildered. "Wouldn't you pronounce the T in your name?"

"In French, the ET sounds like a long A," Lee responded matter-of-factly, still concentrating on the point of her blade. "The T is, as you say, silent."

Diane's eyes grew wide. "I've always wanted to learn another language, especially French. I'd like to travel to France someday," she sighed dreamily. "Would you teach me?" Her eyes pleaded.

Lee looked deeply into her bright green eyes and shrugged. "*Mais, bien sur!*"

"May-bee-n-sewer," Diane repeated. "What does that mean?" she asked keenly.

"But of course!" Lee replied, exaggerating her French accent.

Diane grew silent, pondering. "Aren't you worried about your father coming back to look for you?" she asked, changing the subject to something that was concerning her. She had seen his rage and felt troubled.

"*Non*," Lee muttered, "not really. He probably went back to our camp to sleep it off. He won't wake until high noon or later tomorrow."

"*Voila*, look at that!" Lee said suddenly, gesturing to a large shadowy figure perched on the edge of the roof of the building across the narrow alley from them, with its head cocked curiously, as if it were listening.

"What is it?" Diane asked, under her breath. Squinting through the dim light from the saloon, she could barely make out the shape of a very large bird with a sharply pointed hooked beak and glowing golden eyes.

"You don't often see raptors in town," Lee said, scratching her cap. "By the size of it, I think that's an eagle of some kind. Maybe a golden eagle, by its dark head?"

The bird nodded its head jerkily and shifted its weight, its sharp talons scratching against the wood. It seemed to be peering down directly at them. All at once, the raptor made a loud screeching sound that sent shivers up and down Diane's spine. The girls looked at each other and then up again for the eagle, but it was gone in a flicker of glittering lights.

Hmm, she reflected, t*hat's the second time I've seen those tiny sparkles.* She shook her head slightly, bewildered, and shrugged.

Just then, the baby raccoon emerged from her hidden compartment in Lee's cap. She yawned, stretching her tiny forelimbs, and sat straight up on Lee's head. At once, her ears pricked up and began twitching. Niki's beady eyes were focused on a dark corner opposite them. It was stacked with discarded broken, wooden crates strewn around a large cardboard box. She started chittering noisily, as if she were carrying on a conversation, pausing every so often, seemingly listening to an inaudible response.

Lee and Diane looked at each other and chuckled lightly. Quickly, Lee shooed Niki back into her den to keep her quiet, so as not to raise any unwanted attention to themselves.

"I've never heard her carry on so," said Lee, perplexed.

To their surprise, they spotted two red, beetle-like eyes glowing from the jumbled wooden crates opposite them. "It's just an alley rat," Lee said, relieved that they had at least solved that mystery.

Diane took a slice of jerky out of her knapsack and tore off a small piece, throwing it to the twitching whiskers and sad, pleading eyes. The rat held the morsel in his tiny paws, inspecting it, then scuttled away. Feeling content, Diane glanced down at a sleeping Benji.

The three of them huddled together, wrapped in the warm sleeping blankets they'd bought at the general store, and took turns keeping an eye on the snoring Thorn brothers, who slumbered through the entire night. Duffy slept with his mouth open, a pool of drool growing around his head that covered the side of his face.

"Yuck!" Benji said, as he took his turn squinting through a dusty saloon window. "Still sleeping," he reported upon his return. "The saloonkeeper is dozing, too." He yawned widely, rubbed his tired eyes, and curled up on a blanket next to his sister, falling asleep again.

Diane took her turn to check on the sleeping brothers. "Phew!" She recoiled, scrunching her slender nose. She quietly tiptoed along the stacks of broken crates and discarded bins of moldy, rotting garbage scattered behind the saloon until she reached a back window. Stepping onto a creaky wooden box to peer inside, she grasped onto the windowsill covered thickly in a layer of dirt.

Ick, she cringed, tottering on the squeaky platform. She slowly lifted her head to just above the paint-peeling frame and wiped away years of grime from the window with her father's handkerchief that she pulled from her jeans' back pocket.

Only the top of her new hat and big eyes could be seen from inside. Nobody noticed as she squinted through the smeared glass and spied the snoring brothers at the dimly lit table, where a sputtering kerosene lantern flickered. Ramus shifted in his chair, throwing his head back, his mouth gaped open. He began snoring like a bear.

Carefully stepping back down, Diane crouched low in the dusty alley, gazing up at the dark sky between the wooden buildings.

All the stars, she mumbled to herself. *I've never seen so many stars.*

She remembered the mysterious eagle perched on the building across from her and glanced at the spot where it had disappeared just a short while ago.

What have I gotten myself into this time? She shook her head, shuddering with a smattering of fear, mixed with a larger dose of excitement. *What's the worst that can happen?* she pondered. They had at least a few days for the train to be repaired, maybe more, so no one would miss them until then. She made sure Lee had packed plenty of food, for more days than they really needed, just in case. She considered her new friend, Lee.

Do I trust her? She paused, and dug deep inside herself for an answer. She had learned to always ask herself for the answer—to trust her own feelings instead of relying solely on her parents or a friend's opinion all the time. *Yes, I do,* her feelings revealed.

Things always seemed to work out all right for Diane, no matter the adventure, and she gained confidence in that fact. *Given that this is the biggest adventure of my life so far, am I up for the challenge?* She waited for that feeling to either confirm or reject her thoughts. *Yes, I am. The rewards are well worth the risk,* she decided, feeling a warm glow radiate inside her chest. Setting her jaw squarely, she confirmed her resolve and winked at the glistening stars.

She stepped onto the wooden box again and watched as every now and then, Wadey swatted at a pesky fly in his sleep, successfully smashing it against the bar table. More than once, a squished fly, stuck by its innards to the palm of his huge hand, dropped into his stale beer mug.

"That will be quite a tasty breakfast," Diane snickered, describing the scene to Lee upon her return, who smothered a chuckle. Although it was nearing midsummer, a chilly mountain night breeze swept through the alleyway, swirling up dust that pelted their faces. Diane shielded her tired eyes and wrapped herself tightly in her warm blanket but found that she was too wound up to sleep.

As Lee crept off to check on the brothers again, Diane pulled her book from her knapsack and quietly turned to the pages describing Cibola. Benji stirred and awoke. Spying the stub of a candle discarded in the alley, he pulled out a matchbook from his jean pocket, and striking one aflame, lit the retrieved candle, then nestled close to his sister as she read by the flickering light in a hushed tone.

"Estebanico, the guide, was also known to be a skilled healer and was frequently accepted by many of the native peoples he encountered, collecting hordes of turquoise and other riches in trade for his healing aid. He mysteriously disappeared during a scouting expedition and is believed to have been killed by Zuni warriors, but not before sending a secret message tied to a wooden cross to the explorer, Friar de Niza, confirming the natives' tales of *'seven cities to the north where the people were extremely wealthy, lived in spacious multi-storied villages shimmering in gold, and wore fine-woven clothing made of cotton.'* And he was off to find them."

"What's turquoise?" Benji asked, yawning.

"It's a light blue gemstone, very rare and highly valued by native people of the West, worn as jewelry mostly," Diane recalled from her American history reading.

A gust of wind suddenly blew out the flickering candle. "What about Cibola?" Benji whined in disappointment.

"We'll get there," Diane chortled lightly. "You're making me yawn," she stifled as she hunkered down into her blanket and fell sound asleep, dreaming about the extraordinary adventure ahead and the saddlebags of gold.

CHAPTER SIX

ON TO SILVER MOUNTAIN

A s the eastern sky became a crimson red tinge on the horizon, the waking town of Durango was bathed in an orangish glow. Ramus Thorn snorted and farted, waking himself up. Slapping his two brothers on the back of their heads, he woke them up with a start. Wadey immediately reached for his stale beer and guzzled it down, fly carcasses and all.

Diane nearly hurled at the sight. Benji turned his back and covered his mouth, muffling a giggle.

"Okay, you two!" Lee said tensely. "Let's go!"

They quietly crept to the front of the alley to keep an eye on the doors of the saloon, and patiently waited until the Thorn brothers emerged. They didn't have long to wait. The doors suddenly swung open, and Wadey, Ramus, and Duffy came staggering out. Ramus was rangy, tall and thin like a skeleton, while Wadey was stout, thick-necked, and beefy. All disheveled, Duffy stumbled out last and awkwardly struggled to pull up his pants while he swiped the drool from the side of his face with his tattered sleeve.

Diane watched Wadey pick at the flies between his mossy

teeth, casually spitting their carcasses out into the dirt street, and chuckled. Ramus appeared to be the only one with any wits about him. A dark light smoldered in his piercing eyes. He pulled his addled brother Duffy by his ear and waddled him toward the stable. Duffy howled shrilly, and Diane pinched Benji, who could hardly contain his fit of laughter.

Lee, Diane, and Benji quietly followed behind, blending in with the early risers walking along the dusty streets and wooden boardwalks lined with opening stores. Yawning owners were out in front of their establishments, sweeping the dust from their doorways, turning the hand-painted signs in their windows to "Open." The morning sun shimmered brightly in the handblown glass as they scurried across the creaking planks. Diane grinned as she watched her wavy, distorted reflection ripple by, relishing her new Western image.

The three new friends huddled behind a large brown horse tied to a hitching post, and while avoiding its swishing tail, they kept a sharp eye on the doors of the stable. Only a couple of minutes passed when the stable doors flew open, and they watched as the Thorn brothers rode out, fiercely slapping the thin leather reins against their horses' flanks. It was time.

Diane, Lee, and Benji snuck into the back of the stable and, with a little help from the blacksmith, quietly clambered onto their sleepy horses. The smell of fresh horse dung filled Diane's nostrils and conjured up all kinds of fond memories of the horses back home. Benji rode with Diane on a jet-black horse with a perfect white star on his forehead, while Lee mounted a handsome chestnut with a thick black mane and matching black tail already packed with their supplies. Both horses seemed relieved with their unusually light load. They were stable horses used to being overworked by heavy mountain men or prospectors with their cumbersome loads.

Lee had trapped in these dense woods for the past five years and had grown to be an expert tracker. For their own safety, she said wisely, they should give the Thorn brothers a good head start; that way they wouldn't detect the young adventurers following behind them. She was "woods-wise and street-smart," her papa would say. Lee finally gave the signal to leave.

"Off on a grand adventure!" Diane declared heartily to the woods and the heavens as she gently nudged her black horse forward, walking beside Lee.

"Where did a city slicker like you learn to ride a horse?" Lee asked in surprise.

"One of our neighbors is the milkman and uses horses to pull his wagon. A couple years ago, he had four colts born within a few months of each other. I traded taking care of them— feeding, watering, cleaning their stalls—for riding lessons from his oldest daughter, who learned to ride Western style. I loved taking care of them. It was more of a joy than a chore, really. I'd like to have a ranch someday and raise horses, maybe in Arizona," she replied wistfully.

Lee looked at Diane with surprise. "*Moi aussi.* Me too. I've *always* wanted a ranch with horses, raccoons, and all kinds of wild critters," she said dreamily. "Maybe...someday... somewhere."

They followed the worn trail out of town along the river into the San Juan Mountains for some time. Every now and then, Lee would stop and hang sideways off her saddle, studying the tracks in the grounds. "These tracks are fresh," she said matter-of-factly. "The Thorn brothers are headed the long way up the ridge of the mountain. It's time to take the shortcut I know up this ravine," she said as she pulled the reins of her chestnut horse off the well-trodden trail, leading Diane and

48

Benji to bushwhack through the dense conifer forest. Their travel became more treacherous as they slowly made their way under low-hanging branches, over fallen tree trunks and gnarly roots, around thorny bramble bushes and tree stumps.

"Ouch!" Diane recoiled, her jeans snagged by the thorny vines of a wild raspberry bush pricking her leg. She carefully pulled the grasping vine from her dungarees and rubbed the stinging area.

As the morning sun peeked through the tall pine trees, a soft white aura glistened around every fine needle while plump, white clouds floated below a brilliant azure sky. The warming sun heated the pine sap under the bark, releasing into the air the most delicious scent of ...

Smells like...hmm...butterscotch? Diane thought, smiling softly to herself.

The forest came alive as they rode in silence, taking in the loud, screeching cries of the blue jays and the throaty, guttural squawks of the circling black ravens. The buzz of pesky deerflies was nearly drowned out by the chorus of crickets and the deep drone of croaking tree frogs that hid in the dark shadows cast down from the thick forest canopy. Once in a while, they'd see a hummingbird dip its long, slender beak into a long-necked purple penstemon flower, its wings fluttering so fast its body would hover in place as the tiny bird emptied the flower of its nectar.

"Look over there!" Diane shouted, pointing to a meadow clearing below the small hilltop they were traversing. A herd of elk—females with their spring young, about twenty in all—lifted their heads at the same time. Warily, the elk watched as the horses rode by, and then one by one, returned to grazing the meadow grasses that made up the bulk of their diet, keeping a heedful eye on the curious passersby.

"Buffalo!" Lee quietly said, gesturing to a small number of the lumbering giants—the largest mammals in America—nestled in the shade under a copse of conifer trees. A thousand-pound female cow was nursing her "red dog" newborn. The red-orange colored hair was already starting to turn dark brown, and its shoulder hump was beginning to form along with its tiny buds for horns. "Late in the season for that little one."

"They're actually called bison," Diane chimed in, thrilled to see one with her own eyes. "There were once millions of them roaming the grassland plains and forests in America. Now there are maybe a few hundred," she sighed deeply. "Settlers and farmers have greatly reduced their habitat, and game hunters are killing them just for sport. They're almost extinct!" She shook her head. "Sad, really sad."

"Well, we French call them 'buffalo,'" Lee retorted, grinning. "I think it comes from our word for beef, 'boeuf.'"

Achoo!

"Did you hear that?" Diane asked, alarm tinging her voice as she whisked around in her saddle to look back over Benji's head.

"Hear what?" Lee asked, slowing her chestnut to listen intently.

"I could have sworn I heard something behind us, sort of like a person sneezing!" she exclaimed.

They stopped to listen but heard nothing but the hoot of an owl in the distance. Diane's black horse shifted his weight and anxiously scuffed a hoof against a rock on the ravine floor. The sound seemed thunderous against the silence of the moment. His ears pricked. "You heard that, too?" she said hushedly to the horse, petting his sweaty neck.

Lee turned back in her saddle. *"Rien,"* she said in French.

"Nothing!" And she waved them onward. Nudging her horse forward with her heels pressed against his flanks, she went off again, climbing higher up the ravine toward the layered mountain peaks above. Even with Lee's reassurance, Diane couldn't shake the feeling that they were being followed by someone...or *something*.

They rode for several more hours in silence, just listening to the forest sounds and the breathing of the horses. Pine needles crunched beneath their hooves, and leaves rustled softly over their heads. A warm afternoon breeze blew across Diane's face. Completely absorbed in the beauty surrounding her, she sighed deeply. She had never experienced so much nature before, and her heart soared with every breath of fresh mountain air. When they came to a small winding stream, Lee motioned for them to stop and dismount to give the horses a chance to drink and feed on the thick grasses along the stream's bank.

Benji slid awkwardly off the back of the black horse and fell smack on the ground, his skinny legs wobbly and weak from riding so long. When Diane dismounted, her legs, strained from the stiff, prolonged position, crumpled to the earth as soon as her feet hit the ground. Her stunned look made Benji break out in laughter. His contagious laughter made Diane chuckle, and soon they were both rolling on the ground, their hands held to their mouths, smothering their laughter, trying not to be heard by those mean old Thorn brothers.

Lee came over and stood above them, fists on her hips. "*C'est assez!*" she said tensely.

"What does that mean?" Diane attempted to ask in a serious tone, trying to hold back her laughter.

"It means, that's enough!" Lee replied hotly. "*Ecoutez!*" she said, pressing a finger to her lips and cupping the other hand to her ear. "Listen."

Diane and Benji froze and listened but heard only the wind rustling through the trees, making the leaves quake on a copse of aspens standing like shivering sailors all dressed in white, dappled on the mountainside.

Diane shrugged her shoulders, looking quizzically at Lee. Then, she heard it—a faint scratchy sound, like the shuffle of a restless hoof against a rock. She, too, suddenly felt the presence of something lurking just beyond the row of trees in their shadows, something not wanting to be discovered. They waited in dead silence for several long minutes—*nothing*.

Ree-n, Diane pronounced to herself, repeating after Lee. "Nothing."

Lee finally shrugged, and the tension left her face. She tethered the horses to a nearby tree, giving them plenty of slack to move about easily, then removed her boots, socks, and pants, and folding them neatly, placed them on a sunbaked boulder near the stream. In only her flimsy tan shirt and undergarments, she waded waist-deep into the stream to cool off. The crystal-clear water was a painter's palette of shades of aquamarine green and turquoise blue against a white, sandy bottom. Lee dove and swam underwater through long, stringy strands of green grasses flowing gently in the stream's lazy current. She was eyed warily by a passing trout.

Lee surfaced, sputtering. "Are you a fisherman?" she asked Benji.

"Nah, our rivers stink so bad, nobody can get near them to fish," he said disappointedly. "The garbage in the river actually caught on fire one time!" He wrinkled his nose in disgust.

Lee nodded in understanding, her brown eyes drifting sullenly, "There are hundreds of stinky factories springing up along the Hudson River where I'm from, all polluting the river's water."

Diane sat cross-legged along the grassy bank. She turned her face toward the glimmering summer sun. Closing her eyes, an orange glow sparkled on the inside of her lids, and she allowed herself to bask in its warmth. Slender reeds occasionally rippled in the gentle June breeze, lightly clinking all around her. Using her sleeve, she dabbed away the small beads of sweat that glistened across the tip of her nose as she breathed in deeply the serenity of the pristine mountain stream. She heard a faint buzz and opened her eyes to see two copper-colored dragonflies flit across the surface of the stream, the tips of their wings just touching the water.

So extremely different, she considered. Chicago was the second-largest city in America and one of the most industrialized. Consequently, it was also one of the world's dirtiest, which meant that everything in her gloomy little suburban neighborhood was heavily laden with soot from all the burgeoning factories. The sky above her home was a continuously dreary, faded gray, heavy with an acrid odor, and dismally depressing. She shuddered at the memory. Flowing rivers, like the Chicago River that meandered through the suburbs, were heavily polluted with toxic industrial effluents, harmful waste, and raw sewage.

I never imagined a world so beautiful, she said to herself.

Cupping her hands, Diane dipped them under the surface and watched gleefully as the sparkling, clear water flowed into them. Closing her eyes, she tipped her cupped hands to her mouth and felt her lips touch the cool, almost soft, stream water—refreshing and crisp. A profound sense of freedom and joy coursed through her entire body. She was falling in love with nature, feeling alive, vibrating with its pure energy...and her radiant smile reflected her blossoming feelings.

"Come on, Di," Benji said, shucking his hot duster. Diane

awakened from her forest daze and avidly removed her sweaty clothing, flinging each article slapdash on to the ground. She then followed her brother into the cool mountain stream. Benji furrowed his light eyebrows, then, shrugging his skinny shoulders, plunged into the water and swam away, kicking like a tadpole that had just sprouted legs. Diane chuckled at the sight.

Lee looked at her and grinned broadly.

"I'm just so happy," Diane sighed dreamily. "Really happy, you know. I had no idea nature was *so* magnificent!" She paused, suddenly realizing. "And, I've never felt so...*free*."

Diane glanced at Lee, who seemed to be less tense and enjoying nature, too. Lee gazed into the aquamarine water and nodded slowly in agreement. "I'd forgotten how much I loved these mountains when we first arrived here."

Clambering out of the stream, they collapsed on the warm, green grass and lay there, drying in the afternoon sun. "I'm beginning to understand what Father was talking about," Diane sighed. "You can't experience *this* in books."

As Diane and Benji stared up at the most dazzlingly blue, cloudless sky, Lee retrieved some jerky from her saddlebags and passed it around. The salty dried meat was tough and chewy, and definitely washed down well with the cool stream water.

"Cool beans," said Lee tersely. "That was fun, but it's time to go!"

"And the adventure continues," Diane declared, still vibrating with so much joy she felt she could burst.

They dressed quickly, gathered their things, and mounted their well-rested horses. Lee swung over the side of her horse and hung nearly upside down from her saddle, searching the ground for fresh tracks as they sauntered off.

"This way," she said finally, straightening herself in the saddle. "I see only some faint marks from old tracks, maybe even from our own expedition earlier this spring. No one has been by this way recently." She gave her horse a brisk squeeze with her knees.

"Listen!" Benji yelled out in a muffled tone and froze, staring behind him.

Diane and Lee stopped and looked in the same direction. Hot, prickly fear crawled up Diane's spine. The crisp sound of a breaking twig could barely be heard, but it was there...sure as shooting.

CHAPTER SEVEN

ABANDONED MINE

S *nap!* Another twig broke, this one louder, closer.
Suddenly, Lee's horse's ears began to twitch and perked upright. His eyes bulged wide, nostrils flaring, as he reared up onto his back legs, then circled about, tossing his head wildly. Startled, Lee pulled tightly onto his reins, trying desperately to steady him.

"Let's get out of here!" she shouted, finally gaining control and nudging her frightened horse forward.

The black horse followed instinctively behind, racing through the pines, jumping over boulders while Diane and Benji hung on for dear life.

"Hold on, Benji!" Diane yelled, as their horse galloped over the rough terrain, a fallen tree looming in his path.

Diane leaned forward, grasping tightly onto the horse's flowing mane. The animal flew easily over the trunk, lifting poor Benji off his blanket, his legs flailing, as he struggled to hold onto his sister's waist. He landed sideways hard, nearly falling off the back of the thrashing horse as it twisted around a large rock outcropping too high to jump.

Straining with all his might, Benji finally clambered onto the bumping horse's back, nearly unseating Diane as he did.

"Watch out!" Benji shrieked as the horse went under a low-hanging pine bough, almost swiping Diane off the saddle.

Cold panic drained out of the adventurers as Lee finally slowed to a trot and came to a stop, horses and riders panting hard. "What was that?" Diane asked breathlessly, wiping the sweat from her brow.

"Was that an animal or something?" Benji squirmed, adjusting his cowboy hat that was smashed down, practically covering his eyes.

"I don't know," Lee said, shaking her head, "maybe a bobcat or mountain lion. They live up here in these boulders. But I've never seen a horse react so strangely before, hightailing away like it did."

After a moment's rest, Lee urged her horse onward, and Diane did the same. Benji, still seriously spooked, whispered into Diane's ear as they rode along together. "What do you think that was, sis?"

"I don't know," confided Diane, "but I wasn't sticking around to find out."

"We're getting close," Lee reported when Diane and Benji came trotting up alongside her.

"How do you know?" Benji asked curiously, adjusting again the cowboy hat on his head.

"My papa and *moi* have trapped all of these mountains around here. A few months ago, we came across an old abandoned mine on the north side of this peak that has a large granite overhang surrounded with black veins on either side of its opening, just like the one the prospector described. That has to be the place where he hid the saddlebags packed with gold," Lee deduced.

"I've ridden this wild game trail before. This steep incline leads right up to the opening of the mine. There's a better path just ahead," she continued. "I've heard tell that some years ago, prospectors saw mysterious black smoke coming from this mountain at night—every night. When they explored, they found the opening to a huge cave filled with all sorts of peculiar rocks growing from the ground and hanging from the ceiling. In one part of the cave, they found a large black pool of water with all kinds of odd, pure white animals—all blind."

"Those are cave dwellers," Diane chimed in avidly. "I've read that some animals like eyeless fish and sightless crayfish have adapted to living in the darkness of a cave that even their skin has turned white without sunlight. They're called 'troglobites' because they can't survive outside the cave."

"My friend Anthony is a troglobite," Benji said, chortling. "He stays in his room all day reading comic books."

Lee continued the tale. "The prospectors found that what they thought was black smoke was actually millions of bats flying out of the cave at night. With the gold rush on in these parts, this cave was discovered to be riddled with veins rich in gold scattered throughout the mountain. A large-scale lode mining operation was launched here in the seventies. The bats left their roost while the miners dug out all the gold they could find, then abandoned it. Rumor has it that the bats have returned to the cave since the mine was closed."

"Bats!" squealed Diane, glancing at Benji. She knew he loved all sorts of creepy-crawling and flying things. Although she wasn't particularly fond of the creepy crawlies, they both were intrigued with bats.

The terrain in front of them suddenly became very steep and treacherous. The poor horses struggled, strained, and began breathing heavily. Lee held up her hand, signaling to stop and give them a rest.

"We'd better go on foot from here," she said tensely as she dismounted and led her horse to a thicket of Gambel oaks to hide him.

"Ouch!" Diane cried, tying her horse to a nearby pine. "Those little needles have sharp points, but—" She stopped and sniffed. "What's that delicious smell? It smells like…" she paused pensively, "butterscotch!"

Lee leaned over and put her nose into a crack in the bark that looked like rough puzzle pieces floating on a sea of orange foam.

"Here," Lee said, pointing. "Sniff here!"

Diane hesitated but pressed her face into the rough bark, putting her nose in between the puzzle pieces, and breathed in deeply. "Yum!" She sighed. "That's fantastic! What is it?" she asked, her senses whirling.

"It's the sap of the ponderosa pine tree, the only pine tree that smells like that when the sun warms its bark," Lee stated. "Other pines, firs, and spruces have their own unique smells."

"How do you know the difference between pine and fir trees?" Diane asked, interested.

As she listened to Diane's question, Lee ambled under three distinctly different-looking conifer trees and plucked off some of their needles.

"Well," she paused. "Pine trees have little bundles of needles that grow from their branches. See how the bottoms of the needles are wrapped by this brown fiber here? Some bundles only have three needles, others have four or five, depending on the type of pine tree. Fir-tree needles are like spruce-tree needles. They both grow straight from their branches, with no bundle at all. But the fir needle is flat, soft, and you can't roll it between your fingers. See!" She handed a fir needle to Diane and Benji to experiment for themselves. "Spruce needles are pointy and square, and they easily roll between your fingers," Lee said wisely, as Diane took the spruce needle and rolled it, bubbling with the thrill of newfound wilderness knowledge. She passed the spruce needle on to Benji, who was eager to test the differences for himself.

"You are woods-wise," Diane said heartily. She looked up to smart people who knew things she didn't know. There was always so much to learn from them.

Diane furrowed her brow, thinking deeply. "F for flat-needled fir trees, and S for square-needled spruce trees. This is the best kind of learning," she said fervently. "Learning from real-life experiences, not just from books. The science of nature," she declared. "Someday I'm going to be a teacher of 'nature's science,' with real-life adventures for my students," she continued, as a whole new vision of her future unfolded and a deep passion ignited.

"Did you just make that up?" Lee asked, astonished.

Benji beamed. "She's always making up stuff like that."

They started hiking on foot and quickly stumbled onto a broad, worn path. "This is the path that leads to the mine's opening," Lee said in a most serious tone.

Trudging up the steep path, the valley floor fell further away below them while a cool evening breeze began to blow.

Shivering, Diane and Benji pulled their new smelly dusters tightly around them to keep warm. They were now high up the mountain peak, almost above the height of the treetops, looking down at the Animas River Valley below. The spears of the tallest firs and spruces pointed toward the stars that were poking out from behind the blanket of a darkening blue sky. Diane watched as the silvery edge of a huge orb of fire rose from between the tree spears, silhouetted against a deep red, fading to orange then pearly white, as the biggest full moon lit the rock-strewn path before them.

She gasped. "How beautiful!"

Lee stopped abruptly and pointed to a dark hole cut into the mountainside. All at once, they heard the distant beat of fluttering wings that rose in rhythm with the evening song of crickets as they rubbed their wings together, composing their chirping melody. The forest sounds all blended into a beautiful nature symphony.

The fluttering sound grew nearer, louder and louder, becoming almost deafening. Diane could feel the vibration in the ground as an ominous black cloud, made up of millions of bats, emerged from the gaping mouth of the cave. An eerie, scary sight filled the night sky as the bats flew hither and yon, scattering from the cave to their feeding grounds throughout the Southwest.

As she clasped her hands to her ears, Diane remembered learning that most cave bats fed only at night. Catching insects, such as moths, flying beetles, and mosquitoes, they could eat up to a thousand insects an hour, while other bats liked to eat flowers, fruits, nectar, pollen, and leaves.

"Cool beans," said Lee, shuddering.

"Fantastic," Diane said raptly, her mouth ajar.

"Gee whiz!" screeched Benji, huddling closer to his sister's side.

The three of them remained frozen against the granite rock wall, waiting until the last bat vacated its roost.

"When w-will they come b-back?" stammered Benji, seemingly overwhelmed by the awesome sight.

"Not until morning," reassured Lee. "*Allons-y*! Uh, I mean, let's go!" she said crisply.

The path ended abruptly with an old fallen tree. "This way,"

Lee guided, as she skirted around the rotting stump.

They carefully made their way up a rocky, narrow trail, as if walking on a luminescent moonbeam, to the foreboding hole before them. A last trailing bat exited the dark cave right over Diane's head. To her surprise, she wasn't the least bit afraid. Instead, she was intrigued by its small, brown mouse-like body and leathery black wings. Curious, she reached up to touch it, and it backed away from her grasp, fluttering its wings wildly as it flew off into the blackening sky.

"They're blind, you know," Lee said to Benji, as he flapped his duster open and closed like the wings of a bat, cooling himself off from the tiresome climb.

"Actually, they're not," Diane pitched in. "I used to think so, too, until my classmate Tri told me that they *can* see—as well as we do—but they also have some kind of an echo system to help them in the dark. When they hunt, they make a kind of shouting sound that's too high for most of us to hear, although sometimes children can hear it. The echoes that come back tell them what's ahead, like the size and shape of an insect and which way it's traveling. It was fun to actually see one so close up." She paused, panting, light streams of sweat running down the sides of her cheeks.

Lee looked at Benji and shrugged. "You sure *are* book smart," she chortled.

The three adventurers stood before the dark, gaping hole, and with a unified inhale of breath, they stepped into the mine. A dense blackness immediately gathered around them. Sweat beaded on Diane's upper lip, and she felt like she could hardly breathe. She closed her eyes, swallowing hard to clear her throat of the strangling hold the darkness seemed to have on her.

Lee dropped her canvas knapsack onto the earthen floor and,

rummaging through it, came up with a torch that she struck along the cave wall. Sparks flew brightly, flaming instantly, and she held it before her, lighting their way. Diane opened her eyes and sighed with utter relief as she dabbed the sweat from her face. The acrid odor of the creosote-soaked timbers surrounding her smelled like adventure that set deeply into her bones.

Holding the torch high, Lee squinted into the mine. Its dim light streamed into the narrow passageway, disappearing into the inky blackness. The torch flame flickered onto the low ceiling and chiseled mine walls, bringing the wooden beams and jagged cracks in the rock to life as their shadows bounced to the cadence of their steps. Unearthly, eerie figures of black and orange loomed into view, shimmered, then skittered into the darkness behind them.

Only the sound of the adventurers' labored breathing and the grinding of small pebbles beneath their feet could be heard echoing down the murky passageway.

"This place gives me the willies," Benji said grimly, tugging on Diane's duster.

A light, chilly breeze brushed across Diane's cheeks as she strained to see into the darkness beyond the torchlight. Blowing a dangling strand of hair from her face with a puff of air from her pursed lips, she lightly grabbed onto the bottom of Lee's duster in hopes she wouldn't notice. Lee immediately looked back over her shoulder with a spark of panic in her eyes. She smirked at Diane, who smiled back sheepishly, shrugging her shoulders while mouthing, *Sorry!*

Lee laughed under her breath and squatted. Holding the torch in front of her, she pointed to fresh boot prints stamped into the gravel. Diane saw the torchlight reflecting in Lee's sharply focused eyes. "These must belong to the old prospector.

They're only a couple days old. Let's follow them to where he hid the saddlebags," she said tersely.

They crept along in silence, following the old prospector's tracks into the dusty mine. Just a short way in, they came to an intersection of three tunnels. To their left was an old mine railway leading into a tunnel with a low ceiling heavily supported with beams and rafters. A rusted miner's cart was stationed on the thin metal track. The tunnel ahead was broad, with a much higher ceiling, and looked worn from tired miners brushing up against its walls.

Lee knelt down again to look for the prospector's boot prints. "He went this way," she said confidently, gesturing toward the tunnel to the right. In the dim light, they could see that it was covered from floor to ceiling with a large, spindly spiderweb. Its silvery entangling threads had been recently broken and hung jaggedly—likely the work of a passing intruder too large to succumb to its deathly spell.

Diane and Benji cringed at the sight of the huge spiderweb.

Walking hastily, Lee cleared away the web with a sweep of her torch and led the way down the tunnel until it ended abruptly. The passageway was blocked by a large boulder—part of a tunnel collapse—strewn with broken rafters, splintered beams, and rubble. Lee stopped and stared at the earthly mess, then squatted and searched for the prospector's boot prints.

She found several of them, all jumbled together, along with curious drag marks leading behind the boulder. "Wait here," she directed as she slowly crawled along the trackway and disappeared.

Diane anxiously tugged on an eyebrow while Benji bit his lower lip as they waited in silence. A cold wind blew suddenly through the cave, and they both pulled their dusters tighter around them and shivered. The wait seemed like forever.

At last, a faint glow grew brighter from behind the boulder as Lee finally stepped out, dragging a pair of lumpy, stuffed, saddlebags and grinning broadly.

She stopped, letting the worn saddlebag fall in the dirt at her feet. Diane and Benji gathered around, their hands on their knees, panting excitedly, as Lee unbuckled the dusty leather straps and opened one of the pair of bags.

"Geez!" Benji exclaimed as nuggets of shimmering gold fell out and tumbled onto the earthen floor.

"There's five more just like it," Lee said heartily. "And they're the biggest saddlebags I've ever seen."

Benji held the flickering torch as Diane and Lee dragged the other five saddlebags out from behind the boulder. Diane immediately noticed how much stronger Lee was than she. *All that hard work with her father,* she guessed.

"Whew," Diane said breathlessly, plopping another saddlebag on the ground and wiping her brow. "This is going to take us longer than I expected."

Benji bent down and tried lifting one. His face scrunched and reddening, he strained and quickly dropped the saddlebag to the ground, "That weighs about as much as I do," he muttered, rubbing his sore arms. He quickly did the math. "I'd say each pair of bags weighs about fifty pounds." Looking up at the cave ceiling, "That's at least, uh, eight hundred ounces of gold per saddlebag," he scratched his head, "and we've got six saddlebags."

"So, that's about, hmm," Diane hesitated.

"Four thousand, eight hundred ounces of gold, to be exact," Benji calculated with a smirk.

Diane shrugged her shoulders, inclined her head to one side, and nodded to Lee. "He's a math whiz!"

"Okay," said Lee crisply, patting Benji on the head. "You

both handle one together and drag it to that old miner's cart we saw on the rail track back at the intersection. I can handle one on my own. We'll carry or drag them out from the mine in stages, then down the trail to the horses," Lee said, pondering.

Diane and Benji grunted and walked crab-style, awkwardly dragging and sliding a saddlebag to the growing pile behind the rusty cart, while Lee easily slung one over her shoulder.

"How much do you think they're worth?" Benji asked, rubbing his thin arms.

"*Je ne sais pas,*" Lee responded, swiping her wet, long bangs from her forehead. "I don't know exactly. We'll find out as soon as we get them to the assay office back in town. Thousands, tens of thousands, to be sure!"

Dreaming, as she added the last saddlebag to the pile, of all the wonderful things she could buy herself and her family with this gold, Diane mused quietly, *Won't my parents be surprised?* Her muscles were tired, but her heart was light and thrilled with all the possibilities.

"That's it..." Lee started to say when suddenly they heard raucous laughter coming from the entrance of the mine.

"It's the Thorn brothers," Lee murmured, lowering her torch, placing her hand over the flame to dampen its glow. "Quick, get into the mine cart," she said curtly.

CHAPTER EIGHT

RUNAWAY CART

L ee held up the tattered canvas tarp as Diane and Benji clambered inside, then extinguished the torch in the gravel. The rickety old cart was just big enough to hold them. Only the faint sound of their breathing could be heard in the deafening silence as Lee kept watch through a lifted corner of the tarp. The earthy smell of dust and rusted metal filled the small compartment.

"Stop being so jiggy," Diane muttered to Benji, who quivered beside her.

They didn't have long to wait. Muffled voices, shuffling, and a deep cackling echoed through the mine as the Thorn brothers neared the intersection.

"Which way do we go now?" Diane heard Duffy ask. Peering over Lee's shoulder, she watched as he slapped the dust from his mangy cowboy hat, running his bony fingers through his disheveled, oily hair. Duffy looked like a puffed-up vulture— only with thin, fuzzy hair.

Ramus and Wadey held up their torches. The light flickering on the chiseled rock walls made ghoulish figures that dashed across their rough surfaces, sending creepy shivers up Diane's spine.

Cringing, she heard Ramus sneer, "Well, look at this, fellas. Take a gander at what we have here."

Her heart sank as she watched him walk over to the pile of saddlebags hidden partially out of view behind the cart, grab one, and shove it to the feet of his two brothers. They all smiled; big, toothy grins. Pulling out each of the gold-filled saddlebags, they laid the treasures in the intersection just a few feet from the rickety mine cart.

"How much do ya think we got here?" Duffy guffawed. "Huh, huh? How much, Wadey, huh?" he repeated himself, gabbling like an addle-headed lunkhead.

Wadey thought for a long, hard minute, calculating as best he could out loud, "Six saddlebags, two pouches each, uh, uh…I don't know…a lot…a whole lot…more than you can spend in a lifetime," he said, taking his ragged cowboy hat off to scratch his head.

Duffy whistled. "Whowee! We'd be rich. Richer than rich," he mumbled stupidly.

Diane sighed, feeling a dark hole opening up in her heart.

Just then, Benji's foot slipped from under him and hit the side of the cart with a scraping THUD!

"What's that?" Duffy croaked. Alarmed, his eyes gawkingly wide, he glanced around the intersection.

Suffused bright light filled the tiny cart as Ramus lifted the canvas corner, peered inside, then tossed the canvas tarp sharply onto the cave floor.

"Well, what do we have here?" Ramus drawled with a sinister glare. "Three blind mice!"

"Isn't that the French trapper's son?" Wadey grizzled as Lee held her forearm up across her brow to shield her eyes from the blinding light.

"That's him alright," Ramus scowled, twisting his gnarly fingers and cracking his knuckles. "And look at what we have here," he snarled, rubbing Benji on the head, "This is the kid I nearly tripped over in Jake's Saloon. You did hear our conversation, after all. Didn't you, boy?"

Benji turned his head to gaze directly into Ramus' sallow, gaunt face and quivered in horror. His steely gray eyes were set deeply into hollow sockets, shaded by thick black eyebrows that cast dark shadows over his lifeless eyes. A jagged red scar ran from his curled upper lip to the corner of his eye, and a spasm twitched across his face as he reached into the cart, attempting to pull Benji out by his collar.

"Keep your filthy hands off him," Lee commanded in her male voice as she struggled to push his hand away, "and that's *our* gold. We found it first."

"Now, what do three blind mice need gold for, anyhow?" Ramus sneered, glaring at Lee with poisonous venom in his eyes. "I don't think so, trapper."

Trying to distract Ramus, Diane interrupted, politely and friendly-like, "Mr. Thorn, there's six saddlebags and six of us. Why don't we just each take one, and everyone will be happy? Everyone wins."

Ramus stood back, his weight heavily shifted to one leg, and cupped his bristly chin with his fingers. "Why she's pretty and smart," he cackled loudly, his sinister laughter echoing down the narrow passageways. "No, little lady, I reckon we'll take it all," he said as he stepped forward, reaching for her.

The torchlight flickered across his scarred face; the blue vein on his forehead began twitching horribly—Diane gasped.

All at once, the baby raccoon jumped out of Lee's cap, scuttled down her arm, and leapt onto Ramus' outstretched hand. Sinking her tiny sharp teeth deeply into his hand, Niki dashed back to the safety of her den, sending Ramus stumbling backward in shock and fright, his eyes bulging wide, the vein on his forehead pulsating more fiercely, darkening the red scar on his face.

He fortuitously fell against the brake stick on the cart, and with a screechy bang, released it on the track. Seeing her chance, Lee grabbed some rocks from the bottom of the cart and began pummeling the three Thorn brothers as quickly as she could, hitting Ramus squarely in the face. Diane and Benji joined in as the small cart started rolling slowly at first, then faster and faster, rumbling down the track into the mine tunnel ahead.

A bruised and angry Ramus stood shaking his fist, scolding in a murderous voice, "May the mine swallow you up, three blind mice," as the cart rolled farther and farther away.

When the cart finally turned a sharp corner, they were suddenly plunged into darkness. Benji squealed shrilly, terrified. Diane inhaled in jagged short breaths as they quickly hunkered down into the cart. Facing each other with their backs pressed hard to the cart's rusty side, they squeezed their feet against the opposite side until they went numb, using their trembling legs to wedge themselves in tight. Faster and faster, as the cart gained speed, they could feel the cold cave air whipping violently over the tops of their heads. Diane's stomach wrenched into a knot of utter fear, tinged with excitement, as they grasped onto each other's legs and leaned in, her head squashed against Benji's, both quivering.

Bouncing and joggling down the tracks, the odors from old kerosene lanterns and creosote-oiled timbers filled the black void that engulfed them, almost suffocating them. Deafening was the noise from the clattering cart's metal wheels on the rickety rails. Diane's jaw ached from clenching down so hard, and her opened mouth was dry from the rush of cold air. Every moment or two, she would raise her head up to peer into the darkness, curious and horrified at what might lie ahead.

Lee sat up front on her knees, captaining the runaway cart. "Hold on!" she shrieked, struggling to light another torch. Finally lit, its flames streamed jerkily in the wind, illuminating a ghastly sight. Huge, twisted stalactites hanging from the cave ceiling glimmered and flashed by, like the sharp teeth of a monstrous dragon, as the cart hurtled through them, gaining ever-more speed on a downhill slope.

Over the screeching wheels and the whooshing wind, Diane could hear the loud splattering of water somewhere before them.

"Duck!" warned Lee, as the cart flew underneath a curiously green, luminous waterfall cascading along the side cave wall. The sound of falling water echoed throughout the narrow passageway.

"Whew!" Lee said, wiping her dampened bangs aside.

Suddenly, the cart took a hairpin turn to the right that violently rocked it, lifting two of its wheels off the tracks as it careened toward what looked like a solid wall ahead. The cart tumbled Lee backward onto Diane and Benji, tossing them about until it landed again with a grinding THUD on its four screeching wheels.

"Duck!" Lee commanded again, regaining her position in the front.

Everyone shrieked as the cart crashed through a thin, opaque calcite wall, which had grown over since the closing of the mine, into an inner chamber in the cave's maze of tunnels. Slowly lifting their heads from beneath the rim of the cart, the light from the torch reflected off thousands of facets of amethyst. The walls and ceiling were covered in huge purple crystals with white veins of quartz crystals spiderwebbed throughout them.

"Fantastic!" Diane shouted avidly. Benji ogled the sparkling gems, too, snuggling closer.

"Everything's going to be okay," she said reassuringly.

"Golly gee," he said, panting with an anxious sigh.

There was nothing they could do at this moment, and Diane remembered something her father would say: *so, just make the best of it.*

Just then, the cart slowed, going up a small incline. Diane and Benji sighed deeply, feeling a fleeting moment of relief. Lee released her paralyzing grip on the rim of the cart, exhaled loudly, and just when they thought the miner's cart was finally coming to a halt, it rattled, strained, and tumbling over the top of the hill, fell forward once again, racing downhill at lightning speed into blackness.

Diane and Benji grasped on tighter to each other. She could hear her heart pounding loudly in her ears. She felt a sickening knot in her stomach that tightened with every sharp turn. The dry air became chillier as they whizzed around tight corners. Eyes stinging as the cold air swept past them, her face felt frozen and rigid. Her legs were now numb from gripping the sides so tightly, but she dared not shift her position, in fear she might slip and be thrown from the rickety cart.

Faster and faster the cart hurtled forward, until Lee's torch flickered on a wooden structure blocking the track ahead, the word DANGER written on it in red capital letters.

The runaway miner's cart sped toward it.

Little Niki peered curiously out from her secret compartment in Lee's fur cap and, startled by the frightening sight, whisked around and buried herself deep within the safety of her little den, trembling. Diane could hear Niki chittering madly and wondered if the little critter was cussing them out.

Diane gulped, glancing frantically at the walls of the mine tunnel as they rushed by...terrified...eyes bulging...her heart screaming in her ears...she saw...for a flash of a moment...a small figure standing under a lit torch in a side tunnel archway. She heard Benji scream shrilly, and clutched onto him tightly.

"Grab onto my belt!" she shrieked in his ear as they hurtled toward the wooden barricade. Diane held onto Benji with every last ounce of strength she possessed and braced for a sudden impact.

"Hold onto me!" yelled Lee as the cart crashed through the wooden blockade.

CHAPTER NINE

RESCUE

A bove their heads, Diane saw a rope-and-pulley system. Lee had seen it, too, and lunged, grabbing for the rope just as the cart tumbled from beneath them, bouncing and clattering off the rocky cave walls as it plunged into the black abyss below.

Diane and Benji were jerked and jumbled about, twisting wildly. She managed to clasp onto Lee's long legs and the rope, which flung itself securely around Benji's waist as he held an iron grip on his sister's belt.

There they hung, Benji grasping onto Diane's belt and Diane clinging onto Lee's legs, all entangled in the twisted rope that creaked noisily with every sway.

"Hold tight!" yelled Lee. "And stay still!"

Benji was frozen with fright. Diane looked around, surveying their precarious predicament. She had lost all sense of how far they had traveled through the immense cave, and though she felt like vomiting, she gritted her teeth, determined to find a way out of this mess.

They hung, quivering, not daring to twitch a muscle, when

suddenly, a small light appeared, bouncing down the tracks. It grew larger and larger...and so did their fear that the Thorn brothers were coming to finish them off.

Much to their relief, an odd-looking girl with a long cinnamon ponytail appeared out of the darkness, running awkwardly toward them, swaying a lit kerosene lantern. She stopped at the edge of the tracks and bent over to catch her breath, panting.

"Help us!" Diane pleaded. "Pull the rope! It's tied to the post over there." She inclined her head in the general direction.

Without saying a word, the girl carefully began pulling her end of the rope, slowly bringing the three dangling adventurers closer and closer to the tracks. Finally, safely suspended over the rails, the girl untangled their rope, and Diane told Benji to let go and jump off.

He shook his head jerkily...trembling...paralyzed. He wouldn't let go.

"It's okay, Benji," his sister said tenderly, encouraging him to be brave.

Still, he hesitated until the girl reached up and wrapped her arms around his waist, which must have made him feel safe because he slowly unclenched his grip and fell from the rope into the arms of their peculiar heroine.

"He's alright," she said reassuringly.

Benji then reached up and tugged on Diane's pants. "Come on, sis," he said. "It's only a few feet."

Diane let go of the rope and Lee's pants, landing gratefully on the tracks. She sighed deeply and felt her fear melt away. Color flooded back into her pale cheeks.

Lee then dropped off the rope, flexing her hands. "*Incroyable!*" she declared. "That was close." She let out a gasp of relief and rubbed her exhausted arms.

The girl wore a long black duster that nearly dragged along

the ground over a simple pink, flowered dress with dusty blue bloomers underneath, scuffed brown cowboy boots, and a red bandana slung around her neck. She was a bit odd-looking with her long, skinny neck, rather large protruding ears, and square face dappled with dark cinnamon freckles across her high cheeks and button nose, the same shade as her ponytail. Her eyes were a darker brown with a similar hue.

Don't let looks deceive you, Diane remembered the words of the mysterious woman on the train. *Look deep inside people to see who they really are and have compassion.* Feeling both disbelief and gratitude, Diane turned to the girl on the tracks and asked, "Who are you, and where did you come from?"

"My name is Addie," she said timidly. "That's short for Adeline, and I followed you from town. I was sleeping in the cardboard box in the alley behind Jake's Saloon. When I heard your plans, I thought I might be of some help, so I tagged along," she explained, adding almost apologetically, "I hope you don't mind."

"Well, you certainly were of help to us tonight. Thank you," said Diane. Nudging Lee with her elbow, she murmured, "I told you someone was following us."

"How'd you know where to find us?" Lee asked.

"You wouldn't believe me if I told you," Addie said, looking shyly at the ground. "No one does. That's why my parents left me in Durango," she muttered, with a deep sadness in her voice.

"I'll believe you," Diane said tenderly, feeling compassion for the girl.

Addie looked deeply into Diane's green eyes with hope and trust reflecting in her own. She took a deep breath. "Niki told me," she mumbled. "I can speak to animals. They can understand me...and I understand them," she revealed, physically cringing as if she anticipated being laughed at—or worse.

"I believe you," Diane said sincerely.

Lee and Benji gave each other quick quizzical looks and then stared at Diane with bulging eyes. She flashed her eyes wide and glared back at them, asking with the confidence of a master detective, "Did either of you tell Addie the raccoon's name?"

Lee and Benji looked at each other with stunned expressions and shrugged their shoulders, responding in unison, "No!"

"Then how did she know her name?" Diane asked astutely. "Niki told her, and she told her we were in trouble. Remember when she was chittering right before the crash? That's right, isn't it, Addie? She was talking to you!"

"Yes, that's right," Addie said shyly, but looked relieved.

"How do you talk to animals?" Diane asked.

"I open my mind and picture the animal I'm about to speak to and ask them if I can talk to them," she said, adding, "in my mind, of course. They always say 'yes' because it is as intriguing for them as it is for me to make the connection. I introduced myself to Niki back in the alley behind Jake's early this evening.

"We communicated with some words, but mostly in pictures and feelings—with wild animals, especially. Their vocabulary is nonexistent without human contact. Domesticated animals like Niki have a vocabulary of about a hundred words or so, since they're around humans and all. Though, they complain to me that most of the time, their humans talk too fast.

"Niki communicated very strong fear feelings," she continued, "and sent me a mental picture of the DANGER sign right before you crashed. I followed you into the mine and then hid in the first side tunnel, waiting, until I heard the Thorn brothers come in, then leave laughing. They were bragging about the three blind mice they sent scampering to their deaths," she said with a note of concern. "I occasionally live in this mine, in a small antechamber off the side tunnel, and have explored it from time to time. I've seen that sign before and knew a shortcut to it."

"That's fascinating! That was *you* I saw in the side tunnel," Diane declared keenly. "Can you teach me how to speak to animals?"

"I wish I could. I've tried, but it's not something you can learn. Either you're born with the 'gift,' as my mother calls it, or you're not. My father calls it a curse. He took my mother away in Durango and left me behind with only a horse, a saddle, and the clothes on my back. A few of the townspeople have been very kind to me and help me out in exchange for doing some chores."

She paused for a moment, as if every word conjured up the painful memory that flickered in her sad-puppy eyes, and then continued. "I discovered I had the 'gift'—or 'skill,' I'd rather call it—on my fifth birthday when I had my first conversation with my pet dog, Pipa." Her bright face revealed that she was thrilled to finally be able to talk about it with someone who was sincerely interested and cared.

"Well, *we* believe you, and you're welcome to join us," Diane said, nodding to Lee and Benji as she started walking back along the rail tracks. "Maybe she can help us find the Thorn brothers and where they're camped tonight with our gold."

"I've already spoken to their horses, and I know exactly where they're bedded down," Addie reported gleefully.

"Cool beans," Lee said crisply. "Lead the way!"

CHAPTER TEN

THE DECISION

The adventurers, now numbering four, followed Addie and her swinging kerosene lantern through her shortcut and, in little time, walked hastily out of the mine, grateful to see the starry sky once again. The thin mountain air was cool and crisp, chilling their hot, jangled nerves. Addie led the quiet procession down the rocky trail to their waiting horses. Diane was surprised to see a handsome reddish horse tied up next to her black horse and petted them both warmly.

"It's so good to see you again," she sighed as she stroked the black horse's ears and gently kissed his velvety nose.

They quickly untethered their horses and followed Addie as she led them on foot silently through the dark forest. They'd only gone a short way when she suddenly stopped. A small, smokeless campfire in the distance glowed—the orange, crackling blaze set the tall pine trees in an eerie black silhouette.

Addie made a circle motion with her hands, signaling for them to huddle. "Let's wait here until they're fast asleep. The way they're drinking, it won't take too long," she said hushedly. "Then we'll sneak in and take back a few of the saddlebags."

"Why not all of them?" Lee asked, obviously disappointed.

"Because," Diane agreed, "I'm hoping...that if we take, say, only half of them, they won't bother searching for the rest, so it's less likely they'll chase after us. At least they'll have one saddlebag apiece. That's fair," she surmised naively.

"We can split up the rest of the saddlebags between us," Addie offered shyly.

"It does make sense," Lee said reluctantly. "I don't want those Thorn brothers hunting for us anytime soon," she nodded firmly.

Waiting in the shadows while the brothers ate and drank by the warmth of the campfire, Diane watched as Duffy, stumbling about, accidentally kicked over a burlap sack of beans near his bedroll.

That could spell trouble, Diane reasoned. *Skunks and raccoons can smell that a mile away.* Even in the suburbs of Chicago, a wild critter had occasionally rummaged through their garbage, attracted by its tantalizing aromas.

They huddled silently behind a small thicket of Gambel oaks, watching as the three bumbling brothers started staggering and falling over each other, drunk with celebration. Leaving their dirty plates scattered on the ground with remnants of cooked beans, hard biscuits, and dried meat, they crawled into their sleeping blankets and fell fast asleep. Soon loud, grotesque snoring broke the silence of the forest. Even the crickets covered their ears in their leafy beds.

The four adventurers finally nodded to each other in agreement—it was time to make their move. Just as they were about to come out of hiding, Addie abruptly held up her hand, signaling for them to freeze. A family of skunks had wandered into camp, attracted by the inviting odors of a promising dinner. Addie shut her eyes and quietly waved her hand around up in the air, as if writing magical symbols in the wind, in some sort of peculiar greeting dance that opened a mind connection with the mother skunk.

Diane, Lee, and Benji watched in amazement as the mother skunk stopped in her tracks and looked straight in Addie's direction, her little ears twitching in apparent conversation.

Addie opened her eyes and said, "Let's go now. It's safe!"

"What did you tell her?" Diane asked.

"You'll see," Addie said, snickering to herself. "Stay clear of the skunks, and DON'T step on them!" she cautioned. "They're expecting us!"

The four of them tiptoed quietly around the sleeping men, each of whom had his own unique, annoyingly loud snore. They sounded like a chorus of bullfrogs until Duffy farted, adding his bass to the melody.

They quickly found the worn leather saddlebags hidden under the moth-eaten tarp from the miner's cart. While Benji held it up, Lee passed the saddlebags, one by one, to Diane and Addie, who awkwardly carried them to their waiting horses.

As they slipped back into the shadows, they turned to take one last look at the snoring Thorn brothers and the feasting skunks—who then did the most amazing thing. They encircled the bedrolls of the sleeping men, positioned themselves tail-side in, and waited as if they were standing guard.

"I told them to stay there and wait until the men wake up and then spray them when they stir. That'll keep them busy for a good long while," Addie chortled as the others joined in, smothering their laughter.

"*What sweet revenge,*" Diane reflected.

Under the brightest full moon, Addie mounted her horse, weighed down with a saddlebag full of gold nuggets, while Lee fastened a second saddlebag securely to her chestnut. She then made sure the third saddlebag was tightened properly to the patient black horse. Diane and Benji clambered onto his back, and the four adventurers quietly started off through the forest, dappled in silver moonbeams.

"Can you tell the horses how much we appreciate them?" Diane asked Addie as they rode alongside her.

"I already did," she replied. "They both speak very highly of you all. They told me you're very kind and gentle with them."

"Good. Tell them I love them," Diane said heartily.

"For me too!" Lee added.

"And me!" Benji giggled.

"Where should we go?" Diane asked, bewildered. "We can't go back to town. Eventually, the Thorn brothers will show up, stench and all, at the assay office and discover that we're still alive. They'll know we took the saddlebags then."

"I've heard of another assay office in the Arizona territory at Vulture City," Lee said pensively. "You can send a telegram from Flagstaff, once we get there, telling your grandparents that you're alright and to come and meet you in Vulture."

Diane sat on her black horse, deep in thought, and felt this was the only solution. *My parents are going to worry so,* she fussed with herself, feeling trapped. *They'll skin me alive. But I've got to see this through,* she resolved, clenching her teeth firmly together.

The decision made, she settled into the rhythm of the black horse's gait as she followed Lee into the dark forest. Diane had seen how Lee had smartly bartered for their essential supplies, including plenty of extra jerky, and felt confident that she was a very capable trapper and could provide the necessary food for the longer-than-planned journey. Besides, there was plenty of water in all of the mountain streams she had seen on their journey so far.

Lee had shared with her, as they waited out the night behind the saloon, that she had survived in the wilds of Colorado for weeks on end, sometimes even a month or two at a time, just trapping and hunting, which she did mostly as her father was becoming more and more useless.

Sad, Diane pondered, feeling bad for Lee and her father. *Really sad.* But for their plan, it sounded as reasonable as she could imagine. So, with the decision made, she declared out loud to the forest and the moon, "And the adventure continues!"

CHAPTER ELEVEN

ARTIFACTS

F rom a pine bough overhead, a horned owl hooted in agreement, as if a huge weight had been lifted. The moon's light, too, seemed to intensify, with rainbow colors encircling it in a thick, blurry haze, apparently giving its blessing to their plan.

"How eerie," Diane said, gesturing to the glimmering moon.

"Uh-oh," Lee said, "That means rains on the way. We'd better get a move on. We've got to go southwest from here." Gently kicking her chestnut in the sides, she started him walking swiftly into the night. The black horse with the white star on his forehead, carrying Diane and Benji, followed behind, while Addie on her handsome red horse brought up the rear.

The adventurers traveled in silence for an hour or so, listening to the night sounds of chirping crickets, croaking toads, and the mating call of hidden tree frogs. Winding through a pristine conifer forest, they anxiously watched as dark, ominous clouds filled the midnight blue sky, playing peekaboo with the glistening white orb.

The mountainous valley they left behind in Durango gave way to a landscape of steep canyon walls of yellowish sandstone and shale.

"Look at those rocks, Di," Benji whispered in her ear. "They look like one of Mom's layer cakes with the creamy stuff squished out."

"I think they're made of sandstone!" Diane yelled back over her shoulder, chuckling. They did indeed remind her of an oddly layered vanilla cake with differing thicknesses of yellow cake and white sweet cream. "We learned about the geology of the West in science class. These probably formed in the Cretaceous period—the time of the dinosaurs—when these parts were once covered by a shallow sea. When the sea receded, it left only beaches and sand dunes behind, that later turned to stone."

"How do you remember all that stuff?" Benji marveled.

"I just love learning about the earth—geology. It's one of my favorite subjects," she shrugged, lowering her head into the oncoming wind.

The temperature was dropping quickly with the approaching storm, and the soft breeze soon became a chilly wind that whipped over Diane's cheeks. She pulled up the duster's collar around her ears to keep warm. Benji did the same and snuggled close to her back to shield him from the cold. The smell of rain hung thick in the air.

A light summer drizzle began to dance lightly upon Diane's face as she held it up to a pewter-bottomed cloud that floated by, its rounded top lit by the moon. High up in the canyon walls, fifty feet or so above the canyon floor, Diane spied roughly constructed brick walls with open doorways and windows nestled under a heavy rock overhang. As she gazed around her, she could see more crumbling walls and windows dappled between the layers of rock at various heights on both sides of the narrow canyon they were traversing. She felt as if she was journeying back through time, and the little hairs on the back of her neck prickled.

"Those must be the ancient stone dwellings I've heard travelers talk about at Jake's Saloon," Addie muttered grimly. "They say they're haunted. Many travelers and hunters have reported hearing mysterious drums beating at night and witnessed Indian spirits dancing around ghostly fires."

A chilly silence fell over the adventurers as they considered the possibilities.

"Cool beans," Lee finally said, shivering with excitement.

"Let's go check it out!" Diane agreed bravely.

Addie and Benji just looked at each other, bug-eyed, and, biting their lower lips, shrugged their shoulders.

They continued for a while longer, looking for a suitable dwelling to explore, when suddenly the gathering storm clouds ripped open and poured their contents down in buckets upon them. The torrential rains lashed at their panicked faces, splattering loudly on the trail as they squeezed their horses harder and galloped head-on into the whistling and moaning winds.

"Follow me!" Lee yelled over the pounding rain as a crack of lightning lit up the sky overhead in a huge spiderweb of bright, silken threads and rumbling thunder.

Benji squealed as a lightning bolt exploded a nearby pine tree into a blaze of orange sparks. They swiftly rode by, cringing. Benji leaned hard into his sister's back to shield himself from the fiery flying splinters and shattered debris. Diane bent her head low behind the black horse's driving head, his black mane whipping in her face, her heart pounding in her ears, as lightning flashed all around them.

Up ahead, Diane could see a large sandstone overhang that promised protection from the hammering rain. Lee had seen it, too, and was guiding them there. When they finally cleared the last stand of pine trees, their jaws dropped, and their mouths hung agape at the astonishing sight before them.

A large stone dwelling, at least three stories high, was built into the cliffside in a shallow alcove. Wooden ladders of oak and spruce stood against the walls leading to the upper rooms. From their vantage point, they could see that every exterior room had a T-shaped opening for a doorway, squared windows, and wood-thatched ceilings with their support rafters protruding out of the façade of the dwelling. They noticed open-roof terraces on nearly every floor, with large clay storage pots and black stone mortars.

"Gee whiz!" Benji exclaimed, bubbling with excitement and a bit of apprehension.

They slowly walked their tired, drenched horses out of the chilly rain and onto the main plaza floor. Dismounting, they stood in front of the massive stone structure, observing the walls made of sandstone bricks that had been chipped and chiseled into shape, held together with a mortar of soil, water, and ash. Brushing her sopping hair from her face, Diane inspected the walls more closely.

"Look here," she said fervidly, pointing to some odd markings on the mud mortar. She could see hand impressions and fingerprints from the ancient people who built the magnificent dwelling hundreds of years before. Diane placed her slender fingers into the grooves between the thin ridges.

My hand is as big as theirs, she murmured silently, lost in thought.

Lee stepped back from the wall and lit a torch. It sizzled and sparkled as they explored the first floor of the main building together. Shivering from a mixture of chill and nerves, they entered a low-ceilinged room that was filled with all kinds of wondrous things. The air in the tiny room was musty and stale-smelling. Benji scrunched his face and pinched his button nose closed, wincing.

"Artifacts," Diane said avidly, "made by these cliff dwellers. Something terrible must have happened that they left so many of their belongings behind."

The stone floors were littered with red shards of broken coiled pottery. "They obviously left in a hurry and took only the important things they needed to survive." Diane admired the interior walls of colored earthen plasters that she imagined were once brightly painted, now faded with time. "I studied this in school," she said with astute authority. "I love archaeology, the study of human history, and I've always been interested in the ways of the native Indian people. I admire how they knew how to live with nature and with each other, everyone caring for each other. No one went hungry or was left alone. They had great respect for the earth and the animals, too!" she said fervently.

"That looks like a digging stick," she said, pointing to the long, slender stick with a sharp tip that was propped up in the corner of the room. "They used it to dig up roots and tubers, perhaps even small animals hiding in their burrows," Diane recalled. "And this looks like a bow and quiver of arrows for hunting. Look, the bow's broken; that must be why they left it behind. Many of these things could be easily replaced or were just too heavy or cumbersome to carry, like that black mortar at Addie's feet." She gestured with a wave of her hand.

"What's this?" Benji asked, holding up an unusual-looking basket made of loosely woven twigs.

"Hmm, I think that's a fish trap," she said keenly. "And this is a dipping cup carved from a gourd for drinking water." She was so thrilled to see with her own eyes things she had only read about in her schoolbooks.

"Look at these ground-up pieces of corn," Addie chimed in, catching Diane's infectious excitement. She bent down next to the large mortar—a large black stone, made from volcanic basalt, shaped like a trough—and rubbed her fingers over its smooth surface. Addie picked up some of the pieces of dried, shriveled corn kernels left behind by someone maybe hundreds of years ago.

"They used another stone, called a metate, to grind the corn, or maize, as they called it," she instructed, "like the pestle the pharmacist uses to grind the herbs he gives my mother," Diane added, beaming. "They ground other things, too, like acorns, wild grains, seeds, and pinyon nuts."

"What's this?" Benji asked again, this time dangling a colorfully decorated stick with beads, fur, and some feathers attached. "I found it next to that stone container of white powder."

Diane paused for a moment, her eyes on the ceiling. "The white powder is from the crushed maize that was probably used in their ceremonial rituals. That's a prayer stick!" She suddenly remembered from her book on the American West. "I'm surprised those important things were left behind." *What happened?* she pondered.

Lee and Addie stood amazed at her unending knowledge and enthusiasm; their mouths hung open, listening, while Benji grinned proudly. "You sure are book smart, sis!"

"Well, we can certainly wait out the storm here," Lee said earnestly. "We have everything we need. Look at those blankets!" she shouted, pointing to a pile of them neatly stacked in the corner behind a stone-rimmed hearth.

"Let's get out of these wet clothes and get a fire going here," Lee advised, shedding her soaking outer garments as she walked over to the corner to select a blanket. Wrapping herself in a warm blanket, she promptly stomped off on a search for firewood.

Everyone followed her lead and picked up a mottled woven blanket, shook out centuries of dust, and wrapped one around their rain-soaked bodies, appreciating its warmth. The blankets were made of wool with faded orange, yellow, and black geometric designs, the same colors that adorned the walls.

"Look at this one!" Diane squealed with delight, wrapping a blanket made mostly of turkey feathers tightly around her. "It's so warm!"

"How did they get these wonderful colors?" Addie asked, removing her dripping duster before wrapping her dampened dress in the woolen blanket.

"They made dyes from plants like bloodroot that was used to produce red dyes, while green dyes were made from algae, and yellow dyes came from the lichens that grew on the rock faces and trees near their dwelling. They also used minerals, like ochre and manganese, that they ground up and mixed with animal grease or fatty seeds," Diane offered. "Quite ingenious, don't you think?"

Diane and Benji wandered off together in search of firewood. They ducked in and out of several adjacent dusty rooms. There seemed to be over a hundred rooms; too daunting a challenge to explore them all. But they managed to gather several good logs and some tinder, too. Benji tagged along, wrinkling his nose at all the earthy smells.

"Look how these doorways are made in the shape of a T," Diane pointed out to Benji, who was yawning and beginning to lag.

Diane noticed that many of the T-shaped doorways had a

woven blanket hung from a wooden beam. *For privacy,* she imagined—probably leaving the lower part of the 'T' open for ventilation, allowing fresh air from the outside to flow freely from room to room throughout the dwelling.

Brilliant, she considered, admiring their innovative architectural design and use of natural materials.

Benji got bored and, dumping his wood near the hearth, joined Addie, who was tending the horses.

With her armful of firewood, Diane stopped and stood alone on the edge of the ancient plaza. Gazing out into the chilly haze of rain, she wondered about the cliff dwellers that once lived here, imagining what their lives might have been like while listening to the soft patter of raindrops at her feet. She shut her eyes; a cold mist blew across her face from a stormy gust of wind. For a fleeting moment, the faint sound of the spattering rain sounded like the soft, moccasin-covered footsteps of children running on the plaza, laughing playfully.

Lightning streaked across the sky, a white flash on the inside of her eyelids, startling her from a dream-like memory. She opened her eyes and wrapped her unusual blanket tighter around her. Shivering from the penetrating cold, she watched the full moon duck behind an ominous dark cloud fringed in ghostly silver. Velvety black trees swayed jerkily in the wind against the eerie glow of the moon as the clouds began drifting apart, revealing a speckled sky of twinkling stars.

A movement in the branches caught her eye, as a large, dark shape flapped its huge wings and then flew away under the glistening moon, down-canyon. *That looks like the same golden eagle,* she reflected. Shaking her head, *It can't be—*

Just then, Lee came through a doorway with a lofty armful of dry firewood.

"Let me help you," Diane offered, taking a few branches from the teetering stack.

Finding the hearthstones in the first room, Lee quickly started a warm, cozy fire. They laid their soaking-wet outer garments around the fire to dry, Benji's and Addie's, too. Snuggling into their mysteriously designed blankets to stay warm in their damp undergarments, they snacked on jerky and pemmican bars, passing a water canteen between them.

Addie and Benji joined the huddled circle. "We found a stone trough at the edge of the plaza filled with rainwater, so we brought the horses to it and fed them some grain biscuits. They're on a long tether so they can graze on the grasses just off the plaza," Addie said as she wrapped herself tightly in her blanket and warmed her hands by the small fire.

Benji hunkered down next to his sister and pulled a light blue stone from his pocket. "What's this, sis?" he asked, turning the stone over in the light of the fire.

"That's turquoise, I think," she said in surprise. "Where did you find it?"

"I opened one of the saddlebags and it fell out," he shrugged with a tinge of guilt. "There's a lot more," he said, his eyes gleaming, "and something else…those saddlebags are not like anything we've ever seen. They're *really* old, Di, and each one is branded with a peculiar looking mark, like the letter E, but real fancy like. It's faint, but the mark is there," he said, glancing at Addie.

"He's right," Addie confirmed, nodding. "I've never seen saddlebags styled that way, and the letter is as terribly worn and as unusual as the bags. What could the E stand for?"

CHAPTER TWELVE

HAUNTED CLIFF DWELLING

S tunned, Diane dove into her knapsack, which was always at her side, and pulled out her book of the American West. She flipped to the page with the turned-down corner and read once again out loud, "Estebanico, the black guide, was also known to be a skilled healer and was frequently accepted by many of the native peoples he encountered, collecting payment in turquoise..." she stopped and held up Benji's hand with the blue gemstone in it, glittering in the firelight. "Turquoise, the branded E..." she continued excitedly.

"E for 'Estebanico,'" Benji declared, equally stunned.

"Who is Estebanico?" Lee and Addie asked simultaneously.

Diane proceeded to tell them that in the early 1500s, after great hordes of gold were found in Aztec temples and plundered throughout Mexico, Spanish conquistadors continued to explore the New World in search of more native treasures. A slave guide named Estebanico had supposedly learned of seven cities of gold to the north, referring to the Southwest territories of America, mainly Arizona, Utah, New Mexico, and Colorado.

"Here's the part," she began reading. "He mysteriously

disappeared…but told of native tales of 'seven cities to the north where the people were extremely wealthy, lived in spacious multistoried villages shimmering in gold, and wore fine-woven clothing made of cotton.'"

She skimmed for a moment.

"Estebanico," she finally read out loud again, "called the lost cities of gold Cibola, a Spanish pronunciation for the native name for their adobe dwellings. The Spanish had their own word for the dwellings: pueblo—meaning village. Lost, because the cities were supposedly never found."

Benji's eyes grew wide as he looked at the ancient stone walls around him.

Diane continued. "'The mystery of the lost seven cities of Cibola has never been solved. Explorers and treasure seekers continue to search for gold and other great wealth that may still be hidden somewhere in the pueblos of America's Southwest, waiting to be discovered.'" She sighed deeply and closed the book with a dramatic flair.

"So, the gold of Cibola could be hidden in here?" Benji asked, popping up, "in *this* pueblo?" He darted off to begin again a more earnest search of every nook and cranny of the ancient cliff dwelling. Addie squealed and jumped up to join him.

"I think Benji's got gold fever," Lee chortled. "They both do!"

"Another question," Diane pondered out loud, "Did Estebanico actually *find* Cibola and then mysteriously disappear with these saddlebags filled with gold and turquoise, *and* where did the old prospector stumble onto Estebanico's saddlebags?" Suddenly, a light bulb went off in her head.

"Was that Estebanico's skeleton he found?"

Lee scratched her cap, and little Niki peeked out from her den. "Aren't you going to join the search too?" she said with a skeptical tone in her voice.

"No, I've already scoured most of the rooms. *If* there's gold in this pueblo, Benji will find it." Diane replied and wistfully continued. "Perhaps there *is* gold to be found, like it's written in the book. Maybe, we're in the heart of Cibola!"

Benji and Addie returned sometime later, empty-handed and disappointed. Sulking, they plopped down by the warm fire and, staring into the flames, they reported the details of their exhaustive search.

"Nothing," Benji huffed, rubbing his hands over the flickering flames. He took his pocketknife out and twiddled with it. "We searched every room, I think. Just a lot more *old* stuff."

Lee peered at Diane, who seemed deep in thought as she gazed at the flickering orange and yellow fiery tongues. "What are you thinking about?" she asked, absentmindedly petting little Niki, who had climbed out of her den and curled up on Lee's lap, warily watching the flames.

Diane took a deep breath. "I was just thinking about my family. My mother told us a story once about our great-grandfather, who left his family in Chicago as a young man and went to Arizona to farm the desert Phoenix Valley. He fell in love with a beautiful Indian woman and married. I was wondering if she might have been, or that *I* might be, related in some way to the people who once lived here," she shivered. "One of their daughters married a Phoenician who eventually took their family back to Chicago, where my mother was born," she reflected. "My grandparents returned to Arizona just a few years ago. We're moving out there this summer to live near the rest of my family. Most I've never met."

As they huddled around the blazing fire that leapt, crackled, and sputtered, the weary adventurers drifted to sleep, exhausted by the thrilling events of the day, dreaming of Cibola's gold.

Diane was walking through a thick white mist. As she stepped out of its impenetrable glow, she found herself standing on a stone plaza before a bustling stone structure that felt strangely familiar. A group of giggling children ran by her, gleefully playing with a romping wolf pup. Men and women were all around, busy at their daily chores, and didn't seem to notice her presence. A group of gabbing women dressed in deerskins was grinding yellow and blue maize in black stone troughs, laughing, while teasingly pointing at a circle of young men sitting nearby on tree stumps, knapping stone tools and knives, sheepishly avoiding their stares.

It was a sunny summer day; Diane felt the warmth of the sun on the side of her face and squinted in the dazzling light angling through the surrounding conifer trees, looking toward a rooftop terrace, searching for someone. Putting a hand up to her forehead to shield her eyes, she watched as a tall, slender woman with long, dark, straight hair, an equally slender nose, and glistening brown eyes stood up before a wooden loom. Stretching from hours of sitting and weaving, the woman turned her head and peered down into the plaza. Seeing Diane, she placed her hand over her heart and smiled warmly.

Mother? Diane whispered. *Is that—*

Suddenly, she felt someone nudging her side, waking her. The mist gathered all around her again, swirling, engulfing her, and the scene vanished.

She groaned grumpily and tried to ignore it, hoping that the dream would return. *Was it a dream?* she asked herself, as she drifted into consciousness.

There it was again.

"Diane, wake up!" Lee pleaded tensely with great concern in her voice.

"What's wrong?" she asked, now fully awake, her bones

resonating with alarm.

"*Ecoutez*. Listen!" Lee said tersely. "Do you hear that?"

"Hear what?" Diane replied, a little annoyed as she had been sleeping so deeply.

"*Ecoutez!*" Lee repeated anxiously.

This time, Diane heard it, too. "Drums!" she said, startled.

Immediately she sat up and leaned over to shake Addie and Benji awake, putting her finger to her lips and cupping her hand to her ear, signaling to them to keep quiet and listen.

Addie's eyes grew wide, and Benji buried his head in his blanket.

"Come on," Diane said hastily, as she quickly dressed in her warm, dried clothes. She threw the blanket off Benji and quietly stamped her foot, pointing sharply to the ground—a gesture she had seen her mother make a hundred times that signaled "NOW!"

"Gee whiz!" Benji said grimly, slowly stifling a yawn. Then he heard the drums and quickly went to task. Finally dressed, he shivered in excitement and fear, wrapping himself again in his warm blanket.

Lee led the way out of the dwelling and onto the spacious stone plaza. The pounding rain had stopped while they slept, and only a few light raindrops splattered occasionally from the far edge of the overhang. The drumming grew louder and seemed to be coming from a circular hole cut into the plaza floor. A mysterious, eerie light emanated from the opening. They crept closer and could now clearly hear rhythmic chanting along with the beating drums. Diane's heart was pounding in her ears to the melodious, hollow sound.

Nearing the opening to the kiva, the sacred ceremonial chamber, Lee got down onto her stomach and beckoned for everyone else to do the same. The haunting chanting of male voices grew louder as they inched their way to the kiva opening. Finally, four pairs of eyes peered over the stone-lined edge, and their mouths dropped open, eyes goggling at the most astonishing sight.

Flames reached up toward the sky from a ghostly fire that offered no warmth, seemingly sucking the heat from the room below. Dark shadows loomed monstrously on the circular walls. A cold shudder cascaded down Diane's spine as she stared at the translucent, ghostly Indian spirits dancing around the fire, chanting to the hypnotic beat of the drums. Breastplates made of bone and beads adorned the warriors' glimmering, pale, naked chests. Feather headdresses encircled the silvery hair sweeping down their backs, swaying from side to side as they danced a foot or two above the ground.

The adventurers were thunderstruck! They watched as the ghastly figures bowed up and down, stomping their feet, shaking their war clubs adorned with rattles of deer hooves and polished antler discs to the spellbinding melody.

Suddenly, Addie said hushedly, "Uh-oh!

"What's wrong?" Diane cringed, not sure how much more she could bear.

"The Thorn brothers are awake. They're angry, and they're heading this way," she muttered in a quavering voice.

"How do you know?"

"Ramus' horse just told me so," Addie murmured, knotting her hands.

"Let's hide," Lee said, pushing away from the stony lip of the kiva. She scampered quietly along the plaza and dropped down beneath its side edge, watching.

Diane, Benji, and Addie quickly followed behind. Huddled in the shadows of adjacent pine trees, their eyes peering nervously over the edge, they waited in fear.

CHAPTER THIRTEEN

THORNS' CROSSROADS

A raindrop splatted lightly on Duffy's face, followed by another, then another, until he roused from his drunken sleep, needing to urinate. He opened his crusty eyelids to a bleary vision of fuzzy black and white stripes. Rubbing his eyes roughly, he squinted and blinked, trying to bring the scene into focus. Just then, a flash of lightning lit up the sky, and his eyes flew wide open as he clearly made out the shape of a skunk's hind end aimed directly in his face. He shrieked loudly and quickly threw his sleeping blanket over his head just as a fine, pungent spray was expelled simultaneously from each of the skunks, waking Wadey and Ramus with a fright.

The two startled brothers jumped up into a fog of putrid stench. Gagging, they desperately tried covering their noses and stinging eyes with the filthy bandanas that hung loosely around their necks. Blinded, Ramus reeled backward and tripped over the stones ringing their campfire, tumbling into the hot coals, scorching a hole in his britches. Wadey angrily kicked dirt and rocks at the retreating skunks, cursing as they scurried away, disappearing into the dark forest.

All at once, more bolts of spidery lightning ripped across the blackness, opening the threatening sky. A deluge of thrashing rain poured out from the white, jagged tear in the heavens onto the scuttling Thorn brothers as they hurriedly packed up their campsite, loading their supplies onto their drenched and frightened horses.

Ramus, limping badly, led his anxious horse to the pile of hidden saddlebags. Wadey and Duffy hurriedly followed behind, still gagging. He found the tattered tarp caught against the scaly bark of a dead tree, cast away by the gusting winds. His piercing, cold eyes fell upon the darkened heap of remaining saddlebags of gold.

In a flash of flickering light, he quickly counted just three saddlebags. Ramus stood transfixed, confounded by what he saw, waiting for another burst of light to confirm his bewildering nightmare. As lightning streaked across the ominous sky, he roared with such a menacing, harsh cry that his brothers flinched and cowered. Frightened birds flew from their protective perches, twittering wildly into the thunderous night.

"Well, there's at least one left for each of us," Duffy said, shrugging his shoulders, trying to console his seething brother.

"I want them all," Ramus growled greedily, ignoring the lashing rain. His already sallow face looked white-hot and bloodless in the flashes of light.

Wadey skulked slowly around the dampened pile of worn saddlebags, slumped over, pelting rain splattering off his back, his protruding brow deeply furrowed as he squinted at the ground looking for—

"Over here," he snarled, squatting down, pointing to the soggy dirt.

The three brothers gathered around a muddy boot print

deeply impressed in the rain-soaked earth.

Duffy stood up, scratching his head, then leaned over again and examined closer. "Looks like there are four different boot prints," he mumbled into Ramus' ear, "but some are really small and fat." He shuffled his feet, befuddled.

His brother Ramus slapped him on the back of his head, "They're carrying our gold, you imbecile," he jeered scathingly. "Which way did they go?"

Rubbing the grimy palm of his gaunt hand vigorously up and down his scraggly beard, Duffy followed the boot prints to a jumble of hoof marks. "There's three horses," he croaked, outlining three distinct hoof prints in the soggy dirt with a long, bony finger.

Though Duffy was a bit of a lunkhead, he possessed one remarkable talent—he was an expert tracker. An enraged Ramus was set on tracking the mysterious foursome to recover the other saddlebags filled with gold. So instead of heading back to Durango, the Thorn brothers mounted their shivering horses, frightened by the roaring thunder and lightning, and drove them hard through the torrential rain, with Duffy in the lead.

"I lost my turquoise," Benji squealed, frenetically patting his blue jeans. "It must have fallen out of my pocket." He jumped onto the plaza when suddenly, he heard a noise, like the scuff of a horse's shoe on a rock, that stopped him dead in his tracks.

"Uh-ah! They've passed this way." Benji heard grumbling in the dark shadows from the far side of the plaza, beyond the pines.

Benji slowly crept back down, panting. "They're here," he muttered, trembling.

The soaking-wet brothers stopped abruptly when they heard the faint beating of drums in the distance. Following the sound, they came upon the massive stone dwelling nestled in a sandstone alcove and cautiously made their way up onto the plaza before the ancient structure.

The clatter of horses' hooves on stone echoed loudly against the rocky walls, sending a shudder through Diane. The scared adventurers watched as Ramus emerged from the shadows and held up his hand, signaling for his brothers to stop. A deep scowl flitted across his face as he peered at the mysterious structure before them.

"I don't have a good feeling about this," they heard Duffy grouse; a coyote in the distance cried out to the full moon shining its eerie light upon his frightened face.

The adventurers ducked as the brothers turned toward the howl, right in their direction.

Quivering, they slowly peeked over the edge again and watched as Ramus gingerly dragged his leg over his horse, jumping noisily onto the flagstone surface. Duffy cringed at the thunderous sound of his boots reverberating through the walls of hewn stone, beads of sweat forming on his brow that he roughly swiped away.

"Well, what have we here?" Ramus smirked, picking up a light blue stone, holding it up to the moonlight. "This is worth something, I reckon," he said, tossing it in the palm of his hand.

Benji leaped at the sight of Ramus holding his turquoise. "He's got my stone!" he grumbled and squirmed as Lee yanked him sharply back down.

Diane watched Duffy and Wadey dismount. Tying their weary horses to a heavy wooden beam leaning against a stone wall, they turned to see the ghostly light emanating from a hole in the plaza floor. "Maybe there's more down there," Wadey said, pointing to the kiva opening.

This is going to be trouble, Diane reasoned, shaking her head.

A howling wind suddenly stirred up dust, swirling around the brothers as they listened to the haunting drums and faint chanting carried on the breeze. Each secured a bandana around his mouth and nose, and with long dusters flapping wildly, they slowly approached the circular opening. Shielding their eyes from the blowing sands, they stood transfixed on the edge of the kiva and peered down at the dreadful sight below. Their eyes bulged as they watched in disbelief—Indian spirits dancing around a heatless fire.

"What jiggery-pokery is this?" grizzled Wadey, spitting a blackish wad of chewing tobacco angrily onto the stone floor.

Just then, the drums stopped beating, and the Indian spirits ceased dancing. All ghostly heads slowly turned upward, glaring at the Thorn brothers with hollow, lifeless eyes, then let out a shrieking war cry that caused the brothers to quiver in their boots. They stood on the rim of the kiva, clasping their ears from the raucous shrieks, frozen in fright.

The hair on the back of their necks prickled stiffly when the terrifying spirits started to hiss and whistle some sort of signal. All at once, they reached behind their backs and, in one swift motion, had their bows and arrows poised to shoot. The chief of the Indian spirits with the long, feathered headdress glowered at the intruders, shaking his rattle of deer hooves, and all of a sudden, tossed it to the ground. As if in slow motion, the warriors went down on one knee, aimed, and loosed their fierce ghostly arrows.

They soared through the kiva opening like an array of flying lightning bolts and struck the horrified brothers several times in their chests and abdomens. The pearly, translucent arrows plunged deep, each one feeling like a chilly, freezing icicle. Each time an arrow struck, their bodies would fade to black and only their white, bony skeletons would glow from within and flicker in the moonlight, violently shaking as if they were electrified.

The three skeletons jiggled and joggled on the rim of the kiva and slowly jittered away from the opening, falling to the hard, stoney ground, still jumping jerkily about.

Diane threw her hand over her eyes and peeped through her fingers, watching in horror as the top of a feathered headdress emerged from the kiva.

The chief rose slowly from the circular opening, his translucent face and red, glowing eyes glaring at Ramus and his paralyzed brothers. Diane saw Ramus' eyes flicker, then seemingly drift into blackness, as the gruesome warriors, like wispy white vapors, followed their chief into the inky dark sky.

Benji threw his blanket over his head and clamped to his sister's side, clasping his hands over his ears, and trembled. Diane stared at the scene before her, shivering, feeling Addie shaking at her other side. She glanced at Lee, who seemed paralyzed, unable to blink.

Just then, a small rock clattered across the plaza, awakening the adventurers from their trance. They whisked around and looked in the direction from which the rock was thrown to see a deerskin-clad youth jump over a fallen tree trunk and disappear into the murky woods just off the far side of the plaza. The clouds parted, and the moon beamed a narrow shaft of light onto his angular face as he peeked out from behind a dark pine tree along the base of the cliff, beckoning the adventurers to follow him. Then, he darted into the darkness.

"*Allons-y.* Let's go!" Lee said tersely.

Suddenly, Benji jumped up and, scrambling over the edge of the plaza, scurried to the kiva opening, clearly bent on retrieving his turquoise stone that had fallen from Ramus' hand.

Hiding under his blanket, he slowly stooped to pick up his treasure. Ramus' eyes flew wide open, and he sat straight up, grabbing Benji by his arm. Staring into Benji's terrified face, "You!" he shouted, shaking him. His eyes then flickered, and he fell back, unconscious again.

Benji struggled from his iron grip and ran, leaping off the plaza and into the woods.

"Don't ever do that again," Diane hissed, "You could have been killed." She held his face in her hands, angry yet relieved.

"I'm sorry, sis," he squirmed. "But he had *my* stone!" He patted his pocket to make sure his stone was still there and grimaced sheepishly as they both dashed off to catch up with Lee and Addie.

The storm clouds had dumped their load while they slept and were carried away by the soft breeze that now blew gently through the tall, wet pines. Lee could track, even by moonlight. As everyone gathered around, panting breathlessly, she knelt, feeling the damp ground with her fingertips, and made out the fresh, muddy impression of a soft moccasin that had broken a twig beneath the youth's weight.

"This way!" she said, bristling, pushing a branch out of her way that nearly sprang back in Diane's face, showering her with pine needles and raindrops. *"Pardon,"* Lee said, "Sorry," she added, shrugging.

Diane just raised her right eyebrow and gave Lee a smirk.

"What about the horses?" Diane asked.

"I'll take care of them," Addie offered, following closely behind.

They wandered from the haunted dwelling through the dark pinyon and juniper forest dappled in shifting silver moonbeams along the base of the canyon wall for what seemed like half an hour or so, when they came to a small clearing at the edge of the sandstone cliff. Across the meadow, lit by a full moon in the night sky, they spied several dozen teepees, each with its own fire ablaze in a pit in front of a hide-covered doorway.

"Golly gee!" Benji said tonelessly, and shuddered.

CHAPTER FOURTEEN

ANCIENT MYSTERIES

"What do we do—"
Diane paused mid-sentence when the Indian youth suddenly stood up from his hiding place in the tall meadow grasses and beckoned for them to follow him.

"Cool beans," Lee said crisply.

They walked silently in single file under a now cloudless sky. The chirping of crickets was the only sound heard. They followed their young guide as he entered his village through an archway made of sun-bleached deer and elk antlers. Buffalo-skin teepees were scattered in a semicircle around a main bonfire that was blazing under a dazzling full moon that was slowly setting. Each teepee had a cooking hearth in front of its opening with another skin fastened, acting as a closeable doorway. Fires crackled and glimmered in the family hearths, some with yesterday's hunt of wild game roasting over the smoky coals filling the air with its pungent scent.

Diane had only seen villages like this depicted in her schoolbooks. She slowly breathed in all the unusual aromas and pinched herself to make sure she was really awake and not merely dreaming again. Her heart began to thump hard in her chest with thrilling uncertainty. She took off her white hat and anxiously tucked a few loose blonde strands of hair behind her ear.

Deerskin clad families were clustered around their warm hearths, eating, talking, laughing, with the orange glow of the flames flickering in their happy faces. At this early hour, their young children dozed, cuddled around the crackling fire, hypnotized by the flames, dully listening to the melody of their parents' morning voices. A young one nestled deeper in her mother's lap, wrapped in her reassuring arms, while an older brother leaned his head against his father's shoulder, nodding sleepily.

They all stopped and stared as the Indian youth walked under the antler archway, followed by the young strangers.

The village children awoke and dashed from their fires to greet the guide, their big brown eyes revealing their curiosity about the peculiar procession he led. Their parents rose from their cheerful hearths, alarmed, and walked swiftly to encircle the newcomers as they were ushered to the main fire by the first and largest teepee.

Two giggling little girls scuttled close to Diane and stared up at her, seemingly bedazzled by her blonde hair that shimmered in the fire's light. They tugged on their own dark hair and reached up, motioning that they wanted to touch hers. Diane smiled kindly and slowly knelt down so that she was now eye to eye with them. They innocently touched her hair, giggling behind their tiny hands, and waved, inviting the other children to join in. A few brave little ones stepped forward, smitten with curiosity, and brazenly stroked her hair while grinning at each other. Their sparkling eyes crinkled with delight.

Diane laughed softly, her eyes glinting brightly in the

flickering flames. One of the two giggling girls stopped abruptly, put her small hands on Diane's cheeks, and gazed into her deep green eyes. The girl's little face was so close to Diane's that their noses touched. Her young breath reminded Diane of puppy's breath. At once, she dropped her warm hands from Diane's face and turned, looking for her parents in the encroaching crowd. Finding them, she tottered off, giggling.

"Greetings!" Lee said, holding up her hands in the air before her, palms forward.

"Papa and I have met hunting parties of the native people living in this part of Colorado before," she whispered quickly to Diane. "They were all pretty friendly, to my recollection, and I remember Papa greeting the hunters this way. We traded some of our fur pelts for food, flint, and this hand-carved knife." She looked down wistfully at the elk antler knife in its sheath on her belt for a moment. "It's one of the few gifts Papa ever gave me, the knife and this raccoon cap."

The youth, who looked to be a few years older than Lee, raised his hands and stepped forward to meet her hands in greeting. His light amber-colored eyes glistened in the firelight. "In the name of my village, I greet you," he said in English, surprising the adventurers. His long dark hair was pulled back into a ponytail, accentuating his high cheekbones, slender nose, and smooth bronze face. He wore a colorfully beaded horsetail band around his forehead that blended into his ponytail.

"You speak English," Diane said with surprise and relief in her voice.

"Yes, along with a few others in our village," he replied, sweeping his arm to encompass the gathered villagers. "We have learned many languages from those we have encountered," he said soberly.

Just then, the crowd began to part as an old, wrinkled elder came forth, his high forehead creased with deep lines of age and wisdom. His long, hooked nose separated deeply set, soulful crystal-blue eyes, reminding Diane of the water they'd swum in the day before. *How unusual,* she mused, looking into his clear eyes.

He stood in front of them, tall and proud, his arms crossed high up on his chest. He was draped in a long, deep-red shawl that swept the ground, adorned with hundreds of yellow beads depicting the sun on his back with its rays of light radiating outward, wrapping around to the front of his shawl. His long white hair was tightly pulled back, fastened with horsehair cordage, and adorned with eagle feathers, a sign of great importance.

"And what do we have here?" he asked, his stare piercing into the eyes of each adventurer as he stood stoically, towering over them. He stopped suddenly when he came to Diane and stepped forward, hovering over her. With his huge wrinkly hand, he held up her chin to look even more penetratingly into her bright green eyes. His eyes widened as he gently touched her blonde hair, resting the palm of his hand upon her head. He closed his eyes for what seemed like an eternity.

"Come," he said solemnly, finally opening his eyes, which seemed to be awash with moisture. Turning abruptly, he walked into the largest teepee, their young guide beckoning for them to follow.

In the middle of the large teepee was a huge firepit, burning with a sweet-smelling wood. "Juniper," Lee said. "It's a ceremonial favorite."

Diane breathed in the pungent scent, and her lips curled at the corners. The heat from its flames filled the teepee and warmed her chilled body as she watched thin wisps of smoke drift upward and out of the small circular hole at the top of the teepee, some twenty to thirty feet above her head. The teepee was large enough to hold fifty people or so, comfortably, but with little room to spare.

Around the crackling fire were hides of deer, elk, and bear covering the cold, earthy floor. On the walls inside the teepee were images painted in black charcoal and red ocher of the animals whose hides they were guided to sit upon. A large bear stood on its hind legs, while an elk and a robust deer were both depicted with large racks, each boasting ten points, five on each antler.

As everyone took their place, kneeling or sitting cross-legged, nestled closely together on the worn hair and fur hides, Lee whispered to Diane, "One hunter Papa and I met taught me that the number five is sacred. Five fingers, five toes, five appendages make up the Earth children's bodies. Five— or the pattern of five—is found throughout the plant and animal worlds."

"Hmm," Diane murmured under her breath, nodding slightly. She remembered reading that the number four was also special, representing the four directions; north, south, east, and west.

Just then, their guide stepped forward, standing next to the elder, who sat cross-legged on a raised platform before the fire.

"My name is Asazi," began the Indian youth. "I am apprentice to our zaman and my grandfather, Za-tha, which means 'follower of the Sun God, Za.' We are the Aszanii, *People of the Glittering Lights*, and ancestral friends to the Pueblo People that you witnessed dancing in their sacred kiva on the great mesa." He paused, glancing sideways at Za-tha. "My grandfather would inquire how it is that you were there at their pueblo on this sacred night of the full moon?"

How did he know we were there? Diane wondered, shaking her head. The adventurers were with Asazi the whole time of his return. She never saw him speak to his grandfather privately. *And yet—*

"Well..." Diane spoke up first. She stood up, and began pensively pacing back and forth in front of the fire, talking animatedly with her hands as she went into a full-length story about the last two days' events, recounting the prospector's tale, the saddlebags of gold, their terrifying yet exhilarating cart ride deep into the mine, and their ghostly encounter at the cliff dwelling. All the while she kept a keen eye on Za-tha, observing his expressions and reactions, pondering. *How did he know?* Then, she remembered the dark shadow of the large bird that had flown off from the cliff dwelling—like the same one she saw in the alleyway behind the saloon. *The glittering lights. Could it be—?*

Exhausted, she finally sighed breathlessly, and sank slowly to the ground in a cross-legged position before Za-tha, then, hugging her knees, she looked up into his soulful eyes. Never before had Diane felt so much spiritual energy, quiet strength, wisdom, and confidence, coming from an individual. He reminded her of her pastor. She bowed her head low in complete respect and reverence for the powerful man before her.

The zaman listened intently. The tips of his long, wrinkled fingers pressed together, supporting his chin, deep in thought. "She is most genuine, courageous, and pure of heart," Za-tha whispered to Asazi, beaming.

"Let us see this baby forest creature you're so fond of," he asked.

Lee tapped her fur cap and called out, "*Ça va!* Say, hi!"

The shy little critter emerged to the delighted gasps of their hosts and quickly scurried over to sit on Diane's shoulder.

"She has a great love for animals and nature. Mother Earth

will be most pleased. I *know* she is listening, too," Za-tha whispered again to his grandson.

"And where are your riches now?" the zaman inquired.

"The saddlebags are still on the horses back at the cliff dwelling—or pueblo, as you call it," Diane answered openly.

"And, what do you plan to do with those riches?" he continued to question with curious intent.

"I'd like to buy a home for my family," she said wistfully. "I'm going to become a teacher someday," she replied confidently.

"Ah, a teacher," he repeated, nodding his approval.

Interrupting, Addie cleared her throat. Diane looked at her quizzically, cocking her head with a raised questioning eyebrow. "The horses aren't exactly there anymore," she said shyly.

"What do you mean?" Diane asked, perplexed.

"Well, I showed them how to loosen their tethers. They're free and headed here now," she said, apologetically shrugging her shoulders.

Diane went on to introduce Addie and her special gift.

"A horse whisperer," Za-tha said as a matter of fact. "We've had many among our people before. They are truly special people."

"She can talk to *all* animals," Diane said, proud of her new friend's talents.

"Ah! That is a rare gift indeed," Za-tha said warmly. "We are honored to share our teepee with Addie."

Addie sat straight up and glowed at the words of praise and acceptance.

As Diane watched, she could almost feel Addie's memories of abuse and ridicule at the hands of the ignorant townspeople melt away. She beamed at Addie and winked.

"So, you're interested in riches?" Za-tha asked, with a slight lift at the corner of his upper lip. His piercing blue eyes stared intensely into Diane's, as if reading her mind. "A great and mystical people told us of a quest to discover the ancient mysteries called the Secrets of the Five Rays of Light, offering riches beyond your imaginations. Legend holds that concealed in each Ray of Light is hidden a wondrous secret, and those who find the treasures held within the Rays of Light will be rich forever. Are you prepared to take such a journey?" he asked, waiting patiently for the blonde-haired, green-eyed girl's answer, then solemnly added, "Are you open? Are you ready?"

Diane paused, pondering the meaning of his curious questions, and looked deeply into the eyes of Benji, Lee, and Addie. Awestruck, she remembered the message from the mysterious woman on the train: *seek first the mysteries of the ancients, then the riches of Cibola will be laid before you.* She stared at Benji. Her eyes wide. Standing with his hands in his pockets, he, too, remembered the unusual message and was rocking from heel to toe, bubbling with excitement. They both glanced sideways at the others, nodding affirmatively.

Uncertain of what was clearly transpiring between the brother and sister, Lee and Addie slowly nodded their agreement.

"Yes," Diane said briskly. "Let the adventure continue."

The great zaman looked upward to the heavens and then bowed his head reverently as he said in a low, deep voice, "Let it be so!"

He paused and then slapped his strong, wrinkled hands against his thighs. "You have arrived on a celebratory eve. You will rest with us awhile, but now you will eat as I'm sure you're hungry, and you'll need your strength for the quest that is before you." With the wave of his hand, several village women came into the teepee carrying antler plates of food and gourds of drink.

A young woman with sparkling hazel eyes brought an antler plate heaped with steaming food to Diane. Her little daughter hid behind her, grasping onto her mother's snowy-white deerskin dress, and peeked around her mother at the peculiar girl. Diane grinned tenderly, noticing that her curious eyes were light blue, and both mother and daughter had very pale skin, like the moon, with lighter brown hair. *How unusual! Who are these people?* she asked herself.

As the woman leaned over, a necklace of brown beads swung from the soft, shimmering white deerskin, catching Diane's eye.

"What interesting beads," she said, smiling to the woman, who shrugged sheepishly.

"She speaks Spanish and some Nahuatl of the ancient ones. No English," Asazi offered, explaining to the young woman that Diane was admiring her necklace. The shy woman glanced timidly at her, then bowed away. Diane watched as the mother gracefully swung her daughter onto her hip and scuttled toward a group of chatting women. The little girl glanced back over her mother's shoulder and gave a small wink. Diane cocked her head, pondering, *How curious and—*

"They're called ghost beads," Asazi interrupted her thoughts. "The legend of the ghost beads began with the Navajo people who found juniper berries on the ground, already cleaned of their sticky outer pulp, with a hole bored from one end into the center of the seed—the work of 'ghosts.' Thus, their name. The Navajo taught us that by simply drilling through to the other end of the seed with a bone awl, our village women could make beautiful ghost-bead necklaces and bracelets that we trade with other tribes and the white men at the trading posts or the general store in Durango. That's how I learned English, listening to the white men in town."

"I saw them at Wilcox's Mercantile last night," Lee chimed in. "The sale sign called them cedar beads."

Asazi frowned and shook his head, "We have junipers in this land, not their eastern cousins, the cedar trees that the townspeople mistake them for," he corrected.

"So, how did the hole get there?" Diane asked, always inquisitive.

"Ants," Asazi replied, "seeking the food inside, nibbled off one end doing most of the work. We have learned much from all of the people we have met on our journey here."

"How interesting! Do they have a special meaning?" Diane asked, intrigued.

Asazi nodded, seemingly intrigued by her constant questions. "They represent the interconnection of all things, the earth and its trees, animals, and children. The legend holds that wearing them will bring safety and protection from nightmares, evil spirits, and ghosts. They bring peace and harmony."

"I sure could have used them earlier," she said, chuckling lightly.

Back at the cliff dwelling, the Thorn brothers lay quivering, their yellowed moldy teeth clattering wildly. Finally, their eyelids flickered open, and they slowly came to their senses.

A coyote howled in the distance, and all was unearthly quiet. The bewitching hour had passed. Not even an occasional rain splat could be heard. Only the scent of dampened earth and wet foliage lingered on. The gusting wind had died. The drums were no longer beating, and the chanting fell silent.

The brothers, still shaking, scrambled to their waiting horses and awkwardly clambered onto their backs. Duffy led his horse around in circles, pulling hard on the left rein, his beady eyes scouring the ground.

He guided his horse off the plaza into the dark, wet bush, dismounted and knelt, examining the faintest of muddy traces of boot prints not washed away in the rain.

"They went off on foot this way," he muttered, scratching his head, bewildered. "There's five sets of footprints now. And one's only wearing socks!"

Ramus sneered as Duffy pleaded, "We each have a saddlebag of gold. Let's go back to Durango and be rich forever." His eyes squinted imploringly.

Ramus glanced at Wadey, arched his thick, dark eyebrow in question, and snarled. His thin lips curled upward at the corners. Wadey paused, pondering for a moment, and finally winked at his brother, touching his short, thick forefinger to the brim of his cowboy hat, smirking sinisterly in agreement.

Duffy sighed sulkily, mounted his horse, and pointed his shaky finger in the tracks' direction. The Thorn brothers galloped away, set on a trail of greed.

With the aid of the full moon and Duffy's tracking skills, the brothers made good time by horseback and pulled up just inside the last stand of juniper trees edging the grassy meadow. Dismounting, they tethered their panting horses to nearby pine boughs and turned to watch the scene unfold before them. Silhouetted by a blazing fire, they watched as five small, shadowy figures were surrounded by villagers and corralled into the large teepee.

"Here's our chance," Ramus snarled, his cruel eyes glinting in the moon's reflection, as the last villager stooped and entered the buffalo-hide oval opening.

Seemingly bent on finding out *who* stole his gold, he quietly led his brothers through the meadow bathed in a bluish light from the sinking orb. Following the trampled path through the tall grasses, they sneakily crept behind the main teepee and waited for the chattering noise within to subside.

Clustered behind the large teepee, the brothers pressed their ears to the thick buffalo-hide covering, listening to the muffled voices. Ramus' ears reddened when he heard a strange girl's voice describe how she conspired with the skunks to spray them. Then, his pricked up as an elderly voice described the legend of those that find the *treasures* held within the Rays of Light and how they would be rich forever with immeasurable wealth.

"Those dastardly three blind mice survived the mine," Ramus Thorn muttered in his cold cowboy drawl, twisting his gnarly fingers. "I recognize that pretty girl's voice and had a notion I saw that kid's face before I blacked out. They took our gold, made us into a laughing stock, and now *we're* going to follow them and take *all* of their treasures, the gold to boot, when they least expect it," he sneered, the corner of his upper lip curling.

He motioned to his brothers, and before anyone left the teepee, they silently crept back to their horses unnoticed and waited out the night, plotting their revenge.

CHAPTER FIFTEEN

THE QUEST BEGINS

"**M**mm, mmm, MMM," Diane sighed with her eyes shut, enjoying her food. "This is delicious," she mumbled with a stuffed smile. Benji continued to eat, barely raising an eyebrow. The village women had prepared tender bison seasoned with forest herbs and watercress, mixed with meadow grains, fungi, and pine nuts. It was a hot, scrumptious stew served with vegetables of cattail roots, wild carrots with onions, nettle greens sprinkled with ground wild ginger, a side of beans, and squash garnished with juniper berries and acorns. It was wonderful—flavors she had never experienced before.

"What a fun breakfast, sis," Benji garbled in between chews, his cheeks filled like a chipmunk's, making Diane chuckle at the sight.

"It is breakfast, isn't it? So much has happened, I've lost track of the time."

Lee sat back with her arms folded behind her head, seemingly content. Addie, sitting next to her, nudged her side with a pointy elbow as their horses stepped into the firelight, vigorously nodding their heads, obviously happy to be reunited.

"We'll make sure they are watered and fed," Asazi said as he and two other youths took their reins and walked them into a corral nearby, already brimming with other village horses. In the rough-hewn enclosure of twisted branches, they quickly removed the heavy loads and brought the saddlebags and gear to the adventurers huddled by the crackling fire.

"This is a grand beginning for a quest to discover the ancient mysteries and great riches," Diane declared as she sat back against their shared log covered with a woven blanket of geometric red, black, and white designs. *Looks similar to the ones we found in the ancient pueblo—yet different, somehow,* she noticed.

The flickering flames of the fire danced to the beat of the tribal drums sputtering high into the star-studded night sky, occasionally bursting into a spray of fleeing fireflies from an exploding pine cone.

"Are you sure about this quest?" Lee finally asked.

Diane reached into her knapsack and pulled out the rolled parchment. Handing it to Lee, she told the story of the mysterious woman on the train. Lee's eyes squinted at first, then widened in comprehension as she passed the message to Addie.

"Who's M.E.?" Addie inquired.

Diane and Benji looked at each other and shrugged.

Just then, Za-tha stepped up to the fire and asked as he sat opposite them, "What questions do you have of me?"

Diane took a deep breath, her eyes turned upward to the sky, thinking, then asked, "Who were these mystical people, and how did they come by these riches?"

Za-tha slowly began, "Hundreds of winters ago, people came from a mythical place in the north, called Aztlan. They were very wise and possessed a great understanding of the mysteries of life. The people from Aztlan also possessed wondrous magical powers. The source of their magic was believed to be gold. So, as they traveled south through this land, they met and befriended the many indigenous people living in pueblos," Za-tha paused, taking a sip from his gourd, "Like the one you discovered tonight.

"Often they stayed with them for some time, learning their ways *and* the locations of their gold and other precious metals and gemstones. Over time, they set up a large trading network between these pueblos possessing great riches. You may know these people by another name, the Aztecs."

Benji jabbed Diane hard in the ribs. She gasped, then stared down at him with a scowl before grinning apologetically to Za-tha, who continued.

"Then a great drought came to these lands that lasted too many winters, and the Aztec people decided to continue their trek southward into Mexico. They convinced a few of the native peoples, perhaps the Hohokam and Mogollon, among others, to journey with them, abandoning their pueblos forever," he finished, staring dreamlike into the flames.

"But what happened to all the gold?" Benji chimed in.

"That, you will discover on your quest," Za-tha said, rising to his feet and nodding goodnight.

As he walked off to his teepee, Diane closed her eyes, deeply inhaling the piney smoke, content with life in the moment. *Aztec gold!* Shaking her head slowly in utter amazement, her mind was swimming with even more questions.

Her little brother nuzzled his head against her shoulder. She gave him a warm hug, remembering the kindness the old woman had shown him and the words of the mysterious disappearing woman. All was well in her world as she fell into slumber.

The sky was still black as tar when Diane felt her body shaking. As if climbing out of a deep underground cavern, she finally opened her eyes, startled by the scene of fiery torches whirling around her. From the maze of yellow, orange, and red flames emerged the white-haired Za-tha; eerie shadows from the flickering light flitted across the crevices of wisdom etched into his face.

"Arise!" he commanded, holding out his large wrinkly hand to the awestruck Diane.

"Wake up, Benji," she said hushedly, reaching out for his hand. Benji groaned, sleepily rubbing his eyes. When he finally opened them and focused, his expression of shock matched his sister's.

Za-tha reached down and pulled Diane up by the hand until she was standing. Grasping Benji's hand, she pulled him up, too, and he stood stiffly at her side. In the glow of the torches, she could see that Lee and Addie were already awake and among the village people shivering in the chilly predawn air.

Diane opened her mouth to ask a question, but Benji's tug on her arm quickly silenced her. Za-tha turned away and, with Asazi by his side, solemnly walked through the gathered villagers. The villagers began to move, and she was pulled into the procession of torches with Benji on her heels as they made their way through the still, dark forest. At this time in the wee morning hours, all living critters were still fast asleep, nestled in their earthy burrows, feathered nests, or the crook of a tree.

The procession wound upward on a rough gravel trail, zigzagging on dusty switchbacks to the top of a small butte, high above the tips of the conifers and sparse canopy of deciduous trees. Here they stopped and stood in silence. The heavens above them were so close and dense with twinkling stars, Diane felt as if she were on top of the world. A cold breeze splashed across her face, and she shuddered as she waited—

In the far distance, in the northern sky, a drapery of green, ghostly ribbons of light billowed and shimmered, as if blowing in a sweeping solar breeze.

"That must be the aurora borealis," Diane murmured to Benji under the cloak of silence that lay thick upon the somber gathering. *I've only heard of it. Few people have ever seen it; it's so rare,* she mused in bewilderment. The villagers looked to the heavens in awe at the sight of the dancing lights, smiling to one another, understanding its significance.

Just then, a fire burst forth, almost magically, in a large pit lined with red, angular stones. Great waves of orange sparks burst into the ceremonial sky. The great zaman Za-tha stepped forward, as if from the center of the fire, draped in his red woven shawl, his arms stretched out from his sides, summoning the adventurers to step forward to meet him.

"Asazi, come forth," he commanded in a most serious tone. Asazi moved from the gathered villagers, his fine, squared jaw clenched slightly, and stood in front of his grandfather. "Today, you will be one with these who seek the ancient mysteries of the Five Rays of Light. You'll be their guide and protector. Know that I will be with you and your clan of adventurers, as an intermediary with the ancient spirits of the forest, Mother Earth, and Father Sun, the Great Za. We *all* will be looking over you on your quest." He spoke slowly and with deep feeling as the morning winds swirled at his feet and up around him like a small tornado of a million glowing little sparks disappearing into the darkness above.

In his hand he held a small gourd, shaped like a cup. Dipping his slender finger into the liquid contents, he stepped closer to

Asazi and rubbed a red ochre stripe down his forehead while he quietly recited a sacred ancestral prayer. Reaching into his shawl, Za-tha pulled out a leather necklace with a fine wood carving of a wolf dangling from it and placed it over Asazi's head. He then moved in front of Lee and marked her forehead as well, then Addie and Benji alike. After he anointed Diane, he placed the gourd on a stone that lined the fire. Reaching into his ceremonial shawl, he pulled out something he kept hidden in his hands.

Stepping once more in front of Diane, he held his cupped hands open above her head, his eyes on the sky, and spoke in the language of the ancient ones. He then lowered his hands and revealed a beautiful beaded deerskin amulet, dyed with the same dark red ochre that adorned her forehead. Like a little pouch, the black beads were designed in the shape of a bear paw. It was tied at the top with a drawstring of cordage made from yucca fibers, and it hung from a necklace of braided black and white horsehair interspersed with brown and tan ghost beads.

A bright orangish tinge arched across the horizon, letting all who were gathered know that the sun would be rising soon.

"This day, you begin your quest." Great Za-tha spoke loudly for all to hear. "The Spirit of the Great Bear is in the sky overhead and has chosen you as one of his own," he said as he swiped his powerful hand across the heavens.

Diane looked above her and saw, to her astonishment, the star constellation Ursa Major directly above the sacred butte. She had just studied Greek mythology and their star legends in her world history class and was thrilled to see the twinkling bear with her own eyes. *The handle of the Big Dipper is the tail of the Great Bear, and the "dipping cup" is its flank,* she remembered, raising an eyebrow.

"The Great Bear Spirit will be your guide and protector, too. Trust him. Call upon him in need," the wise zaman advised.

Diane's eyes brightened, and she bowed her head in respect and shivered with an innate understanding as Za-tha placed the protective ghost necklace over her head, positioning the amulet over her heart.

"With each Ray of Light you discover on your quest, you will receive a talisman, an object with magical powers to dispel evil and bring good fortune on your journey, to place inside your amulet." He spoke sagely, looking deeply into her green eyes. "Something to help you always remember the treasures you've discovered."

Above his head, the first ray of the morning sun struck the sleepy, dull clouds, turning them vibrant shades of magenta and orange. The entire sky was suffused with a deep pink aura as the heavens awoke to a new day, a new adventure.

As the small procession wound its way down the forested butte, the tall, straight pines stood as if at attention, saluting and bidding farewell to the brave adventurers. Their horses were patiently waiting for them at the bottom of the last switchback, weighed down with clean blankets and fresh supplies. Everything was neatly packed in deerskin carrying bundles, secured with hemp cordage, and fastened alongside their saddlebags of gold. Water canteens made from dried deer stomachs were filled with spring water and tied to their saddle horns.

Za-tha gathered the clan of adventurers one last time. Before speaking, he took a small deerskin pouch from his shawl, and opened the drawstring, poured a white powder into his hand. "Your quest will begin where our people first encountered the ancient Aztec Trail," he said solemnly, as he sprinkled the juniper ash onto the adventurers.

"Travel west into the setting sun until you reach a stream that will lead you into the valley of the Superstition Mountains. Follow the path upward, between the towering black pinnacles, until you reach the saddle with the solid black wall. Wait and watch vigilantly for the last ray of light to shine on *the flow of Mother Earth's sorrow and collect a black tear from its mist.* Be cautious," he continued, sprinkling the last of the sacred white powder on Diane, "for many warriors have tried to gather her tears and have never returned. The juniper ash that I have sprinkled on you will protect you on your journey."

These terrifying words struck fear into Diane's heart that coursed down to her toes, and she glanced sideways at the clan, willing to bet the other adventurers felt the same. Za-tha stepped in front of Diane and, from his deerskin zaman bag, removed a fine-woven white shawl with a ghost-bead fringe. He placed it around her neck, summoning the ancient spirits of the forest and the sky.

"Protect your daughter and her clan," he commanded, looking to the stars, and somehow—deep inside her—Diane felt comforted, for she sighed in relief. "Let it be so!" he finished, as the morning sun finally broke through the now colorless clouds and cast a luminous yellow light on the clan in confirmation.

The five adventurers mounted their horses, and with a tug on their reins, turned them toward the west, away from the rising sun in the eastern sky, as Diane proclaimed heartily, "And the adventure continues…"

CHAPTER SIXTEEN

THE RAGING BEAR

They traveled in silence, absorbed in their own thoughts of the events of the past couple of days and of the promise and the warning for the journey ahead.

"Di?" Benji whispered, nudging his sister's side as he rode behind her on the back of their black horse. His scrawny legs hung over the saddlebags filled with gold nuggets.

"Yes, Benji," she replied, shaking away her thoughts.

"Do you think we'll ever see the Thorn brothers again?"

"I've been wondering about that myself," she admitted. "I've been thinking about the choices we've had and the decisions we've made that have led us to this incredible adventure." Shifting around in her saddle, she smiled at her younger brother's new western appearance. His brown duster and black cowboy hat made him seem a tad older and taller.

He grinned back at her. "I know, right? If our train hadn't stopped in Durango at the exact time that it did, and if we had never followed Lee into the alleyway, we would have never overheard the tale of the saddlebags of gold from that old prospector."

"And when the train broke down," Diane continued, "we could have just stayed in town, but instead, we decided to go and find the gold for ourselves." Pausing, she pondered out loud, "And we would have never had that fantastically scary ride in the abandoned mine, found the saddlebags of gold, *nearly* died, was saved by Addie, discovered the haunted cliff dwelling," she sighed heavily, "followed Asazi to his village, learned of the Secrets of the Five Rays of Light offering immeasurable wealth, and started this adventure."

"Golly gee, sis! That's a lot to think about," Benji said, panting.

"We've had a lot of choices thrown at us these past days, and we've had to make a lot of decisions." She scrunched her forehead with a most serious look. "We weighed the consequences the best that we could so, I'm feeling good about the decisions we've made. But honestly, I have no idea what decisions those nasty brothers are going to make once they've realized that someone has taken half of the saddlebags, they stole from us. They're really at a crossroads, as Father would say," she said, twisting around in her saddle to face the front again. "They may not think sharing half of the saddlebags is fair, like we do!"

"I guess we'll just have to wait and see," Benji grimaced, seemingly not at all comfortable with the thought of the Thorn brothers and their decisions. "I hope they take their gold and go back to town and we're through with them forever."

In the late morning, they traversed a meadow filled with white-flowering yarrow plants and soft green mullein bursting with tiny yellow flowers atop tall, straight stalks. Asazi shared with them that his people used the light dead stalks from last summer's growth as arrow shafts, while Lee chimed in that the broad, fuzzy leaves were known as "cowboy toilet paper," their use being self-explanatory.

"The women of my village dry the thick mullein leaves, flowers, and roots and grind them into a powder that is then steeped in hot water to make a tea to treat their children's winter colds, asthma, and other lung ailments," Asazi said solemnly. "The yarrow plant is big medicine, too, and a tea of its leaves is used to treat fevers, colds, hay fever, diarrhea, and toothache, among other illnesses."

Diane was fascinated, learning about the different uses for nature's wild plants, particularly as medicine. *I want to remember that,* she decided. *I've got to write it down in my field journal.*

The sun was now high in the sky, beating mercilessly on their tiring horses, so they stopped at a meandering stream to let them drink, rest, and feed on the tall grasses along its banks. Diane took off her boots, rolled up her dungarees, and stepped cautiously into the cool, clear stream. The gentle flow of water soothed her chafed legs, which were sore from their constant rubbing against the leather saddle straps. Digging her heels into her aching calf muscles, she kneaded them up and down, sighing loudly.

"Come on!" she shouted, gesturing to everyone, none of whom seemed to need further coaxing. They quickly stripped off their boots and socks and jumped into the water, splashing and laughing. Benji tripped on a rock and fell, face-first, into the stream. Lee reached down under the water, and grasping him by his belt, raised him out of the water while he continued to stroke with his arms and legs. He looked like a frog, and everyone laughed and splashed him in affectionate delight.

Diane couldn't remember ever having so much fun and feeling so free. She stood silently and faced the warmth of the sun, closed her eyes, and breathed in the joy and peace she felt in the moment.

Suddenly, a large crash resounded over the rushing current upstream—like several willow trees breaking all at once— followed by an ear-splitting, menacing roar. Something big was rushing toward them, splashing and turning the stream into a torrent of angry water sprays and fountains. The five of them stood transfixed in shock and awe, forming a haphazard line across the stream. Addie stood by Diane's side while Benji hid behind her, trembling, his eyes squeezed shut, as a giant black bear galloped furiously toward them, his huge paws like paddles on a steamboat, churning up the water in his wake.

Asazi let out a screeching war cry and started waving his arms over his head, sending an icy chill up Diane's neck. Lee flapped her duster open and closed, making herself look like a formidable opponent, shouting as loudly as she could. Addie quickly waved her hands about, conjuring her magical symbols, trying to make contact with the raging bear. Diane instantly stood straight up; her feet planted squarely in a strong, courageous stance. Her heart pumping in her throat, she tightly gripped her white shawl that was wrapped loosely around her neck and extended her other hand straight out in front of her.

She *had* to do something. Sweat beaded up on her forehead, dripping into the outer corners of her eyes, stinging them. "I command you to STOP!" she shouted at the oncoming bear, breathing heavily.

In a flash, a brilliant white light, like a rippling wave of energy, radiated from the scarf in every direction and enveloped the clan in a white aura of protection. For a fleeting moment, she saw within its silvery edge, like a gleaming lasso, the giant bear stopped and dropped before them. Just then, she *knew*—

"Tell him to stop for the sake of love, Addie!" Diane shouted shrilly to her friend at her side. Blinking her eyes, the image faded away.

Addie, frenetically waving her hands, finally broke through the animal's thrashing rage and communicated her greeting along with Diane's message. The big black bear reeled, then lurched, and lunged, finally falling at the adventurers' feet, his heavy, hot breath blowing in Diane's and Addie's faces. They both stared into his fierce dark-brown eyes for what seemed like an eternity as their eyes remained fixed and unblinking, exploring each other's souls. His ragged breathing slowed, and his eyes softened from a crazed rage into a glimmer of excruciating misery.

"He's hurt," Addie said, "and in horrible pain."

Diane slowly placed her hand on his huge, bristling head. "Tell him we will help him if he will let us," she said tenderly, listening to his strained and rattled breathing.

Addie relayed the message, and the giant bear lowered his head and lifted his front paw. The stream water had cleansed a large, visible gash on his foreleg that now ran crimson red with fresh blood. A huge obsidian tear glittered in the corner of his eye, against his dark fur, and trickled down his black, bristly muzzle.

Asazi now moved into action. "I saw some desert willow plants and sacred datura along the stream and an agave plant growing in the meadow we passed earlier," he said. Jumping onto his painted horse with one leap, he quickly rode back to where the meadow began.

As if released from a spell, Lee sprang back to life and said, "There's some sage and prickly pear cactus back a ways, too."

Mounting her chestnut horse, she sped away in a mire of dust clouds, splattering clumps of dirt and grass.

"Now, what do we do?" Diane asked, feeling a bit at a loss, staring down at the huge black bear at her feet.

Resolved, she clambered out of the stream, quickly put on her cowboy boots, and stood waiting for Benji and Addie with her hands on her hips and a serious look scrunched upon her face.

With Addie's help, they coaxed the bear onto the bank of the stream and guided him to lie down under the cool shade of a Gambel oak tree. Collapsing into the grass under the leafy branches, the bear whimpered softly with a low rumbling sound in his massive throat.

"Gee whiz, Di!" Benji exhaled, slowly creeping up beside the bear and sitting cross-legged next to him, gently patting his head. "That scarf is magic!"

Soon Lee and Asazi returned together and went right to task. Asazi found a rounded stone in the stream to use as a hammerstone. He directed Diane and Benji to make a fire to heat up some water in the kettle Lee had packed for the journey. He then took the large white flowers of the sacred datura plant and ground them, along with the seeds from its thorny seedpod, into a fine powder. Next, he smashed the tiny, slender leaves of the desert willow into a clump of fibers and mixed them with a little water, which made a paste-like substance, called a mash, that had great astringent—toxin-absorbing—medicinal qualities.

Removing three small gourds from his deerskin bundle, he placed them on the rocks Diane had collected to ring the fire, acting as a windbreak protecting the flames. He then gave the hammerstone to Lee, who needed it to grind up the sage leaves she had collected.

"That smells wonderful!" Diane exclaimed. "What is it?"

"It's sage," Lee answered, as she smashed the tiny leaves. "It makes for a good germ-killing wash," she added, handing a fresh sprig to Diane. Lee showed her how to twist the stem and crush the silvery green leaves with her fingers to release its aroma. "It's got another name, Cowboy Cologne," Lee said, chuckling.

"Mmm," Diane inhaled, making a mental note to add sage, along with ponderosa pine and juniper, as another one of her favorite wilderness smells.

Asazi put a pinch of each of the powdered wild herbs into separate gourds and then poured hot water over them so that they could steep for a while, releasing their healing medicines into the water. He asked Lee for her sage powder, and he steeped it as well in the third gourd.

The agave plant was next. Asazi used the hammerstone to pulverize a leaf of the agave, breaking up the pulp, and separated it from the fibers that were attached to a sharp, hard point. He then artfully twisted the attached fibers into a strong single strand, making a perfect needle and thread.

As he worked on the agave needle and thread, Lee took her hunting knife and cleaned the prickly pear pad by craftily removing its long spines, and then cut it in half, lengthwise, revealing the gooey slime inside. She cut long, shallow slices in a checkerboard pattern on the inside of the pad to release more of its healing goo. She explained that it made a perfect astringent that drew toxins—even rattlesnake venom—out of wounds.

Finally, everything was ready. The big black bear was resting and waiting, drawing in breath in painful muted gasps and throbbing moans. Asazi and Lee carefully planned out his treatment and shared their plan with Diane and Addie, who was to translate it to their bear patient.

The bear immediately sat up, his ears twitching, as he carefully listened to the directions that Addie was translating from Asazi.

"First, we need him to sip the sacred datura tea—but only *one* sip though. It is a powerful medicine that acts like a sedative in small doses and a hallucinogen in higher dosages. If he sips too much, it could kill him," he began.

"The young boys in my village drink the sacred plant as part of their manhood ceremony. If they survive, they are deemed warriors," Asazi explained, looking pensive.

Everyone cringed and shuddered.

"After he drinks the tea, Lee will clean his wound of any debris with the mullein leaf and sage cleanser. Next, I, Asazi—" pointing to his chest "—will sew up the gash with the agave needle and thread that has been soaking in the sage liquid. Finally, we will apply the desert willow mash, as a poultice, to the gash in his leg and place the prickly pear pad over the wound, tying it in place with some bandages that Diane tore from her dress."

"Does he understand?" asked Asazi soberly.

The bear cocked his head as he listened, his eyebrows scrunched and paused, as if considering the surgery, then answered by lowering his head and blinking his dark, sad eyes.

Addie closed her eyes and then nodded, "He understands, basically," she confirmed.

Asazi carefully poured the sacred datura into another gourd cup and lifted it to the bear's mouth. "One sip only," he cautioned the bear, whose eyes glinted, looking as if he understood, and took one small lick.

Asazi put the gourd cup down and spoke to Diane, "You should be prepared to catch his head when he falls asleep and hold it so that he doesn't hurt his eyes. A sharp stick could damage his sight as his eyes may stay open under the influence of this powerful medicine, and—"

Before he could finish his sentence, the giant bear began to teeter. Rocking dangerously from side to side, he suddenly crumpled and very slowly fell toward Diane, who was ready and awkwardly caught the giant black bear's heavy head in her sleeping blanket, guiding it jerkily to the ground. The solid THUD of his body hitting the ground made the earth quake beneath their feet.

"Whew!" she said breathlessly, as she fell hard on her bum, straddling the bear's head aside her legs.

His eyes did indeed remain open, which was sort of eerie, as they seemed to stare into blank nothingness. And so was his mouth, opened slightly with his tongue hanging down over his teeth.

How strange! Diane mused.

She held his head in her blanket and gently rubbed his ears as she often did with her little schnauzer at home, soothing her when she trembled from fear of a thunderstorm. The act made her feel a little homesick. Remembering her Daisy dog that she loved with her whole heart, she realized just then that she hadn't thought of Daisy once since this wild adventure began—until this very moment—and sighed deeply.

Asazi and Lee soon had their patient's wound completely cleansed, stitched up, and wrapped in bandages. His task completed, Asazi sat back and grinned, pleased with their efforts.

"I've never seen a black bear this large before. My ancestors speak of a time long ago in our homeland of great cave bears that weighed over two thousand pounds. This one must weigh at least a thousand pounds or so. He must be a descendant of those great ancient bears. I'd like to name him Sa'ami, the Gentle One," Asazi continued solemnly.

The bear suddenly sighed in relief, seeming to understand that the operation was complete. Still sedated, he shut his eyes, moaned slightly, and began to snore.

Diane chuckled to herself and just couldn't hold back her curiosity any longer. She slowly lifted the sleeping bear's black upper lip to peek at his huge canine teeth. With her small finger, she tapped ever so lightly on the exposed white tooth as the bear continued to snore.

"It's so big," she said in disbelief. She then placed her small hand over the bear's huge paw, shaking her head in amazement. It was bigger than her hand in every way. She ran her fingertips along the rough pads down to the curved dark claws. They were longer than her fingers!

CHAPTER SEVENTEEN

CIRCLE OF RESPECT

The excitement and intense strain of this wondrous day left the small clan drained and exhausted, so they unloaded the rest of their gear and made camp by the snoring bear. The sun was sinking low in the west, getting ready to retire for the evening. Addie and Benji were sitting around their campfire, talking quietly about the big black bear sleeping peacefully at Benji's side, not wanting to awaken him. Asazi and Lee ventured off, weapons in hand, looking for a tasty evening meal.

Diane sat on her bedroll with her back against a fallen tree, deeply content, in front of the flickering flames. She loved the sound of the crackling fire and the smell of burning pine. Taking a small black book, her field journal, from her knapsack, she began recording the events of the day: the injured bear, the native plants and their medicinal uses, her favorite wilderness smells, and her thoughts about Daisy, home, and her family.

"Is something wrong with me?" she asked Asazi, who had just returned from their hunting foray, joining them by the fire. "I haven't thought much at all about my family or my little dog,

Daisy," she implored, seriously concerned.

"No, Diane," he said, pausing to think about this unusually odd question. "You live in the moment, the here and now—which most people don't do. People tend to live in the past or in the future. They miss the beauty of what's happening right now, all around them."

"Hmm! Live in the moment," she repeated to herself, jotting it in her field journal. *Something to always remember,* she decided as she continued to write feverishly about the gold, their quest, the village of the Aszanii, and all those she'd met along her journey and what she'd learned so far since they had left the train. *I've got so much to write about, I'll never get caught up,* she thought, thrumming her pencil anxiously against her thigh.

"That was delicious," Benji said, fervidly licking his fingers. The aroma, like roasted chicken, settled over the happy clan. Asazi and Lee had a successful hunt and together downed several wild game birds that were a little smaller than a chicken, with plump bodies and feathered legs. They were all ravenously filling their hungry stomachs.

Diane was still picking the cooked meat from the bones when, all at once, Addie, having finished her veggie stew of wild carrots, nettles, and mushrooms, stood up and formally announced, "It's time that we made proper greetings to our traveling companions." Everyone looked at her quizzically as she used her foot to draw a large circle in the dirt next to the fire. "Let's get our horses and bring them into our Circle of Respect."

This is going to be most interesting, Diane considered. With curious anticipation, she led her black horse with the white star on his forehead into the circle.

The five adventurers stood in the circle with their horses by their sides. Even the bear rose groggily into a sitting position to participate. Addie shut her eyes and began waving her hands above her head in large swooping circles and then lowered them to seemingly include the small gathering of travelers.

When she opened her bright, round eyes, she said, "Let's each introduce ourselves and share one special thing about ourselves so that we can get to know each other better and honor each other," she directed avidly.

Addie began, "I'm Adeline, speaker to and for animals, and this is Rohan," Addie said, with a wave of her hand, introducing the clan of adventurers to the red horse given to her by her father. "And, he told me that he is very proud of his red tail."

She then turned to Diane, who was grinning. "Okay," Diane gulped, "I'm Diane, and I love books and science, geology, archaeology, and my favorite—*dinosaurs!*"

Addie focused her attention on Diane's horse, shutting her eyes for a long moment, then opened them again. The jet-black horse with the white star had been transfixed on the flames, almost in a trance. Suddenly, he raised his head, the fire reflecting in his soulful dark eyes, and looked directly at Addie. His ears perked, standing straight up and forward, twitching, he nodded his head as if he were listening to and answering her.

"This is Mavric," she introduced formally. "He likes his name given to him by his first owner, and he's very proud of his perfect white star and the way he prances, and...oh!" She added, smothering a giggle, "He loves to run fast and break wind." Everyone burst out in laughter and then immediately silenced themselves to show respect to their new animal friend.

"I'm Benjamin, but I liked to be called Benji, and I love baseball," Benji said heartily, patting Mavric gently on his long snout with newfound affection.

Lee was next. "I'm Lee Planchet." She stomped her foot for dramatic emphasis. "I *was* once the greatest French trapper in the West," she declared crisply, standing in her familiar pose of strength and confidence, with her fists on her hips and her head held high at an angle. Pausing then with a concerned look on her face, she cleared her throat and proclaimed solemnly, "And I will never kill another animal for money again, only for food."

Addie turned to Lee's gleaming chestnut horse and shut her eyes. "This is Bentley," she said, finally opening her sparkling eyes. "He is afraid of mountain lions, on account of one stalking him for nights when he was just born. He hates their smell," she said grimly. Then on a lighter note, she continued, "and he loves his name and black mane. His name was given to him by a very nice young woman who treated him kindly."

Asazi stepped forward. "I am Asazi of the Aszanii people and apprentice zaman to my grandfather, Za-tha."

Turning to his painted horse dappled with large patches of white and brown, accented with a long black tail and thick mane, Addie closed her eyes once again. When she opened them, she frowned.

"This is Forjon. A rattlesnake spooked him when he was a young colt, and he badly gashed his back leg. It took a long time to heal, and it still hurts him from time to time. Needless to say, he is afraid of snakes," she translated sadly. Everyone looked at Forjon with a new sense of understanding and appreciation because most of the clan were afraid of rattlesnakes.

Amazed, Asazi said, "This story is true. I was there and saw it all unfold. I treated his leg for many moons."

The groggy bear swayed and startled them with a low grumble and groan. "Oh yes," said Addie. "This is Sa'ami. He likes his name given to him by Asazi, and he wants to thank his new friends for treating his leg, as it's feeling better already." Addie paused and looked timidly at the ground, "I hope you don't mind, but I've asked him to join our clan and travel with us on our journey if he'd like to, and he said yes."

"That's wonderful," Diane said, smiling widely. Her warm smile lit up her face.

Addie sighed with relief, and Asazi nodded approvingly, as if he seemed to know this would be so.

"Sa'ami is our protector," Asazi said in a most serious voice, "sent from the Great Bear Spirit to be our guide and to protect us on our quest."

Diane shivered with the memory, and Benji just beamed, enamored with his new furry friend.

Just then, Niki popped her head out of Lee's fur cap. "We mustn't forget our littlest friend," Addie chuckled lightly. "This is Niki, and she loves her new home. And she is very proud of her striped tail and banded mask."

Everyone stood in silence, realizing that their relationships had reached a new depth of understanding and connection. Even the horses and the bear seemed to accept each other and their inclusion in the clan. It was indeed a Circle of Respect. They would never feel the same again.

Their animal companions were now and forever their friends, and they cared for them as deeply as they cared for their human brothers and sisters.

A sudden rustle in the pine boughs caught Diane's attention. "Look," she said in a hushed tone, pointing to the shadowy movement in the conifer trees above their heads. From within the limber branches and fine-bundled needles, a beautiful snowy owl appeared. Its white feathers shimmered in the moonlight, and Diane noticed an oddly familiar string of brown feathers around its neck, like the beads of a necklace. Glancing down at them for just a moment, the owl's large hazel eyes blinked, and then the beautiful bird of prey took flight, flying north into the clear night sky. A silvery moonbeam glistened on the owl's white, outstretched beating wings as it flew over the gently rippling stream, disappearing over a distant valley ridge.

"So graceful," Diane sighed. *It sure seemed like it was in a hurry,* she considered.

Just then, another small movement caught everyone's heed as tiny white wings fluttered anxiously on the pine bough. A young snowy owl, only a few inches tall, blinked its startling light blue eyes and awkwardly took flight, following the path of its mother.

"Did that little owl wink at you, sis?" Benji murmured in awe.

Diane shuddered, shaking her head in bewilderment.

CHAPTER EIGHTEEN

THE AZTEC STONE

The first rays of the morning light peeked over the tops of the conifers and fell upon the sleeping faces of the adventurers, waking them ever so gently. Diane lay still, her eyes closed, feeling the soft breeze blow through her hair, breathing in the sweet forest scents, remembering. *I saw the bear stop and lie down at our feet before it actually happened,* she reflected, thinking about her white scarf and the silvery image she saw outlined in its brilliant white light. *It showed me what was about to happen. Or, was it showing me what I wanted to happen, what I was thinking?* She shook her head, trying to make sense of it.

Just then, a bird began its morning song directly overhead. She opened her eyes to a world bathed in a soft yellow light— hundreds of glowing sunbeams breaking through the branches, melting into a pearly morning mist that rose from the forest floor. The scene felt magical, and moisture filled her eyes.

Just beautiful, she mused, sighing deeply as she watched a small aspen leaf float on a breath of air that brushed across her cheeks, lightly landing in the palm of her hand.

Listening to the horses grazing nearby, she glanced over at the others still sleeping and saw that Asazi was awake, too.

"Twist the leaf until it breaks and then smell it," he guided, shifting to his side to look at her directly.

Diane did so. "It has a strong smell; something like aspirin," she said, exhaling contentedly.

"All plants have their own unique smell. Twist them to reveal their essence. We use the aspen's sap for pain and the white powder found on the bark of its trees as sunscreen," Asazi shared. Reaching into his medicine bag, he removed a small deerskin pouch.

"I'd like to use some of that aspen powder on my nose and cheeks. I'm getting a little sunburned. Benji too!" Diane said, patting her face.

He opened the pouch and, dipping his finger inside, removed it covered in a white powder. "Here," he said as he gently smeared the powder onto her nose and cheeks. "That should protect you today. I'll apply some on Benji when he awakes. Addie may need some too."

Then noticing the look of peace on her face, he continued, as if he were hearing her thoughts, "The Great Mother Earth is pleased that you love her forest so."

"I do," she replied serenely, and then shivered as large goose bumps rose to the surface of her little arms.

"That is a sign that Mother Earth has heard you and is pleased," he continued, his voice as gentle as falling leaves. "Today, we should reach the Superstition Mountains as the sun sets, just as Za-tha predicted."

With those words, Diane stretched her arms to the sky and declared loudly, "Good morning, forest and friends. Let the adventure continue..."

Diane noticed their sleeping blankets were surrounded with

a thick dark-twined rope. "What's this?" she asked, inspecting the unusual fiber.

"That's a horsehair rope," Asazi replied. "It protects us from rattlesnakes. Rattlers, like many small creatures, can be drawn to a warm place at night when they're cold. You don't want to wake up with a snake curled up in your sleeping blanket, do you?" he asked, chuckling. "Unlike other fibers, horsehair scratches the rattler's belly uncomfortably, so they won't slither across it. My people know that snakes don't openly attack people, but they *will* be attracted to mice that may find tasty morsels in your bedroll. Be sure to not eat or have food near your sleeping blanket."

Makes good forest sense, Diane decided, hugging her knapsack.

She nodded appreciatively for the lessons on aspen trees and rattlesnakes and took out her field journal to jot down what she had just learned. From her bedroll, she could hear Lee say, "*Ça va, la monde!*"

"What does that mean?" Diane asked, always interested in learning Lee's native language.

"Roughly, 'How's it going, world?'" she replied sleepily, yawning.

Once they packed up their campsite, they doused their fire thoroughly and loaded their gear and saddlebags of gold onto their waiting horse friends and mounted. Before clambering onto Bentley's back, Lee took a small fallen branch from a pine tree thick with needles and swept away their footprints and sleeping blanket impressions from the ground. All traces of them had magically vanished.

"'Leave no traces, take only memories,' my papa would say," Lee recited, riding alongside Diane and Benji. They snacked on their breakfast pemmican bars made of grains, seeds, fat, and dried meat for energy and headed off to the black mountains to the west and the first Secret of the Rays of Light.

As Addie and Asazi rode up beside them, Lee handed them each a breakfast bar. "Za-tha mentioned that our quest would begin where your people first encountered the Aztec Trail. Where is that, exactly?" Lee asked, pressing further, "Where are these Superstition Mountains?"

"Arizona," Asazi replied with a glint in his eye.

Diane suddenly pulled hard on the reins, bringing Mavric to an abrupt halt. "Where did you say?"

Asazi took a deep breath and went on to explain, "Remember my grandfather's words, 'In their journey from the north, the Aztecs met and lived with many Pueblo People, creating secret storehouses of treasures; gold, silver, turquoise, and other wealth. They created a vast network of these storehouses along what we call the Aztec Trail as they proceeded to the south, finally settling and building their civilization in Mexico.' They continued to trade with the pueblos of the north until their great capital was conquered by the Spanish conquistadors and the Aztec empire was destroyed. The pueblos and their storehouses of treasures remained hidden," he paused, looking intently into everyone's staring eyes.

"Their secret locations," he continued, "were known only to the Aztec *Tlatoani* or rulers and a clan of people they entrusted as the *Keepers of the Tlatoani Treasures*. The mystical Aztecs were a powerful people, possessing great magic. They created a way for the *Keepers* to travel easily throughout the Aztec Trail, in order to retrieve their treasures at the ruler's command," he paused once again. Sitting up tall in his saddle, his chest out, he solemnly proclaimed, "My people are the Keepers! The Aszanii were entrusted to protect the hidden treasures of the Aztecs."

Thunderstruck, Benji fell backward and awkwardly rolled off Mavric's back, "You know where the lost cities of Cibola are?" He gulped hard; his eyes as big as baseballs as he dusted off his dungarees. He stood in the dirt, staring up at Asazi.

"The pueblos," he corrected, "are not lost to my people," Asazi said in a somber tone. "Gold, silver, and greater Aztec treasures still remain, those of the ancient mysteries—the Rays of Light. And it is the *Secrets of the Rays of Light* we seek," he said, snickering at the sight of Benji's befuddled face.

"And we're supposed to start this journey in Arizona?" Lee blurted out incredulously.

"How exactly are we going to get there?" Diane asked, a bit more politely, squinting sideways at Lee. "And, when... h-how...your p-people?" She stuttered, words tripping and sliding over her tongue. Her head was buzzing with so many questions, her mouth couldn't keep up.

Asazi reached into his deerskin medicine bag that always hung across his chest. "With this!" He held up a long, slender four-sided blue crystal. It was about five inches long, an inch or so at its width, tapering to a point that was capped at both the pointy top and rounded bottom with a soft yellow metal that brilliantly reflected the sun.

"That's turquoise!" Diane exclaimed.

"Is that gold?" Benji squealed, his gold fever boiling to the surface again.

Asazi nodded his head. "Yes, this is an Aztec Stone, and it possesses great magic."

Lee shook her head in complete puzzlement. "And how is that going to take us to Arizona and the first Ray of Light?"

"I'll show you when the time comes. But that time is not now," Asazi said patiently, looking into Lee's doubtful eyes. "We continue our journey west, just as Za-tha instructed."

Breaking the uncomfortable moment, Addie shouted out with glee, "Look, here comes Sa'ami!"

Miraculously, the bear's wound was nearly healed as he lumbered up to his new clan. Asazi had checked his wound when he awoke and treated it with more natural herbs. Benji sauntered over to Sa'ami to give him a good morning pat on the head, when all at once, the bear whisked his large torso around, knocking into Benji's little body, toppling him over onto the bear's huge bristling back.

Benji frantically grasped onto the coarse, prickly hair at the nape of his thick neck, squealing and grunting, his feet struggling to find a foothold. Asazi hurriedly rode over and lifted Benji up by the back of his britches, and he finally clambered onto the bear's back. Sa'ami swaggered playfully with Benji straddling him, wearing a huge grin on his face. The horses all nickered, tossing their heads, in seeming acceptance of their fellow clan traveler.

Diane's and Lee's mouths dropped open in speechless awe at the sight of Benji riding the huge black bear. Asazi smiled slightly, marveling at Mother Earth's creature. Addie chortled first, and then one by one, they all joined in the laughter as the bear picked up his pace and started to strut even more, seemingly proud of his little antic and the joy it brought his new friends.

"And the adventure continues..." Diane declared again as she gently squeezed her knees to nudge Mavric forward, following Benji on Sa'ami's back.

CHAPTER NINETEEN

ASAZI'S PORTALS

In the warmth of the afternoon sun, the weary adventurers were silent, listening to themselves breathe in rhythm with their horses' gait and to the occasional buzz of a pesky passing fly that interrupted their peaceful harmony. Suddenly, Sa'ami stopped and leaned back, rising up on his strong back legs, his nose straight into the soft wind, sniffing the air. Diane knew that bears had an incredible sense of smell and had read that they could smell food up to ten miles away.

Poor Benji was startled as he desperately clutched onto Sa'ami's bristly neck and scrambled to stay on. His legs slid off Sa'ami's slick flanks, dangling freely in the air, frantically searching for a foothold. Then, in another sudden move, Sa'ami fell down on all fours with a hard thud that rocked Benji forward, as the bear lurched in a full-speed dash deeper into the dense forest ahead.

Diane yelled, "Hold on, Benji!" but she lost sight of him among the boughs of the tall pine trees and leafy Gambel oaks. "Giddy up!" Diane shouted, and everyone in unison gently kicked their horse friends to swiftly chase after the crazed bear with a panicky Benji glued to his back.

It seemed like forever before they finally stopped in front of a most bewildering scene. Sa'ami was digging vigorously into the dirt beneath the branches of a juniper tree, his huge paws deeply clawing into the soft ground. Every moment or two, he stopped and plunged his nose into the earth, his hindquarters poised up in the air, a stub of a tail wiggling and waggling in what seemed to be utter ecstasy. As he continued to dig, dark, blackish-blue berries began floating upward from the ground. The adventurers watched in wonder as Sa'ami snapped at the escaping berries and, catching them in his mouth, ravenously chewed them down while swaying side to side.

"Magic berries!" Asazi offered.

Much to their astonishment, they found Benji digging right alongside Sa'ami, catching the berries in his mouth as they floated toward the sky. His mouth and face were covered in a dark-bluish stain, and as the clan approached on horseback, he gazed at his sister with a twisted grin, giggling.

"Hey, Di!" he slurred, teetering a little tipsily as he sauntered toward the approaching clan. Waving, Benji fell over, chortling, and wrapped his arms around his stomach. He couldn't stop giggling and snorting.

Aghast, Diane jumped off Mavric—who had raced, breaking wind the entire way, completely pleased with himself—and ran to Benji, grabbing him by his upper arms and holding him up straight.

"Are you alright?" she asked firmly, in a mixture of fright and amusement.

"I feel a little fuzzy," he mumbled, "but great, sis. Try this," he said as he held up a magic juniper berry to her lips and then fell over laughing again.

"What's wrong with him?" Lee asked, a concerned look etched deeply across her furrowed brow.

Asazi shook his head, smothering a chuckle, and carefully removed the Aztec Stone from his medicine bag. It was glowing with a soft blue light. "There is great magic in this place. We must be near the Aztec Portal. That may explain the magical behavior of the juniper berries and their curious effect on Benji and Sa'ami."

Diane hugged her brother, holding him tight, "Are you okay to travel?"

"I'm okay, sis, really," Benji giggled, squirming out of her grasp. "Why do you ask?" Just then, he glanced over to his bear friend. "Oh!" He swallowed.

A seemingly intoxicated Sa'ami swayed, and toppling over, rolled onto his back, his four huge paws suspended stiffly in the air. And the giant bear began to snore.

"I guess we'll just leave him here for now," Asazi shrugged, placing several broken pine boughs over the sleeping bear to conceal and protect him from the sun. "He'll probably be awake when we return."

"What's a portal?" Diane asked, completely intrigued and relieved that Benji did appear to be all right.

"It's an ancient gateway, an opening," Asazi replied, anticipating her next question. "Only the ancient Aztec mystics knew how it worked, for they built it long ago. I just know the Aztec Trail is an extensive maze of these magical portals. I've used them many times in my zaman training. This is how my ancestors, the Keepers, traveled vast distances in short moments of time to the northern pueblos to retrieve the Aztec rulers' stored treasures and brought them back to Tenochtitlan, the capital city of the Aztec Empire."

Lee rolled her eyes, her fingers making the motion of zipping and buttoning her mouth shut. Diane squinted her eyes and grimaced slightly at Lee.

Asazi, ignoring the girls, continued, "Once we enter the ancient portal, we'll travel swiftly, unlike anything you've ever experienced, then magically exit the portal in Arizona nearest to the location of the First Ray of Light."

"How will we get back here?" Addie asked, concerned for her bear friend.

"Once opened, the portal will remain so for many hours," Asazi answered, shifting his weight on Forjon's bare back. He held out the glowing Aztec Stone in the palm of his hand and nudged his painted horse forward.

"This I want to see," Lee said skeptically.

Asazi helped Benji clamber onto the back of Mavric and signaled for the clan of adventurers to follow close behind. His eyes were sharply focused on the Aztec Stone as they slowly took steps further to the west until they came upon a circular clearing of pockmarked limestone.

All at once, Diane shrieked, "Look at my scarf! It's glowing white!"

"And look at the stone!" murmured Addie, stunned.

The Aztec Stone began glowing brilliantly, radiating white light in every direction.

"We're here!" Asazi proclaimed. "At the place of the Aztec Portal." He summoned everyone to gather around him. "It's going to be very windy once we enter, so hold onto everything tightly. Addie, can you tell the horses to stay calm and that they'll be alright?"

Addie closed her eyes, waving her hand above her head in mysterious circles. "They understand," she said finally, opening her eyes.

Asazi held the Aztec Stone high in front of him in the palm of his hand and placed the forefinger of his other hand on its golden tip. Averting his eyes to the sky, he quietly spoke in

Nahuatl, the ancient language of the Aztec mystics, a Keeper's command to release the stone's magic.

Suddenly, the Aztec Stone started spinning around and around, slowly at first, then faster and faster, while its glowing radiance grew brighter still. The clan's eyes grew wide as the brilliant light seemed to begin swirling in front of them. Dazzling, tiny sparks began popping in the whirling light. Like a tornado of light, a funnel grew and expanded high over their heads until the mouth of the light funnel turned and moved in front of them, forming a large round circle of light, like a sheet of frosted glass with a glowing white edge.

"I've seen that white lasso before!" Diane shouted. "That's what I saw when Sa'ami charged us."

"That was magic," Asazi said, his keen eyes on the portal as the frosted-looking glass began to clear and another scene of a distant landscape was visible within the portal. "Those are the Superstitions. It's time to enter."

The ancient portal was large enough to allow a horse and rider to easily enter. Asazi patted Forjon on his neck reassuringly and nudged him forward.

Diane turned in her saddle and looked into Benji's bugging eyes. "Hold on tight," she said firmly, as he wrapped his arms around her waist and pressed his hat against her back. She followed Asazi's lead and gave Mavric a reassuring pat, then pressed her knees into his sides. The horse nickered, tossing his head jerkily and hesitantly stepped over the white-glowing edge and entered into the portal.

All at once, the scene around her blurred into a stream of earthy colors whizzing by. Shades of blue, green, brown, and red all trailing like flowing ribbons along their route. Sound was muffled, but for an occasional soft buzz, crack, or chirp that was instantly cut short, just as it began. She felt sick to her stomach and grabbed onto her hat as the wind blasted them as they moved forward.

"Cool beans!" Diane heard Lee yell, her voice quickly whisked away, as she brought up the rear, clutching onto her cap and a shaking Niki inside. Addie was stone silent, grasping her duster, hunched over, leaning into the wind. The horses seemed to be standing still, one after the other, as if on a flatbed railcar, as the world flashed by at lightning speed. And the wind! As if they were swimming in a river current, it washed over them, howling in their ears.

Her eyes stinging, Diane could barely see Asazi's horse step forward as she saw the approaching edge of another gleaming white lasso. Asazi raised his hand, signaling that they were about to exit the portal.

Mavric, his head hanging low, pressing hard into the invisible force, finally stepped tentatively over the glowing rope-like edge and into a world very different from the cool pine forests of Colorado. Benji, releasing his grip, yelled into his sister's ear, "Look, Di!"

Glancing up, she saw the glint of the stream Za-tha had described and their first glimpse of the green valley leading into the Superstition Mountains. It was lined with huge black pinnacles made of basalt, standing guard like sentinels along its flanking ridges.

Next, Addie reappeared, swiping her brow and breathing heavily. "I'm fine, I'm fine, really," she repeated when she saw the concerned look on everyone's faces.

"*Incroyable!*" Lee said breathlessly as she and Bentley finally exited the portal. "That was unbelievable!"

She smirked sheepishly at Diane, who grinned from ear to ear, thrilled to see some of Lee's skepticism melt away.

The sun was slowly descending toward the rocky horizon

as the adventurers found the promised trail that led into the V-shaped valley and up to the jagged black pinnacles along the saddle of the mountain crest.

The river trail crossed fine-grained alluvial sediments of volcanic tuff, breccia, and granite that were weathered from the unusual rock formations above them, then eroded, washed down by monsoon rains onto the valley's floor. As the adventurers climbed higher, the trail gave way to a coarse-grained black basalt that had a glass-like sharpness. The rocky trail meandered up the side of the valley through stands of lanky saguaros with oddly twisted arms and stout barrel cacti that baked in the blaze of the late afternoon sun. It then switched back to the opposite side, zigzagging through the welcoming shade of catclaw and mesquite trees that grew cooler at every ascending turn.

Benji excitedly tapped Diane on the shoulder. "Are those stone walls?" he asked, pointing to a pile of light-colored rocks scattered on a ledge, reminding his sister of the man-made walls at the haunted cliff dwelling.

"You have the eyes of an eagle," Asazi said, turning around on his horse. "Those are all that remain of the people that once lived in this area, and that..." gesturing to ancient petroglyphs carved onto the dark brownish-black rock face next to it. "Once these lands were filled with gold, silver, copper, and precious gemstones of turquoise, azurite, and malachite. The Keepers removed much of it from the hidden storehouses before the prospectors came. We're getting close," he said solemnly, and turned back around, not seeing the frown on Benji's face.

Disappointment dripped from his eyes. "So, where's the treasure?" he muttered. Slumping in his blanket, he gave his sister a sad punch in the back.

"Wait and see," was all that Diane could think to say, and shrugged.

Not far ahead, they could see the solid black rock wall Za-tha had described, and it became a race to get to the wall before the tired sun set.

CHAPTER TWENTY

SA'AMI'S TEARS

T wo thousand feet above the valley floor, with the blazing summer sun long past its mark, the evening winds began to blow cooler, as they always did right before sunset and sunrise, especially at this altitude. A gush of air lifted Diane's hat, and she quickly clamped it back down on her head. Wrapping the white, gauzy scarf around her neck, she buttoned up her duster to stop shivering from the cold and the thrill of what might be waiting for her around the next bend. Even in early summer, the evenings were chilly in this mountainous terrain.

Glancing up at the ominous black peaks, Diane noticed a large, dark bird with a golden sheen along its head, floating effortlessly on the evening breeze.

Hmm, looks almost familiar somehow, she pondered, then shrugged. *It's so high! I can't...*

"Hey, Di, look!" Benji interrupted her thoughts.

The promising black wall was just on the other side of the monstrous cliff face before them.

In front of her, Asazi began to cross a narrow black ledge

composed of large, smooth obsidian orbs, known as volcanic glass, when suddenly, Forjon's back left hoof slid out from beneath him. Diane gasped in horror, tugging hard on Mavric's reins to stop, and froze.

As if sliding on black ice, the frightened horse screamed and struggled desperately to regain his footing and balance, tossing Asazi off his back. Tumbling over Forjon's shoulder, Asazi hung under the painted horse's strong neck, panting. Forjon continued to strain, frantically snorting, his nostrils flared, eyes bulging, whinnying a desperate cry.

Asazi quickly lowered himself to the slippery ledge and stepped safely onto the coarse cinder along its edge. He grabbed Forjon's reins to steady him and then pulled with all his might. Working together, Forjon finally stepped off the slick black obsidian onto the stable cinder. Everyone sighed loudly in relief.

Asazi stood quietly with his forehead pressed against Forjon's, both horse and rider breathing deeply. With their eyes shut, Asazi's lips moved soundlessly in what Diane assumed was a solemn prayer of gratitude to the ancient spirits that protected and rescued them. Everyone dismounted and ran to embrace the exhausted brave ones. Addie waved her hands and shut her eyes to communicate with Forjon directly.

"He's alright," she reported breathlessly, "just shaken. He wants to thank you, Asazi, for saving him from the great danger. He could have easily tumbled off that cliff ledge." At her words, Forjon vigorously nodded his head up and down, flicking his ears, and pawing the ground.

"Come look!" shouted Lee as she appeared from around the other side of the cliff face. She had vanished just before the commotion, scouting ahead, but returned, eagerly beckoning the adventurers to follow her.

As they rounded the cliff face that formed the back side of the ledge, their eyes widened simultaneously. In front of them, the glittering sun was shining upon a huge black wall of jagged basalt—a wondrous sight, and frightening.

Eons before, a violent volcanic eruption had thrown up molten lava from the depths of the earth, which seemed to freeze in midair, forming ragged peaks, jagged pinnacles, and cliff faces shredded with gaping holes now filled with hanging gardens of wildflowers.

Looking a bit like pulled taffy, the trapped gases had exploded in the molten lava, cooled immediately, and solidified, creating an eerie, holey structure in the black wall before them.

The jagged wall had the appearance of a grisly gathering of dark, screaming ghoulish faces, all twisted and contorted, giving Diane the willies.

Scary. She shivered at the sight of it.

From the cliff's ridgeline at their backs, the setting sun shot its last beam of glistening light across the chasm before them, illuminating Za-tha's black wall. Its intense light lit up a stream of water flowing out from one of the gaping, ghastly mouths. A twilight breeze dispersed the cascading spring into a sparkling spray of fine mist that carried its nourishing waters to the far side of the flow, allowing velvety green mosses and bright orange lichens to flourish on nature's lavishly gardened rock wall.

Diane reflected on Za-tha's words. *Collect from the flow of Mother Earth's sorrow, a black tear from its mist.*

"That's it!" she said, elated. "The place where we'll find Mother Earth's tears."

Quickly, Diane grabbed Lee by the elbow. "Let's go!" she said, pulling her onto the narrow cinder trail along the jagged cliff face. In fear of falling, the girls slowly made their way, hugging their backs to the rock wall. Benji started to follow, but Asazi pulled him back. Grumbling again, he reluctantly waited behind with Addie and Asazi, both holding their breath with every step.

"*Attentif.* Careful," Lee directed tersely. "Hold onto the holes."

The wall of volcanic basalt rock felt like sharp, edgy glass. Recent summer storms had flashed torrents of water down the little box canyon's black walls, washing away large sections of the trail, making the path too dangerous for animals to pass— *and too dangerous for humans as well,* Diane reasoned. Using the holes in the frozen taffy wall as hand and footholds, they carefully made their way across a wide gap in the swept-away trail. One wrong move, and they would most certainly fall to their deaths.

Clinging to the cliff wall with one hand, Diane grasped onto her white scarf with the other and said a silent prayer of protection for their safe passage.

All at once, Diane turned and watched Lee step onto a rock jutting precariously out from the wall. It suddenly crumbled and gave way, tumbling hundreds of feet down the cliff face to the bottom of the valley, noisily crashing and bouncing off other boulders in its path. Diane saw the panicked look of molten fear on Lee's face and reached out, firmly grasping Lee by the arm, and pulled her to safety.

"*Incroyable!*" Lee said, panting. She exhaled jerkily, still catching her breath, as she carefully stepped onto a solid remnant of the washed-away trail.

"I know Mother Earth is protecting us," Diane said breathlessly.

Just then, a large red-tailed hawk screeched loudly from the top of the cliff and lurched forward into the evening wind. Its whitish underbelly, in contrast to its dark-brown hooded head and throat adorned with a necklace of light feathers, gleamed in the setting sun as it hurriedly flew north to deliver its message.

Wiping her brow and adjusting her hat, Diane and Lee finally stepped safely onto the solid part of the trail and carefully made their way along the base of the black wall. Beautiful hanging gardens grew out of the gaping basalt holes in the rock, which were filled with lush green ferns and miniature plants with colorful, tiny flowers. The air was filled with their wild, delicate fragrance. Diane, taking just a quick moment, closely inspected all of their beautiful shapes and designs, making a mental note to learn more about wildflowers. *I need to write that down in my field journal tonight when we camp,* she mumbled silently.

Kneeling at the small black pool beneath the flow of spring water, Diane and Lee cupped their hands and filled them. The water was cold and crystal clear in their hands, magnifying the lines in their palms. Testing the water, Lee first sniffed the water for any unpleasant scent that might indicate it was poisoned by natural toxic minerals. Satisfied, she took a small sip and held it in her mouth, waiting for any strange reaction. After a minute or so, she was content that the water was safe to drink and swallowed.

"Cool beans," she sighed, "This is incredibly sweet water."

Diane joined her. Delight twinkling in their eyes, they freely drank the thirst-quenching liquid. Diane was in heaven. Her heart soared as she gently splashed water onto her face, reveling in the chilly sensation.

In a natural state of ecstasy, Diane recited once again to herself the words of Za-tha, the zaman, spiritual leader of the Aszanii, and Asazi's grandfather, *Collect from the flow of Mother Earth's sorrow, a black tear from its mist.*

Tethering the horses to a boulder along the trail, Addie and Asazi, holding a squirming Benji by the collar, carefully sidled along the precarious path and joined them, drinking from the spring, almost giddy with glee. Diane moved along the black ledge to the other side of the pool, where the fine mist blew onto the cliff face, and discovered a small pool of water hidden within. She cautiously reached down into its depths and felt small, rounded pebbles at the bottom. Gathering up a handful, she brought them to the surface and into the last remaining ray of light for everyone to see. In her hand were several smoothly polished pebbles of black obsidian—volcanic glass—that glistened in the setting sun.

"They look like Sa'ami's tears," she gasped, remembering the giant black bear's pain. Everyone nodded in agreement.

"Bear tears represent the Mother Earth's tears for all her children, including her animal children that suffer at the hands of her human children," Asazi said sagely.

"Sa'ami's tears!" Diane exclaimed again, joyfully.

Peering into the dark pool of water, Benji saw the faint gold glint of stone buried in its depths. "Look at this, sis!" he said excitedly as he held a shimmering gold nugget up to the sun's vanishing rays. Tucking his found treasure into his pocket, Benji absently stepped backward, and all at once, his boot heel slipped on the loose cinder, and teetering wildly, he started to fall over the edge of the cliff, screaming in fright.

"Benji!" Diane yelled, clutching onto her white scarf. Her heart pounded in her ears. Diane's stomach was in her throat, and she could hardly breathe.

Suddenly, something enormous soared overhead and blocked the last ray of light, casting a dark shadow across the terrified clan. The thunderous beating of a heavy bird's wings filled the air. Everyone looked up in shock and surprise to see the fluttering wings of the largest golden eagle they had ever seen.

The raptor flapped its huge wings and, extending its sharp talons, grabbed onto Benji's flailing duster, and lifted him. Dropping a stunned Benji back onto the trail, the terrifying eagle landed on a nearby perch of jagged basalt. Its piercing eyes looking curiously and almost kindly at them.

Diane squeezed her brother tightly. "Please," she pleaded as he squirmed, "be more careful. This trail is treacherous!"

Just then, to the adventurers' astonishment, the majestic golden eagle magically faded away, and in an explosion of tiny glittering lights, Za-tha now stood in its place. His long red shawl with the sun depicted in yellow beads shimmered in the last rays of light from the setting sun. Billowing open, it rippled in the wind along with streams of his flowing white hair. He raised his hands, palms outward, facing Asazi, his grandson, in a sign of greeting. Asazi grinned widely and, stepping forward, touched his own palms to his grandfather's.

"Greetings," Za-tha said warmly.

Diane stood in awe in front of him. Swallowing hard, she asked shakily, "*How* did you do that? What *are* you?"

Befuddled, she slowly raised her cupped hands high above her head so that the tall zaman could see the black pebbles she had collected.

"Behold," he said and nodded with approval. Reaching into her hands with an old, crooked finger, he selected one of them and held it up to the diminishing ray of light. Its soft beam lit up the stone with an eerie, blackish glow.

"This is a tear of Mother Earth's sorrow for her Earth children who have lost their way into the darkness of self, forgetting the way of togetherness, which is the only path to oneness. They have forgotten how to respect each other and the beautiful earth, as well as its small creatures that were created for them, for their joy."

Opening her amulet, he reverently placed the stone within and said, "May this talisman always be a reminder to you to respect and appreciate all life, large and small, and the environment that we share. You have learned well the secret to the First Ray of Light: *let kindness always be your first impulse.* You have shown great kindness to your new friends, especially to Addie, your horse friends, and to the great black bear, Sa'ami. In this, Mother Earth is most pleased," he continued solemnly.

Still astounded, Diane looked up into Za-tha's wrinkled face, etched with age and secrets, and peered deeply into his soulful crystal blue eyes, questioning warily. *The mysterious woman on the train said the exact same thing,* she reflected. *How did he know—Who was she?*

Za-tha saw the bewildered expression on Diane's face, a glint sparkling in his eyes.

Gently taking her by the chin, he raised her head so he could look deeply into her troubled green eyes. "You have done well," he finally said after a long pause. "Asazi will explain everything when the time is right. Until then, be not afraid. Trust your feelings."

She sighed deeply; a weight of concern suddenly lifted with his words. Somehow, deep inside her, she *knew* that she was safe; *they* were safe, and feeling protected, her smile began to grow broadly. "Thank you," she said breathlessly. "Thank you for saving Benji." Her eyes glistened appreciatively.

"Now," he said, nodding. Taking a step back to look at all of the adventurers, "Once you return to your bear friend, you will journey to the west to find the Cave of Ages and discover the secret to the Second Ray of Light. You will cross a green river whose far bank of sandstone contains large bones from ancient monsters that long ago were turned into stone. Follow the bank of bones northward, upriver, until you locate a large sandstone ledge with the letter 'A' carved into it. Be at the ledge at sunrise. The morning ray of first light will reveal the opening to the Cave of Ages. In it, you will find *the remnants from the birth of Mother Earth's children.*"

With these words, Za-tha turned his face upward, grasped his amulet, then slowly raising his powerful arms out from the sides of his body, he magically changed back into the golden eagle. With a screech into the howling wind, he flapped his huge wings and flew away with a trail of tiny glittering lights.

"*Incroyable*," Lee murmured in a slow, low voice.

Benji lightly tugged on Diane's duster as they both stared, wide-eyed and speechless.

Asazi stood with his left hand over his heart, his right arm extended as if he were holding a connection with the flight of the golden eagle, his beloved grandfather. "Fly safely with the Mother," he whispered.

CHAPTER TWENTY-ONE

TLATOANI TREASURES

"**M**ore jiggery-pokery?" Wadey grouched warily, slapping his cowboy hat to his thigh and scratching his head as he stood before the swirling white light.

"Yup! Yup!" stuttered Duffy, circling the ground before the Aztec Portal, closely examining the jumbled array of hoof prints. "They went into the light, sure as shooting."

Ramus sat back on his horse, slowly rubbing the scruff on his chin, pondering. "If they went that away, so can we," he glowered, and with a slap of the reins against his horse's flanks, he leaned forward and jumped his horse into the portal.

"Wow-wee!" could be heard trailing from inside the portal as Ramus' cowboy hat came rolling out.

Wadey swaggered over and picked it up, then climbed onto his horse's back and, with a hard slap on its hindquarters, followed his brother into the light.

Duffy gulped hard, the apple in his scrawny throat visibly shaking. He reluctantly clambered onto his horse, swiped his brow, and squeezed his knees tight, motioning his horse to proceed cautiously forward.

"They're coming!" Ramus drawled scathingly as he cracked his gnarly knuckles. He scowled as the adventurers passed. Huddled in a black lava bubble big enough to hide the three brothers and their horses, the glint in Ramus' eye was murderous. As he loomed out of the darkness, his shadowy figure glared and sneered, "Where there's some treasure for the taking, surely there'll be more!"

Still unsteady from the jarring jolts they received during their Indian spirits encounter, they left their horses hidden and proceeded shakily on foot, hobbling up the rocky trail to the black wall.

The three brothers walked the short distance side by side, and together stepped onto the glassy obsidian ledge.

Duffy screeched as his foot slid forward along the slippery black rock, stretching him into a perfect 'splits' position. "Yahoo!" he screamed in horrific pain.

Ramus reached down to help him up. Suddenly, both feet slipped from underneath him, and he lurched forward, landing on Duffy, making him shrill even louder. Wadey bent backward in cruel laughter at the sight of his brothers, when all at once, his boots flew forward high into the air, plopping him hard on his buttocks while kicking into his two brothers, hurtling them over the ledge.

Ramus turned quickly and grasped tightly onto Wadey's outstretched leg, while his brother Duffy, dangling from Ramus' pants belt, was shrieking loudly. Gritting his teeth, sweat from his brow overflowing into his eyes, Ramus strained as he slowly hauled himself upward, all the while pulling a frenetic Wadey skittering closer to the edge. Ramus sneered, thinking he had conquered the situation, when all of a sudden,

Wadey's sweaty hands slipped on the smooth surface, and—
WHOOSH! He slid over the ledge, taking his brothers with
him. They screeched and tumbled, falling over boulders on
their way down the cliffside until they landed in a large patch
of prickly pear cactus, yowling shrilly.

From a ways off, Diane heard a spine-tingling yowl. She
couldn't make out whether man or beast had made it.

"Did you hear that?" Lee asked, alarmed, as Asazi and
Forjon stepped over the white-glowing edge back into the
Aztec Portal.

Diane and Benji both nodded. "Let's get away from here!"
Diane yelled, over her shoulder, seeing the frightened look
on Addie's face as they trailed Asazi. Lee brought up the rear
once again. Diane clutched onto her hat as Benji pressed his
head into his sister's back, and the howling wind washed over
them again. *I'll never get used to this,* Diane thought, patting
Mavric reassuringly.

The windblown clan reached the placid grassy meadow
tinged with juniper trees at dusk and stopped abruptly at
the sight before them. Still nestled under the boughs of the
juniper lay Sa'ami, sleeping soundly and snoring loudly. Diane
snickered quietly while everyone stood silently encircling the
sleeping, snoring bear with warm smiles on their faces.

Sa'ami slowly raised his huge head. Peering through pine
needles with bleary eyes, he seemed to grin groggily at his
new friends, and then dozed off again.

Lee and Asazi went straight to work gathering dry tinder,
twigs, and logs to make a fire for the night. Diane watched in

amazement as Asazi spun the long, slender stick between his palms, moving his hands vigorously down the length of the drill stick. She had read about this hand drill method of fire-making in her books and was thrilled to see it demonstrated. *Seems pretty simple,* she figured.

He released one hand when he reached the bottom, and grabbing the drill at the top again, he brought the other hand up and started the downward pressure again upon the flat wooden base. Fast and steady, he twirled the drill, creating friction on the soft juniper wood of the fireboard that had a small notch cut into its side.

Beads of sweat streamed down Asazi's cheeks and his breathing was labored.

Just then, wisps of smoke drifted up from the fireboard as a red, glowing ember dropped from the board through the notch into a dry tinder nest positioned below. Asazi grunted his relief.

The nest was filled with cattail fluff and finely shaved juniper bark that smoldered immediately. Once the flammable fibers held the precious glowing ember, Asazi dropped his drill, picked up the tinder nest, and holding it close to his face, started gently blowing into it.

Within moments, the tinder nest exploded into a blaze of flames. He then dropped it into the campfire pit and stacked little twigs, dried leaves, and pine needles over it. Thick tendrils of white smoke gushed forth from the small tinder pile as it burst into serpentine-like tongues of flames. Once caught, Asazi added larger branches and finally, a couple logs to the burning fire that would last throughout the night.

At last, Asazi sat back on his haunches, panting hard, but seemingly pleased with his efforts. "My people have learned much from all the people we have encountered on our journey northward," he said respectfully.

The scrumptious aromas of food cooking finally woke Sa'ami, who wandered off for his own dinner, while everyone enjoyed sitting around the fire, telling their version of the evening's extraordinary experience.

Diane had been waiting for this moment. Bubbling, unable to contain herself a moment longer, she blurted out, "How did Za-tha turn into an eagle? And how did your people become the Keepers of the Tlatoani Treasures?"

Benji, Lee, and Addie all sat up, wide-eyed, and leaned forward, waiting for Asazi's answer.

Asazi stared into the flames, his amber eyes seeming to glow brightly in the firelight, but his mood was somber. Uncertain how the clan would react, he hesitated, then looked deep into their eyes and proceeded slowly. "Long ago, my people, the Aszanii, lived in a distant land far, far to the east. We lived a quiet, isolated life in small villages along the sea. The people of my village were born with a rare gift, making us very different from those of other villages around us. So, we purposefully stayed as distant from them as possible," he paused, looking down while stirring the fire. "We were born with the ability to change our shape to those of birds of prey and other animals." Sighing deeply, he glanced up and went on, "This is how we move among other people, observing them and learning from them without their knowing of our presence. This is how I learned English. It is also how we have survived all these years."

Peering deeply once again into the eyes of each adventurer, seeing only rapt interest, he continued, "One day, an injured stranger wandered into our village. The zaman, our healer and spiritual leader, took him into his home and cared for him, sending him back to his village healed and well. Unfortunately, during his stay, the visitor accidentally witnessed the zaman's magical transformation and reported it to his village authorities upon his return."

"That's horrible!" Diane cried out. Benji nodded vigorously in agreement.

"That's just not right or fair!" Lee chimed in, throwing her hands up in utter disgust.

Addie was silent, her chin in the palms of her hands, glued to every word of this incredible story.

"This was during the time of the great Inquisition, and my people were persecuted for witchcraft and hunted almost to the point of extinction. With the help of our village brothers, we that remained, escaped across the Great Waters to the west and to the New World recently discovered, later called the Americas. Here we learned to blend in with the people we first encountered, the Aztecs," he sighed, stirring the fire again. His golden-bronze skin shimmered in the blazing light.

"The Aztecs!" Diane shouted fervently; her eyes wild with excitement. She was just beginning to understand how truly complex and special the Aszanii people were.

Asazi nodded solemnly and continued, "The mystical Aztecs appreciated and respected our transformations as powerful magic and considered us their animal protectors, a divine gift from their Sun God. We became a trusted and valued part of their great civilization and learned many of their ancient secrets. In time, we became the *Keepers of the Tlatoani Treasures*, which means their 'ruler's treasures,' and were given the magic spells and stones to travel throughout the ancient portals of the Aztec Trail," Asazi paused again, seemingly considering how much of the story he should tell.

"When the Spanish conquistadors arrived sometime later,

the elders of my people recognized our age-old enemy, and with the help of the Aztec Stones, they secretly fled into the northern territories of the Americas, where we once again lived in harmony with the indigenous people, learning from them and adopting many of their ways," he finished, satisfied he shared just enough.

La-to-a-ni, Diane said silently to herself, wanting to pronounce the ruler's treasure correctly.

Tears ran down Addie's face. She turned from the fire, swiping them away. "That was an amazing story and so sad," she finally murmured. Benji patted her softly on the shoulder, looking soulfully into her eyes, consoling her in his gentle way.

Diane smiled at the kind gesture and noticed that while they were listening, Lee had picked up a piece of juniper wood and started quietly, pensively, carving it with her knife.

"What are you working on?" she asked, her mind still swimming from all that she had heard.

"Do you remember Za-tha's warning, something about encountering ancient monsters?" she replied seriously. "I would never have believed my eyes—or ears! Between Addie's talking to bears, raccoons, and horses, the Aztec Portals, and Za-tha appearing as an eagle, anything is possible," she finally accepted. "We'd better be prepared."

CHAPTER TWENTY-TWO

THE BOOMERANG

D iane shuddered, recalling Za-tha's words—a *warning*. In all the excitement, she had forgotten. Lee saw the sudden look of recognition, then the look of grave concern come over her face.

"I'm making a weapon a trapper from Australia showed me how to make a few summers ago. He had heard of the Pike's Peak Gold Rush in these parts and had high hopes of becoming a rich 'Fifty-Niner,' like Buffalo Bill Cody and so many of the immigrants that came at that time. Fortunately for the Australian, he was also an expert trapper, and rumors tell, he ended up making his fortune in the fur trade," Lee said, as she continued talking and whittling away. "He called it a 'boomerang,' and it can be highly effective."

She stopped to look at it in the firelight. "He also taught me how to throw it. It can kill a small animal or stun a large one. I had one until my papa used it for tinder," she sighed sadly. "Feels like the right time to make another."

"Good idea," said Diane, somewhat relieved and excited again. "Will you make one for me, too, and teach me how to use it?"

"Me too!" said Asazi. "I'm interested in such a weapon."

"Me three!" chimed in Addie.

Benji just nodded his head and looked to Lee with a hopeful glint in his eyes.

The juniper wood was strong but also soft enough to carve easily, and within a couple of hours, Lee had roughly carved the angular, flat shape of the boomerang for everyone. She showed them how to finish it by smoothing it down to a polished surface with a knife blade or the flat edge of a sharp stone shard.

Even Benji took out his pocketknife, as he was an avid carver, something he'd learned from his grandfather. He went to work on his by the light of the fire.

A while later, Diane held hers up to inspect it in the glow of the flames against the backdrop of stars in the night sky. She felt a deep sense of satisfaction.

Asazi scrunched his eyebrows in serious concentration as he inspected his creation. "How does this work?" he finally asked, perplexed.

"I'll show you in the morning," Lee said, continuing to polish her boomerang.

Asazi's eyes grew large. "I'd like to paint our weapons for a successful journey," he said soberly.

Diane quickly offered her boomerang to him. "Here's mine," she said, tossing it to him.

"On Diane's, I will paint the symbol of the bear," he proclaimed, "as this is her totem." Seeing that he had everyone's attention, he continued sagely, "In my village, my people believe in the power of animal spirits, that each animal possesses certain unique characteristics that are similar to those found in each of us. The totem—like the bear for Diane—is a symbol of great spiritual significance. It represents the animal and its special qualities, like courage, strength, and leadership. The bear symbol is a good omen and is known as *the Protector.*"

"*Oui*, yes, that was one *bear* of a challenge," Lee chuckled to herself, "the way you *faced the bear.*" She continued, "I could *bearly* contain myself." Lee's sense of humor was emerging, and everyone joined in as Lee laughed at her own play on words.

With that, Lee threw a couple large logs onto the flames, and the rest finished polishing their boomerangs by firelight. Handing them to Asazi, they snuggled contently into their sleeping blankets. Looking up into the starry sky, Diane sighed and marveled at the number of stars that twinkled overhead. *Countless*, she mused. She was certain that the streak of light across the sky, looking a little like a bony spinal vertebra, was the Milky Way, which she had only read about in her schoolbooks, and pointed it out to Benji.

"Why can't we see this at home?" he asked groggily.

"Too much pollution from all of the factories," she said, listening to him suddenly blow sleepy puffs of air. *He's sound asleep,* she smiled to herself.

She loved this moment. There was no place she'd rather be than right here, right now. She could hear the crackling of the fire, the horses grazing the meadow grasses among the purple thistles and owl clover, the crickets and tree frogs serenading her with their evening song. A cool night breeze gently swept across her face as she breathed in the delicious smell of the ponderosa pine trees and the sweet fragrance of burning juniper. *And the stars! So many stars.*

Just live in the moment and appreciate the NOW. She reflected on Asazi's wise words. Face the bear! she thought, recalling Lee's words. *Let kindness ALWAYS be your first impulse!* She pondered the wisdom of Za-tha's words and from the beautiful vanishing woman on the train. *I must write this all down in my field journal in the morning,* she said to herself as she drifted off in a deep, peaceful slumber.

Its razor-sharp three-clawed feet slashed at the ground as the enormous two-legged beast crashed through the dark trees, chasing her. Diane's heart was pounding in her chest; her throat felt raw and tight with fear. She felt the earth shake beneath her feet, and she could feel the hot breath of the terrifying creature on the back of her head as it lunged and snapped its fierce, powerful jaws, just missing her. She glanced over her shoulder as she dashed through the reeds along a river's edge and saw a flash of its gnashing dagger-like fangs glistening in the sunlight as it roared a most terrible growl, just above her head, that was deafening, and...

Diane woke to the sound of something whizzing over her head, followed by a dull THUD. *There it is again,* she said to herself, barely able to pry open her eyelids. THUD! She slowly opened her eyes to the first beams of morning light. Shielding them from the sun's penetrating glow, she opened her eyes wide and focused on Lee giving Asazi and Addie boomerang-throwing lessons.

WHIZZ! She heard it again as the boomerang sailed through the air, hitting its mark on the dead pine trunk with a THUD!

"Cool beans!" exclaimed Lee, thrilled with Asazi's successful throw. "Your turn, Addie," she said, obviously proud of her fledging students—and her instructing.

"You're a natural," Lee said, giving Addie a strong slap on

the back as her boomerang hit the charcoal-drawn circle, just a few inches below Asazi's.

"Hey!" Diane jumped up from her sleeping blanket. "How long have you been practicing?" she asked, a tad disappointed. "Why didn't you wake me?"

"Only a little while," replied Addie timidly. "You seemed to be dreaming, so we didn't want to disturb you."

"Who could sleep with visions of ancient monsters in your head?" Lee muttered, shuddering.

"Me too!" Diane said, nodding her head. "I was having a scary dream right before I woke up—it seemed so real—a terrifying monster was creeping about in the dark shadows... its growl was like a whistle or a whooshing sound...I could hear it stomping...THUD...THUD...and felt the ground shake."

Lee glanced at Addie and both snickered.

Diane shook the vision from her head and yawned. "Show me how to throw this thing," she said, jumping over her log headboard as she stomped flat-footed up to the group, swinging her arms widely to loosen her muscles in a display of athletic confidence.

"Where's my boomerang?" she asked, forgetting that she had given it to Asazi the night before.

From his traveling pouch, Asazi pulled out a beautiful boomerang decorated with bear pawprints in black manganese and stripes of red and yellow ochre painted across its blade.

"This is beautiful," Diane said, holding it up to the morning light. "When and how did you paint this?"

"Last night by the fire," he said, glowing. "I mixed a few crushed minerals with dried fish eggs that I carry in my traveling pouch. After adding some water to the fish-egg binder, I mixed it with the minerals in separate small wooden bowls to make my paints; yellow, black, and red—the sacred color of Mother Earth—representing her blood spilled during Creation, the birth of new life!"

"Hmm," she pondered. "How did you get it to look so shiny?" she asked, turning it over in her hands and admiring the fine craftsmanship.

"I rubbed beeswax over it to seal and protect the colors and the designs," Asazi replied, his smile revealing that he seemed pleased that she appreciated his artistry.

"It's wonderful!" Diane said, beaming radiantly. "Thank you so much!"

Lee showed her how to hold her boomerang and then demonstrated how to throw it. With a little instruction, she was ready to cast her first throw. She wound up and released it like a pro. It went whizzing through the air toward the target marked on the tree trunk...and sailed right past it. Disappointed, she tried it again, and missed again.

This isn't as easy as it looked, she thought to herself. *But never give up!* And, she continued her attempts without much success but tried all the same.

Finally, Benji woke, and lifting the sleeping bear's paw from around his waist, he joined in the morning training. Asazi pulled out another boomerang from his pouch and handed it to Benji, whose eyes glistened at the sight of it. He scampered off to get instructions from Lee.

Each boomerang had similarly painted stripes and a bear paw designed into it, reminding everyone they were united as the little Sa'ami Bear Clan. Sa'ami had finally risen and wandered off to find some breakfast. Diane knew that black bears had a very diverse diet of nuts, berries, plants, insects, and meat—mostly mice, rodents, peccaries, and young deer.

Disgusting, Diane shuddered, feeling sorry for the cute little forest animals. *They're omnivores,* she recalled from her school lessons. *They eat both plants and animals.* Her favorite "bear" word was "crepuscular," which meant they hunted at twilight, both at dawn *and* at dusk.

Sa'ami lumbered into camp sometime later, licking his lips, seemingly content from a successful hunt. Addie had a conversation with him the day before, making it quite clear that Niki was a part of their clan and not to be mistaken as a bear snack. He had to find food away from camp unless it was offered.

The boomerang lesson over, they loaded up their horses. After dousing the campfire with creek water, snuffing the life of the embers, and scattering the fire-ring stones, they helped each other onto their saddles. Benji stood in front of Sa'ami with a quizzical look on his face, pondering. Suddenly, his eyes brightened as he spied a large boulder among the pines. Tugging Sa'ami by an ear, he led him to the mossy boulder, fleetly stepped onto it, and clambered onto Sa'ami's waiting back. Diane's clan watched, amused at Benji's antic, and grinned at his ingenuity. Applauding, they nudged their horses forward and continued their quest northward to the Cave of Ages and the ancient monsters.

CHAPTER TWENTY-THREE

JUST BE

I t was a beautiful summer day. A soft golden haze flooded the tall field grasses of the meadow, buzzing with busy bees, butterflies, and ladybugs, all at their day's work of collecting nectar, pollen, and such. The tender young shoots of green grasses were intertwined with multicolored wildflowers that attracted the noisy insects. Diane rode silently alongside Asazi, just enjoying the moment. He noticed the peaceful look on her face.

"Close your eyes," he said softly, breaking their silence.

Diane did so immediately with complete trust and curiosity.

"Now, breathe in slowly through your nose as deeply as you can, then exhale freely through your mouth. Do this four times," he instructed.

She did as he guided while he watched, counted, and waited.

"Now, still your mind," he guided. Taking her wrist, he swiped her hand in the air across her forehead. "Wipe away all thoughts."

"Keeping your eyes shut, tell me what you smell," he inquired.

This feels like a game, she mused and slowly, deeply inhaled, as she was told.

"I smell the scent of the ponderosa pine trees," she began. "It's like warm butterscotch," she said, bubbling. "I can smell the dirt, wet and earthy. It reminds me of my uncle's can of fishing worms," she said gleefully, breathing in again. "I smell the grasses and plants, all kinds of different plant smells." She was enjoying this game. "Nature is filled with so many smells!" she chortled. "I can smell the horses, the leather of the saddle, and PHEW, my clothes are starting to reek! They need a washing," she snickered, wrinkling up her nose.

"Good," Asazi said. "Now, what do you hear?"

"Hmm," she murmured as she refocused her attention. It was like turning off one of her senses and turning on another. "I hear the creaking of the saddle and the breathing of the horses." She began the game again, concentrating first on the sounds closest to her. "I hear the clinking of the bridle and Mavric's steps crunching the twigs and needles beneath his hooves."

Now, expanding her circle of sounds, she said pensively, "All the horses. I can hear them all breathing," she said with delight. "I can hear the insects—the crickets rubbing their wings together, the buzz of the bees sucking nectar, pesky flies, and the fluttering wings of a passing bird," she said in wonderment. "I can even hear the field grasses hitting their long, slender stalks together in the breeze and the wind rustling through the trees." She sat up in her saddle as if the whole world had opened to her. "It's a nature symphony!"

"Now, what do you feel?" he asked in a serious tone.

Again, she took a deep breath to refocus her attention and paused to turn on her feeling senses.

"The breeze on my skin, tickling my hair," she began. "I feel the warmth of the sun on my face and the motion of Mavric's gait, rocking me from side to side in my saddle. I can feel him breathing under my legs." She laughed, truly enjoying this game.

"Finally, take four deep breaths again and let all of these

senses come to you at once," he concluded.

It was like a floodgate had been lifted. She felt overwhelmed with all the sensations, and her body tingled all over in response, goose bumps bristling on her arms, and the hair prickled on the back of her neck.

"I feel like I'm vibrating," she said, shivering.

"You're 'at one' with nature," Asazi explained. "You are completely alive, and you're feeling your connection to Mother Earth and all her creations. Sit quietly, when you feel this connection, and let go of any concerns," he continued. "Let them blow away like leaves in a wind and remember to keep all thoughts from your mind," he said, as he raised his own hand and swiped it in the air across his forehead, as if clearing a blackboard.

"Remember to always take four deep breaths and relax your shoulders. Let them drop to your pockets. And be mindful of your whole experience—use all your senses to connect with nature and your animal friends. *BE present in the moment*," he offered.

"Being in the BE," she murmured, considering the wisdom of his words. *This just feels good. Feels right,* she reflected, learning to connect with everything around her.

"The past is gone; the future has yet to come; all we have is here in the present. By doing this every day for just a short time, you'll find true peace and happiness your whole life long—a gift from Mother Earth to you," Asazi finished.

"Just BE! Something I've been kind of doing all along, without knowing it, but not like this," she shared with Asazi, looking deep into his gleaming amber eyes. "Thank you for showing me how to *BE present*."

And she promised herself, right there, right then, that she would always try to *live in the moment* and BE truly present by acknowledging and appreciating her connection with nature. "Just BE," she repeated. Such a deep, profound peace fell over her that a tear welled up in her eye and trickled over onto her cheek. Deep in her soul, she knew the truth and importance of this life lesson.

"And when you are in the moment, feeling your connection to Mother Earth, you have the power to create, as she does," Asazi added sagely. "This power is in everyone who knows it and recognizes it. Simply *think* of something you want to create, *see* it in your imagination, *feel* like you already have it, and *know* that you have this power and that you're worthy to receive it—and you'll *create* it. Then thank the Mother for giving it to you. By always *being* in a state of appreciation and gratitude for what you *already* have, you will *manifest* whatever more you want from the World of Spirits into your physical World of Life in the here and now."

Diane fell silent, pondering the wisdom of these words. Somewhere deep inside her, she knew these words were true. With a deep breath, she sighed heartily and felt her entire body tingle again in recognition.

Think it, see it, feel it, know it, create it, she repeated to herself. Just then, she remembered her white scarf and the brilliantly white circle she saw with the silvery image of the bear stopping and dropping at her feet. *Is my scarf showing me how to create? Picturing what I want all within the white lasso?*

"I have the power to create whatever my heart desires? I'm the designer of my life experiences?" she asked Asazi pensively.

"This is the truth," he confirmed.

Swinging down from his horse, Asazi scooped up something hidden on the ground. Brushing it against his deerskin, he handed it to Diane. "This is your Joy Stone," he said, handing her a glistening piece of orange calcite. "Anytime you want to connect to the creative powers of Mother Earth, rub this stone, then hold it tight, and remember something that brings you that special feeling of joy, then *see* what it is you want to create within your white lasso, *feel* your joy, and *know* that it is on its way to you."

Diane accepted the Joy Stone gratefully and quietly tried to think of something that brought her joy. Suddenly, she remembered her Daisy dog and how much joy she felt smelling her puppy breath. "Puppy breath," she proclaimed, chuckling. "That's my joy thought!"

It was around noon when they stopped to give the horses a little break to graze on the forest grasses and sweet wild plants. The bright western sun was at its zenith, infusing the air with Diane's favorite forest smell—warmed butterscotch.

Leading the clan of tired horses, Asazi turned Forjon around and rode back to the adventurers. "We're close to the Aztec Portal that will take us to the green river," he said excitedly. "Let's stop here and rest first."

Diane dismounted her sweaty horse and pulled out her boomerang, determined to learn how to throw it. Mavric wandered off to graze with the rest of the horses.

"Time to practice," she announced briskly. "Show me again, please. How do I throw this thing?"

Lee patiently showed her how to hold it properly and then, once again, demonstrated how to throw it. The boomerang flung out of Lee's hand and soared, ripping through the air, then amazingly turned in a sweeping arc and returned again to her hand. Everyone clapped enthusiastically and pulled out their own boomerangs to commence their practice.

Diane clenched her teeth, squinted her eyes, and furrowed her forehead in concentration, determined to be able to throw her boomerang, too. She was once, after all, very athletic, and enjoyed healthy competition. That is, before she became a bookworm. Taking a firm stance, she quieted her mind and took a deep breath. On the exhale, she threw her boomerang with all her might.

It immediately left her hand, flying sideways across the heads of the other throwers, all of whom ducked in succession as it flew straight toward Benji, still sitting on Sa'ami's back, and hit the pemmican bar out of his hand just as he was about to take a bite from it. The whizzing sound scared Sa'ami, who darted off so fast that he threw Benji backward, somersaulting down his long, bristly back.

"Oops!" Diane said under her breath, and she dashed toward Benji, crying out, "Are you alright?"

Lying on his back, staring up into the tree branches, startled, he began to laugh while rubbing his stinging hand, and everyone joined in.

"Cool beans," chortled Lee heartily. "That was quite a throw!"

"I think I'll have some lunch instead," Diane said glumly, helping her brother to his feet and soothing the returning Sa'ami with a scratch behind his ears.

"But I will get this," she said firmly. "Wait—you'll see. I *never* give up!"

"Let's go!" Lee shouted crisply a little while later, swinging her leg over the back of Bentley while scooting a chittering Niki back into her raccoon cap.

Asazi helped Benji onto Mavric's back behind his sister and

started out, Addie following on Rohan.

"We'll find the Aztec Portal in a sandstone arch not far from here," Asazi said, gently slapping the reins against Forjon's flanks.

The stately conifer trees gave way to a dwarf pinyon and juniper forest dotted with outcrops of red sandstone and white limestone. Up ahead, a stone arch, like an inverted 'V,' dominated the landscape.

"Look at my scarf!" Diane said, "It's glowing again."

As the clan approached the red sandstone arch, towering thirty feet over their heads, Asazi pulled out the Aztec Stone from his deerskin pouch. It was glowing too! "Everyone ready?" he asked in a solemn voice. Everyone gulped hard and nodded, anchoring their belongings to their saddles and grasping onto their hats.

Asazi held the glowing turquoise stone in his open palm and placed his forefinger on its golden tip. As he repeated the ancient words of the Keepers, the stone started twirling again, faster and faster.

"Here we go again," Benji said, wrapping his arms around Diane's waist.

The brilliant light emanating from the Aztec Stone began swirling in front of them. "I like the popping sparks of lights," Benji whispered into his sister's ear. She squeezed his arms in hers as he pressed his hat securely to her back.

Once again, the tornado of light grew before them, expanding as it rose high over their heads until the mouth of the light funnel turned and moved into the space within the arch of sandstone, filling it completely. As the frosted-looking glass began to clear, magically revealing a very different landscape of a high desert, Asazi pressed his legs against Forjon's sides and signaled to enter.

CHAPTER TWENTY-FOUR

ANCIENT MONSTERS

I n a short time, the weary adventurers came through the windy portal and upon the raging green river. Even Sa'ami fared well. Addie had a conversation with him during their rest and explained, as best she could, what was about to happen when he went into the light.

The howling sound hurt his ears, but he liked the wind gusting through his fur. It tickled, he told her once he was through the ancient gateway, still shaking his head wildly, trying to get the wind sound out of his ears.

"He's okay," Addie said with relief.

"The water *is* really green," Benji said, jumping off Mavric and running to Sa'ami to scratch his irritated ears and ride his furry friend. Struggling to get on his massive back, Asazi rode by once again, picking him up by his pant belt and helping him clamber onto his back.

"Whew, thanks!" Benji sighed, swiping his brow.

The extreme wind had blown Asazi's headband askew, revealing a distinctive pale tan line across his forehead. He casually adjusted the band back into place, the beaded black horsehair in dark contrast to his golden, bronzed skin. Signaling with his hand, he nudged Forjon forward, following the green river northward as Za-tha had instructed.

"How do you know which way is north?" Diane asked Asazi, who was clearly their guide in this unexplored territory. For there was no sight or sound of man for many, many miles, only the constant drone of flies and bees on the occasional desert breeze.

"Moss grows on the north side of trees where there is less sun," he explained, "but here in this hot desert, I follow the path of Father Sun across the sky. He rises in the east and sets in the west. You can always trust him to guide your journey," he said wisely. "Father Sun is always caring for his children, for we are all pieces of him—the glittering lights."

Pieces of the sun, hmm, glittering lights, Diane pondered. *Not so different from my own beliefs. We're all children of God.*

"We should keep on eye open now for the cliff of bones and the large sandstone ledge with the A carved into it," Asazi guided.

"But first, we must find a way across. It *is* a fierce river, indeed," Lee said, riding up next to them. *"Incroyable!* How are we going to find a way to the other side?"

The river was not that wide, but it seemed deep, dark, and foreboding. Filled with back eddies, deadly whirlpools, and large submerged boulders, that caused the rushing waters to tumble and roar into great swells over them. The water then flowed swiftly into deep troughs and exploded, splashing onto boulders downriver that were above the waterline. It was a tumultuous, frightful sight, and everyone stood on the bank, silent in trepidation.

"There's got to be a way across," Diane finally said, breaking the silence. "Let's keep going upriver until we find one." Diane remembered Asazi's words. *Think it, see it, feel it, know it, and you'll create it!* She grasped her Joy Stone in her pocket and closed her eyes. *Puppy breath,* she whispered to herself, then pictured the white, circling lasso and inside, everyone standing on the far bank, feeling safe and happy.

Okay, let's create it! she said, feeling happy, knowing that they could achieve it. *Let it be so!* She remembered Za-tha's parting words, and they seemed to fit perfectly into her new sense of empowerment.

They traveled for a while when they came to an elbow bend in the river. The far bank had been just a small rise when they first spotted the green river, but it had been gradually increasing in height along their way. Now, at the bend in the river, the far bank turned into a sloping cliff wall of sandstone. Thirty to fifty feet high and protruding from the wall were what looked to be the skeletal bones from huge...*ancient monsters.*

"Dinosaurs!" Diane shrilled excitedly. "Those are dinosaur bones!" She pointed, in total disbelief, to the huge skull and vertebrae of a sauropod, probably from the Jurassic period over 150 million years before. She loved studying dinosaurs. Her desk at home was stacked with dinosaur books, and she fancied herself an amateur paleontologist, at least from the confines of her room or the school library. But this...

"This is what Za-tha must have been talking about," she declared astutely. "His 'ancient monsters' are actually extinct *dinosaurs*! Look at the femur—the thigh bone, of that sauropod. It's bigger than I am." She chortled. "Oh, oh, oh, look!" she cried out as she jumped off Mavric and ran down the riverbank, pointing avidly. "That's got to be the braincase and lower mandible of a carnivorous predator like *Allosaurus*. See the distinctive brow horn over each eye? Look at those teeth— they're at least *six inches long*," she said breathlessly. She spun around in circles; her arms stretched out to the turquoise sky in complete ecstasy. This was the most thrilling moment of her life, and she was *living* it!

Nothing could top this, she decided.

She took a deep breath and exhaled loudly in complete and utter surrender to this most exquisite moment. Never in her wildest imagination did she ever see herself actually experiencing what she loved so deeply in her books. Staring at the radiant afternoon sun through the young summer willow leaves, feeling her oneness with everything around her, as if she were floating above the earth, Diane dropped her eyes to the level of the river and started yelling. Jumping up and down, she waved wildly to everyone to follow her as she quickly ran upriver, disappearing around the bend.

She stood—her right foot forward, hands on her hips, a stance of a champion—confident, powerful, and playfully cocky—waiting for her friends to meet up with her with a huge victorious smile on her face.

As they reached her, she gestured ahead and said, "Look, behold our bridge!" She laughed heartily when all their mouths dropped open. From this new vantage point, they could see that a large cottonwood tree had fallen across the river. Its huge trunk—at least four to five feet wide and worn flat on the topside—was easily strong enough to support the weight of the horses with their passengers, at least, one at a time.

Mavric trotted up to her, tossing his head, nickering softly, curious about all the commotion, and nestled his muzzle against her back.

"Are you ready for an adventure, Mavric?" Diane asked, stroking his long nose as she grabbed his reins, mounted, and led him upstream to the base of the fallen tree trunk. Its enormous gnarly roots were twisted and anchored deeply into the earth, and obviously worn from previous use. *I wonder who else has passed this way?* she considered as Mavric easily clambered onto the old trunk, sunken and half-buried in the riverbank, but his bravery suddenly drained away when he saw the raging river below him. He balked, nostrils flaring, and took a few frightened steps backward, snorting harshly.

"Whoa!" Diane cried tensely, a jolt of fear coursing through her. "What do I do?"

Lee and Addie dashed to her rescue. Lee crossed alongside Mavric's flank and grabbed his reins to steady him. "*Ca va,* Mavric, it's okay," Lee said encouragingly.

Scampering behind, Addie made her way along the trunk, and stood in front of the frightened horse. Gently holding his face, she looked reassuringly into his bulging eyes. She spoke tenderly to him, slowly stroking his ears to calm him down.

"This may help!" Asazi said as he came along the other side with a handful of wild carrots he had gathered along the river's edge. He had seen the Queen Anne's lace growing wild and made sure it wasn't poison hemlock, which looked very similar with its beautiful umbel of tiny white flowers and carrot-like root but lacked the fine little hairs along its stalk.

"Addie, may I have your bandana?" Asazi asked stroking Mavric.

Addie gladly untied it from around her neck and gave it to him. Asazi folded it into a blindfold and gently wrapped it around Mavric's terrified eyes. It immediately calmed him, as his attention now turned to the scent of the carrots, one of his favorite treats. His nose began to twitch, and his upper lip undulated like a wave reaching for the beach.

Asazi took the reins from Lee, who nodded in understanding as she stepped aside and let Asazi pass. He stepped backward along the trunk, holding the tantalizing carrots in front of him, just out of reach of Mavric's nose and searching lips.

Slowly Asazi proceeded, step by step, while Mavric cautiously stepped forward, one hoof, then another, until the sound of the raging river was silenced by his intense desire for the handful of wild carrots. Finally, they crossed over the river and reached the far bank. Asazi slipped off the blindfold and guided Mavric—with Diane still clutching the saddle horn— off the giant tree trunk.

Diane exhaled loudly. "That was fantastic," she exclaimed, still breathing heavily.

Mavric tossed his head up and down in agreement, happily munching the carrot reward for his bravery. In no time at all, the other horses and their riders made their way across the precarious tree bridge and gathered together on the far bank.

Sa'ami seemed at home on the large trunk and easily scampered across with a terrified Benji hanging onto his thick neck, arms wrapped tightly, with his eyes closed.

"*Incroyable*! Uh, unbelievable!" Lee finally said, panting.

Diane snickered in relief when Benji finally opened his eyes and, turning from the clan, she began in earnest to investigate the magnificent cliff wall of dinosaurs. The fossilized bones were partially buried and scattered throughout the rock face. Sometimes, just the edge of a bone or the head of a femur were visible. Other times, almost all of a bone was exposed from years and years of erosion, wind and rain sweeping the cliff wall, slowly revealing the dinosaur treasures hidden within it.

She placed her hand raptly on an eroded ilium, or pelvic bone, that was protruding from the rock and many times bigger than her little hand. Shutting her eyes, she took a deep breath, feeling the smooth, sculpted stone with her fingertips, making a connection to a life and a time long past. *Dinosaurs dominated the earth for over 200 million years and vanished about 65 million years ago,* she reminded herself.

Inhaling the earthy, ancient smell that filled her nostrils, she never imagined this adventure would turn into such an epic journey and fulfill one of her life dreams—*digging dinosaurs!*

Now, she was standing next to a dark gray femur, a thigh bone longer than she was tall, looking up at the light gray, yellowish sandstone cliff wall, the burial place of dinosaurs, containing hundreds of bones from carnivores and herbivores alike.

"Look at this." She gestured to an extremely long line of partially exposed vertebrae that stretched some forty feet across the wall of bones. "This is probably a tail of a sauropod like *Diplodocus* or *Apatosaurus.*"

"My teacher, Mr. Edwards, is a dinosaur fanatic and digs dinosaurs every summer with a team of museum paleontologists," she laughed. "He says he's as *old as dirt and dinosaurs,* but really, he's a genius when it comes to these terrible creatures. That's what 'dinosaur' means in Greek, 'terrible lizard.' My hand nearly falls off trying to take notes on all of his discoveries and theories," she shook her hand in painful memory.

"He says that the things we're learning in class won't be in textbooks for years. Like, he thinks these giant herbivores held their immense tails high in the air as a counterbalance to their long necks and as a high-speed, powerful whip against their predators instead of just dragging them across the ground," she paused.

"Dinosaurs had all kinds of ingenious ways to defend themselves. See these tail spikes and bony plates on this *Stegosaurus* skeleton?" she said, stretching up on her toes to point to a partially buried backbone lined with elongated, triangular-shaped flat plates ending with a tail tipped with four deadly spikes, each two to three feet long.

"Ouch!" Benji squealed, ogling the long, pointy spikes with a grimace.

Diane affectionately rubbed her brother's head. "Mr. Edwards has found lots of spikes like these with broken tips that suggest to him they were used to ward off predators. He once excavated an *Allosaurus* fossil with a partially healed puncture wound in its tail vertebra that perfectly fits a mighty swinging *Stegosaurus* tail spike. They're kind of similar in purpose to the tail club of another herbivore that was built like a tank with armor," she continued as she walked slowly beneath the fossiliferous wall, hoping to find some more defense mechanisms preserved in stone.

"Mr. Edwards still doesn't know what quite to make of the bony plates. Were they for defense, protecting the neck and backbone of the *Stegosaurus*? Were they used for regulating the dinosaur's body temperature? Or were they simply for display, to attract a mate, or to just show off?" She chuckled and shrugged her shoulders.

"Predators defended themselves with their speed, intelligence, and teeth," she said, running her finger along a serrated tooth of the Allosaurus skull she had spied from across the river. "See the saw-like blade edge? It was designed to rip flesh."

Benji's eyes bugged at the *Allosaurus* tooth.

"Carnivores like *Allosaurus* could rip over two hundred pounds of flesh with a single chomp!

"My favorite defense mechanisms are the large frill of the *Triceratops*, another herbivore that appeared later during the Cretaceous period. Mr. Edwards excavated one and found that it was six inches thicker than the human skull and made entirely of solid bone. It was virtually impossible for a predator like *Allosaurus* to sink his teeth into its neck—that's *if* it could get beyond the thrust and deadly blow of the *Triceratops'* four-foot-long brow horns," she paused, inspecting the gritty sandstone wall more closely.

She sighed breathlessly. It felt good, and it was fun to share her knowledge and love for dinosaurs with her new friends. *I'll really enjoy being a teacher someday,* she realized in that moment, feeling quite content.

They sauntered along the sloping fossil bed, talking about dinosaurs and contemplating their possible demise.

"How did all of these bones get here?" Addie asked, sincerely curious and interested in her paleontology lesson. Diane stood in silence, putting her hand to her chin in a thoughtful pose.

"I think the dinosaurs died upriver somewhere, and their bodies—or just their sunbaked bones after the flesh were eaten or decayed—were swept away by floodwaters, perhaps in the spring and deposited here. Millions of years ago, this area may have been a bend in the river or a shallow sandbar. In either case, the water slowed and was no longer capable of carrying the weight of its load—the bodies or bones—and dumped them here. This probably happened for years, maybe centuries or even thousands of years, judging by the hundreds of bones," she paused, pondering.

"Mr. Edwards would be proud of you, sis!" Benji said, beaming.

"Look here," Diane said, pointing to another set of bones in the wall. "Some of these bones are articulated, meaning still connected, which tells me that the bones were still encased in flesh when the water slowed, and the carcass got caught in the river bend or stuck on a sandbar. Over time, the dinosaur decayed here in place, in situ, allowing the whole skeleton to be eventually buried and fossilized."

"Gee whiz, Di!" Benji exhaled, shuffling his feet.

Diane smiled brightly. "These bones over here," pointing higher on the wall, "are separated, or disarticulated, telling me that their bodies must have laid on the ground somewhere upriver. The flesh either decayed in the hot sun or was eaten by meat-eating predators or scavengers."

Addie gasped. Diane continued. "Once the spring waters came, the remaining bones were picked up, jumbled, and swept away downstream, which would explain why we're finding only one or two bones of an individual here or there, and not the whole skeleton.

"The smallest and lightest bones were carried faster and farther than the heavier ones—"

Addie grasped Diane by the elbow and tried interrupting her in midsentence, slightly tilting her head in the direction upstream.

Diane only paused, not really paying attention to Addie's gentle attempt, and continued, "So the lighter bones were carried downstream, collecting together—"

Addie tugged more forcibly on Diane's duster, angling her head more sharply upstream, but still to no avail as Diane paused again, getting a tad annoyed, then continued, "While the heavier ones sank and—"

Absently brushing the nagging hand from her duster, Diane finally stopped. "What?"

Following everyone's gaze, she slowly turned to see a large sandstone ledge with a letter A roughly carved into it up ahead.

Diane's mouth fell wide open.

"Cool beans." Lee chuckled. "We thought you'd never stop and notice. You sure were in some dinosaur fog. We *are* on a quest, you know?"

"I guess so," she mumbled, staring at the weathered A. "I'm sorry."

I'd better pay more attention.

The sun was now sinking behind the wall of bones, casting a long shadow across the green river, making it look even more ominous and foreboding—the river of death and bones!

The clan made their way to the base of the cliff beneath the sandstone ledge and unloaded their gear to make camp in the cool shade underneath it. Diane gave Mavric a gentle kiss on his nose, scratched his ears, and took off his gear so that he could forage in the riparian woods lining the green river. She patted him on his rump as he walked away.

Everyone fell into their usual evening routines. Lee and Asazi went off to hunt while Diane, Addie, and Benji gathered firewood, spread out their sleeping blankets, unpacked the cooking utensils, and readied them for whatever the hunters would bring back to camp.

Diane struggled with starting the fire using Asazi's hand-drill method. *My book certainly gave clear instructions, and Asazi sure made it seem easy,* she reflected, bearing down harder on the drill as beads of sweat trickled along the sides of her reddening cheeks. Her hands were starting to burn from the friction, and the salty sweat leaked into her eyes, stinging them and blurring her vision. Wearisome as it was, she persevered and finally managed to create the ember that started the fire smoldering.

"Whew!" *That sure was harder than my book made it out to be,* she panted, but felt deeply content.

The sun turned from a hazy yellow to a glowing magenta as it finally slipped behind the Jurassic wall, plunging the clan into a quiet twilight. The fire leapt into blazing tongues of orange and red flames tinged in bluish-white flickers, crackling and popping.

While they waited, Addie announced that it was time to

formally introduce little Niki to Sa'ami. Though they had been introduced to the whole clan in the Circle of Respect, Niki spent so much time sleeping that this was the first opportunity for them to meet directly. Addie had asked Lee for her raccoon cap before she left, so she slowly opened the top of the fur cap to find Niki curled up, sleeping in her secret den.

"Niki," she said hushedly, holding out her hand to the stirring baby creature.

CHAPTER TWENTY-FIVE

MOST UNUSUAL CONVERSATION

W aking up suddenly with the chilly evening breeze, the young raccoon stretched its little black paws and yawned. Addie held out her hand, offering a little piece of carrot. Niki sniffed the air with her cute black nose and crawled out onto Addie's hand. She grabbed the carrot with one paw while she appeared to be looking for something else that seemed to be missing.

"Oh yes!" Addie realized. "Raccoons like to clean their food before they eat when they can," she said.

Diane sprang up from the blazing fire and rummaging through their cooking utensils, found a small tin bowl that she filled with water and brought it to Niki. The baby raccoon dropped the piece of carrot into the water and moved it about with her tiny front paw, giving it a thorough washing.

"I read that Niki's behavior is called 'dousing,' how she washes her food before she eats it," Diane said, intensely interested in observing Niki. "I also read that raccoons frequently dabble for food near the shoreline of lakes or rivers, finding their food underwater, like mollusks, crawfish, frogs, and the like."

"I've seen them pick up their food, inspect it, then rub it to remove the dirt," Addie added.

"An Indian tribe has a name for raccoons that means, 'the one who rubs, scrubs, and scratches with its hands,'" Diane chortled. "They're omnivores, just like bears, that eat both plants and animals. I read that they also like insects, berries, nuts, grains, particularly sweet corn—farmers don't appreciate them much—egg farmers either—rats, squirrels, birds, fish, snakes, worms, even baby alligators." She scrunched her face in disgust. "Of course, they're scavengers, too, and eat human garbage, which makes them quite naughty in neighborhoods."

Finally satisfied, Niki used her nimble five little toes, much like fingers on a human hand, to pull the bit of carrot out of the water and began chewing it happily. Then to their surprise, she climbed into the bowl of water and splashed about, giving herself a needed bath. Diane and Addie laughed at the sight. Niki then crawled out onto Addie's hand again and vigorously shook herself off, turning into a little fluff ball with tiny black eyes peering out from behind her bristly black mask.

"I wonder why she has that black mask?" Benji questioned as he observed the bathing raccoon. "She looks like a forest bandit," he giggled, wandering off to find Sa'ami.

"I remember reading that it's an adaptation that may help her with her night vision by deflecting glare, as raccoons are nocturnal animals," Diane offered, intrigued with the masked, puffy kit.

Addie held Niki in the palms of her hands and lifted her up to her face to look directly into her beady eyes. Once she had the raccoon's attention, Addie became silent and closed her eyes. Diane knew that she was about to start a conversation. After a minute or so, Addie finally turned to Diane and reported that Niki was agreeable and ready to meet Sa'ami.

"Now, you hold her while I speak to Sa'ami," Addie directed.

Diane held out her hands next to Addie's, and Niki, understanding just enough of what was expected of her, crawled onto Diane's hands and sat staring up at her. Diane giggled heartily. Raccoons were one of her favorite forest animals. Once, a raccoon had wandered into her backyard and hid under the back stairs of her home in Chicago. It was the first wild animal she had ever encountered. She loved how they used their hands, just like people's hands. They were clever, intelligent, social, and a bit mischievous.

Just like me! she realized, chuckling to herself as she stared into Niki's black eyes.

Addie found Benji playing tag with the huge bear in the shadows of a copse of willow trees along the river nearby and stopped them to have her conversation with Sa'ami, reminding him that Niki was part of their clan and *not* a bear snack.

She frowned and looked at Diane, befuddled. "Sa'ami wants to know if Niki will bite his ears!" she shouted back to Diane, sitting by the warm fire with Niki snuggled close to her chest. "What should I tell him?" Addie asked, quite concerned, shrugging her shoulders.

"Tell him the truth," Diane replied, after a moment's thought, smothering a chuckle.

"Maybe...she's a baby, but I doubt it would hurt very much. Her teeth are very tiny, and I'll tell her biting is forbidden," Addie reassured the big, lovable bear. "She is the littlest member of our family, and you are to protect her like you protect the rest of us." Addie laid down the ground rules sternly and reported that Sa'ami understood. Diane's eyes gleamed as she watched in amazement. The bear actually looked as if he slightly nodded his big fuzzy head.

Benji and Sa'ami scrabbled out from the shadows and

followed Addie to the campsite, stopping in front of Diane. Sa'ami groaned, tossing his head, and sat down so that his head was level with her hands. She held the baby raccoon out in front of her. Its little eyes glinted in the firelight.

Sa'ami curiously lifted his large black nose up to sniff the little raccoon, resting his muzzle on the edge of Diane's fingers. Niki suddenly scooted back away from the giant nose—seemingly terrified—and scampered up under Diane's chin, hiding. Addie came close and spoke to her out loud so all could hear.

"It's alright, Niki," she said, soothing her jangled nerves. "Sa'ami is our friend, and his size will protect you."

After a moment, Niki tentatively crawled back onto Diane's hands and up to Sa'ami's moist nose. Niki stretched her neck forward and touched her little nose to Sa'ami's.

How adorable, Diane chuckled.

They stayed like that for a while, nose to nose, the big black bear and the tiny baby raccoon. Then Niki stood up on her hind legs, and stretching her two little black paws up into the air, she gently patted Sa'ami's nose, chittering acceptingly. They were friends, now and forever. All at once, Niki jumped up and ran up the bridge of Sa'ami's muzzle and sat on top of his head, pawing the air, proclaiming their friendship.

Just then, Lee and Asazi returned with an armful of wild vegetables, casually swinging a couple of birds. They could barely believe their eyes when they saw Niki standing on Sa'ami's head, waving, as if in greeting. They both grinned, waved back, and went straight to work.

"What are those?" asked Diane curiously, pointing to the plump birds dangling over Lee's shoulder. "They look like miniature chickens."

Lee nodded in agreement. "They're called grouses," she said, pulling the antler-handled knife out from the sheath on her belt. "You ate them the other night," Lee said, concentrating on the task at hand. She carefully ran her finger down the sharp edge of the blade as Diane watched her take charge of the evening's meal.

"Oh! I guess I didn't see them before you started dressing them," Diane said, a tad perplexed. "What a curious saying, *'dressing the grouse.'* It's more like undressing the bird," she said, throwing another log on the fire, then squirmed as she watched Lee slice off the bird's head and pull out its feathers by the handful. Moisture hidden in the log suddenly expanded and began to hiss and sputter, spewing twinkling orangey sparks into the night sky.

"Don't you think this is dressing the bird?" Lee said amusingly, turning around, holding a handful of feathers arranged like a bowtie under her chin, her deadly serious expression now making the funniest face. She burst out laughing at her own joke, and Diane joined in.

"You make me laugh, Lee Planchet," snickered Diane.

Lee turned serious again for a moment, her warm brown eyes turning sad. "I always tried to make my papa laugh when he would drink and turn mean. If I could get him to laugh, I would usually avoid a whooping." Then Lee wiggled her bowtie, crossed her eyes, and began to laugh again. Her toothy smile was framed at the corners with deeply creased dimples.

"En-cry-a-ble!" Diane pronounced slowly, trying to imitate Lee and her native French tongue.

"Incroyable!" Lee repeated, surprised. *"C'est tres bien!* That's very good, or well done!" she praised, her eyes glistening.

"Say-tray-bee-n," Diane said, beaming. "How do I say 'thank you'?"

"Merci beaucoup!" Lee responded, saying it slow, enunciating

clearly. "'Please' is *'S'il vous plait!'* Which translates as 'If you please.'"

"Mare-see-buttercup," Diane chortled with a note of mischief in her voice. "Sil-ver plat-ter?"

Lee scowled and then chuckled at her wit.

"Okay," Diane turned serious again. "Mare-see-bow-coo' and 'See-view-play!'"

"*Tres bien!*" Lee said, slicing open the naked grouse to remove its innards.

That evening, they sat around the blazing campfire, listening to a chorus of forest crickets in the background, talking about the day's adventures. They laughed, recounting the sight of Niki and Sa'ami, now all cuddled together and sleeping with Benji at the edge of the fire, warmed by its glowing flames and lullabied by its melodious crackling.

Content from a delicious wilderness meal, Diane stirred the fire with a long stick and leaned back against her saddle draped over a thick fallen tree branch. Reaching into her knapsack, she pulled out her field journal to record her latest discoveries and experiences.

"What are you writing?" Addie asked timidly as she sat down beside Diane, sharing the log.

"I like to write about my adventures of the day, along with other things I've learned, people or animals I've met...and I like to sketch things that I want to remember." She was drawing as she was talking with Addie and turned her journal around so that she could see the scratches on the parchment.

"That's wonderful!" Addie exclaimed as she viewed the

drawing of the dinosaur fossil wall, the bones outlined and shaded artistically.

"Here are my science notes," Diane said, pointing to line after line of scratchy writing. "Someday I'll use my field journal to teach my students and take them on exciting science adventures. And this is turning out to be quite the adventure."

"I'd like to do that, too!" Addie said faintly as Diane flipped through her journal, sharing with Addie her drawings and daily journal entries. They sat by the fire, laughing, oohing and aahing over their shared experiences, deepening their friendship.

"Addie, can you talk with any animal?" Diane asked curiously.

"Yes, I've communicated with all kinds of animals, even rattlesnakes!" Addie said shyly. "I once had to convince one to turn away from Rohan's stall. It was a most difficult conversation. They're very stubborn, you know," she giggled.

Diane contemplated Addie's answer and made a point to jot it down in her field journal.

"It's been quite a day." Diane sighed, putting aside her field journal, as she snuggled into her warm sleeping blanket between Addie and Asazi, who was listening quietly to their conversation. She took off her hat, hung it on the horn of her saddle, and tucked her arm behind her head, propping it up to have a better view of the blazing fire that was smoking lightly—strands of wispy smoke rising upward against the black sky.

"All the stars," Diane said hushedly, gazing through the smoky haze into the vastness of space. Millions and billions of twinkling, brilliant tiny lights strewn across the fathomless heavens.

"My people believe they are the campfires of our ancestors—

those that came before," Asazi said pensively, the light from the flames flickering in his amber eyes.

"I like that," Diane mumbled as she yawned and felt her eyelids growing heavy, drooping slightly. A deep pang for sleep overwhelmed her. Wispy tendrils of juniper smoke rose from the sputtering fire. Caught on the chilly night breeze rustling through the nearby trees, they swirled and wafted over her face filling her nostrils. Soothing and promising, she inhaled and signed deeply.

Nestling deeper, she pulled up the woven blanket to cover her nose. With only her eyes peeking out, she glanced once more at the starry sky. Suddenly, a falling star streaked across the blackness, a long firetail trailing behind. *"Ooh!"* she marveled.

Campfires of our ancestors, she repeated to herself, gazing one last time into the red, glowing embers that hissed and crackled. As she began to slip into a deep sleep, she could have sworn she felt the earth tremble—just for a second— accompanied by a distant...deep...primeval roar. *Those that came before...*

CHAPTER TWENTY-SIX

CAVE OF AGES

"**D**id you hear that?" Lee asked, nudging Diane to wake her.

It was daybreak, and the morning sun would be rising soon. An eerie sense of foreboding loomed in the chilly morning air.

"There it is again," Lee said, alarmed. "It sounds like it's coming from within the wall of bones."

"I thought I was imagining it when I fell asleep last night," Diane murmured, rubbing the sleep from her eyes, stretching. "I felt the earth shake, too!" she said soberly through a half yawn.

"*Qu'est-ce que c'est?*" Lee asked, repeating in English with a shudder, "What *is* that?"

"I have no idea," Diane muttered, equally concerned, scrunching her forehead.

"The birds are not singing this morning," Asazi said grimly, rolling up his sleeping blanket quietly, as if someone or something might be lurking nearby. Their Aszanii guide and apprentice zaman was clearly unnerved.

Benji detangled himself from Sa'ami's grasp, both groaning

groggily. "What's going on?" he asked, listening to his sister's stilted whispers. The giant black bear swatted at a pesky fly.

"That's very curious," Addie pondered. "Something's certainly not right today. The animals feel it, too! They're unusually still and listening, as we are," the animal whisperer continued tensely.

Not a chirp, a buzz, or a snap of a twig could be heard throughout the riparian trees, only the muffled rolling sound of the river flowing by. The clan's nerves were jangling as Asazi wisely directed, "Let's get into our Circle of Respect and call on Mother Earth for her protection today." His soothing voice was betrayed by his deeply furrowed thin, dark eyebrows.

Everyone gathered around the smoldering campfire, folded their arms across their chests, bowed their heads in silence as Asazi did, and closed their eyes.

"Great Father Sun and Mother Earth, we bow before you and ask for your protection today. Be with us on our quest, keep us safe, and guide us with your wisdom," Asazi prayed fervently, his forehead smoothed once again with confidence.

All at once, the first ray of the morning sun shot a beam through the willow trees along the east bank of the river that gleamed golden on the top of the dinosaur cliff. Its narrow shaft of light lit up a cluster of desert sagebrush, saltbush, and a scraggly creosote bush growing in the shade of a large boulder under the sandstone ledge with the 'A' carved into it.

"Look!" Benji shouted, pointing up, bouncing on his toes. "There's a hole in the wall, an opening behind the boulder near those glowing bushes," he said anxiously, staring at the dark hole. Everyone could now clearly see in Za-tha's second Ray of Light, that the shadow behind the boulder was actually a cave opening.

"The Cave of Ages," Diane said, astounded, as she watched

the sun rise slowly through the black, silhouetted trees. Its ray of light slowly crawled down the cliff wall, lighting a path to its hidden entrance, and the secret held within. "See that?" Diane shouted fervidly. "The sun's showing us the way! Look at all the dinosaur bones! They're making a ladder to its entrance."

They'd decided that whatever the day brought; they would camp here again that night. So, they hastily gathered up just what they reasoned they might need in their knapsacks: rope, matches, torches, tinder, and boomerangs, among a few other things. They had no way of knowing what lay ahead or where their journey might lead them. It was thrilling and frightening, all at the same time.

It was also decided that Benji, Sa'ami, and Niki would stay behind and take care of the horses, who would enjoy a day's rest.

"Are you sure, Benji?" his sister asked.

"I hate caves!" he said, glowering, his face scrunched into a sour grimace. "You're not getting me in there after our last adventure in one, and anyway, who's going to look after the saddlebags of gold?" He smirked, standing firm.

Reluctantly, Diane gave Benji a big bear hug and shrugged, knowing that once his mind was made up, there was no convincing him otherwise. She sighed deeply, then turned, gazing up to the ledge with the letter A. Confidently, she grasped ahold of the head of a dark gray femur jutting out from the sandy wall and stepped up onto what looked to be a smooth, almost polished shoulder blade partially buried in the cliff face.

Millions of years ago, these magnificent, terrible creatures dominated the earth, she thought. Now, I'm using their bones to climb to the Cave of Ages. She shook her head in utter disbelief.

A rib bone, followed by a humerus, all made of stone. A hand on a lower jawbone, or mandible, a foot on an eroded tibia. The fossilized bones seemed to be lined up with some intentional purpose. One after the other, they followed; Lee, Addie, and Asazi climbing the dinosaur ladder upward until they all stood on a bony-plate ledge of a *Stegosaurus*, waving to Benji and their animal friends below.

The dazzling morning sun rose above the leafy cottonwoods and slender willows, blinding Diane as she gazed down at her stubborn brother, feeling a little lost without him. Water glistened in the corners of her eyes, and tears of concern trickled down her face. She wiped them away and, with resolve, turned slowly to face the ominous, gaping hole in the cliff face beside the boulder.

Diane took a deep breath and then stepped into the darkness. A chilly gust of wind, carrying a deep, earthy odor, filled her nostrils and brushed across her face, whisking her hat away. As if the cave were inhaling, it sucked her hat inward, rolling it on its brim into its depths along the musty floor. She dashed into the cave, chasing after her disappearing hat, finally catching up to it in the fading light. Skittering across the craggy surface, she reached down and swooped it up with one hand.

Whew! she sighed to herself, panting heavily, her cheeks flushed. Standing up in the cave, she swiped her hair from her face and put her hat on her head as her eyes adjusted to the dim light. She had run just a short way down a slight incline, her head nearly touching the ceiling, and now stood in a long, narrow passageway at least five times her height and only two times as wide. This was a whole new realm of darkness, filled with bleak silence and the most unusual pungent smells. The last vanishing rays from the outside world illuminated the cave wall directly before her. Squinting, she could make out the faded dark lines of a written message.

"Come here!" Diane yelled back to her friends, who were cautiously following behind.

Lee, Asazi, and Addie made their way to her, their blazing torches creating monstrous shapes and curious designs on the inner cave's chiseled surface. They stopped before her, holding their torches high to read the peculiar lines scratched helter-skelter onto the cave wall.

BEWARE 1815
GREAT DANGER LIKE DAGGERS 1552
TURN BACK 1629
RUN FOR YOUR LIFE 1791

The scattered messages were scrawled in black charcoal across the tan mudstone—except for the last one. Diane looked closely at the stained message; it seemed to be written in red.

Could that be human blood?

She swallowed hard. A cold shiver prickled up the back of Diane's neck, and the hairs on her arms stood straight up as huge goose bumps formed on her skin. An awful sense of foreboding seared through her entire body. She drew deep, shuddering breaths and closed her eyes. Grasping her white scarf tightly, she envisioned herself and all her clan in the brilliant white lasso, gathered once again around the campfire later that night, safe, sound, and happy. A feeling of peace came over her. She opened her eyes, clenched her teeth, and said quietly under her breath, "Let's go!"

Diane glanced around, looking for her friends, and saw Lee on one knee at the base of the cave wall. While the others were busy ogling the ghastly messages, she had put the finishing touches on her own mark on the wall, *Sa'ami Bear Clan 1893.*

When Lee looked up, Diane shrugged and nodded her approval.

"Here," Lee said, handing Diane a lit torch of her own.

Lee lit another one for herself. Holding their torches high, Lee led the clan down the winding passageway that disappeared into dense blackness. As they walked along the narrow cave corridor, tripping and occasionally stumbling on the uneven surface, they goggled upward, openmouthed, discovering more ominous warnings.

Pointing to a badly worn message scratched on the rock surface above their heads, Lee asked, narrowing her gaze, "Can anyone read what that says?"

Everyone stopped and stared at the scuffed markings on the wall. Asazi stepped forward, removing a small deerskin pouch from his medicine bag. Opening the drawstring, he carefully poured out a fine black powder of manganese onto the palm of his hand. He held it up to the wall as far as he could reach and gently blew the powder upward onto the ancient surface.

The black powder, dusted with Aztec magic, swirled up into the air and clung to the wall over the mysterious writing. The eroded letters began to blacken against the light rock face, and Diane's eyes flew wide while Addie nearly fell backward. "It looks like an 'E' followed by a 't-e-b,' then 'i-c-o,'" spelled out Lee, struggling with a few smeared letters. Finally, Lee stopped and stared as the name "Estebanico" began to appear on the stone surface.

"There's a date!" Diane shouted with uncontrollable glee.

Asazi blew a second time, and the magic black powder twirled and settled once again on the scratched impressions, revealing the date *1544* just after his name.

"My book said that he was presumed killed in 1539. This proves that he was still alive after his disappearance. Alive with the gold of Cibola!" Diane exclaimed, suddenly feeling very sad that Benji wasn't there to see it.

Wait till I tell him, she reflected, missing her brother terribly, praying that he was okay. *He's going to be mad!*

Lee saw the perplexed look on Asazi's face. "I'll explain who he is later," she said, as she headed down the winding passageway again.

Their torches flickered, casting eerie black shadows onto the uneven cave walls. Grotesque, shimmering shapes and terrifying figures skittered beside them, as they proceeded deeper into the looming darkness.

"Look!" Addie pointed to a spot high on the wall.

Everyone gathered beneath it, their necks straining to look up at a drawing that defied time. In black, red, and yellow was a faded cave painting depicting primitive stick figures wielding insignificant spears, aggressively fighting off a giant monster with great pointy plates along its back.

"There's another one," Asazi said alarmingly, pointing farther down the wall. Suddenly, in the flickering light, the wall seemed to come alive, like a mural in a museum with all kinds of images of giant beasts—creatures that no longer roamed this world—fighting with a band of brave warriors.

"Look, that's a *Stegosaurus*!" Diane said fervently, sweeping her arm over the scene. "And this is a *Triceratops*," she grimaced, "Yuck," watching in horror as it plunged its great brow horn into a warrior, his broken body lifted into the air. "That's gruesome!" She shuddered.

"What is this place?" Lee asked tensely.

"These are my ancestors," Asazi said somberly, extending his torch to shed light on a mysterious symbol painted on the cave wall. His amber eyes glistened with sorrow in the torch's light. "The circle is an ancient symbol of great spiritual significance. It encircles an 'A' for *Aszanii*. It has been the symbol of my people for all time."

"Is that the letter 'I' overlapping the 'A' in the middle of the circle?" Diane asked, squinting a tad. "What does it mean?"

Asazi seemed stunned and pondered for a moment, "It means, 'I' the individual, the descendant of the great Sun God, Za, and the circle represents him, the great I AM and my relationship to him and to ALL that is. I am 'one' with him and all creations. I AM forever. We are all like threads interwoven in a blanket. Do you understand, Diane?"

"Hmm, I think so," she answered, "Like the colorful threads in my sleeping blanket, we are all unique yet connected, and each is important in its own way. It's not so different from what I've been brought up to believe. Just another shade of understanding."

"Let's go," Lee interrupted tersely.

The light from their torches danced across the wall of dinosaurs and warriors actively fighting, as if locked in an eternal battle.

"That's impossible!" Diane declared, completely bewildered as she slowly made her way along the wall. She took off her hat and nervously ran her fingers through her hair, lifting her blonde strands to their tips, "Dinosaurs and man are separated by sixty-five million years." And yet, before them, an epic battle was clearly depicted between Asazi's ancestors, the Aszanii, and Diane's beloved dinosaurs.

She was exhilarated—and terrified to the roots of her spine. *Where is this cave taking us?* she pondered. *What's in here?* Remembering the scary sounds and creepy sensations from the night before, the hair on her arms stood up again in trepidation

"Look over here!" Lee shouted from ahead, waving at the quivering clan of adventurers. She was gesturing to an opening in the wall that was so low she had to get on her hands and knees to peer inside.

"It's a small tunnel. It might lead deeper into the cave," Lee said crisply.

"Should we check it out," Diane asked, "or should we continue our search farther along this passageway?" She was waiting to hear what the clan wanted to do when, suddenly, she heard—

"Oops!" Lee yelped before they could respond.

Lee had crawled just a short way into the tunnel and then *disappeared*. They could hear her muted screams trailing deep into the wall before they faded into a terrifyingly dead silence.

CHAPTER TWENTY-SEVEN

UNDERGROUND RIVER

D iane, Asazi, and Addie scuttled to the low opening and peered into the small tunnel, using their torches to light the way.

"Lee, are you alright?" yelled Diane. "Can you hear me?" she pleaded, suddenly afraid for her friend's life. A clammy chill prickled up the nape of her neck.

"*Venez ici*! Uh, come here!" Lee finally shouted back from deep inside the tunnel, her voice tinged with excitement.

Relieved, but now flooded with a whole new set of feelings, curiosity mixed with a little fear, Diane felt her heart beating hard in her rib cage; its pounding rumbled in her ears as she got down on her knees and placed her hands on the floor.

"Yuck!" she squealed, recoiling. The tunnel floor was soft and gushy.

"This is like wet clay!" she said, hypothesizing that this section of the cave must have more porous rock layers above it, allowing groundwater to seep through, creating this icky, wet passageway.

Holding her torch in front of her, she cautiously crawled a

few feet in, when her hand suddenly slipped and she began careening downward, as if on a giant mudslide, twisting and turning ever downward into a black abyss. Screaming like she was on a roller coaster, she fell back onto her bum and skittered the rest of the way down on her back until she came to an abrupt stop, plopping hard into a pile of squishy wet clay.

Lee stood over her, fists on her hips, laughing at the sight of Diane all covered in brown clay, and held out her hand to help her up.

"Very funny," Diane muttered, "but that was really scary." Grasping Lee's extended hand, Diane struggled to stand up, feeling like she weighed an extra thirty pounds or more. She staggered slightly to regain her balance, wet clay dripping from her like a melting chocolate ice cream cone.

"Are you okay?" Addie yelled down.

"I'm okay!" Diane shouted back, wiping the clay from her face.

Ever practical, Lee called back up to Asazi, "Make a ladder of knots with your rope and tie it up there somewhere before you come down, so we have a way to get out of here later. It's a good twenty feet or so and too slippery, otherwise."

"Good idea!" Asazi replied.

In a few minutes, the end of a rope ladder came tumbling down, followed by Addie and Asazi. Hunching over in the small, low-ceilinged room, Diane and Lee stood before them in the flickering light of their torches, looking like mud goblins, all clad in brown garb. Addie and Asazi couldn't help but chuckle until they looked down at themselves. Stunned, eyes bugging, they realized that they were also clothed in drippy goo. Everyone laughed.

"Okay, now where do we go?" Diane asked as she waddled stiffly from the clammy clay. "I sure could use a bath."

"The tunnel turns this way," Lee said, already on the move. The tunnel widened a bit, and the ceiling was now high enough for them to stand erect and walk about easily. Lee led the procession of ghastly figures farther into the tunnel when suddenly, she stopped.

"*Ecoutez*," Lee said. "Do you hear that?"

They all quieted and listened. Diane could hear running water—a lot of running water! They followed the tunnel that turned sharply to the right and immediately opened into a larger dark corridor, filled from wall to wall with an underground river.

"You wanted a bath," Lee laughed heartily. "You got what you asked for!"

Asazi stood at the edge of the flowing river, surveying their surroundings. He raised his torch high enough to scatter beams of light farther down the watery passageway. Great roots from the trees up above dangled like dark giant spiderwebs from the ceiling, casting unearthly shadows, giving the cavernous channel an eerie look and a creepy feel.

Finding a piece of dried, broken root about five feet in length, Asazi plunged it into the river to test its depth. The river was a little less than three feet deep here and flowing slowly, so he jumped in, holding his torch above his head so it wouldn't get wet. A cloud of brown mud bubbles floated downstream from his body. Everyone followed him in, keeping their torches held high, enjoying the cleansing, cool water.

"What do we do now?" Diane asked as she squeezed the water from her clothes, releasing the last clumps of clay.

"I think we should walk downstream," Asazi answered, pointing to the damp stone wall where another cave painting depicted his ancestors' symbol. "They're guiding our journey," he proclaimed sagely.

They removed their knapsacks from their backs and steadied them on the top of their heads, keeping the contents dry as they walked, single file, down the shallow river. One hand firmly held their knapsack, while the other held their torch, lighting their way into the chilling darkness.

Lee was leading the procession of river walkers when, suddenly—whoosh—she slipped underwater and disappeared. Only her knapsack could be seen floating. In another quick moment, she shot straight up out of the water, spraying everyone as she shook her wet head.

"It's getting deep," she spluttered.

Startled, Diane spun around, looking for a solution.

We need something to float on, she reasoned. Taking a deep breath, she closed her eyes to settle and center herself.

Puppy breath, she said in a hushed voice. With her imagination and good feelings, she pictured the white lasso, and within it could *see* her adventurers safely floating down the underground river channel, having fun. She could *feel* the joy in their laughter.

Opening her eyes, the white lasso disappeared, and she took another slow look around. In the dim glow of their torchlights, she saw a pile of debris collected in a dark corner and pointed to it.

"Look!" she shouted excitedly.

As all eyes turned to the corner, Asazi carefully made his way over to it. Clambering out of the river onto a narrow ledge, he inspected the cache of debris. He waved everyone over in astonishment. One by one, they waded through the underground river as he pulled the twisted branches, twigs, and rotting leaves from the corner. Buried beneath was a stockpile of several large logs, at least five feet in length. He put his foot on the first log closest to the water's edge and leaned his body against the rest of the pile to pry it free. It rolled straight into the river, splashing Diane, who eagerly followed behind him.

"Climb on!" he guided Diane. He held her knapsack and torch as she scrambled onto the log, and straddling it, he handed her the knapsack, which she quickly slipped onto her back. He cradled her torch in a hollow notch carved into the log. Pushing away, she took hold of a flat wooden plank that Asazi had also found in the pile.

"Use it as a paddle," Asazi instructed as he gestured through the air.

"This is perfect!" she said, as she paddled awkwardly from side to side, steadying and balancing the log as it slowly inched its way forward.

With the use of a long, sturdy branch as a lever, Asazi released another log from the stack for a very soggy and dripping Lee, who immediately—and adroitly—paddled off. She, too, cleverly put her torch into a crack in the log, freeing her hands and lighting her way.

Plunk! Another one splashed into the water for Addie, and then he tumbled the last log into the river for himself. Asazi helped Addie onto her waiting log, then expertly jumped onto his own like he was jumping onto Forjon's back. He floated next to Addie and put her torch in a hollow knot in her log as well. Soon, all four of them were paddling down the underground channel, laughing and splashing as the current floated them slowly toward a mysterious destination.

Despite the fun, for a fleeting moment, Diane worried about getting back to Benji as the underground river turned sharply to the left and entered yet another damp chamber in the vast cavern. She shook the concern from her thoughts, trusting that all would happen as she had envisioned in her white lasso.

The ceiling was filled with beautiful formations of stalactites and hanging wavy ribbons of crystalline calcite that looked like strips of crispy bacon. A huge honeycomb of white gypsum crystals shimmered in the flickering light of the clan's torches.

"What do you call those stony icicles hanging down from the ceiling?" Addie asked as she floated up next to Diane's log, her torch dimly lighting the underground passageway with a suffused golden glow.

"Stalactites," Diane said keenly, adding, "My teacher shared with us that 'stalactites' have a 'C' in the word for 'ceiling' and 'stalagmites' have a 'G' to remind us they grow from the ground."

Addie nodded, seemingly thrilled with the simple way to remember some cave geology.

As they meandered along, they floated into a maze of large roots, like spindly vines, that hung down from the roof of the cave and stretched to the thirst-quenching waters below, frequently blocking the river adventurers' way. Every now and then, they would have to awkwardly back up and untangle themselves from the dense, slimy vines before continuing their forward trek. It was exhausting but exhilarating work.

"What are those?" Diane gasped, pointing to hundreds of luminescent, double-winged insects that clung to the woody vines, their long abdomens glowing an eerie yellow light. They reminded her of the lightning bugs she and Benji chased and collected in their suburban backyard at home, but these were a hundred times larger and looked like giant lightning dragonflies.

"I've never seen anything like them," Lee marveled as she floated by to take the lead with Asazi, who was drifting up ahead.

The river turned once again as they entered into another chamber, where bioluminescent green plants grew from the white sandy bottom of the river. Glowing yellow algae, orange lichens, and giant red fungi clung to the wet cave walls, cascading downward into the crystal-clear water. The enchanting chamber glowed brightly. Large arthropod creatures, dark gold—mottled with inkblots of brown—like armored shields, crawled along the illuminated bottom; their segmented exoskeletons, cephalons, and pygidiums really got Diane aflutter.

"Heads and butts!" she yelled. "Those are trilobites!" She was deeply befuddled. "They're extinct," she exclaimed, awestruck. "They lived in the seas of the Paleozoic era over three hundred million years ago. Some were terrifying swimming predators, while others were just ocean floor scavengers or filter feeders, and *all* seventeen thousand known species disappeared during the mass extinction at the end of the Permian Period," she paused, remembering her lecture notes. "Some trilobites were very small, with all kinds of unusual, curvy spikes on their pygidiums—or tails. Others were up to twenty-eight inches long with a cephalon—head—displaying large bulbous eyes. These are huge!" She continued, "Their name refers to the three parts of their body. 'Tri-lobe' means three lobes," she shook her slowly, scrunching her thin eyebrows together. "What *is* this place?"

They took turns oohing and aahing, fascinated with all the wondrous and mysterious sights and creatures.

"*Ecoutez*," said Lee. "Listen!" she said sternly, holding her cupped hand to her ear. "Do you hear that?"

In the distance, they could hear the sound of trickling water that grew ever louder as they continued to float slowly with the current toward it.

"Look!" Addie shouted in a panicked voice. "The water's moving faster."

Indeed, the current was moving swiftly, and the trickling sound became a loud, rumbling roar ahead that turned into a distinct sound of water cascading over itself.

"Hold on!" Lee yelled over her shoulder as she disappeared into the black abyss.

"Cool beans!" They could hear her voice trailing from the shadowy depths below.

Then Asazi disappeared into what looked like a dark, gaping hole in the earth and let go a frightening war cry that sent shivers up Diane's spine.

She beckoned to Addie, and they paddled their logs together. Holding onto each other's forearms, they locked arms to stabilize their logs in anticipation of the scary unknown. All at once, their logs plunged downward over cascading rapids.

The roar of the falling water was deafening but not as loud as the pounding of Diane's heart in her ears. She clenched her teeth and squinted into the blackness, breathing heavily as a chilly blast of air blew into her face, lifting her hat. She quickly smashed her hat back onto her head, nearly covering her eyes. She wasn't too sure she wanted to see, anyway.

"Whoa!" Diane shrieked as sprays of water splashed into her face. "This is like riding a bucking bronco!" she screamed to Addie, who was grasping onto her arm so tightly, Diane felt as if she was bruising her. Her stomach was queasy and was churning wildly, like the dark water flowing over the submerged boulders.

Their logs bounced along, shifting forward and backward, engulfing them momentarily in thick blackness, then into the flickering light from their steadfast torches. Finally, the tumultuous rapids gave way to calm waters again as they glimpsed the blazing torches of their friends up ahead.

The fear and thrill over, Diane swiped the moisture from

her face. "That was a blast!" she said breathlessly to her grinning friends.

The four of them, relieved and happy to be together again, laughed and splashed each other in a victory celebration. They were happy to be alive. Ecstatic to have faced their fears and conquered them.

Face the bear, Diane mused.

Suddenly, the river turned yet another corner, and they entered a mysterious, foggy chamber filled with puffs of clouds that looked like cotton balls hovering over the water's surface. A blanket of white fog crept slowly across the underground channel and grew heavier as the puffy white clouds became more numerous and melded into larger ones before their eyes.

Thickening, billowing, and wafting toward the ceiling of the cave, they combined to form an airy, opalescent wall. The light from their torches, reflecting off the millions of minuscule molecules of water vapor, obscured their way with a glowing white haze.

"Look!" Diane yelled briskly, pointing ahead as a golden iridescent light grew brighter, and the heavy clouds began to thin and fade away, marking the end of the cave. As they emerged, the sun shone brightly above them, blinding the weary river travelers, who shielded their eyes from its radiance.

"Where are we?" Addie asked, nervously peeping through her fingers.

CHAPTER TWENTY~EIGHT

THE LOST WORLD

J ust then, dark, shadowy objects fluttered above them, blocking and distorting the sun's light.

"That's impossible!" Diane said tensely, as three giant flying reptiles glided into view. Their immense wingspans—over thirty feet in length—arched into the sky in front of the sun, blocking its light, casting monstrous shadows onto the ground. As if on cue, all three of their nine-foot crested heads with long, pointy beaks turned toward the river travelers as they dove from the sky, sailing directly toward them in a blurry descent.

"Hide!" yelled Asazi in a panicked voice, jumping off his floating log. The adventurers quickly scrambled off their logs, splashing noisily toward the river's edge, and struggled to climb up the steep, muddy bank. Diane's hands desperately clawed and grasped for any handhold in the slippery mud. Finally, scrabbling wildly, she found a rock anchored into the mucky bank and with one strong yank, she hoisted herself up, rolling onto the grassy edge, breathless. Quickly turning over onto her stomach, she reached down to give Addie a hand, pulling her up and out of the muddy grave.

"Come on!" shouted Lee, waving frantically for the girls to run toward her. Diane grabbed Addie by the hand and together they dashed toward Lee and Asazi, who were crouched down hiding behind a huge buttress root—shaped oddly like a brown scaly sail—supporting a very tall, primeval tree with dozens of aerial roots. Appearing as gnarly vines, the roots hung from thick branches to the ground, creating a deadly mesh of entanglement.

The frightful flying creatures swooped down from the sky like streaming rockets toward their intended prey. Suddenly, they reared back, their wings flapping fiercely, suspending them in midair, as they lost sight of the adventurers who disappeared into the woody weave of dangling branches and roots.

Defeated, one by one, the carnivorous reptiles flew away into the sun, in the same direction from which they had emerged just moments ago. Though it had seemed like a terrifying lifetime, the menacing monsters were gone and the four adventurers finally took a deep breath and simultaneously sighed their relief.

"What *were* those?" Lee asked, her voice still trembling.

"Those were pterodactyls—*prehistoric flying reptiles*! They lived during the Cretaceous Period, over 100 million years ago," Diane reported soberly, shaking her head in disbelief.

"*Incroyable!*" Lee mumbled, breathlessly.

"Where *are* we?" Addie asked for the second time, still a bit in shock.

"I would guess by the name Cave of Ages and the flight of the pterodactyls, we've travelled to a place untouched by the mass extinction that happened 65 million years ago—when dinosaurs ruled the planet," said Diane astutely. "A lost world of dinosaurs!"

"We haven't seen any dinosaurs," Addie said timidly, "you said they were reptiles!"

Diane's eyes widened as she tilted her head upward, indicating they should look downriver behind them. Addie, Lee, and Asazi slowly turned around to see a herd of *Hadrosaurs*, duck-billed dinosaurs, coming to the river's edge for a long midday drink.

Like an odd cross between a duck and a hairless, earless kangaroo with its long tail, powerful back legs and short forelimbs, the long-necked *Hadrosaur* was the size of an African forest elephant, weighing about three tons. The herd found a place where the bank was depressed so they could easily stretch their distinctive elongated duck-shaped heads with square-lipped beaks to the thirst-quenching waters.

"Will they hurt us?" Addie asked, anxiously twirling her ponytail.

"I don't think so," Diane said avidly. "They're herbivores, but very protective of their young. My teacher shared with us that his team of paleontologists have found some of their nests in Montana. The nests contained hundreds of tiny pieces of eggshells, even baby dinosaur bones. The mother dinosaurs *must* have cared for their young for some time in the nest, making dinosaurs more like warm-blooded animals than cold-blooded reptiles. At least that's what my teacher thinks."

"Why?" Addie asked, furrowing her brow. "How does crushed eggshells show that the mother dinosaur cared for her young?"

Diane paused, wiping beads of sweat from her upper lip, "Well, when baby turtles are born, they immediately leave the nest and turtle scientists find the eggshells broken into large, almost whole pieces. But when paleontologists study the dinosaur's nest, they find the eggshells broken into tiny fragments." She paused again. "How would that happen? What does that tell you?" She asked, making Addie think like a scientist.

Addie pondered, "I guess, something would have had to smash them into little pieces." Grimacing, as she was thinking so hard it almost hurt, her eyes suddenly widened. "The baby dinosaurs stayed in the nest stomping around on their eggshells because their mother was feeding them, taking care of them." She bubbled with the thrill of discovery.

"That's what my teacher thinks, too!" Diane said. "The crushed eggshells and fossil bones of babies found in the nests also tell us that the hatchlings were about fourteen to sixteen inches at birth and that when they left the nest with their mother, they were about three and a half feet long—" Diane stopped midsentence.

"That's it! Didn't Za-tha tell us that we should find something representing the birth of creation?" Diane said fervidly, walking back and forth while talking with her hands in her very animated style. "The eggshells! That's what we need to find. We need to follow this herd to their nesting grounds."

All at once, the herd turned away from the river's edge and headed inland.

"Let's go!" Diane directed, already stomping away flat-footed.

Addie, Lee, and Asazi picked up their knapsacks and, with a united deep breath, took their first steps forward to follow Diane and her herd of *Hadrosaurs*.

"Look at them walk," Diane said with glee. "They're bobbing their heads just like chickens." She chuckled. "And their tails are sticking straight out behind them. They're not dragging their tails like earlier dinosaur theory envisioned." She felt as if she were in heaven. Diane loved dinosaurs and hung on every word her teacher taught in class regarding them.

"They don't have feathers, do they?" Addie asked, catching a smattering of dinosaur fever herself.

"These don't," Diane responded, "but my teacher has excavated some that *did* show impressions of feathers. His discoveries and theories are way ahead of his time," she said proudly. "For instance, he believes that based on the fossil evidence, dinosaurs evolved into birds."

"Birds are dinosaurs?" Lee chimed in; a tad skeptical. Diane raised an eyebrow, cocked her nodding head, and smirked.

Living, breathing dinosaurs! Oh, I wish Benji were here to see this, she sighed, shuddering—uncertain for a moment, when and *if* she'd ever see him again. She shook her head to clear away the negative thoughts, grasped her scarf, and envisioned herself once again by a blazing campfire, thrillingly sharing this wondrous experience with him.

The adventurers followed the herd for some time until they came upon a broad open space covered with big mounds of dirt and leaves. Each mound was spaced about twenty-three feet from the others in every direction.

"Those must be the nests," Diane said ecstatically. "See how they're spaced—roughly the length of the mother's body. That way, one mother won't trample the nest of another mother." Glancing around, she was certain—this was the *Hadrosaur's* nesting colony.

"Aren't they smart," Diane continued, glowing with pride for her newly adopted friends.

"What are we looking for?" Lee asked, finally intrigued.

Diane closed her eyes and took four deep breaths, as Asazi had instructed. *What do you want to create?* she could hear him asking her. She grasped her Joy Stone, closed her eyes, and envisioned a nest filled with crushed eggshells within her white lasso. She could *see* the nest, see herself picking up an eggshell, and she could *feel* the exhilaration of it. She then opened her eyes.

"I know what to do," she declared. "Addie, do you think you could talk to a dinosaur?"

"I don't know," Addie hesitated, shyly. "I've never tried before."

"Well, you're about to find out!" Diane said eagerly. "Let's go!" She grabbed Addie by the hand and pulled her into the *Hadrosaur* colony where a mother was bobbing toward her mound on the fringe of the nesting grounds. Diane had noticed this particular dinosaur on the herd's way back to her mound. She had lowered her head to pick a small, nourishing fern when another mother bumped her and plucked it away. Now, this mother was returning to her nest with an empty mouth, while all the others had plenty of food for their hungry young.

The girls made their way quietly, running from tree to tree, hiding behind each one as they followed the mother to her nest. Panting, Diane glimpsed down at the base of their tree and found the same fern-like plant she had watched the herd foraging on their way back to their colony. She bent over and picked a handful of it.

"Come on!" Diane whispered. She and Addie then made another dash to the last tree before the mother's mound, with Asazi and Lee trailing stealthily behind—boomerangs in hand, just in case. They watched as Diane and Addie stood behind the conifer tree, waiting for the mother to settle down beside her nest.

As they gazed intently, one lonely hatchling clambered out of the nest and stood up on its hind legs, touching its hungry mouth to its mother's duck-billed lips, obviously hoping for food and finding nothing but the warm, exasperated breath of the mother's sorrow.

"This is our chance!" Diane said, nudging Addie. "Talk to her!"

"What do I say?" Addie pleaded, with a quiver in her voice.

"Tell her that we're friends wanting to help. We have food for her young," Diane replied patiently.

"Okay, here goes!" Addie murmured timidly, closed her eyes, and started her magical aerial hand dance that summoned her connection to the good mother lizard.

Immediately, the *Hadrosaur's* head jerked up in alarm. Grave concern reflected in her eyes that darted frantically about, seeking the source of this most unusual communication. As Addie continued to speak slowly and soothingly to the concerned mother, the fear in her eyes diminished and her shoulders seemed to relax. Her whole body seemed to absorb the love and sincerity Addie was transferring to her.

"Now," Addie instructed, "keep your eyes to the ground and walk slowly toward her with the food held in front of you—and don't smile. Showing your teeth is a sign of aggression. Only predators bare their teeth. Oh, and take off your hat."

The mother sat back and waited patiently in a posture of wary acceptance. Her little one scrambled between her forelimbs, chasing a flying Cretaceous insect. Diane took a deep breath, slipped off her hat, and slowly came out from behind the tree. With excitement mingled with fear, she stood in front of the tall primeval tree and paused, thinking, *you can do this. Steady, slow, don't look up and don't smile,* repeating Addie's instructions.

She took her first tentative step, then another, edgily, slowly making her way to the waiting, three-ton mother. Diane could hear the *Hadrosaur's* heavy breathing as she neared her. The cute grunts and cries from the playful hatchling helped her relax a little, and a small smile came over her face.

Oops! Don't smile, don't smile! Diane reminded herself.

Without thought, almost instinctively, Diane stopped, sank slowly to the ground, and sat with her legs crossed in front of her. She lowered her head out of respect for this magnificent animal before her and in deep appreciation for this most incredible experience—a living dinosaur! This was the single-most thrilling moment of her young life.

She held the clump of ferny leaves out in front of her, a little beyond her lap, quivering slightly. The hatchling immediately stood up on its hind legs and stretched its nose into the air, sniffing the plant, jerkily bobbing its head toward the peculiar creature offering it. Suddenly, the baby chirped and dropped down onto all fours, taking an uncertain step toward Diane. The protective mother stomped her large foot down in front of her little one, blocking its advance and grunted a loud, alarming sound.

A sharp, fiery feeling of fear coursed through Diane's body. She took a slow, deep breath, steadied herself, and remained still. The mother leaned forward onto her two short forelimbs and stretched her horny lips toward Diane's head. She felt the hot breath of the dinosaur as the mother sniffed her blonde hair, then the plant in her hand. The *Hadrosaur* then stopped and stared, her elongated snout at Diane's eye level, silently waiting.

Diane couldn't resist. She slowly raised her eyes upward and found herself peering directly into the face of a duck-billed dinosaur. Looking deeply into the mother's questioning eyes, Diane's heart nearly burst with respect and love for her.

The mother's eyes softened. Diane slowly tore off a small piece of a leaf and placed it on the ground in front of her. The mother grunted a soft, low, grumbling noise in her throat, and the hatchling immediately dashed for the nourishing plant. Swallowing the tiny offering, the baby startlingly leapt into Diane's lap. It sat on her thigh, munching noisily away at the rest of the plant, devouring it completely in a matter of minutes.

Satisfied and seemingly curious, the baby stood up on its hind legs, looking up into Diane's face, then fearlessly scampered up her arm and sat on her left shoulder. Diane froze, uncertain of the little one's intent, then slowly turned her head toward the inquisitive baby and looked into its tiny muzzle. The baby sat back on its hind legs, chirped lightly, and hesitantly reached forward with its short forelegs, placing its two front feet on Diane's cheeks. The two of them stared at each other, examining every feature, crevice, and cranny of each other's faces.

Live for the moment! She remembered Asazi's words. *Just BE!*

Diane could feel the baby dinosaur's heart beating through the pads of its feet. She could feel and smell the chlorophyll breath as it exhaled wheezily into her face. The newborn's feet were still soft and supple, unlike the hardened, well-travelled pads of its mother. Diane slowly raised her other arm and brought her hand up to the baby's face. With a newfound trust, the baby touched her nose to Diane's palm, then licked it. Diane giggled and the baby alarmingly jerked its head upward, looking again into Diane's eyes, reaffirming its trust in this new, unusual friendship.

When the little one seemed satisfied, Diane slowly placed her fingers behind the baby's head and softly rubbed its neck. For a moment, the baby stood completely still and tense until, with an audible sigh, it finally relaxed into the petting, clearly enjoying the touch of human hands. Just then, the baby crawled down into Diane's lap and turned over onto its back, exposing its soft, young tummy.

Just like my little schnauzer puppies, Diane reflected, swallowing a chuckle. Her Daisy would come to her and fall right over with her little, fuzzy legs in the air, begging for a tummy rub.

Diane tickled the tender, newborn skin and again giggled slightly to herself. *What an experience!* she thought, and then remembering her classmates that loved dinosaurs almost as much as she did.

I can't wait to tell Hannah, Jayden, and Caleb about this. Natali and Gabby will go bananas! Vivian too!

The baby dinosaur squealed in delight as the mother came forward, unsure about the sounds her little one was uttering. She dipped her huge head into Diane's lap and sniffed her gleeful baby. Content, she backed away and lowered her head to Diane in approval.

Then the mother turned and began to walk away, but stopped, as though she had just remembered something. The *Hadrosaur* grunted, and the baby immediately jumped out of Diane's lap to follow her. Diane got up, dusted herself off and followed the mother, who led Diane to her nesting mound. She dipped her head down, and glanced up into Diane's warm green eyes, nodding her permission.

Peering down into the nest, Diane could see the numerous eggshells remains from several babies that were nowhere to be seen.

Probably lost to marauding predators, like the Troodon, a bird-like raptor that frequently stalked nesting grounds, Diane remembered sadly.

The shells were crushed into small pieces, about the size of Diane's pinky fingernail, evidence, indeed, that the babies had remained in their nest for some time under parental care.

Diane reached down and gratefully selected a few choice pieces to fit into her amulet, talismans of birth and creation. She stood up and nodded her head in gratitude to the mother and then held out her hand, palm up. The mother paused, and then gently touched her nose into Diane's palm. Diane reached down to the playful baby one last time and rubbed behind its head, then turned and walked back to the trees.

"*Incroyable!*" Lee said to Diane and Addie, who finally joined them. "Who would ever believe what we've just witnessed? Look at you, Dino Diane, holding a baby dinosaur. That's a good nickname for you—Dino Diane!"

They all laughed as much at the humor as from the feeling of relief.

"I love it!" Diane proclaimed avidly. "Dino Diane, that's my name now and forever more!"

"Well, you've certainly earned it," Asazi agreed, heartily.

"And thank you, Addie," Diane sighed. "I couldn't have done it without you."

"Cool beans," Lee said tersely. "Now, what?"

"Well, let's head back to the river and find our way out of the cave of ages," Asazi said wisely.

CHAPTER TWENTY~NINE

ATTACK OF THE ALLOSAURUS

R elieved and ecstatic, they turned from the nesting colony and made their way back through the forest of strange conifers, giant ferns, and tall reedy horsetails—species of plants that went extinct long before or evolved into the smaller descendants that now populated the young clan's world.

"Stop," Asazi said tensely, holding up his hand, his broad shoulders rigid, as he quietly crouched down into the grasses and reeds. The adventurers froze and listened. Up ahead was a clearing adjacent to the river's edge filled with a herd of foraging herbivores.

"I've never studied anything like them," Diane exclaimed with glee. "Look at those long crests on the top of their heads. They're obviously some kind of bipedal herbivore, plant-eaters that walk on two legs. See how they're walking on their two back legs, but look how those over there are foraging on all four," she said, scratching her head. "That makes them both bipedal and quadrupedal dinosaurs!"

Diane paused, brushing an annoying loose strand of hair behind her ear. "They're herding, too!"

All at once, the crested dinosaurs started bellowing a loud, low sound that echoed throughout the herd. "That must be how they communicate," Diane said excitedly. "What an amazing defense mechanism."

"Looks like we're going to need it," Lee said in alarm as she pointed to the trees nearest the herd, her eyes bulging wide.

From the other side of the clearing, the four startled adventurers saw the protruding chest and enormous head of a fearsome *Allosaurus* lurking from within the trees. Now, the herd *and* this ferocious predator stood in their path to the river—and their hopeful escape.

"I have an idea," Diane said keenly. "Do you think you can talk to them, Addie?"

"I'll t-t-try," she stuttered, and hesitated. "What am I going to tell them?"

"Tell them when they see four small, two-legged creatures come out from the forest, they should bellow all together at once. Tell them there's a meat-eater about to attack their herd and that we are here to help them."

"Okay," Addie said, gritting her teeth with resolve. "I'll do better than that!" Addie immediately went into her hand-dancing trance and warned them. Almost instantly, half the herd of about fifty dinosaurs looked their way as the four adventurers stepped simultaneously from the trees into the clearing. Just then, the *Allosaurus* broke through the trees with an ear-splitting roar, charging the herd in a full-speed run.

The twenty-five or so dinosaurs with which Addie had connected burst into a synchronous bellow that caused the ground to tremble with its powerful vibration. The others soon joined them, and the *Allosaurus* suddenly reeled around in circles, confused and disoriented. Tottering, it staggered and fell to the ground, struggling to get back up again. Its small forelimbs were of little help in picking up a five-thousand-pound wriggling dinosaur!

All at once, the bellowing stopped. "Run!" yelled Addie as she bravely dashed into the field toward the crested dinosaurs. Diane, Lee, and Asazi stood stunned, their jaws dropped, but quickly followed. Suddenly, four crested dinosaurs broke from the herd and ran directly toward Addie, stopping right in front of her, lowering themselves to the ground. Addie fearlessly jumped onto the back of the nearest one and swung her knapsack around its long, muscular neck, holding onto the shoulder straps like reins on a horse. The others followed her lead and leapt onto the backs of the waiting dinosaurs.

"*Incroyable!*" Lee shouted, awestruck, swinging her leg over her ride's broad back.

The four crested dinosaurs with their strange new friends on their backs raced across the field toward the river. The ferocious *Allosaurus* still lay on the ground, momentarily defeated, thrashing its hind legs and tail, deeply clawing the earth, desperately grappling to get back onto its feet. It opened its huge jaws and growled a deep, terrifying roar.

Diane had never heard anything so frightful before; its roar was deafening. She could feel it vibrate as it echoed loudly in her head. Burying her ears in her shoulders, her heart pounding in her throat, she grasped tightly onto her shoulder-strap reins and dashed after Addie, escaping across the grassy field.

Petrifying and exhilarating at the same time, Diane held her breath as she watched her timid, fearful friend—the sun shining on Addie's face, the wind blowing wildly through her hair—looking so strong and free as she clung to the neck of her crested dinosaur. She could almost feel Addie's joy and sense of empowerment, shedding years of abuse and ridicule.

Unexpectedly, the four crested dinosaurs made a quick turn

to their left to avoid crashing into a herd of grazing *Triceratops.* The four riders twisted, slipping sideways, and were thrown off their dinosaurs' backs. They tumbled to the ground right at the feet of the surprised herd of frilled dinosaurs that looked a little like elephants with bony ruffled collars, but with three spiky horns instead of a long trunk.

"Lie still," whispered Lee tensely.

The four adventurers lay like stones flat in the cool, thick grass as the curious herd slowly approached and encircled the strange, breathing stones. The oldest, largest male Triceratops stepped cautiously forward and sniffed Diane's hair. She stiffened as she felt the approach of this six-ton herbivore, his enormous weight shaking the ground with a rumbling vibration she could feel deep in her bones.

Boy, if Treston could see me now. Triceratops is his favorite, she thought as she fondly remembered her classmate, even at this frightful moment.

Diane felt—*and smelled*—the old *Triceratops'* warm, stale breath. *Yuck!* She wrinkled her nose at the unusual stench, and then surprisingly, the *Triceratops* nibbled a few strands of her hair with his huge, scaly lips.

"Ouch!" she cried shrilly, remaining motionless.

The huge male immediately stepped back jerkily, alarmed, swinging his long brow horns menacingly from side to side as he shook his head over her, apparently disappointed in the taste of her blonde hair and equally surprised by the talking stone.

From a distance, the clan heard a too-familiar roar resounding through the conifer trees. Giant-winged Cretaceous insects took flight from the trees, rattled by his horrifying roar. Their clamorous screeches, croaks, squawks, and fluttering wings filled the afternoon sky, darkening it. The recovered

Allosaurus...breathing hard...his chest heaving...eyes aflame ...nostrils flaring...had caught the scent of the adventurers on the wind and was now on a fierce mad-dash charge toward the clan and the herd of *Triceratops*. Great clumps of dirt and grass were ripped from the earth by his tremendously sharp claws and splattered like a muddy wake behind him as he plunged toward them.

Diane shrieked with a look of panic toward Addie with pleading eyes, holding her hands over her ears. Addie quickly made contact with the leader of the herd, the old *Triceratops*, who turned his attention to her, listening. In a flicker of a moment, the *Triceratops* leader snorted a grunting command to his herd, and males and females alike immediately arranged themselves into a solid defensive line across the field, bumping shoulder to shoulder nervously.

"Come on!" Lee shouted crisply as she raised up from the ground onto all fours.

Diane, Addie, and Asazi carefully did the same, crawling on their hands and knees between the legs of their huge protectors to get safely behind them. The dinosaurs shifted their weight and pawed the ground in a display of aggression, making it most difficult—and dangerous—for the adventurers to pass.

A jittery young female lifted her trembling foot and nearly stomped on Diane's hand as she skittered past. *Yikes,* she muttered to herself, moving her hand away just in time. "Whew!" She exhaled jerkily, crawling even faster.

The *Allosaurus* fiercely approached the formidable barricade of *Triceratops*, with their deadly brow horns lashing about, pointed directly at his vulnerable stomach and legs, then stopped abruptly. Their distinct bony frills were glowing bright red from the increased blood flowing through them as they gazed threateningly at the frustrated predator. Their frightening display of defense, along with their four-foot-long brow horns, made the *Triceratops* a mighty opponent.

The bewildered and frustrated *Allosaurus* finally lowered his head, barked out a terrifying, defeated cry, then reluctantly turned and stomped sulkily away, a loser today in the game of survival.

As Addie watched the vanquished bipedal carnivore disappear into the shadows of the distant trees, she communicated a huge burst of appreciation and gratitude to the leader of the herd. Receiving her message, the old *Triceratops* lowered his huge head in acknowledgment and grumbled a farewell as he turned his huge torso and led his victorious herd downriver.

"That was fantastic, and horribly scary!" Diane exclaimed as she lay exhausted in the grass, barely able to breathe.

Lee and Addie lay nearby breathing heavily, but relieved.

Asazi was the first to regain his strength and stood up, brushing off the weeds and Cretaceous dirt from his deerskin pants.

"Look," he said, pointing toward the river. All three heads popped up as they stared at the river before them. It was at least fifty feet wide at this point, a tad rough, and judging by its dark color, quite deep.

"How are we going to cross that?" Addie asked incredulously, finally putting words to the fear they all were feeling.

Diane shut her eyes. Rubbing the Joy Stone in her pocket, she waved her hand across her forehead, clearing her mind, "We need a way across. Show me a way!" she whispered, opening her heart to receive an answer from deep within herself.

Feeling empowered, she opened her eyes and gazed downriver. To her surprise and utter amazement, she saw a herd of *Lystrosauruses*, herbivores that looked a little like a cross between a cow and a hippopotamus, with turtle-like heads. They had a small horny beak for biting off pieces of vegetation, and their robust, heavily built bodies were about the size of a modern farm pig.

"I've got an idea!" Diane shouted avidly as she darted down the grassy field toward the herd of *Lystrosauruses* that were making their way down the stony bank to cross the river.

Addie, Asazi, and Lee quickly followed behind and gasped as Diane jumped off the three-foot embankment onto the back of a swimming *Lystrosaurus*. As if they were floating stones, Diane made her way, leaping from one *Lystrosaurus* to another across the fast-flowing river. The *Lystrosauruses*' attention was focused intently on the opposite bank, so they hardly noticed the brave adventurer stepping momentarily onto their backs.

Addie, Asazi, and Lee stopped at the edge of the bank—thunderstruck—their mouths gaped open, and watched in amazement as Diane stepped off the last floating stone onto the opposite bank, panting, waving frantically for them to come across. "Hurry, hurry!" she screamed as they hesitated. "Come on! Come on!" She signaled to them to turn around and look! Simultaneously, they slowly turned their heads, glancing over their shoulders to see the *Allosaurus* angrily charging once again toward the herd of *Lystrosauruses* and directly toward them.

Hot-footed, Addie and Asazi swiftly jumped onto the moving backs below, and with adrenaline pumping through their veins, they hurtled across the floating stones with lightning speed and onto the safety of the opposite bank.

"Whew! That was close," Asazi said, gasping, trying to catch his breath. "Where's Lee?" he asked in alarm, looking around for her. "She was right behind me."

Lee was last in line, and was about to leap onto the back of the nearest floating dinosaur when she spied a mother

Lystrosaurus downstream, screaming at her baby that was frozen in fear on the bank. She was desperately trying to coax her young one into the frightening, rushing water.

Lee instantly changed her direction and dashed downriver, the *Allosaurus* hot on her heels. With one arm, she scooped up the baby *Lystrosaurus* and then jumped onto the mother's back, running across the living stone bridge over the river. The mother followed hastily after her screeching baby, which Lee dropped safely on the opposite grassy bank. The mother clambered out of the river and rushed to her baby, sniffing and nuzzling its small nose to make sure it was all right. Lee stood bent over with her hands on her knees, struggling to catch her breath.

The last *Lystrosaurus* waddled into the rushing waters just as the *Allosaurus* came to an abrupt stop at the edge of the river. His meal had eluded him again.

CHAPTER THIRTY

ESCAPE

"**W**hat do we do now?" Lee asked breathlessly. "H-how do we get b-back to our world and Benji?" Diane stammered worriedly.

"Let's follow the river and see where it goes," Asazi replied, with a calming note in his voice.

"He must be worried sick about us," Addie said, clearly concerned, "But, I'm sure he's okay," she murmured, glancing sideways at Diane reassuredly.

They quickly picked up their knapsacks and walked hastily along the river, leaving the docile grazing herd of *Lystrosauruses* behind.

"Look over there!" Addie cried out. On the other side of the riverbank, basking in the hot sun, were seven large reptiles, ancestors to the modern alligator, at least thirty feet in length, weighing about ten tons each. Their huge pointy heads were nearly six feet long and contained rows of crushing, robust teeth.

Too lazy to be bothered, they, too, missed the floating Lystro-meals that had just crossed the river. Half hidden in the shade of an unusual-looking plant with a short, barrel-shaped trunk and a feathery crown of small-leafed stems, perhaps a member of the extinct genus *Cycadeoidea*, one of the largest reptile's glimmering, scaly hide twitched slightly.

All at once, he jerked his head upward and to the side, as if to get a good look at the clan goggling it on the opposite shore. Suddenly, he snap-opened his huge jaws with rows of sharp teeth glistening in the sunlight and hissed loudly.

Everyone froze and shook their heads warily—they'd had enough excitement for the day—and one by one, they cautiously tiptoed away from the bank and continued their trek downriver. "I hope none of *those* are sunbathing on *this* side," Diane muttered, expressing the clan's thoughts.

The warm afternoon sun was calming as they walked among the peculiar Cretaceous plants growing along the river's edge—palmlike cycads, maidenhair gingkoes, and feathery, nonflowering ferns. The air was so fresh and clear, free from the industrial pollution Diane had grown accustomed to in the city. She inhaled and grinned softly.

Finally, they could see up ahead that the river turned sharply to the right. As they approached the bend, they found the water flowing into the mouth of a small cave.

"That's it!" Asazi said assuredly. "Our way out!"

They ran up to the cave opening to see that the rushing current stretched from wall to wall, with no walking path in sight. They had only one choice!

"We're going to have to float our way out," Asazi declared soberly, shrugging his shoulders. The water was obviously too deep for them to walk through and too fast.

"On what?" Lee asked, a little anxious and perplexed. She brusquely swiped aside her brown bangs that stuck out from beneath her raccoon-skin cap, scrunching her eyebrows.

"On these!" Diane said keenly. She was pulling on a huge green leaf, an ancestor to the dramatic elephant-ear plant she had seen pictured in her schoolbooks. She learned it grew in the tropical rainforests of the Hawaiian Islands and dreamed of visiting that exotic place someday. The leaf was bigger than she was, and she carried it awkwardly on top of her head, to the river's edge. This peculiar species was surprisingly thick and rubbery and perfect for her intended purpose. The others scrambled to the giant, lustrous plants, plucked off a leaf raft of their own, and lined them up on the bank. Lee and Asazi went back for a few more, on account of their weighing more, and gave an extra one to Addie and Diane, just to be safe.

"Are we ready?" Diane asked excitedly, putting her leaf raft into the water and quickly clambering on board. The others did the same and were surprised to see how well they floated.

The fast waters rapidly whisked them into the main part of the rushing river, and they swiftly entered the dark cave once again, this time floating in complete darkness. The damp walls of the cave squeezed closer, and the river ran faster in the narrowing tunnel.

Careening through twists and turns, they floated along ever faster, hunkered down in their leaf rafts, quivering. They lay on their backs with their knapsacks on their stomachs, firmly holding onto the leaf's spaded edges for dear life.

The cave walls were suffocatingly close, and the ceiling so low, it occasionally brushed across Diane's knapsack. Diane shut her eyes tightly, wondering about Benji. *How long have we been away?* she worried, holding her breath. Her heart began to pound wildly in her ears. Fear twisted her stomach into an aching knot. She grasped her amulet and asked her bear totem to protect her brother as she concentrated on seeing his shiny face beaming in the sun once again. She felt a release of panic and a sense of peace wash over her. She somehow *knew* deep inside her that *all* was well, and she exhaled loudly.

Finally, up ahead, she could see a soft yellow light growing bigger and brighter. A sound of roaring water that began as a trickle, quite faint at first, now grew louder as the clan approached the brilliant haze that clearly marked the end of the cave.

As they sailed into the world of light under a dazzling sapphire sky, their leaf rafts all at once, fell from beneath them. Drifting over a stony cliff ledge, they fell with the cascading water into a deep pool forty feet below. Screaming all the way down, the four adventurers plunged—one by one—into the pool of water, slipping deep beneath its cool surface. Frantically kicking with all their might, they made their way up to the surface and the blue sky again, gasping for air as they swam to the pool's edge.

"Look," Diane said, gesturing to the fossiliferous cliff wall as she heaved herself out of the water and scrambled onto the grassy bank. "This is the same rock formation we found yesterday. I think we're in the right place," she said, panting in cautious relief. "Benji should be around here, somewhere, I hope," as she spun around three hundred and sixty degrees, looking frantically for her brother.

Indeed, the pool overflowed into the same river they had crossed the day before they entered the Cave of Ages. So, they followed the river downstream, meandering along the base of the familiar cliff wall filled with fossilized dinosaur bones, the only remnants of the majestic, terrible creatures they had left behind but would certainly never forget.

Up ahead, they saw Sa'ami sitting on his haunches with Niki straddling his head, both swatting playfully at little yellow butterflies that fluttered around them. Benji dozed under the nearby willow tree. Just then, he opened his eyes to see his four companions sauntering up to him, still soaking wet.

"Benji!" Diane shouted out. A huge smile lit up her face as he dashed into her arms, giving her a squeezing cub hug. She hugged him back, beaming.

That night, they sat around the warm, friendly campfire, sharing thrilling and terrifying stories with Benji of their great dinosaur adventure in a lost world. The fire crackled and popped merrily.

Diane finished sharing her wondrous experience with the *Hadrosaur* mother and her baby, then leaned back into her saddle perched over an old log. Her hat hung from the leather horn as she continued feverishly drawing in her field journal. She glanced up at the moon, glowing through melty marshmallow clouds that reminded her of the topping on her mother's Thanksgiving sweet potato casserole—all bubbly, gooey, and golden—always a little burnt along the edges.

Benji squirmed closer beside her. "What are you drawing?" he asked, straining to look over her shoulder. Just then, Sa'ami lumbered up, licking his lips, and plopped down heavily next to Benji, nearly sitting on him. "Phew! Sa'ami, I don't even want to know what you had for dinner," he grumbled, smelling his pungent fishy breath, vigorously waving it away.

Little Niki leapt from Lee's lap to Asazi to Addie to Benji and scampered up Sa'ami's slippery black fur to sit on top of his head, noisily chewing a piece of carrot, dropping tiny orange shavings onto Benji.

"Hey," he giggled, swiping the carrot peels from his face. "Can I see your drawings?"

His sister turned her field journal so everyone could see her rough sketches of their memorable experiences. In the glow of the fire, they could make out the rough outlines. To the clan's oohing and aahing, she continued to turn the pages.

"I'll shade them in later," she said, closing her book, laying it reverently on her lap. The clan nodded their approval.

"Wait, Di! Go back to the picture of the message wall," Benji asked, sitting up straight with a most serious look on his face. She wondered if her brother had noticed, and opened her field journal to the drawing of the message wall. Benji squinted—his eyesight wasn't that good—and straining, he paused, then his eyes bugged wide, "Does that say *Estebanico*?" he read slowly, excitement dripping off every syllable.

Diane grinned from ear to ear. "Yes, it does!" she said fervently.

Now Benji was grinning, rocking back and forth in utter disbelief. "That means he did survive and found the gold of Cibola, or at least some of it, and we now have it! Geez!" he exclaimed, letting out a huge breath. "There's got to be more out there then," he surmised, thrilled again about their quest.

Diane promised herself in that moment, no matter how much he might protest or how red he got in the face, that she would never leave her brother behind again.

"Let me see the eggshells," Benji finally asked, exhausted from their heroic yet fearful stories and the news of Estebanico and the gold.

"Okay, but first, I have something for you, for all of you," she said, with a glint sparkling in her eyes. She rummaged through her knapsack and pulled out a handful of long, curved dark claws. Benji's eyes widened.

She had inspected the fossiliferous dinosaur cliff while dinner was roasting and found a perfectly preserved articulated upper body of an *Allosaurus* protruding from the rocky surface. Weathering had eroded out several of the forelimb claws that lay jumbled at the bottom of the cliff face, a few hidden in a pile of dust and debris. Leaving the bones in place in the rock wall, Diane had knelt next to the cliff face and slowly sifted her fingers through the fine sediment. *Best to leave those on the wall there for someone else to find and enjoy,* she considered.

Suddenly, having felt something hard and curved, she wrapped her fingers around it and brought the treasure up into the sunlight. Within minutes, she had found not one but several raptor claws along with a few impressive serrated teeth and now, surprisingly, handed everyone their own fossilized claw as a keepsake, giving Benji a dagger-like tooth, too.

"Thank you, Di," he murmured breathlessly, ogling his terrifying fossils. He tucked the claw in the back pocket of his blue jeans and wrapped the carnivore's tooth in his bedroll.

"This is wonderful!" Addie said, smiling widely, her big front teeth glistening in the firelight.

"I will cherish this always," Asazi said heartily, admiring the deeply grooved and pointy claw.

"Cool beans!" Lee whistled. "But her name isn't Diane anymore," she said, glancing at Benji. "I gave her the nickname 'Dino Diane,'" she said spiritedly.

"Golly gee, sis," Benji said, shuffling his feet.

Diane then reached into her amulet. Carefully finding the delicate eggshell fragments, she removed them one by one and held the little pieces of dinosaur talismans in the palm of her hand, showing Benji the tiny treasures.

Admiring the peculiar bumps on the surface of the eggshells, "I can't believe all that happened. It seemed like you were gone for only a few hours," he muttered, disappointment now melting every word into a low grumble.

Just then, a strong breeze blew through the trees and over her palm, lifting one of the light pieces into the air and whisking it straightaway into the bluey-white flames of the campfire.

All at once, with a burst of brilliant light, Za-tha appeared from the blaze and hovered above the flames.

"Greetings," he said in his low voice. The flames beneath him exploded into a fountain of red and orange sparks that danced to his words. He held his hands up, palms forward, in his familiar way.

"Well done!" he exclaimed as he nodded his approval. "You have shown great courage and ingenuity. Addie," he said, turning toward her, "In you, this day is born a great awakening to the powers within you. When you let go of your fears and trust in yourself, you can accomplish anything your heart desires. When you stop clinging so dearly to what people think of you and care more about what you think and feel about others, then only are you *truly* free. Don't let others define who you are. BE the magnificent you, just as you are."

Addie sighed deeply, the firelight glinting in her round cinnamon-brown eyes.

Za-tha reached down into Diane's palm and retrieved one of the eggshell fragments. From inside his red shawl, he pulled out an amulet with the image of a crested dinosaur burnt into it, and placed the eggshell fragment in it, then hung the amulet around Addie's long, thin neck. Addie lowered her head in reverence, a glistening tear trickled down her freckled cheek.

Za-tha placed his large, gentle hand on her head, as if anointing the birth of the new Addie. "You've always had this power within you," he told her sagely. "You simply have to acknowledge it, know that it is there, and choose to be in your power in everything you do."

He turned and swept his eyes over each of them. "You've

learned well the Second Ray of Light: you have the power within you to be whatever you want to be and have anything you desire. You simply have to THINK it, SEE it, FEEL it, KNOW it, then CREATE it. You are the creators of your life experiences." The flames of the fire danced in his soulful eyes as he spoke. "You are confronted with choices every day. You make decisions that either bring you closer to your dreams or push them further away, simply by what you think and the feelings you send into the universe," he paused.

"Your feelings are vibrations of energy. The universe is all energy and recognizes feelings of love, joy, and peace as high energetic vibrations, which will, in turn, bring you even more experiences of love, joy, and peace. But the opposite is also true," he warned somberly. "If you're feeling anger, guilt, or fear, you send those low vibrations into the universe as well, which will return them in kind, filling your life with more of the same misery."

The flames of the fire licked up around Za-tha, bursting red sparks into the cool night breeze. "May your eggshell talismans always remind you that *you* create your life by what you think, see, and feel," he said with a hint of promise in his voice. "Your thoughts are the pictures of your life that you are painting. Your feelings breathe life into your pictures, creating your physical reality," he paused. "Your *feelings* are the fuel that powers your creations. *Trust* your feelings and follow them. They will always guide you. Remember this always!" he finished, with a warm look of love in his wise, fathomless eyes. Long, wavy strands of his silvery-white hair swept across his deeply creased forehead.

The five adventurers felt the truth of his words in the depth of their young souls and smiled at each other with a sense of inner knowing.

"Now," Za-tha spoke again, "Rest tonight, sleep well, and tomorrow head southwest to the Canyon of the Hoodoos and the Red Rock People. In one day's ride, the last ray of the setting sun will shine on a huge red rock wall, the color of ancient blood, which will block your passage. There, you shall be given the third secret by the ancient ones, the Red Rock People hidden in the hoodoos. But beware of the Canyon of the Coyotes," he cautioned gravely. The yellow beads depicting the sun on his shawl gleamed in the flickering firelight, mirroring the twinkling stars in the heavens.

With these final instructions, Za-tha raised his powerful arms from his sides, palms open to the little clan, and said, "Let it be so!" He vanished into the flames of the fire, accompanied by a swirl of tiny sparks flying into the dark skies above.

"Red Rock People," Lee repeated out loud, quavering. She shuddered, and goose bumps rose up on her strong, young arms.

The clan sat silently around the fire, each lost in their own thoughts, pondering the wisdom of this secret of the ages and their extraordinary dinosaur adventure.

Suddenly, Benji punched his sister hard in the arm.

"Ouch! What was that for?" she cried, rubbing her arm.

"That's for not *making* me go with you," he said, sulking grumpily.

After a moment of pondering, "Choices!" Diane finally said softly, shrugging sympathetically.

CHAPTER THIRTY~ONE

TICKLING A FISH

CRASH! The morning came with a loud crash of tin plates that were stacked neatly by the smoldering campfire. Everyone woke suddenly from their slumber to see the largest raccoon they'd ever laid eyes on scamper back into a nearby thicket. As it disappeared through the brush, a baby raccoon tumbled out into the clearing before them. The mother had accidentally run over her young in her hurried escape. She paused, turned, then frantically ran back to rescue her stunned little one, swatting it back into the thicket with her large black paws.

At once, the five sleepy-eyed adventurers saw not one but three pairs of little masked eyes peeping back at them. The harried mother raccoon had apparently been scavenging for food to feed her numerous young kits.

Rummaging in her knapsack, Diane quickly found a pemmican bar that she broke into small pieces. *I don't want to scare them,* she whispered to herself as she gently tossed each morsel just before the thicket. The mother raccoon cautiously came out to inspect the offering. Sniffing it first, she picked up the piece with her dexterous black fingers, carefully inspected it, then held it to her mouth, taking a small, tentative nibble. She paused. Seemingly satisfied, she stood up on her hind legs and began chewing it heartily.

Sensing her approval, the three little kits slowly crawled out from beneath the safety of the green leaves of the thicket, and each finding its own tasty morsel, imitated the mother's etiquette. The adventurers watched as all three baby raccoons sat up on their hind legs, noisily enjoying their breakfast gifts.

Just then Mavric came up behind Diane and nuzzled his nose into her back. She turned and placed her hand on his forehead and kissed his velvety nose.

"It's good to see you, too," she said kindly, looking into his caramel-colored eyes, lined with long black lashes. "You're right. It's time to go," she said, turning to her friends.

The four raccoons scampered back into the leafy thicket as the clan loaded up their horses and mounted them, thrilled for the adventure ahead. Placidly sitting on their horses, they waited patiently for Benji and Sa'ami. Niki, riding atop the bear's head, waved her black paw goodbye to the departing raccoons.

Diane had noticed that her brother was still quite glum.

With a mad dash, Benji ran and tried to leap onto Sa'ami's back from behind, as he had seen Asazi do, and smacked hard into Sa'ami's hind end, his stubby tail poking Benji in his eye. He staggered backward and fell heavily on his bum.

"Golly gee," he muttered dispiritedly. Lying with his legs splayed out on the trampled wild grasses, he slowly rubbed his sore eye, seemingly feeling the whole affair just added insult to his already injured heart.

Asazi rode by, smothering a grin. He reached down and lifted Benji up by the hand, swinging him onto Sa'ami's back, who trotted off, tossing his head as if he were chuckling. Everyone but Benji was amused by the sight.

With the gleaming sun rising in the east, tiny rays of white light intertwined with muted shades of gray streamed through the cottonwood and willow trees across the green river. The shimmering drapery of light angled from the treetop canopy above to the lush riparian floor in a most beautiful, radiant display. An enchanting soft glow illuminated the shrubs, ferns, and wildflowers of the delicate ecosystem along the river's banks, making everything appear magical.

Birds were once again singing their morning songs in greeting to the nourishing sun as Asazi and Lee rode up alongside Diane. In a few hours' time, the elevation changed drastically, and the clan once again entered a montane forest community of ponderosa pines and Douglas firs.

Asazi was chewing something. He handed a pine needle to Diane and gestured that she should chew it, too. "It's good medicine," he said soberly. "I chew it whenever I can to stay strong and prevent illness."

Diane looked at him quizzically and raised an eyebrow, but trusting him, she tentatively put the slender needle into her mouth and began to chew. "Yumm!" she mumbled.

Asazi offered one to a passing Benji, who shook his head glumly and sauntered off with Sa'ami and Niki.

"It's nice. Tastes a little like lemon. I wonder what gives it so much power?" Diane pondered out loud.

"It's good for colds and influenza. And it helps your eyes and skin, too," Asazi replied as he plucked off another needle from its bundle and handed it to Lee, who cautiously put it into her mouth and chewed slowly.

Asazi and Forjon rode away to meet up with Addie to give her the last pine needle from the ponderosa bundle and to keep her company, leaving Diane and Lee alone to chew their pine needles in silence.

Just then, Lee spat out her chewed needle. *"C'est assez!* I think that's enough," she said disgustedly. "It's down to a ball of stringy fibers, and the taste is gone. I don't think he meant for us to swallow it, too." She pulled out her canteen and drew a swig of water. They had filled their canteens from the river before they broke camp that morning and had plenty for the day's ride ahead.

"Always get your water from the rushing surface where the water is the cleanest. Most of a river's sediment settles to the bottom. Never drink standing water," she recited.

"Where did you learn that?" Diane asked.

"My papa taught me," Lee murmured.

"He's taught you a lot," Diane said earnestly.

"Oui, I mean, yes, I suppose so," Lee said quietly, almost under her breath. "How to drink, how to kill, how to be mean," she continued bitterly.

"How long have you been away from home?"

"Too long! Five years since I've seen my mama and two sisters. My little sister Suzette must be almost six years old now. She was born just before we left. My papa felt that my older sister could help my mama with Suzette while we were gone. It was fun in the beginning, an adventure, *bien sur,* but as time went on, things got really hard, animals got fewer, the money dried up, so he began to drink and got mean. He was angry that things weren't going as he'd hoped, and he took his disappointment out on me when he drank."

"Why didn't you just turn around and go home?" Diane asked, feeling her pain.

"His pride wouldn't let him. He wanted to go home rich from trapping and was determined not to return until he was," Lee said, clearly exasperated.

"That's not fair to you," Diane said, sincerely concerned.

"Tell me about it."

They fell into silence again.

The sun was sinking low in the late afternoon sky as the clan of adventurers broke through the last line of dwarf trees of the semi-desert woodlands that lined the hot badlands before them.

It was Diane's favorite time of the day, when long shadows were cast across the landscape and the sky was an intense azure blue. A warm breeze rustled through the remaining junipers and pinyon pines, signaling that night was soon approaching. Diane felt at peace in the long shadows, and connected with all around her.

Off in the distance, they could see painted rock canyons glimmering colorfully in the setting light. Millions of years before, the interbedded red and white sandstones were formed in an ancient shallow sea that once lay across the now-barren horizon. Carved by wind and water erosion, the beautiful rock formations looked like a painted desert of scarce shrubs deeply cut with colorful canyons. Banana yuccas, broom snakeweed, and desert sage dotted the canyon floors.

Swiping a loose strand of blonde hair and securing it behind her ear, Diane gazed out over the expansive badlands. She tried to imagine a time long before when a shallow sea edged with sandy beaches teemed with primitive life forms stretched for miles across. Wandering rivers flowing through forested floodplains dominated by dinosaurs dumped their sediment, forming silty deltas at the mouths of the shallow salt waters. Her favorite dinosaurs, the *Hadrosaurs*, lived on the western shore of this interior seaway while their cousins lived on this east side.

"We must be nearing the hoodoos," said Diane with excitement—and a smattering of apprehension. "But, how are we going to cross *that* before nightfall?" she asked, a bit befuddled.

"Yes, those red rock canyons will lead us to the hoodoos Za-tha spoke of," confirmed Asazi, as Diane and Lee rode up beside him and Addie. Benji and Sa'ami lumbered up from behind.

Reaching into his deerskin medicine bag, Asazi removed the Aztec Stone. It was glowing softly.

"We're near the portal that will take us there swiftly," he said.

Diane looked down and discovered that her white scarf was glowing lightly as well.

"Can we take a break first?" Benji asked, wearily eyeing the magical stone. "I'm hungry, and so is Sa'ami." The giant black bear tossed his head in agreement and pawed the air for emphasis.

Just then, Sa'ami paused, his muzzle stretched up to the sky, and jerkily sniffed the air, then suddenly took off running with Benji bouncing on his back, hanging on for dear life.

"Whoa!" he yelled as Sa'ami dashed toward a small creek ahead.

"Good sniffs, I'd say," guessed Addie.

"Here we go again," Asazi chuckled. "Let's go!" He signaled, and gently nudging his painted horse's flanks with his heels, Forjon galloped off. Everyone quickly followed behind, still laughing at the sight of Benji bobbing and yelling through the diminishing grassy plains before the badlands in the distance.

"Giddy-up!" Diane said, chortling, giving Mavric a squeeze with her knees.

When they finally caught up to Sa'ami and Benji, they were sitting in a thicket of raspberry bushes, happily picking and eating the tasty wild berries. Diane, Addie, and Lee quickly dismounted and joined them, searching through the thorny brambles, their hearts light with this simple pleasure of nature. A gift from the Mother.

"I've never eaten raspberries fresh off their viney canes," Diane said with delight as she plopped another juicy berry into her red-stained mouth. "They're so sweet! Mmm, mmm, MMM," she sighed, her eyes shut in ecstasy.

She was glad to see that Benji was in a better mood. She had made a grave error in judgment by leaving him alone, even if it was at *his* request. She knew then that wasn't her father's idea of watching out for him, being responsible for him. She sighed deeply and vowed to take better care of him. After all, they were in the wilderness, far from home, lucky to still be alive. She shuddered, and swiped her hand through the air across her forehead to clear away her negative thoughts, which were clearly running her down a dark, emotional rabbit hole.

She plopped another sweet raspberry into her mouth and sat in the grass with the others, who were happily stuffing themselves, while they curiously watched Asazi skulk along the meandering creek nearby. In the lazy sun, shaded by their hats, they gazed as he slowly entered the creek through a stand of bulrushes and slender horsetail reeds. Beautiful wildflowers were intertwined in the grasses: penstemon, western iris, and delicate golden columbine flowers that looked like pointy falling stars with trailing firetails. He moved slowly, purposefully, through the water with his head down, and his eyebrows deeply furrowed in focused concentration, searching carefully for—*something.*

But, for what? Diane considered, always inquisitive.

Their stomachs content, they quietly tiptoed on the bank alongside Asazi until he stopped and held out his hand, signaling for them to do the same. Then, in snail speed, he slowly lowered his hand into the water, holding it still for what seemed like forever. All at once, he jerked his hand out of the creek with a good-sized fish dangling from his thumb and forefinger. Everyone on the bank applauded in astonished surprise.

"You caught a fish with your bare hands!" Diane proclaimed with glee.

"How'd you do that?" Lee asked, genuinely amazed.

"I tickled the fish," he said, with a faint note of humble pride. "I'll teach you," he said, throwing the fish onto the bank for a quick dinner.

Everyone got into the water except Sa'ami. He was already downstream, splashing in the water, and catching his own fish for dinner, bear-style.

"Fish always rest with their heads pointing upstream *into* the flow of water. In the heat of the day, they like to hide in the shade where it's cool, usually in the undercut of a bank or under floating debris of branches and leaves. You must move very slowly and reach under the bank to find the fish with your fingertips. When you feel a fish, lightly move your fingers along its stomach and slowly make your way, 'tickling' the fish until you reach its gills. You'll feel the opening and closing of the gills as it breathes. When you feel it inhale, quickly thrust your thumb into the open gills and out its mouth, securing it with your forefinger, like this."

He showed them, making an O-loop with the tips of his

thumb and forefinger. "Then, pull it out of the creek and toss it onto the bank," he said, concluding his lesson.

Everyone enthusiastically spread out along the banks of the stream and began exploring its edges, searching for a shady undercut. Diane eagerly shed her boots, rolled up her dungarees, and followed Asazi's path into the cool stream water.

Appreciating the delicate and colorful wildflowers, she made a mental note to take a few samples afterward and press them into her field journal. *I'll ask Asazi about them later,* she decided. *Maybe they have some medicinal use.* She found that she really enjoyed learning about the wild plants on their journey.

The water felt so refreshing after their long ride, she sighed deeply. The clear stream was flowing gently, and she reveled in the soft, squishy mud bottom, scrunching her toes, as she stood surveying its banks. Diane found a shaded undercut in the slight bend of the creek, and following Asazi's instruction, she slowly reached into the darkness. *This is icky,* she recoiled, a little concerned at first. *What else might be lurking under these banks?* She didn't want to think about it and shook the twinge of fear from her head.

There it was! She could feel the cool, slender body of a fish resting in the shadows. With her hand just short of the tail fin, she started tickling the fish ever so lightly with her fingertips, amazed that it didn't move at all. She had expected it to dart away at any moment. When it didn't, she continued to slowly tickle her way up its stomach until she felt the gills opening and closing with every breath.

Panting slightly, she suddenly held her breath and with one quick motion, she thrust her thumb into the open gills of the dozing fish and out its mouth, locking it with her forefinger as she squealed. She yanked it out of the creek and threw it onto the bank, still squeamishly screaming and jumping about. Her face blushed beet red and crinkled in disgust, she watched Addie and Lee almost simultaneously throw their dinners onto the bank nearby.

Just then, a loud, raucous sound erupted downstream, startling them. They turned and watched, in utter awe, as Sa'ami violently splashed the stream water with his huge paddle paws, churning up the silty bottom, catching a few dazed fish in the turmoil. When one escaped out of the water, he swung and smacked it with his paw, sending it sailing onto a pile of flopping fish on the bank. They all chortled as his pile grew larger and larger. He did have an appetite, and fish was clearly one of his favorites!

"This is fun!" Addie yelled shrilly.

"It's icky!" Diane shouted back, deeply satisfied, though, that she had mustered up the courage to do something that made her so absolutely uncomfortable. *I never read about this in any of my books,* she reflected.

Lee gathered the flopping fish on the bank and quickly ended their suffering. Asazi had a cooking fire blazing and was seated on a nearby log. On his lap were several thin branches from a young willow tree that grew near the creek. Everyone gathered around to watch what he was doing. First, he peeled the bark from the branches in long strips, which he piled next to him, keeping them for later. The bark came off easily. He then took a long, thin, bare branch and bent it into the shape of a large hoop—ten or so inches across—bringing the two ends together, making a handle. He made another similar hoop, placed them on top of each other, and tied the two overlapping handles together with the peeled, flexible bark strips. Finally, he broke six shorter straight pieces from another thin branch and tied three of them horizontally across each hoop, spacing them evenly.

From a deerskin pouch, he took a black stone flake, made from flint, and with its very sharp edge, filleted the fish, feeding the guts and entrails to the waiting, hungry Niki. He finished by cutting the fish's head off and pulling out its vertebrae.

Yuck! Diane squirmed as she marveled at the precision, speed, and skill of his crafty hands. Determined to learn everything, no matter how disgusting, she observed his every move and gulping hard, picked up a lifeless fish. Asazi reached into his pouch again, pulled out another stone tool, and showed her how to fillet her dinner. She'd seen her mother clean fish before, but never quite like this. And, she certainly hadn't cleaned any herself. It was actually pretty easy, and Diane decided that she enjoyed working with her hands and learning how to survive in the wild—catching fish with her bare hands—*something a bookworm would never have dreamt of experiencing.*

Lee pulled out her antler-handle knife and filleted her own fish, as well as two more for Addie and Benji, who grinned from ear to ear, his face completely stained red with splattered berry juice.

"Gee whiz!" Benji mumbled, his cheeks bulging. "These raspberries are great!"

Just like him, Diane chuckled quietly.

Once the fish were filleted, Asazi opened the double hoops and laid them inside. He used the remaining peeled bark to securely fasten the two hoops together, and then he held the ingeniously contrived contraption by its handle over the flames of the fire, grilling the fish, Asazi-style. In a few minutes, the smell of roasting fish filled the air, making everyone's stomachs rumble with hunger pangs.

Asazi had also collected some cattail roots, which tasted like starchy potatoes, and wild asparagus that he roasted on the hot rocks around the firepit. He then went to work making a green salad of watercress, dandelion, and curly dock with a trimming of barrel cactus fruit that had a sort of citrus flavor.

"Mmm, mmm, MMM," Diane sighed as she picked a piece of grilled fish from its skin and dramatically dropped it into her salivating mouth. "What are these seeds sprinkled on the salad?" she asked. "They're tasty."

"Those are seeds from the hemp plant," Asazi replied sagely. "My people use hemp in many ways. The women use the fibers to make clothing. The seeds are edible and have great medicinal uses. It is considered a treasure from the Great Mother Earth, and the elders burn it as incense during their sacred ceremonies."

"*Incroyable!*" Lee joined in licking her lips, handing a few morsels of fish to Niki, who sat on her lap, waiting patiently. "Growing kit," Lee snickered.

"This is yummy!" Benji added heartily.

Addie said nothing, but her eyes glowed bright with a glint of contentment.

"*Merci beaucoup,*" said Lee, finally falling back into the grass, rubbing her stomach, utterly stuffed.

Asazi bowed his head, pleased.

Refreshed and stuffed with fish, salad, and berries, the adventurers continued their journey toward the red rock canyons and the waiting hoodoos in the far distance.

CHAPTER THIRTY-TWO

SWARM OF BEES

A s they neared a thick pillar of crimson stone, like a monument on the horizon, Diane's scarf began to glow brightly. "Look!" she shouted, holding her scarf up for everyone to see.

Asazi removed the turquoise Aztec Stone from his deerskin pouch and held it out on his palm in front of him. It, too, was much brighter than before, signaling they were nearing the ancient gateway. "The eastern face marks the entrance into the portal," he said, angling Forjon in that direction. Everyone followed behind.

The large pillar of stone was at least fifty feet high and thirty-some feet long, reminding Diane of a giant tombstone. She shuddered as she crossed over into its deep shadow.

Asazi stopped in front of the solid wall of rock and looked to the clan. One by one, each nodded that they were ready.

"Is Sa'ami ready?" Benji whispered to Addie, whose eyes were closed.

Opening her eyes, "Yes, he's prepared, and so are the horses," she said reassuringly. "Niki, too!"

Benji hunkered low on Sa'ami's back wrapping his arms around the big bear's thick bristly neck. "It's okay, Sa'ami," he murmured reassuringly.

Asazi sat up tall on Forjon's back and placed his finger on the golden tip of the stone and closed his eyes, repeating the magical incantation of the ancient ones.

At once, the Aztec Stone began to twirl in the palm of his hand, radiating brilliant light in every direction. Engulfing Asazi in the swirling light, the adventurers' horses stepped back from the awesome sight as the light funnel grew around him, expanding to the heavens. Then in a flash, the tornado of light flew to the face of the rock, splashing onto its surface. Once again, it looked like a frosted glass surface surrounded by a thick white rope. The frosted appearance cleared, revealing the red rock canyons directly in front of them. Asazi leaned forward, signaling Forjon to enter the Aztec Portal. The rest of the clan hesitantly trailed behind.

"How are we going to find the 'red wall' Za-tha spoke of amongst all these rock formations?" Addie asked as she rode out of the portal and up next to Diane, who was adjusting her hat and swiping blown-away strands of hair from her face. The red rock walls loomed now directly in front of them.

"We'll follow the path of the sun as it makes its way to the horizon," Asazi replied, turning around on his blanket, watching Sa'ami and Benji saunter along, shaking off the effects of the blasting portal winds. Little Niki rode curled up on Sa'ami's head, seemingly exhausted.

The painted desert badlands of sage and cacti had given way

to scrubby uplands of Rocky Mountain junipers and Colorado pinyon trees, edged with low-growing manzanita, as the clan continued to gain elevation and enter the red rock country of the hoodoos before sunset.

The beautifully smoothed and twisted cherry mahogany branches of the manzanita shrub with its drought-resistant, shiny green leaves were an instant favorite of Diane's. *I can't wait to draw it,* she mused, paying close attention to the details of the artistic structure of the plant, which looked like a mahogany octopus with wild spindly arms. Asazi explained that its tiny red ripened or slightly sour, green berries were a preferred food source of the local deer, elk, and antelope herds—and raccoons! Diane reached down and collected a few green berries as an evening snack for Niki, placing them in a pocket of her knapsack.

Noticing her field journal, she recalled her science teacher lecturing about the geology of the West. She pulled out her journal and flipped through the pages until she found her notes.

"Would you like to hear this?" Diane asked Addie.

"Yes, of course. I'm really interested in learning about the earth," she said. "I had no idea!"

Diane read aloud:

Seventy million years ago, during the Mesozoic Era, the West was once covered by a shallow seaway that stretched from the Gulf of Mexico to the Arctic Ocean. Ancient streams and rivers deposited silts and sands in beaches, lagoons, and swamps along its banks and coastal shelves.

"So, right where we're riding, right here in this spot, there was once a sea?" Addie asked, shaking her head in disbelief.

Diane nodded her head and continued.

Over eons of time, sedimentary rocks—limestone, siltstone, dolomite, and shale—were all formed in these prehistoric depositional environments. Oxidation of the iron in the sediments gave many of the sedimentary layers their pink and red colors, while other layers formed were dark-gray to black.

Diane glanced up. "Look at those!" she shouted, pointing to several large, straight-shelled, and coiled ammonite fossils embedded in a dark, grayish-black shale. "They lived over 200 million years ago and are the only remnants of the ancient sea that once dominated this area. They went extinct with the dinosaurs."

"They look like huge squids," Addie said in amazement. "And, that's our evidence that this was a sea at one time, right?"

Diane beamed and continued reading:

As time progressed, areas in the West were uplifted by unknown forces deep inside the earth that transformed the seaway into a floodplain of meandering streams, deltas, and shallow lakes. Periodic flooding spread mud, cobbles, and fine silt over the broad plains while large quantities of sediments were laid down in the numerous lakes nearby. As they did so, layers of differing thicknesses of calcium-rich muds and limey oozes were stacked atop one another, creating the white siltstones and red limestones coloring many of the West's fabulous canyon formations.

She closed her field journal, patted it respectfully, and placed it back in her knapsack.

"That's how we get different-colored rocks, by the minerals and things that make them up, isn't that so?" Addie asked, seemingly thrilled with her blossoming understanding of how the earth worked.

"What's this, sis?" Benji asked, holding up a small, smooth rock shaped like a shell.

Diane took the white shell and inspected it carefully. "It looks like a fossil clamshell, probably from the ancient lake that formed after the..." Then she stopped mid-sentence, and her jaw dropped. "Look where you're standing, Benji," she said in awe.

Beneath Sa'ami's huge black paws, the distinctive impressions of dinosaur footprints were carved into the white lake siltstone. Lots of them!

"Sa'ami's standing in a dinosaur trackway," Diane exclaimed in delight. "Look how they're coming from there and going to..." she paused again.

Off in the distance, Diane noticed a mysterious black cloud swiftly drifting toward them. It moved in the strangest of ways, as if it were alive, moving, twisting, contorting closer and closer. Then the clan heard a most peculiar sound, like the buzz of a—

"Watch out!" Asazi shouted warningly. "That's a swarm of bees!"

"They're coming this way!" Lee croaked in a panic, frenetically looking for a place to hide.

There were no boulders or tree trunks or rocky outcrops— *no place to run and hide.* They were out in open scrubland, completely exposed.

Diane had read of a swarm of bees but had never seen one, and this one was huge! As the swarm of thousands of buzzing bees neared her clan, she grasped her deerskin amulet, hanging on her chest.

My white scarf of protection! she suddenly remembered,

panting breathlessly.

Above the threatening drone of the bees, she yelled to the clan to huddle around her. Her voice was barely heard, muted by the deafening buzz, but the look of panic and yet confidence etched deeply on her face told the clan what she wanted them to do.

"Come on," she clamored, waving her arms in a circle, beckoning them to join her.

The sky grew darker. The buzz grew louder, shattering the peace they'd enjoyed just moments before. The riders hurriedly dismounted and quickly led their anxious and agitated horses into a circle surrounding Diane.

Mavric and Bentley's bulging eyes and flared nostrils made it apparent that they sensed something was horribly wrong, too. Lee stood quietly next to her chestnut, stroking his sweaty neck to calm him. Asazi, a pained crease in his brows, pressed his forehead against Forjon's long snout. Both horse and friend had closed their eyes. Asazi's thin lips were moving slightly in silent prayer.

Addie sat on the ground, horrorstruck, her arms wrapped tightly around her knees, rocking backward and forward, breathing in sharp gasps beneath Rohan, who snorted jerkily. "Too many bees, too many connections," Addie mumbled grimly between gasps, "Impossible to communicate."

The horses nervously pawed the ground. Sa'ami, Benji, and Niki snuggled under the steamy breath of the frightened horses and quivered in fear. Sa'ami's fuzzy ears twitched as the buzzing mass grew louder—and closer. He hung his head low, his massive body protecting Benji and Niki, who were curled up between his front legs, swaying between them.

Diane hurtled her magical scarf into the air and twirled it about, round and round, high above their heads. She glanced at the horizon and the quickly sinking sun, frowning. She was worried. *Would they get to the red wall to find the Red Rock People in time? Would they survive this?* she whispered to herself.

All at once, the gauzy scarf began to glow, and the swirling blur created a dome of brilliant white light that emanated from the scarf itself, making her little clan magically invisible to the approaching bees. The sky was like dark molasses as the black mass now rumbled overhead.

Straining to hold on, droplets of sweat drained into her eyes, stinging them. Diane could feel the bees' small bodies flying into the scarf and ricocheting away, hither and yon. She held tightly, her arms tiring, breathing heavily, until finally, at last, they flew past them. The angry buzz, almost ear-piercing, faded, and drifted away.

"Whew!" she exhaled, rubbing her sore arms. She wrapped her beloved scarf around her neck once again, holding it dearly, appreciating it for their protection.

"Gee whiz!" Benji spluttered, choking down fear and disgust, as he wiped away Sa'ami's spittle that had oozed down from his trembling muzzle onto the crown of his head. He turned and gave the protective big bear a crushing hug. Niki violently shook her little fuzzy body and scampered up his black, bristly forelegs to sit on top of Sa'ami's head.

The clan, as if waking from a trance, slowly mounted their horses. And, with a wave of his hand, Asazi turned slowly toward the red canyon walls, leading the way.

Not far off, three bloodcurdling screams could be faintly heard; their shrill shrieks, carried on the evening breeze into the canyon, were lost among the hoodoos.

"Did you hear that?" Diane asked alarmingly, sure that she had heard muffled cries behind them. She turned in her saddle, eyes transfixed on the horizon, saw only the black cloud undulating against the early evening rose-colored sky, and shrugged.

She suddenly noticed movement beneath the fibrous branches of a scrubby sage bush. The upland floor was pockmarked with scattered holes, remnants of a prairie dog town, now abandoned. From a small hole, Diane saw a feathery head emerge with two large round eyes blinking widely at her. Bursting forth into the sky, a small burrowing owl fluttered its tiny wings, flying up and hovering right in front of Diane's face. It chattered softy and bobbed its head as if in greeting. The brown, spotted, feathered raptor blinked its sharp yellow eyes a last time and then flew off in a great hurry to deliver its message.

Startled and perplexed, Diane slowly turned back in her saddle, shaking her head slightly, and rode off to catch up with Lee, who was patiently waiting.

CHAPTER THIRTY~THREE

HOODOOS

The clan of adventurers cantered along the eroded edge of the uplifted plateau, making up lost time. Diane ducked under a long, spindly pine branch that was tipped with clusters of tiny cones and bristly needles that reminded her of a bottle brush.

"This is an unusual pine tree," Addie noticed, picking one of its tiny purplish cones from its branches. "Ouch!" she muttered, wincing. "It clawed me."

"That must be a Bristlecone pine," Diane paused, "I've read that it's the oldest plant on the earth. Some trees live over five thousand years. I'm sure Asazi has something to take away the sting."

"Thanks," Addie said somewhat abruptly, and immediately rode off to meet up with Asazi.

As Diane passed by the trunk of the Bristlecone pine, she noticed that some of the exposed bark of the tree looked dead and twisted, like the gnarly, wrinkled skin of her neighborhood milkman.

I'd like to draw that in my field journal tonight, she decided, pulling it out once again to make a rough outline of the coarse texture of the bark, best as she could as she rode along.

Long, slender walls of colored rock layers, called fins, jutted out from the semicircular canyon the clan was entering. Just then, Benji and Sa'ami sauntered up beside her.

"Look, Benji," Diane said, pointing to a large, colorful trunk of petrified wood that lay at the base of the fin they were passing. "It's evidence that this ancient floodplain was once heavily forested with large, primitive trees nearly a hundred feet tall. And see those," she said keenly, motioning to the fossil remains of snails and clams embedded in the fin's white layer of siltstone. "That's more evidence that a lake environment once existed here millions of years ago."

"Geez, sis," was all Benji could muster and moseyed away.

She flipped the pages in her field journal again to her notes on physical and chemical weathering and erosion. "Oh yes, here it is," she mumbled, as Lee quietly moseyed up beside her, listening.

The fins of the West are made mostly of soft pink limestone that has large, vertical cracks running through it. In the winter months, sun-warmed melting snow seeps into the cracks and then freezes overnight. As the frozen water expands, it further widens the cracks.

Year after year, the forces of weathering, and later erosion, carry the crumbling rock fragments away, separating the once-solid fin into a row of free-standing, vertical rock columns, called hoodoos.

"Sure is a funny name for a pile of rocks," Lee interrupted. "But how did they get that strange shape?"

Diane narrowed her gaze at Lee, then smiled, thrilled to see that she was interested, too. Diane continued reading aloud as Addie and Asazi met up with them, both grinning broadly.

> *Summer rains also play a part. Combining with carbon dioxide in the atmosphere, they form a weak solution of carbonic acid that, over time, "chemically" weathers the limestone in the hoodoos. Harder layers of mudstone, conglomerate, and siltstone, intermixed with the softer pink layers of limestone, are more resistant to chemical weathering, giving the hoodoos their peculiarly bulging, lumpy shapes—creating a mystical landscape.*

"*Incroyable,*" remarked Lee as she rode under the towering spires and oddly sculpted pinnacles. "They look like gargoyles or tall, scary goblins."

"They look like totem poles," Asazi added, with a hand to his brow, shielding his squinting eyes from the slanting rays of the early evening sun.

"These must be the hoodoos Za-tha spoke of," Addie chimed in eagerly. "But I think they look like fairy chimneys."

"I think they're beautiful," Diane declared. "It looks like an enchanted fairyland," she sighed, returning the field journal to her knapsack.

The tired sun was now setting, casting long, eerie shadows of the hoodoos onto the still-resistant cliff walls and fins before them. Through a yellowish haze, movement on the top of one of the hoodoos caught Diane's eye.

"Up there!" she shouted, gesturing in alarm to the top of the hoodoo on her left, her green eyes wide and sharply focused.

"This must be the right way," Lee replied. "*Voila,* that's a coyote!"

The clan stopped dead in their tracks as they watched more

and more coyotes step forward to the edge of their lookouts atop the spooky hoodoos nearby. They were surrounded.

"This is Coyote Canyon," Asazi confirmed in a most solemn tone. "Sit up tall in your saddle, look them fiercely in the eye, bare your teeth, and growl loudly," he instructed, then shutting his eyes, he offered a silent prayer to Mother Earth and the ancient spirits.

Feeling a pinch silly, everyone followed his instructions, and the adventurers took on a menacing, formidable front. Diane took off her white hat and flailed it above her head as she bared her teeth and growled as loudly as she could. Benji waved his cowboy hat. Addie flapped her duster, while Lee removed her raccoon cap and swung it about wildly in a most frightening display that baffled the guardians.

Even Sa'ami raised up on his hind legs and roared fiercely, his growls reverberating off the rock hoodoos, confounding the coyotes even more. Niki stayed curled in the bear's fur, trembling. The guardians slowly stepped back from their perches. Cowering, the thick gray and red fur on the back of their necks stood up stiffly as their piercing yellowish-green eyes glittered in the setting sun, allowing the clan passage.

"Whew!" said Benji, blotting his brow as Sa'ami's front paws hit the ground with a heavy thud, rocking Benji on his back. "So now, how do we find the Red Rock People?"

"We follow the path of the sun until it reaches the horizon," Asazi answered, nudging Forjon.

They slowly continued through the meandering canyon walls and scary hoodoos, under Limber pines, by Greenleaf Manzanita shrubs until they reached an open amphitheater, where the canyon spread wide to the left and to the right, blocked by a solid wall of red rock. The clan reverently got off their horses, walking them solemnly into the open semicircular space beneath the immense "red wall," and stood silently still—waiting.

After some time, "Now, what do we do?" asked Addie, leaning slightly toward Diane, whispering into her ear. Diane shrugged her shoulders, closed her eyes, and clasped her white scarf, asking her inner guidance for an answer.

At that moment, the last ray of light of the setting sun beamed over the red wall before them and cast its magical light onto several huge hoodoos tottering directly behind.

All at once, the coyotes began to howl on top of their hoodoos, their voices echoing loudly through the canyons, magnified by the countless reverberations. The sound was deafening, terrifying, and exciting all at the same time.

Suddenly, dark, voluminous clouds boiled in the sky above the shaded red wall. Thunderous cracks of lightning sparked bright flashes across the ominous sky, casting spidery veins of lightning bolts shattering onto the hoodoos, electrifying them in an explosion of dazzling lights. The ground began to shake, and delicately balanced boulders fell from the hoodoos, crashing noisily onto the canyon floor. The clan scrambled back to avoid the crushing debris.

"*Attentif!*" Lee shouted, jumping back from a tumbling boulder.

Another thunderclap echoed off the canyon walls as Diane pointed to the top of the hoodoos. Her mouth fell wide open, lips barely moving, and no sound could be heard. Following her gaze, all eyes turned slowly up to the hoodoos, then stared in horror as they saw five pairs of giant rock eyes glaring back.

Taking a deep breath, Diane took a step and stood with her hands held high. Asazi squared his shoulders and stepped forward with his palms up in his familiar sign of greeting. His amber eyes stared, locked with the piercing red eyes of the Red Rock People.

Lee, Addie, and Benji followed suit, hands held high, silent, and waiting. Sa'ami stood up on his hind legs and waved his paws in the air. Even little Niki finally peeked out from the fur atop his head. Surveying the others and spying the huge rock giants, the little raccoon, too, stood on the bear's head and waved her paws at the silent stone people that had now taken full form in front of them.

The tallest one in the middle, with a long train of red-rock-carved feathers cascading down his back, stepped forward, holding his hands high in the air, reciprocating their greeting. The ground trembled below the adventurers' feet, and a cloud of red dust showered down upon them.

"Who seeks the Secret of the Ray of Light?" asked the apparent leader, his deep voice rumbling and echoing off the canyon walls. "For its secret is protected, as we are, by the coyotes. They have alerted us of your coming. I know you encountered them on your journey here." He paused. "You heard them tonight, it is certain, giving tribute to the last ray of light."

"I do," said Diane, straightening up, taller and confident, as she looked into his stony eyes. His head towered over hers, at least ten times her height or more. "I seek the Secret of the Ray of Light."

"There is one among you that needs to hear the wisdom of our words. One whose heart is full of anger and resentment. If you are brave enough to hear our words, show yourself," commanded the leader of the Red Rock People.

After a long silence, "*C'est moi*," Lee said, "That's me," taking a long stride forward.

"You show great courage," the leader said warmly.

"Let me tell you a story," he began solemnly. "A long time ago, as the Spirit of the Great Mother Earth looked down upon her world, she saw a handsome young hunter in the woods and fell in love. With a cast of her hand, she caused a great wind to blow through the trees, and within the swirling dust, she appeared in human form as a beautiful young woman. She married the hunter and bore him twin sons.

"After a time, Father Sun grew lonely, missing his conversations with Mother Earth. So, one day, while walking along a cliff near the sea with her sons cradled on her back, a great storm came upon her. Bolts of lightning were cast from the sky and struck Mother Earth, returning her to the Spirit World. There she pleaded for the lives of her two infant sons. So, two more lightning bolts were cast, one striking each infant.

"When the lightning bolts struck their small bodies, they were magically changed. One infant tumbled into the sea and was saved by a pod of dolphins, magically becoming one of them. The other son was found by a wolf mother with two cubs of her own. She adopted the crying infant, who instantly changed into a wolf cub."

"But..." Diane interrupted, completely absorbed in the story and filled with a thousand questions.

Benji gave a quick tug on her duster, signaling for her to wait.

The leader glanced sharply at her and nodded to Benji, acknowledging his wisdom, as he continued, "The brothers grew healthy and strong, learning the ways of their animal forms. In time, Mother Earth whispered to each of them, telling them of their magical powers to change shape from their animal form into their human form at will. She also told them they were not alone, that each had a twin brother. The next day, she arranged for them to meet on the shore beneath the cliff where fate had changed their lives forever.

"The twin brothers became fast friends, and one day, they

found a village of people not far away and stayed, learning the ways of humans. In time, each brother married and had children of his own. To their astonishment, the children born from the seed of the shapeshifters inherited their magical powers. Children of the wolf father became animals of the forest, influenced by whatever animal came near them at birth. An owl sitting in the tree outside the window at the time of birth gave its spirit to the child, and that child grew to be able to change into the owl of that kind. Many of the Forest Children were born as birds of prey, while most others were born of the wolf spirit or other forest animals.

"The children of the other brother were born at the seashore and became dolphins or whales. In time, it became difficult for the children to hide their magical powers, so to protect their secret, the two families moved together to an isolated area that was in a dense forest near the sea, far from the villages of humans. For hundreds of winters, the families lived secretly in peace and harmony, and prospered. The forest and sea provided for the hunters, while the women and children farmed their fields and gathered nature's bounty. The descendants of the twin brothers grew in number until they became two separate villages.

"On a dark, stormy night, their secret was discovered, and the authorities were sent to destroy them. The Forest Children gathered up all they could and hurriedly embarked in their wooden boats and escaped into the raging sea. The Children of the Sea escorted the wooden boats; the dolphins provided fish to eat along the long journey, while the large whales often carried the wooden boats on their backs safely and swiftly across the Great Waters to the West. Finally, they found land and were accepted by mystical people of a great civilization in a New World. Once again, they prospered for a time, only to be discovered and pursued by their enemies from their old land. The shapeshifters escaped and made their way north, ever so far from the sea."

"That's when they met the Aztecs and became the Keepers..." Diane swallowed back her words and shrugged apologetically. All the while, Benji tugged on her duster.

The leader ignored her outburst. "Over time, fewer and fewer Children of the Sea were born with the magical power to change form and eventually, their power was lost. Until one day, the descendants of the Children of the Sea no longer worked together for the good of their village, turning their backs on the Forest Children, for their hearts grew to be filled with jealousy, contempt, and anger. Their hearts had turned to stone, for there was no compassion to be found. Their spiritual leader, a powerful zaman, invoked the Spirit of the Great Mother Earth and asked her to put a spell upon her children, for the Forest Children had done nothing to provoke their hatred. She heard the cry of their zaman, who banished them to these magical canyonlands and turned them all into stone until they learned the lesson of forgiveness."

He paused, looking intently at Lee. "Whatever has happened in your life, whoever has caused you harm or hurt, have compassion and forgive them. Until you've walked in their moccasins, you cannot judge the journey of another. Anger becomes a prison that affects only the bearer of it." With great warmth in his eyes, he paused. "Lastly, and most importantly, forgive yourself. This is the hardest thing to do, for it fills you with guilt. You must also learn to be open and accept forgiveness from others," he concluded. *"Forgiveness is the way to true freedom."*

With these words, great tears welled up in Lee's eyes.

"I forgive you, *mon père*," she said with deep regret. "And...I forgive myself for being angry with you."

Her tears overflowed onto her face and dropped onto the red dust of the earth beneath her feet. The darkened stain looked like blood as it began to magically flow, widening and spreading toward the feet of the hoodoos of the Red Rock People.

All at once, Asazi spoke, standing tall before the leader, seemingly understanding the meaning of the story. "And have the Children of the Sea finally learned the lessons of compassion and forgiveness?"

The great red stone leader lowered his head toward Asazi and glared into his amber eyes. "In you, I recognize my forest brother of the Aszanii, and so I ask, on behalf of my Aszua people, for your forgiveness," he said solemnly.

"Today, the Children of the Sea, known as the Aszua people, will once again join the Forest Children as the Aszanii-Aszua people of one village," Asazi said, reaching into his medicine pouch and taking out a small deerskin bag. From the loosened opening, he poured into the palm of his hand a fine red powder of ochre, sacred to Mother Earth. He blew the red ochre onto the flowing tears of forgiveness. "Accept our forgiveness and forgive yourselves," he said wisely.

As the magical flow touched the red-stone-carved feet, a great swirl of sand from the ground whirled swiftly upward to the top of each hoodoo.

One by one, out popped from a hoodoo the human form of an Aszua freed from the curse of hard-heartedness. Last, and finally, the leader was transformed before their eyes and knelt on his right knee, his head bowed in humility and gratitude at the feet of Asazi. With his people freed from their prison of stone, he turned to his wife and each of his children and gave them a huge hug filled with love and appreciation. He greeted and embraced each of his brethren with warmth and delirious joy.

That night, the adventurers celebrated with the reunited Aszanii-Aszua people around a huge, crackling bonfire. The men had hunted together and downed a deer and javelina while the women foraged for berries, cactus fruit, squash, and all kinds of wild, edible plants. They once again ate together, enjoying the company of one another in a cooperative spirit of neighbor helping neighbor. Hunters and their families danced around the blazing fire after dinner, creating wondrous shadows against the canyon walls that reflected their jubilation and gratitude to the Great Mother Earth for their freedom. And, for their lessons, finally learned.

The Aszua leader sat with the clan of adventurers and asked who led them to this canyon. Diane shared with him the story of their quest for the Secrets of the Five Rays of Light and true wealth, and about the great spiritual leader, Za-tha, who sent them on this most amazing journey.

"I would like to meet this zaman, Za-tha," said the leader of the Aszua people.

"I believe I can arrange that," Diane said with a glint of surprise dappled with a smattering of mischief in her eyes. Opening her amulet, she took out one of the few remaining dinosaur eggshell pieces and tossed it into the bonfire. Once again, great bursts of sparks exploded into the darkened sky and danced with the stars above.

With a puff of white swirling smoke and tiny glittering lights, Za-tha appeared in front of the bonfire. He stepped forward, his hands held high, palms opened.

"Greetings, my beloved brother," Za-tha said to the surprised leader, his silvery-white hair and the yellow beads embroidered on his red shawl shimmered brightly in the firelight.

The startled leader, mouth slightly agape, hesitated, then finally returned the gesture. "In the name of our Great Mother

Earth, thank you, Za-tha, for your wisdom in sending your grandson Asazi to finally free us."

"This quest has served two purposes. You have learned well, my brother," Za-tha said, "and so has our brave clan. Lee, come forward," he commanded.

Lee stepped in front of Za-tha, her head bowed.

"You have shown great compassion and wisdom in releasing your anger, and forgiving your father *and* yourself, just as my brothers have learned the power of forgiveness. You are to remember this moment always," he said solemnly.

With these words he removed an amulet from his long red shawl and draped it over her head, placing it gently around her neck. The tan deerskin amulet was painted with a red hoodoo. He took her hand and held it, palm up, in front of her. He placed his other hand over the heart of the leader and closed his eyes. In a flicker of a flame, he pulled his hand away from the leader's chest and dropped into Lee's open palm a red, rounded pebble of jasper, smoothed and polished.

"Put this talisman in your amulet to always remember the heart of the Red Rock People and the lessons of forgiveness," Za-tha said, the firelight glimmering in his soulful eyes.

Za-tha then turned to Diane and motioned for her to hold out her hand as well. He placed another polished red pebble in her hand and pressed his hand upon her head.

"You have learned well and unlocked the Third Secret of Five Rays of Light; *forgiveness is the way to freedom.* Tomorrow, you will travel southwestward and find the stream that will take you to the place of the Three Patriarchs. When the sun sets between their peaks, it will light the way to Angels Landing, where, *with crystal clarity, you'll discover the fourth secret of true wealth.* But BEWARE! It is well guarded, and only an innocent heart filled with joy can pass and possess its secret."

With that, he turned to Addie and smiled warmly, placing a red jasper pebble in her amulet, and then turned to Benji, patting him lovingly on the head.

At last, Za-tha turned back to the leader of the Aszua. "This night, I will send a messenger to guide your people to our village where we will once again be of one heart.

"Behold. Let it be so!" he said, and he stretched out his arms toward the starry sky and disappeared into the fire.

Huddled around the blazing campfire, the leader of the Aszua people, pensively staring into the flames, looked up into Diane's bright green eyes. "So, your quest is taking you on a journey to find the secrets of true wealth," he said, stirring the fire.

"Yes," she said, nodding.

"Surely you must be wise and courageous for such an undertaking as this," he said, reaching into his deerskin pouch that was strapped around his waist. He removed five oddly rounded stones of gleaming amber and held them up to the firelight. "Amber has powerful earth energy that will give you wisdom, patience, and confidence. It will help you make good decisions and bring balance into your life," he said sagely.

Hmm, balance, Diane reflected. *Something my father is always talking about.*

He took Diane's hand and held it palm up, placing a glistening stone in it. "May this amber aid you on your journey." He turned and gave each clan member one as well.

When he came to Benji, he stopped. "You have shown respect and wisdom this night as I told the story of our people.

For that, I'd like to give you a very special stone," holding up the largest of the five pieces of amber in the light of the flames.

Benji squinted and saw the black silhouette of a... grasshopper? His eyebrows furrowed, bewildered.

"This grasshopper was captured in this stone, thus capturing its essence. The grasshopper's totem removes any obstacle that may stand in your way to success and prosperity. It brings the bearer of this stone great abundance and good luck. You shall be the keeper of its magic," the leader said, handing the quarter-size stone to an awestruck Benji.

Benji, ogling the amber, mumbled, "Thank you," and gingerly placed the stone in his pocket along with his other treasures.

That night Lee danced with the freed Aszua people. She danced with the stars, her heart freed from anger and filled instead with the light-heartedness and peace only forgiveness can bring. She danced as if she could fly and soar off the earth, glide among the clouds and around the moon.

Diane, Addie, Asazi, even Benji joined in the dance of freedom around the fire, lifted by the joy and jubilation Lee and the Aszua people felt in their hearts.

Tomorrow was another day, another adventure, but tonight they danced—wild and free!

CHAPTER THIRTY-FOUR

ROCKSLIDE IN THE NARROWS

T he huge yellow orb slowly rose in the sky while its morning light silently crept down the red wall toward the canyon floor. Nestled next to Diane's head, little Niki placed her tiny black paw on the sleepy-eyed adventurer's forehead, as if purposely holding her down, and began to lick her nose. Diane opened her bleary eyes to see two little black sparkles in a bandit mask staring down at her and chattering away while the baby raccoon cleansed her face.

"Niki!" she squealed, sitting up quickly, rolling Niki away in a somersault. "Oh, I'm so sorry," Diane said. "Come here, little one," she coaxed, holding out her hands. Cautiously, Niki hesitantly crawled back into her waiting hands, with her little striped tail tucked between her hind legs.

Diane scooped her up and held her right to her face, nose to nose, and gave her a little kiss on the bridge of her nose, that special space between her black eyes, where she always kissed her Daisy dog back home. At that moment, she thought of Daisy and her mother and father, feeling a little homesick. It seemed like forever since she had said goodbye to them on that train platform.

Gazing around her, she realized that the Aszua people had vanished. She guessed that the messenger must have come in the night, and they had gone to rejoin the Aszanii village. *I wonder who the messenger was,* she pondered, as she put a squirming Niki down, who quickly scampered off to wake Lee in a similar fashion. *I would have liked to have met them.*

Still pondering, Diane shook Benji awake from his bear hug with Sa'ami and heard Lee giggling. She then rolled over to Addie, who opened her eyes immediately, a little startled at first, then sighed as she looked into Diane's friendly green eyes.

"Where's Asazi?" Diane asked.

Addie shrugged her shoulders as she looked toward his empty bedroll laid out next to hers. Just then, he sauntered up to the sleepy clan, still snug in their blankets.

"I've watered and fed the horses and filled our water canteens," he said, looking quite content.

Someday he'll make a great leader, Diane considered.

"The village people departed sometime before sunrise and left us traveling food for our journey. I've packed it, so we are ready to go. If we leave now, we should make the place of the Three Patriarchs before sunset," he said, offering his hand to help Addie out of her sleeping blanket.

He is indeed responsible and considerate, Diane decided, propping herself up on an elbow. *Something I'd like to be more of myself.*

"Let's go then," Diane said with glee. "I can't wait to see what the next secret will bring." She sprang from her sleeping blanket, rolled it up quickly, and fastened it to Mavric's saddle. "And the adventure continues!" she shouted as she mounted her black stallion and trotted off, then stopped abruptly, looking for Benji.

She spied him tugging on Sa'ami's ear, headed to a nearby alligator juniper tree with low-hanging branches. Its thick gray bark, broken in deeply cut layered squares, looked just like the rough hide of an old alligator. He dragged, pushed, and pulled, carefully positioning Sa'ami under a branch, then nimbly climbed the tree.

Straddling the branch, he shimmied across the scaly bark and then swung under it, dropping artfully onto Sa'ami's waiting back. Grinning from ear to ear, looking quite pleased with himself, Benji patted Sa'ami on the head and hugged his bristly neck. Diane smothered a chuckle and gently gripped Mavric's sides with her knees and squeezed, urging him forward. "Let's go, Mavric," she said, patting his black, sleek neck.

Cheering Benji on, everyone quickly followed her lead, and soon the clan was on the dusty trail again, headed to the stream that would lead them southward to the Three Patriarchs and the secret hidden at Angels Landing. The sun was radiantly white overhead, the dry western air hot and almost suffocatingly still.

A few turkey vultures circled high in the powder-blue sky. From the ground, they were marked by their V-shaped grayish-white flight feathers and wrinkly, red, naked heads as they floated effortlessly on thermals, sniffing for carrion, the decaying flesh of dead animals.

Diane watched the buzzards' effortless flight, feeling a sense of their freedom as they flew through fossiliferous clouds, reminding her of bony sections of broken vertebrae scattered across the sky.

She brushed away a pesky deerfly that kept circling her sweaty neck. "Ouch! That hurt," she cried hotly, slapping her neck, as it successfully landed and bit. A red welt was already swelling.

Asazi rode by and offered her a small container of the

aspen salve he had used on Addie's pricked finger. "Here, put this on the welt," he said, "It'll soothe the pain. A gift from the Mother."

"Thank you," she said as she smeared it on. *I've got to write this down in my field journal,* she promised herself, already feeling its healing power. "What's in it?"

"I made this from aspen bark and bear grease," he said as he rode off to find Benji.

They found the stream around noon and guided their horses into the shallow, clear water, then headed downstream. The cool water refreshed them as it splashed against their legs, and the horses seemed to enjoy it as well. The soft, silty bottom was easy on their hot, tired feet. They had covered a lot of miles over the past few days, and this part of the journey was the best so far, from the horses' point of view.

Mavric pranced along with his head held high, black mane blowing in a warm, summer breeze, and whinnied his approval continuously.

Sa'ami lumbered along, dragging behind with Benji slumped over on his back. Noticing, Asazi rode up to the giant bear and asked, "What troubles you, my little friend?"

Benji scowled, hating the word "little." Ignoring the comment, he muttered, "Did the Children of the Sea become jealous and angry because they didn't feel special anymore?"

"I believe that may be where the seed of contempt grew," Asazi responded tenderly.

Benji took a deep breath, pain etched into his face, as he looked up into Asazi's warm eyes. "I feel that way sometimes."

"Ah," Asazi said, nodding his head, "Your sister is indeed special," as if reading his mind. "Can I tell you a secret?"

Benji sat up tall on the back of Sa'ami, listening intently.

"So is a boy who rides the back of a giant black bear!"

Asazi said kindly. "We are all special in our own way. It is your journey to discover *how* you are special and to use your uniqueness for the good of everyone. Most importantly, honor and respect what is special in others. Then, you are free to enjoy your own."

Beaming, like a huge weight had been lifted from his young soul, Benji thanked Asazi and gave Sa'ami a quick kick to catch up with his sister.

Growing bored of the endless landscape, Benji clambered from Sa'ami onto Mavric's back and turned, riding backward, to practice his boomerang. Diane could hear him grunt as he threw it and then giggled when it came flying back into his waiting hand. He was getting really good with it and growing in confidence. Her heart smiled, enjoying his giggles of accomplishment.

Still tired from the night before and the exertion of his boomerang practice, Benji turned back around. Wrapping his small arms around his sister's waist, he rested his head against her back. Before nodding off to sleep, he mumbled, "Di, where's the gold of Cibola?"

Diane just grinned as she held his stubby hands in hers.

Up ahead, the grassy plains became dotted with oddly shaped domes of white sandstone crisscrossed with lines, like a shimmering, stony checkerboard. As they approached, the domes seemed to grow surprisingly larger and stretched all the way down to the stream's edge.

Remnants of sand dunes long past. These peculiar rock sculptures evidenced the continuous layering of drifting sands from winds that once blew across the ancient desert basin that once dominated this landscape, creating the cross-bedding feature on the eroded relics. Turned to stone, the sandstone formations were exposed to the weathering ravages of freezing and thawing that caused the vertical striations, or fracture lines, on their surface. The unusual combination of horizontal layers, crossed with vertical lines, gave it the look of a giant stone checkerboard.

The clan of adventurers rode by and marveled at one of the huge checkboard domes with a flat top.

"That's called a mesa, which means 'table' in Spanish," gleamed Diane, the amateur geologist, as she pointed to its flat top. "'Checkerboard mesa' would be a fun name for it," she chortled.

The stream entered a meandering canyon of steeply sculpted red sandstone whose walls were the highest they had yet encountered on their journey, towering over a thousand feet or so. On the smooth red rock surfaces, high above their heads, were beautifully carved arches where the cliff face had fractured and weathered, causing huge pieces of its surface to fall away, exposing the true white sandstone behind it.

"Sandstone naturally breaks this way—in magnificent arches," she continued her geology lesson. "The red color comes from iron oxide in the sedimentary layer above. It's like the stone rusts," she chuckled. "Rains and springs seeping through the rock layer wash the red color downward, staining the white sandstone below. See there?" She pointed, thrilled again to be witnessing with her own eyes, earth's wondrous creations and processes that she had only read about in her schoolbooks.

Along fracture cracks that ran horizontally across the cliff faces, lush hanging gardens of wild plants and flowers flourished, their roots fed by the seeping water percolating through the semiporous sandstone as gravity pulled it downward. The canyon walls grew higher and closer to the edges of the stream, creating a dangerous, narrow passageway completely shaded from the sun.

"Why are the walls stained black along the bottom?" Addie asked, catching the geology bug, too.

"I think it means that this passageway is flooded occasionally, probably in the spring," Diane surmised. "The black is most likely from the minerals in the water."

"I wouldn't want to be caught in a flash flood in here," Lee muttered, cringing.

They stopped and jumped off their horses to let them rest and drink from the stream, relishing the cool breezes of the narrow canyon's shade.

"Look here," Asazi said, standing next to a low-hanging garden. "This is alum." He held up a plant with a broad green leaf in the palm of his hand. "You take the root and break it, then hold it on a cut. It will instantly stop the bleeding." He wrapped his fingers around the stem of the plant and gently pulled the roots from the rock crevice, placing the plant in his medicine bag. "The Great Mother Earth has provided all the food and medicines her Earth children need to survive and thrive. It is up to us to protect these natural gifts by first learning about them. Knowledge brings appreciation. Appreciation brings responsibility to preserve for all to benefit and enjoy," he sagely concluded.

"My papa uses that root when he cuts himself shaving," added Lee. "I've seen him pull it out from underneath boulders, or he sometimes finds it in cracks in rock walls like these."

Diane shook her head, marveling at all the gifts nature provided. *How many plants?* she pondered.

Asazi saw the quizzical look on her face. "My village uses almost all of nature's plants for either medicine or food. The few we don't, offer us their beauty," he said pensively.

"See this?" Addie asked, walking up to them with a long,

slender, reed-like plant in her hand. "This is a Chinese puzzle," she shared, pulling the plant apart into nature-cut segments and laying them in the palm of her hand. "Here, Benji. Try and put the puzzle pieces back together," she directed.

Benji took the sturdy green pieces from her hand. He loved puzzles and immediately went about the task of putting the cylindrical reed back together in proper order.

"My people call that plant 'horsetail,'" Asazi offered. "It's glass-like fibers are very strong, and the women use it to scour their bowls when they clean them."

Diane loved learning about the medicinal and useful qualities of nature's plants and decided to add them to her studies when she settled in Phoenix. *I must remember to add horsetail to my notes tonight,* she promised herself.

They clambered back onto their horses and continued down the narrow canyon. Blocked by the high, sculpted walls, they saw only a sliver of the sky above and had no idea of the time. Suddenly, they heard a loud, thundering crash, followed by an avalanche of sound, presumably from the flaking off of another large arch of sandstone somewhere upstream, but not so far behind them. The raucous noise echoed through the placid canyon, bouncing off the walls in a deafening chorus of falling stone.

They covered their ears with their hands as the horses reared up at the terrifying, ear-shattering sound. Diane reached forward and cupped her hands over Mavric's aching ears to shield them from the painful clamor, and he immediately calmed down and steadied himself. Everyone else did the same. Even Sa'ami held his big bear paws over his ears, lashing his head wildly from side to side. Poor little Niki just buried herself deeper into Lee's fur cap, trembling.

Just then, a rolling cloud of rock debris filled the entire

canyon like a flash flood flowing toward them. The horses had enough of the narrow canyon and darted forward, frenetically galloping downstream to escape the mysterious cloud of choking dust as their riders held on for dear life.

Benji squeezed Diane so tightly, he practically cut off her ability to breathe. She leaned forward and hugged Mavric's neck, grasping strands of his black mane in her fingers. Benji lay snugly across her back, squeezing even tighter, burying his head in her back. The ride would have been exhilarating if it weren't so frightful. They both shut their eyes and breathed in heaving bursts in rhythm with Mavric's expanding chest.

"Hold on!" she screamed, out of instinct and fear more than anything else.

Finally, the sandstone walls opened into a wide canyon surrounded by steep cliffs and majestic peaks. The dazzling sun poured in, blinding horses and riders alike. The sightless horses, as if afraid of what might be lurking ahead, came to an abrupt halt, panting, snorting, and hoofing the ground nervously.

"Is everyone alright?" Asazi yelled, pulling hard on his reins, turning Forjon furiously in circles to make sure his clan was safe and unharmed.

"Cool beans!" responded Lee breathlessly. She clearly seemed to enjoy the speed of the harried ride.

"We're good!" Diane called from behind, her cheeks flushed red, at last released from Benji's suffocating hold.

Rohan came to such an abrupt stop that he threw Addie off. Tumbling over his head, she landed awkwardly on the rock-strewn canyon floor, injuring her ankle. Asazi jumped off Forjon and ran to her rescue. He lifted her gently off the stony ground. She winced with pain when she tried to take a step, putting pressure on her lacerated and swelling ankle. He helped her hobble to a boulder in the cool stream and instructed her to keep her ankle submerged in the chilly water.

"It'll keep down the swelling and cleanse that bleeding gash," Asazi advised, as he reached into his medicine bag and retrieved the alum he had collected earlier.

Breaking the alum root, he lifted Addie's leg from the water, dried it with deerskin, and applied the broken end of the root directly along the cut. Watching over his shoulder, Diane could hardly believe her eyes as the wound almost magically stopped bleeding. "That was fantastic," she mumbled, convinced that she was definitely going to learn more about medicinal plants.

"It's only a sprain," Asazi reported after closely inspecting the reddening ankle and applying some aspen salve to keep down the swelling. "It'll be fine, but sore."

"Where's Sa'ami?" Benji yelled in a panic.

All heads turned, looking anxiously for their beloved traveling companion. Streams of minuscule rays of light created the soft golden haze that engulfed the canyon narrows from which they emerged, blinding their ability to see.

"There he is!" shrieked Benji, pointing upstream. Sa'ami came hurtling through the curtain of light, bouncing and tossing his head wildly. Benji jumped off Mavric and dashed toward his beloved friend but stopped suddenly as Sa'ami knocked him over onto his back and began smothering him with bear kisses and slobbering licks.

"Yuck! Sa'ami, stop that," he chortled, swiping bear saliva from his cheeks. He grabbed Sa'ami by his bristly jowls and kissed his muzzle, happy to see him, too.

Just then, the shrouded sun broke from behind the pewter clouds that had scattered its light, revealing its location in the sky. They had traveled longer than they realized in the narrows of the canyon, and the sun had already begun its evening descent.

CHAPTER THIRTY-FIVE

ANGELS LANDING

"**L**ook!" shouted Diane, gesturing toward the horizon below the path of the burning orange orb. "The Three Patriarchs!" Just beneath the sinking sphere were three monumental peaks tipped in gleaming white sandstone. The sun was clearly on a trajectory between the two peaks on the right.

"*Incroyable!*" resounded Lee. "Look at the Ray of Light!"

As the setting sun began its lazy descent between the peaks, it shot a white beam to the canyon floor that slowly climbed up the face of the huge rock formation opposite them.

"There it is!" said Diane briskly. "That's Angels Landing!" She pointed to a protruding ledge high up on the monolith, where a curious rock carving that looked like an angel with outstretched wings was sculpted into the wall above it.

"How are we going to get up there?" Lee mumbled back, a quiver of fear spasmed across her face.

"Over there." Asazi pointed to the narrow path carved into the rock cliff.

"*Incroyable,*" Lee muttered jerkily.

Asazi saw the look of panic on Lee's face and knew the challenge immediately. He turned to Benji and Diane.

"Are you two up for a climb?" he asked soberly.

They both nodded vigorously.

Asazi would lead the way, but before leaving, he spoke quietly to Lee. "You stay here," he directed, "and protect Addie and the animals. Keep her leg in the cool stream to bring down the swelling. Her injury is not too bad, but the swelling could be a problem for her later." He then reached into his medicine bag again and removed a pouch of coarsely ground aspen bark and leaves. "Make a fire and boil some water to make a tea of this medicine for her pain. Tell her to sip it slowly."

Lee exhaled with relief, looking content to sit out this adventure, and immediately set to task gathering firewood.

Diane watched their encounter. She appreciated Asazi's method of leading with compassion and making sure Lee still felt important and offered value to the clan. Even if she was evidently afraid of heights.

A rocky trail had been carved into the sandstone wall that would take them to the ledge at Angels Landing, perched a thousand feet above the canyon floor. Diane gulped down her fear as she gazed upward and took her first step. She had no particular fear of heights, but this was definitely putting *her* to the test. She could hear her heart pumping in her ears, and beads of sweat moistened the bridge of her nose.

Benji glanced sheepishly at his sister but mustered his courage and took a step onto the trail behind her. They hiked the steep switchbacks until the path narrowed treacherously to only a foot wide. Pressing their backs hard against the rock wall, they cautiously inched their way upward. The wind-polished rock surface was solid and flat, offering few pockets or crevices for handholds. The path zigzagged higher and higher across the tall monolith of white sandstone, glittering in the beam of light.

The sun was nearing the bottom of the V-shaped valley between the peaks, and with its cooling effects upon the earth, the evening winds began to blow, and blow strongly indeed. A sudden gust could easily push a person off the perilous trail. The wind rippled across their clothing like billowing sails on a windjammer. Benji was nearly lifted from his feet in the gale and scuttled closer behind his sister, quivering slightly. The last ray of light now shone brightly on Angels Landing.

"There it is!" Diane cried out above the sound of the howling winds.

"I wonder what's guarding the secret!" Benji yelled back, remembering Za-tha's warning.

"We'll soon find out!" his sister shouted back, finally stepping onto the huge stone ledge.

With crystal clarity you will discover the secret to true wealth, she repeated to herself as she stood on the landing and peered over the edge one thousand feet below, waving to her friends. Lee could hardly look up. She waved weakly, and quickly glanced away. Diane turned to inspect the cliff wall itself, and her jaw fell open.

The last ray of light illuminated a small stony cavity in the cliff wall beneath the angel rock sculpture. A geode embedded in the rock wall was broken open and filled with clear quartz crystals that sparkled like brilliant diamonds in the setting sun.

"Benji, look!" she shouted, dipping her hand into the rock cavity and scooping out a handful of glistening crystals to show him.

"Golly gee!" he mouthed, his words lost to the gusting winds as he inched his way onto the landing. Asazi was following not far behind, struggling against the forceful winds.

All at once, Diane saw a blur of movement behind Asazi,

just a few feet farther down the treacherous trail. She shouted a shrill warning, but the howling wind carried her voice away and swept it downward through the canyon walls to the ears of her friends, who now looked up at her in shock and horror.

A gathering of guardian rattlesnakes was slithering up the narrow trail behind Asazi. Benji couldn't hear what his sister was saying, but the look of terror etched on her face pricked the hairs on the back of his neck. He stopped dead in his tracks. Behind Diane he saw the triangular-shaped head of a gigantic rattlesnake. Its body was at least twenty feet long, with shimmering dark diamonds patterned down its thick body, the size of a large tree branch, with orange eyes squinting through slits of fury. It was coiled and poised to strike—icy venom dripping in silvery threads from yellowish, razor-sharp fangs.

Lightning-quick, Benji whipped his boomerang off his belt and, steeling himself, flung it with all his might toward his startled sister. Her eyes bulged. Goggling the oncoming projectile, she dropped to her knees just as the boomerang whizzed over her head and struck the rattlesnake directly in its open jaws. The snake flailed and thrashed about, trying to dislodge the weapon from its throat as horrible, guttural gasps spewed forth from the struggling monster. Diane hadn't seen the ghastly giant behind her until it dropped exhausted across her back. Its long, forked tongue flopped over her shoulder with a lingering hiss.

Screaming and waving her hands wildly, she jumped up and down as she tossed the twitching body off her back. Regaining enough strength, the snake turned and slowly slithered away, still choking on the boomerang. Benji dashed to his sister, hugging her tightly. Diane squeezed him back, her eyes watering, so very appreciative of her courageous brother. Asazi followed quickly behind and joined them on the landing, alarmed.

"There's more behind me," he said, catching his breath, and then hesitated, "and more behind you!" He pointed to another gathering of rattlesnakes wriggling on the trail from beyond the landing.

The sight was bewildering. Diane's mind reeled. She had read that rattlesnakes were known to sometimes den together, but they were solitary hunters! This swarm-like behavior was as if they were possessed or bewitched in some way. It was frightening and spine-tingling.

Suddenly, Asazi grasped onto his amulet, mouthed a magical spell, and in a glittering of tiny lights, changed into a large gray wolf with glowing amber eyes. The wolf turned his bristling back to Diane and Benji and, taking a powerful protective stance, snarled menacingly at the approaching rattlesnakes.

Shaking her head in utter disbelief, Diane grasped her white scarf tightly in her hand and closed her eyes, calling upon her inner guidance for assistance. *Help! Oh, please help us!* She was screaming in her head, desperate for an answer. All at once, a brilliantly white light emanated from her scarf and, from the corner of her eye, she caught movement on the rock face above the crystal-filled geode.

From the white rock that looked like the spread wings of an angel, she watched in awe as the enormous wings and body of a huge golden eagle emerged and swooped down, perching on the edge of the landing behind the frightened adventurers. The golden eagle turned its head and nodded, beckoning for them to climb upon its back.

"Jump on!" yelled Diane, as she dashed across the stony landing and leaped onto the huge eagle, clutching ahold of its slippery feathers with her long fingers.

Benji followed, then Asazi, transforming back into his human form in a cascade of glittering lights as he leaped from the landing. Grasping onto each other, the eagle spread its huge wings and fell forward, gliding effortlessly into the wind just as the two gatherings of rattlesnakes met on the landing, coiled, and sprang off the ledge after them. As they fell, the rattlesnakes turned pale as ghosts and vanished, wriggling into the wind.

Cold air whipped over Diane's cheeks as she smashed her hat flat on her head and leaned into the raptor's powerful neck. Squinting hard, her watering eyes stung. The eagle turned and soared along the red canyon walls. The three adventurers squeezed their knees into the sides of the golden rescuer as they clung to its back, swiftly circling downward.

Just then, Diane glanced toward the valley floor and saw three bedraggled, dust-covered figures skulking in the canyon shadows just behind Addie and Lee as they tensely watched their friends soaring hundreds of feet above their heads. Her stomach tightened into a sickening knot of helplessness.

Emerging from the shadows, Diane recognized the three hobbling Thorn brothers as they crept along the cliffside, hiding among the darkened trees. *Caught in the rockslide,* she surmised, as their clothing was ripped and shredded from the sharp rock shards that had fallen upon them like broken glass.

Their horses must have thrown them, she guessed, looking up the canyon and spying three bucking horses darting off like outlaws, taking the rest of Estebanico's gold with them.

"What in tarnation?" Diane heard Ramus thunder, as the biggest black bear he ever laid eyes on growled at his backside, swatting the ground with his forepaws. Emitting rumbling, blowing noises, the bear mock-charged them several times, then stood on his powerful hind legs, towering high over their heads, his sharp claws thrashing the air.

Lee and Addie turned to see what all the commotion was

when they heard the three brothers shriek and watched them scamper hurriedly toward the rock trail to Angels Landing with Sa'ami hot on their heels.

Both Benji and Asazi followed their gaze as the brothers quickly scurried up the pathway that was too narrow for the large bear. Lumbering behind, Sa'ami stopped abruptly at the trailhead and paced back and forth, seemingly frustrated that he could go no further. He snarled a threatening low grumble, then ROARED—foaming spittle flew from his huge open jaws through his large white canines. The hair on his powerful neck spiked with rage, he angrily swayed from one front paw to another as he glared at the ascending brothers.

In no time, spurred by Sa'ami's growls, the Thorn brothers were standing on Angels Landing at last, glowing in triumph. Ramus haughtily led the way to the geode of crystals in the cliff face, his brothers scuttling behind him, smirking. He scooped up a handful of crystals. Wadey and Duffy did the same. Looking quite smug, they turned and stood on the edge of the landing, holding up their riches into the diminishing light.

Diane realized just then that the brothers must have seen her holding up the handful of crystals and thought they were "diamonds" glimmering in the setting sun. In a flicker of a moment, it was obvious to her that the greedy brothers had made up their minds that they were going to take all of the clan's treasures—the whole kit and caboodle—if they could get their hands on it.

All at once, the crystals in their hands started to vibrate and wriggle, transforming into tiny, squirming rattlesnakes that grew in size before the outlaws' bulging eyes. Shrieking, they threw the squiggling rattlers up into the sky, and as they fell, the enormous diamond-backed vipers engulfed the brothers in a swirling mass of venomous wrath. From their gnashing fangs burst forth radiant streaks of blinding light, flashing into the twilight.

Standing in the flailing mass, Diane could almost feel Ramus Thorn seething, his face contorted and twitching. With sickening cries of pain, the brothers began to wither and fade before her eyes. Ramus' pale, gaunt face and shaking arm appeared for a last time from the serpentine swirl. His dark eyes glared savagely down at Diane as he waggled a threatening fist at her. And then, in a final explosion of light, Ramus, his brothers, and the mass of rattlesnakes vanished from sight, leaving only an eerie green vapor floating above the landing.

As they soared along the red canyon walls, spiraling downward, Diane stared, transfixed, at the bewitching scene above them on the landing. Benji cringed, burying his head into his sister's back. Diane tore her eyes from the grisly sight and looked to the red rock walls to clear away the vision. *Awful, just awful.* She felt a tad sick to her stomach. The chilly evening air swept over her. Shivering, she pulled her duster tightly around her and pondered. *Their greed gobbled them up. So sad,* she mumbled to herself.

As the golden eagle made its last swooping circle along the steep canyon walls, it suddenly turned, diving sharply downward, its riders grasping tightly as it finally reached the canyon floor. Its huge, powerful wings fluttered as the eagle's talons touched the ground, and the adventurers dropped one by one, landing safely. The raptor squawked loudly, and flapping its massive wings, changed once again into Za-tha in a flood of glittering lights.

He stood before them, his robe billowing in the chilly wind as he held his hands high, extended forward in his familiar greeting. In a flash, Diane ran into his outstretched arms and gave him a great big bear hug that nearly toppled him.

"Greetings, child," he said, somewhat taken aback by her outpouring of innocent affection.

"I know what the fourth Secret of the Ray of Light is," she said ecstatically, tucking a wisp of hair behind her ear.

"And what is that, my child?" he asked, surprised.

"Joy!" she said fervidly, her heart still racing, "Joy from appreciating what you have."

He smiled approvingly, nodding his head with great pride. He raised a wiry white eyebrow. "And how did you come by this great wisdom?"

"When my brother Benji saved me from that horrible giant rattlesnake and ran into my arms, I *knew* how much I loved and appreciated him. I saw the greatness in him, and I'll never see him any other way again. In that moment, I felt so much love and joy that I thought I was going to burst," she panted, pausing a moment to catch her breath. "And then, when we were flying, I felt so—*free*. I knew it all came together—love, appreciation, joy, and freedom. I think it can all be summed up with joy, the greatest feeling of all. That is true wealth—*joy*." She finally stopped and waited patiently.

With a glint in his eye, Za-tha smothered a chuckle. "You have learned well." He nodded once again. "Appreciation is indeed the key to joy!"

Diane dipped into her vest pocket, then held out her hand filled with crystals. "These represent the clarity of life, the seeking of joy in all that we do, don't they?" she offered.

"And so they do!" he agreed as he reached into her hand and selected a perfect crystal, which he dropped into her amulet. She bowed her head humbly in respect for this wise old zaman.

"Thank you," she said, beaming.

"Now, it's your turn." He motioned to her, and she understood.

She selected crystals for Lee and Addie and dropped them into each of their amulets. The quiet ceremony electrified the air with a sense of awe and reverence. She turned to Benji and looked soulfully at Za-tha.

"He has earned one, too!" she said pensively.

"Most certainly, he has," Za-tha said, turning to look into Benji's hopeful eyes. "What have you learned from this quest?" he asked solemnly.

Benji was startled by the zaman's question and gulped loudly, pondering. His furrowed eyebrows lifted, his eyes wide and bright as he replied, "Riches are not just in your pocket but also in your heart." Nervously, he shuffled his cowboy boot in the red dirt, awaiting Za-tha's reaction.

"And so they are," said Za-tha. He gladly acquiesced and pulled from his red shawl an amulet, the size of a small change purse, with a picture of a coiled rattlesnake painted on it, and draped it over Benji's small neck.

Diane stepped in front of her brother and selected the largest, clearest crystal of all and placed it into his amulet. Tears of joy trickled down her cheeks, and she gave her precious brother a loving hug.

"You're not little anymore, Benji," she said proudly. "From now on, it's just Benji, my courageous brother. You're forever tall in my eyes." She squeezed him hard.

"You hug just like Sa'ami," he said, squirming and laughing as he hugged her back just as tightly.

She paused in front of Asazi, reflecting on those amber eyes as she stared into them, "Thank you," was all she could muster. Feeling speechless, she shrugged and gave him a tender hug.

"You're welcome," he said, understanding her bewilderment.

"Rest here tonight," Za-tha instructed. "In this valley, you'll be safe, and the Three Patriarchs will watch over you and protect you. Tomorrow, you will complete your quest with the last part of your journey to the grandest canyon of all. Head southeast to an enchanted forest lake, then due south from there to reach the canyon. You will cross a raging white river and follow along the river's southern trail until you ascend the Devil's Corkscrew. It will lead you to the ancient Indian Gardens of the Ancestral Pueblo People, Hualapai, and the Havasupai—People of the Blue-Green Waters. There, you will *be greeted by the Fifth Secret of the Ray of Light as the sun sets on this sacred place.*"

Za-tha then stretched out his arms and said, "Let it be so!"

Changing back into the majestic golden eagle, he flew away toward the white peaks of the Three Patriarchs with a trail of glittering lights, then vanished into the darkening sky.

CHAPTER THIRTY-SIX

MORNING FROLIC

A speck of golden light glinted off the highest white peak of the towering stone fathers as the first crimson splashes of dawn began to paint the cliff walls below. The monolithic peaks stood majestically against a turquoise sky, remnants of ancient times and ancient environments long vanished. Wispy white clouds, like ostrich plumes, feathered the blue horizon.

Rock swallows swooped down over the heads of the adventurers as they slept in the canyon under the protective shadows of the Three Patriarchs. Their sweet morning songs echoed against the deceptive red walls, carried on a cool canyon breeze, waking Diane from her restful sleep. She stretched and yawned; her arms raised in open greeting to the dawning day.

She rolled over to see Benji sleeping, nestled in his bedroll next to her. His mouth was open, and a small canyon butterfly was flying gently up and down on the current of his breathing. Sa'ami was snoring nearby.

I could live here forever, she said to herself. "I love nature," she whispered so the Great Mother Earth could hear her. She then started a game that she decided she would play every day when she awoke.

What do I appreciate right now in this moment? She began the game. *The cool breeze across my face that's tickling my hair. The sound of the running stream as it trips over boulders and splashes onto rocks. That blue sky above, and those magnificent, powerful white monuments glistening in the morning sun. My brother and my mother and father and Daisy back home. Za-tha and his great wisdom. Great Mother Earth and all her creations. My new friends and their kindness and willingness to go on this journey with me. This quest and all that I have learned and experienced.*

As she continued to enumerate the things that she appreciated, a feeling of peace came over her, and she sighed out loud. *This is what joy feels like,* she mused, and feeling deeply contented, she snuggled back into the warmth of her sleeping blanket and said a prayer of gratitude for all her blessings.

Just then, she heard Sa'ami grumble and moan his morning greeting, and a loud THUD of his paw as he swatted an annoying fly buzzing around his head. Diane watched as little Niki crawled sleepily out of Lee's cap and slowly crept toward her. She pretended to be asleep as Niki gently plopped down next to her ear and placed her little black paw across her forehead, holding her down to begin the morning face-washing routine. Niki's tiny tongue was rough, and her whiskers tickled Diane's nose. She began to squirm, so Niki pressed down more firmly, determined to complete her task.

Addie awoke and chuckled at the scene.

"Why is she doing this?" Diane asked her, smothering a giggle.

"I don't know. I'll ask her." Addie went into her dancing-hand trance.

Niki immediately stopped and looked directly at Addie, her little ears perked and twitching. For a moment or two, they carried on a seemingly magical conversation. Finally, the twitching stopped, and Niki resumed her face washing, the conversation apparently over.

"So, what did she say?" Diane asked impatiently.

"She said she was taking care of you. That it's her job to do so," Addie replied brightly.

Diane looked at Niki lovingly. Picking her up under her two front legs, Diane held her close to her face, looking deeply through her mask and into her beady black eyes. She gave her a kiss on her little nose and hugged her gently to her chest. "I love you, Niki," she said tenderly.

"She knows," Addie assured her. "She can feel the love in your heart for all animals."

At their giggling, Benji awoke, and the butterfly flew away. "W-what's going on?" he stammered, yawning and wiping the drool from the corner of his mouth.

"Nothing really," Diane murmured, "just getting my morning face washing from Niki."

The girls giggled again, and with that, Niki scampered off to wake Lee in the hope of some breakfast morsels.

Diane sat up, stretched her arms out, and announced, "Let the adventure continue!"

"I have something that will take care of Addie's ankle," Asazi said as he walked into view carrying a shrub with some delicate-looking orange flowers.

"What's that?" Diane asked.

"The globe mallow plant," Asazi offered.

"Yum! My mother makes marshmallows with it," Lee said as she picked Niki up to stop her from licking her eye. "Are you making us marshmallows for breakfast?"

"No," Asazi said regretfully.

He sat by the smoldering fire, and Diane watched as he took

the root of the plant and began to pound it with a stone.

"How do you make marshmallows?" Diane asked Lee, suppressing a yawn along with her disappointment that they weren't getting the sweet confection.

"You whip the sap from the roots with eggs and mix in some honey and nuts," Lee said wistfully. "It's my favorite candy."

Lee turned her head aside abruptly, but not before Diane saw a tear rolling down her cheek.

She really misses her mama, Diane pondered. She couldn't imagine being away from her family for as long as Lee had been. She wished she knew what to say to make her friend feel better.

A sudden idea occurred to Diane, and she turned back to Asazi. "Wait, you said you were going to help Addie's ankle. Are you going to use all of the globe mallow to do that?"

He angled his head and raised a questioning eyebrow. She leaned in close and whispered into his ear. He grinned, then turned his attention to Addie.

"I'm going to mash the root into a sticky paste and use it in a poultice for her ankle. It's good medicine for sprains and swelling. It's also good for broken bones and other kinds of wounds. It should help heal her ankle faster," he said, carefully applying the paste.

"Thank you," Addie said, her voice filled with gratitude and perhaps, something more. "It feels a lot better, but it's still sore and a little swollen." She grimaced.

"You shouldn't be riding with it for another day or two, but we don't really have a choice," Asazi said, looking at her with concern in his eyes. He shrugged. "Let's break camp as soon as we get Addie's ankle taken care of."

Diane quickly got out of her bedroll and started her morning routine.

The cool stream felt wonderfully invigorating as she stood in the shallow water and splashed her face. Little fish darted between her legs, tickling her toes with their tiny fins. Holding her hands together like a large spoon, she dipped them into the crystal-clear water, closed her eyes, and drank from her hands.

"I love taking a nature bath," she said, feeling especially peaceful this morning.

Walking over to the stream's edge, Asazi reached into his deerskin pouch always slung over his chest and took out a small wrapped package. "Hold out your hands," he said.

Diane cupped her hands and held them in front of her. Asazi placed an amber-colored piece of dried pulp in her palms. He then scooped up some water and sprinkled it onto the twisted fibers. "Rub your hands together."

She did, and the pulp in her hands immediately started to foam. "What is this?" she asked excitedly.

"Yucca soap!" he said. "*Now* you're taking a wilderness bath."

Suddenly, Lee leaned over, a glint of mischief in her doe-like eyes, and pushed her in. Diane slipped under the surface and immediately spouted up out of the chilling water, splashing and spurting water from her mouth like a sea squirt.

Laughing, Lee said, "*Now* you're taking a nature bath."

Diane splashed Lee, who in turn splashed Asazi, and soon Addie and Benji joined in the morning frolic. Even Sa'ami and Niki came to the water's edge and seemed to appreciate their human friends' joyful play.

Like all raccoons, Niki loved the water, and she quickly scooted into the water and swam around Sa'ami's huge legs while he stood in the cool water, licking it up.

Dripping wet, the adventurers came splashing out of the stream.

Just then, Benji squealed. "Look, sis!" He was squatted over the water, gazing down to the pebbled bottom, digging. "What is this?" He stood up, holding a strange piece of what looked like a cluster of reddish-orange snowflakes with a bright metallic luster. "There's lots of it down here," he squealed again, diving down to collect some more.

Asazi glanced over, narrowing his gaze. "That's copper. It is a precious metal to many of the Pueblo people living in these parts. Much of it is used to make tools, weapons, and jewelry. Copper knives, arrow points, spearheads, and axes were also traded among the different tribes. The Aztecs heavily mined the mineral and traded it, and even created a copper money system."

Diane, Lee, and Addie quickly jumped back into the stream to hunt for copper snowflakes, splashing and laughing again. Benji found a few more small treasures and tucked them into his blue jean pockets.

"Every Ray of Light has had its challenge, reward, and unexpected surprise," Asazi said sagely, as he gathered the tethered horses grazing by a copse of Gambel oaks nearby, and brought them to the stream to drink.

Loading up their sleeping rolls and knapsacks, the clan walked over to their quenched horses. Diane tied her sleeping roll under her saddle and climbed onto Mavric's back, then turned around looking for Benji.

"Come on, Sa'ami," said Benji, tugging on the giant black bear's fuzzy ear. Sa'ami grumbled and lazily got up to follow Benji to a small outcrop of rocks. Benji pulled him until his huge body was next to the pile of rocks and then put his palm out in front of his nose, signaling him to stop. Benji climbed the outcrop of teetering rocks, using them as stepping stones, and just as he was about to clamber onto the back of the lovable old bear, Sa'ami, following a good sniff on the wind, moseyed away. Poor startled Benji shrieked as he slid down the side of his bristling flank and landed with a thud at the base of the outcrop in a dried-up puddle, covered in dust.

Smothering a chuckle, Asazi rode by and reached out his hand to help Benji, swinging him onto the back of his painted horse. He then trotted up next to Sa'ami and motioned for Benji to jump down onto his back, which he did with ease, brushing the dust away. Diane smiled, squeezed Mavric's sides with her heels, and began their morning ride to find the Aztec Portal at the enchanted lake.

CHAPTER THIRTY-SEVEN

JACOB LAKE

The rock swallows swooped for a last time overhead as the adventurers and their animal companions made their way downstream. The red canyon walls opened wider and wider. The monumental peaks of the Three Patriarchs faded away behind them as the shaded forest thinned, turning into a grassy prairie of wildflowers with purple lupine, orange Indian paintbrush, and white sego lily. A morning dew blanketed the tall prairie grasses with millions of tiny droplets of moisture, exposing a miniature city of glistening spider tents that clung to their blades. Glimmering beads on fine silky threads, woven by tireless spiders working through the night, created crystalline webs of death and survival.

"They look like miniature teepees," Asazi commented as they rode by.

They then dropped in elevation even more into an open desert of purple sage and spiny yuccas.

"I wonder what you can use this plant for?" Diane pondered out loud, riding by the pointy-bladed plant.

"That's the yucca plant," Asazi said, tucking a loose dark

hair under his braided horsetail headband. "You bathed with the soap made from its roots this morning."

"From that spiny plant?" Diane interrupted, amazed.

Asazi smiled, nodding his head.

"The women of my village also use the fibers from yucca's waxy leaves to weave into baskets, mats, and sandals," Asazi continued, handing her a small basket from his deerskin pouch. "I keep small things in it."

Diane turned it over in her hands, admiring the fine craftsmanship. *I'd like to learn how to make this,* she decided. *Hmm, I guess I never really thought much about how things were made. It would be fun to actually make things with my own hands. More fun,* she considered, *more rewarding than to just read about them.*

The radiant sun was searing overhead, and Diane was happy that she had her hat to shade her from its intense, burning blaze. In the distance, she could see that the dusty desert gave way once again to a green meadow that fringed a forest of tall Douglas firs, quaking aspens, and ponderosa pine trees as the elevation rose dramatically.

The cool pine breezes felt refreshing after the heat of the desert, and their intoxicating scent filled the air. As the clan approached the green meadow, Diane saw a herd of female elk and their young grazing lazily under the noon sun, seemingly not bothered by the passing horses with curious creatures attached to their backs. The lumbering giant black bear was far more alarming, however, so the small herd scampered off into the nearby forest.

She could hear their thundering hooves on the thin-soiled, grass-covered bedrock, when all at once, she spied a large bull elk with a huge rack prancing across the open field, following the herd. His head held high, steamy breath exhaling through his flared nostrils, he looked majestic as he leaped gracefully over the tall field grasses and summer wildflowers.

Diane watched in awe as the bull elk's bulging muscles rippled and strained in his powerful neck. A blanket of sweat streamed down his shimmering hide. *The epitome of freedom,* Diane pondered, *I can almost feel how free he feels just watching him.*

A little after the sun's zenith, the adventurers reached the beautiful forest lake, and Asazi signaled for them to stop to rest and water the horses. As Diane dismounted, she noticed that Asazi continued on mysteriously in search of—something. *This was the enchanted lake, after all,* she considered.

The golden orb gleamed high above the lake and exploded onto its surface like a million gleaming diamonds reflecting its glorious light. A strong summer wind whipped through the trees, and Diane, squinting her eyes, watched as the dancing sparkles expanded with the breeze across the lake surface right to her feet.

It looks like a pathway to heaven, she marveled. Unable to resist, she took off her boots and socks, rolled up her dungarees, then stepped into the refreshing water and onto the soft brown lake sediment that squished through her bare toes. It tickled, but it also felt soothing, and she giggled with joy.

The wind rippling across the surface was reflected in the curvy silt ripples embedded in the lake bottom. She shuffled through the miniature landscape, flattening the rounded hills with her feet, and walked out into the array of dancing sparkles to find herself completely surrounded by them.

She took off her sweaty hat, turned her face to the warm sun, and shut her eyes for a moment to listen to the wind as it rustled through the forest branches, making a most indescribable yet peaceful sound.

Like waves gently crashing on a beach, she imagined as she listened, enjoying the cool breeze on her face and her moment communing with nature.

When she opened her eyes, she dipped her cupped hands into the lake water and scooped up one of the sparkles of dancing light in her palms, intrigued with her captured treasure.

A colorful blue jay fluttered overhead, cawing loudly. Diane had never experienced anything like this in her city life—the serenity and her connection with nature. Her heart soared, and a tingling sensation that started at her legs, zinged up through her body. She was overwhelmed with a complete feeling of joy and a oneness with nature!

As she stood in the sparkling waters, a beaming glow on her face, she took note of the marsh areas scattered along the edge of the lake, thinking, *What a great habitat for birds.* Just then, she spotted a long-legged great blue heron stalking its fishy prey within the tall, slender reeds. The bobbing of its head as it slyly walked through the thick green plants reminded her of the way the *Hadrosaurs* walked toward their nesting mounds.

They both bob their heads when they walk and on only two legs. Even their feet look similar, remembering all too well how the feet of the *Allosaurus* were structured. *Dinosaurs evolved into birds indeed,* she considered again. *My teacher was right!*

Atop the blades of the coarse marsh grasses were scattered double-winged dragonflies, just sitting, absorbing the warm sun glistening through their thin, veiny wings. *Make a wish when you see a dragonfly, and it'll bring you good luck and prosperity,* she remembered her mother once saying in their small garden at home, and, *when you see dragonflies, it often means it's time to shed some old habits and make better ones.*

She also recalled her teacher saying that dragonflies and their aquatic larvae were voracious predators. Just then, the heron stretched its long neck into the reeds, and the startled dragonflies flittered away.

Along the base of the reeds floated a water-soaked log lined with five small lake turtles basking in the sun. *"I love turtles,"* she mused fondly, watching one munching lazily on a water plant, while a baby turtle crawled clumsily over the back of another to catch an insect, then gulped it down.

Diane recognized a few other species of birds as well— flycatchers, starlings, warblers, and woodpeckers. A gobbling wild turkey made its way along the marsh's edge while colorful ducks floated through the sparkling diamonds between the green lily pads. Their beautiful white flowers opened for only a few fleeting days before they curled up and sank to the bottom of the lake, turning into seedpods for next year's blossoms.

She scrunched up her toes to feel the soft sediment squish through them again and watched as tiny water spiders zigzagged effortlessly across the water's surface, their little feet designed by nature to take advantage of the tension created between the molecules of water.

But Diane remembered that it wasn't their feet, really, that allowed them to skitter across the surface. The secret of the water "striders" was in their legs. Their legs were lined with tiny hairs that captured and held air, acting like miniature buoys, enabling water striders to move about easily, rippling the water like delicate raindrops falling in a summer rain.

They're fun to watch, Diane thought, as they glided around her legs as if playing a game of tag. She passed an intrigued Benji entering the maze of water striders as she clambered through the horsetail reeds back onto the grassy bank. She quickly put on her socks and boots, then sat quietly under a copse of aspen trees.

Enchanted, indeed, she whispered to the breeze.

A mourning dove cooed, and robins sang their sweet song, well hidden in the tall pines and the firs. Life was abundant in this secluded forest lake. A chittering sound came from the trunk of a nearby ponderosa, and Diane spied a tassel-eared squirrel with a big bushy tail collecting the seeds from the conifer's pine cones.

"Conifer," meaning cone-bearing, Diane recalled learning in a biology lesson.

"That's the most unusual squirrel I've ever seen," she said to Addie, who sat down next to her, sharing the shade of the quaking aspen. "Look at its beautiful white tail and grayish-black belly. I've never seen tufted ears like that before. What kind of squirrel do you think it is?" she asked Addie, and then Lee came over to join in the conversation and share the cool shade.

"I've heard of them," Lee said matter-of-factly. "They're called Kaibab squirrels and only live out West here. I think they're cousins to the Abert's squirrels we've already seen. They mostly eat acorns and mushrooms, along with seeds, bark, and the twigs of these ponderosa trees where they make their home."

"I've heard other trappers from Arizona tell tale of them. Look at these tracks," Lee said, pointing. "These belong to a bobcat that probably preys on the squirrels and other wildlife that live around this lake, like rabbits or mule deer. I've seen many of their tracks, too. This place has *beaucoup* wildlife," she said, swiping her long bangs from her eyes.

"I'll write about them in my field journal tonight," Diane said keenly.

"Speaking of wildlife," Lee said, with a faint note of mischief in her voice, as she held a curious-looking brown pine cone in her hand. "This is the cone from a Douglas fir tree. Mice love to hide in it. See their tails?" she said, trying not to laugh.

Intrigued, Diane looked closely at the cone. To her surprise, it did look like dozens of tiny mice were trying to hide under the woody scales of the cone, and only their two hind legs and tail were exposed.

"Mice butts!" she chortled, and shared the funny cone with Addie and a dripping Benji, who joined them and laughed in agreement.

Just then, a loud splash rippled over the lake, and everyone turned toward the source, immediately alarmed. A large buck with a huge rack of velvety, fuzzy antlers had jumped off a stone ridge on the other side of the lake and was swimming across, his head just barely above the water, his nostrils flared.

"I didn't know deer could swim," Diane murmured in shock. *Why would he jump into the water like that?*

The clan watched in amazement, shaking their heads. "Golly gee," Benji mumbled.

At once, they noticed that Asazi and Forjon now stood on the stone ridge vacated by the escaping buck. Asazi's palm was raised before him, and the Aztec Stone was glowing brightly.

"Time to go!" Lee said tersely.

Everyone quickly gathered their things, and mounting their horses, rode swiftly to the stone ridge across the lake. As they approached, Diane's scarf began to radiate a soft white light, becoming more intense with every step Mavric took as they neared the ancient Aztec Portal.

Before them, the water in the lake began to swirl as it joined the vortex of light rising up above the ridge. The mass of whirling fluid of water, air, and light magically transformed into the frosted-looking surface of brilliant white light. Like a giant glass pane roughly edged in a radiant glow, hanging in midair, it began to clear. Asazi signaled the clan that it was time, and on Forjon's back, leaped into the mystical gateway.

"Here we go! Hold on tight," Diane shouted to Benji, who was nestled against her back. Sa'ami followed close on the hooves of Mavric as they stepped over the glowing white edge into a colorful, magnificent landscape.

CHAPTER THIRTY-EIGHT

THE GRAND CANYON

"**W**hoa!" Asazi commanded Forjon, pulling hard on his reins while he raised his hand, signaling for everyone to stop.

Before them lay the deepest, widest canyon they'd ever seen. They halted their horses on a rock precipice jutting into this most extraordinary hole in the earth. Mavric pawed the ground nervously, shifting his weight from leg to leg, still agitated from his journey through the windy portal. Diane drew a deep breath, took off her hat, resting it on the saddle horn, and gazed out over the ledge.

From their exquisite vantage point, the clan looked at least one mile down into the depths of the huge canyon and easily over ten miles across to a colorful, rock-layered rim. They stood at the edge of a ledge that dropped thousands of feet over white cross-bedded sandstones, red sloping shales, and blue-green layered limestones. Massive cliffs with royal arches and eroded slopes were punctuated by rocky pinnacles and monumental buttes, all adding to the majesty of this incredible terrain.

Below, they could see the raging river Za-tha had referenced, winding through the lower canyon walls like an emerald-green snake. Even from this vast distance, they could see areas of white patches that marked formidable rapids, the most violent and tumultuous the adventurers had ever encountered or could even imagine.

"This *must* be the Grand Canyon," Diane said, awestruck. "I've learned about it in our geology lectures, but the pictures..." she murmured incredulously. "The pictures don't come close to showing how truly magnificent it is." The view was surreal, with large boulders perched precariously on slanted ledges, hulking monoliths of stones, and spindly spires dappled throughout the vividly dynamic landscape.

"Cool beans!" Lee exclaimed, leaning back in her saddle, her hand to her brow to shade her eyes. "And that must be the Colorado River that helped carve it," she added, scratching Niki behind her tiny ears.

"Water carved that?" Benji asked, stunned. "Gee whiz!" He exhaled disbelievingly.

"Not exactly," Diane instructed in her blossoming teacher voice. "Water, wind, freezing and thawing, weathering, and erosion all had a role to play. But yes, water from the mighty Colorado River and all its tributaries running down into it from its North and South Rims did most of the work. Hey," she said excitedly, "we must be at the North Rim. It's about a thousand feet higher than the South Rim over there." She pointed across the deep chasm. "We're about seven thousand feet in elevation.

"I always dreamed of seeing the Grand Canyon when we moved to Arizona, but I never imagined I'd see it like this," she said, a bit choked up.

"Well, not to burst your bubble," Lee said tensely, flipping her cap's striped raccoon tail over her shoulder. "But *how* are we going to get across it?"

"I read in my book of the American West that there are old Indian trails the early prospectors took down into the canyon with their mule trains in search of gold and silver. The Spanish conquistadors in the early 1500s came across the Grand Canyon on their expeditions, searching for the fabled seven golden cities of Cibola. They never found the legendary cities, not here anyway," she paused, then went on, "and not with any gold—only native people farming on the canyon floors, living in stone dwellings carved into the walls of the canyon. Probably the Havasupai people Za-tha spoke about," Diane paused again, dabbing the sweat from her face with her sleeve. Mavric anxiously scratched his hoof against the stony ledge and nickered anxiously.

"But the stories remained," she continued, gently petting his twitching neck, "attracting prospectors, trappers, and photographers alike to this magical landscape. Photographers would risk their lives climbing up these steep canyon walls, balancing their equipment on perilous perches to take their dramatic images. It was an incredibly dangerous undertaking to capture the magnificence of this enchanting place. I would love to become a photographer someday," she said, "so that I can document my adventures and share them with my students. It's a great way to teach and learn," she concluded avidly.

"But *how* are we going to get across?" repeated Lee, Asazi, and Addie in unison, while Benji tapped incessantly on her back, and Mavric pawed the ground once again.

"Oh!" She paused. "There's a place upriver from here I read about called Lee's Ferry. It's at the beginning of the Grand Canyon. There we can take a ferry across with the horses," Diane replied confidently, pulling the reins firmly to back Mavric away from the ledge, turning him around.

"I saw a rim trail back a ways," Asazi said, taking the lead.

With that, the rest of the clan turned their sweaty horses and headed back to find the old Indian trail that would take them eastward to Lee's Ferry. Because the trail was well used, it was easy to find, but it took them most of the afternoon to finally break from the forested rim to descend the many treacherous switchbacks to reach the river below.

The stony trail cut through thick sedimentary layers of sandstone, shale, and limestone, and every step downward took them farther back through eons of time represented in the colorful rock formations. Hundreds of millions of years were traversed in a matter of hours. Each rock layer represented not only a different time, but also a different environment.

"It's amazing to think that right here, in this very spot, were once ancient seas, then floodplains where dinosaurs roamed, huge sand dunes crawling with lizards and scorpions, and before all of that, enormous mountain ranges as tall as the Himalayas," Diane sighed, in awe of the astonishing beauty before her. "The Grand Canyon spans from 225 million years ago to over two billion years ago. A lot of changes occurred during that time, all preserved in the story of the rocks," she said fervently.

"Geez, sis!" Benji said, squirming behind her. As Sa'ami lumbered by, he clambered onto his bear friend's back.

When they finally walked their tired horses onto the sandy beach, it was late afternoon. A gangly man on a large ferry waved lazily as he crossed the river toward them. The long, rectangularly shaped floating raft was big enough to haul several passengers, horses with a carriage or two, and cargo across the slow-moving water.

Diane dismounted and stepped forward to meet him as he limped off his ferry, grinning broadly.

"Howdy, little lady," he said, as he tied the flat, wood-planked ferry to a large boulder on the shore. "Just how many passengers do we have here?"

"Good day, sir," Diane responded with a friendly smile. "There's five of us, four horses, and, oh yes, a bear," she said matter-of-factly.

The old man wearily shook his head, looking both amazed and befuddled. He nervously removed his dusty cowboy hat and scratched his bald head. "You say...say—a-a bear?" he stuttered, looking fearful, and squinted his eyes to shade them from the blinding sun as he peered through the clan of adventurers for this mysterious bear.

"Have you ever ferried a bear across before?" Diane asked earnestly.

"Well, no, I haven't," the ferryman responded hesitantly, now pulling on his scraggly beard. "Can't say that I have. That *would* be something to see, I reckon." He looked down at his dusty boots, shuffling anxiously, and drew lines in the sand with his badly scuffed heel.

"Well then, sir, how much would that be worth to you?" Diane asked shrewdly as her plan began to unfold. The other clan members just watched this curious exchange silently and chuckled to themselves, smothering their grins.

The old ferryman slapped his mangy cowboy hat against his leg and scratched his head again, taking a long hard look at this little blonde girl before him and her clan of travel-worn adventurers. Surveying the situation, he finally asked, "How old are you, little lady—if you don't mind me asking?"

"I'm twelve-and-a-half years old, sir, nearly thirteen," she stated. "My brother, Benji, is ten, almost eleven; my friend Lee is fifteen; Addie's fourteen; and Asazi is seventeen years old," she said, smiling kindly.

The old man eyed Asazi warily. "I don't ferry Indians," he said cantankerously, digging his boot heel into the ground and spitting to make his point a bit more distasteful.

"Asazi is not an Indian," Diane protested politely. "He is an American, just like you, and just like me, like all of us who were born in this country, and he's our friend," she stated calmly yet definitively. "Underneath our clothes and skin color, aren't we all really alike? Aren't we all Earth's children?" she questioned, looking sternly into the eyes of the old ferryman.

He thought for a moment, his eyes to the ground, biting his lower lip, then finally looked up into her sparkling green eyes, nodding his cocked head slightly. "I don't see your brother," he drawled, squinting his eyes again.

"He's riding the bear!" Diane declared.

"Riding the bear?" the ferryman shouted in genuine astonishment.

Her plan had worked. "That *would* be worth a trip across the great river, indeed, by golly," he said incredulously. "Show me the bear! I want to see this with my own two eyes."

"We have a deal then?" she confirmed, with a glint in her eye.

"Yessiree, Bob! Little lady," he said impatiently. "Let's see the boy riding a bear before I change my mind."

With that, Diane waved downriver toward the last stand of pine trees. Benji emerged atop Sa'ami and sauntered cautiously toward the old, stunned man. The ferryman tightly clutched his worn hat with both hands, wringing it into a twisted knot, while his lower jaw dropped wide open.

"For land's sake! That's the biggest black bear I've ever seen," he said, shuddering. "And the boy is riding on his back!" he exclaimed in awe as he took a few stumbling steps backward, as if drunk on Red Eye. He awkwardly regained his composure as the bear came to a stop in front of Diane, and gesturing toward them, she once again made proper introductions.

"This is my brother, Benji, and our bear friend and protector, Sa'ami." The old man just stood still, seemingly transfixed in fear. "Mister," Diane said with pleading eyes, tugging on his soiled shirt sleeve.

"Yes, yes, yes!" He finally spoke. "A deal's a deal." He spat a large grisly wad of chewing tobacco at her feet and shook his head.

She stepped out of the way as the befuddled ferryman took Mavric and Bentley by the reins and led the horses onto the ferry, tying them to a hitching post in the front of the wooden raft. He then came back for Forjon and Rohan and tied them to the back. He hesitated when he turned around to Benji and Sa'ami. He took off his moth-eaten cowboy hat and bowed, motioning them with a sweep of his hat to come aboard before scuttling quickly out of their way.

Sa'ami was suddenly hesitant to step onto the manmade floating platform and stopped abruptly, shaking his furry head, refusing to get aboard. Diane motioned to Addie.

"Talk to him," she murmured under her breath. "Tell him it's safe, and we'll be with him. We need him to protect us."

With that, Addie began her hand dance and then stood quietly with her forehead pressed to Sa'ami's.

"What's she doing?" the old man drawled.

"She's talking to him," Diane responded in an offhanded sort of way. "It's a gift she has."

The old man scratched his head and pulled on his beard

again. "Balderdash!" he proclaimed. "A boy who rides a bear and a girl who talks to him," he guffawed. "I've seen it all today!"

Addie slowly walked backward onto the ferry, keeping eye contact with the old bear, and Sa'ami immediately followed, stopping in the middle of his clan. "That was brilliant," whispered Addie squeakily, as she passed by Diane.

The ferryman chuckled to himself, then slapped his thigh and shook his head disbelievingly.

"Never in my life!" he cackled, releasing the rope from the boulder, and jumped on board.

The emerald-green water was slow-moving at this section of the river, and the old man easily moved the ferry along the rope tethered to the other side. Hand over hand, he pulled the hemp-coiled rope, ushering the ferry closer and closer to the opposite shore.

White puffy clouds drifted across an unimaginably blue sky, their shadows moving like black cattle crossing the river on a southward drive. Lee's Ferry was the only place for hundreds of miles that the Colorado River was accessible from both the north and south sides of the region, allowing prospectors, settlers, and travelers to cross.

"Where y'all headed?" the old man asked, as the horses and their riders, and one giant black bear, stepped off his ferry.

"We're headed for Indian Gardens above the Devil's Corkscrew," Diane said innocently.

"Devil's Corkscrew?" the ferryman shouted in awestruck dismay. "That trail is treacherous! The sun beats on it so, you and your horses will perish in a flash if you attempt it in the heat of the midday sun," he warned, looking very concerned for their safety. "Stay on this trail and head west into the setting sun. You have a few hours of daylight left—make the best of it. You should make the Little Colorado by nightfall. You'll know it by its turquoise-blue color. Camp on this side and cross it in the morning. Don't drink the water—horses neither. It's poisonous! You should make Devil's Corkscrew by late afternoon tomorrow. Wait and get a wiggle on once the sun has set over the trail," he advised gravely.

"Thank you," Diane said. "Thank you so much!" she repeated.

"Hey, what's your name?" he shouted as they rode away.

"Dino Diane," she shouted back brightly, wrapping a strand of blonde hair around her ear.

"Dino Diane and her clan of adventurers," the ferryman mumbled. "Wait until I tell my travelers tomorrow, what a tale — *a boy who rides a giant bear and a girl that talks to him.*"

CHAPTER THIRTY-NINE

THE INNER GORGE

The path was well defined but narrow and rocky as they headed into the descending sun with the green river flowing swiftly alongside them. The Colorado River was at least two hundred to three hundred yards across; it was indeed the widest, most powerful river the adventurers had ever seen. They felt like little ants in comparison. Riding along, they could hear the occasional thud of huge boulders rolled along its bottom, pushed by the mighty force of water. Crashing into other boulders beneath the surface, the ground trembled with each collision. They watched the river swell over the top of a submerged boulder and then flow into a deep depression, or hole, on the opposite side. When the submerged rock pile broke the surface, dangerous, raging white rapids were formed.

"Why is the water so green it's like emeralds?" Addie asked.

"I think it's from the algae growing in the water," Diane responded, scrunching her brow in thought, "which means the water is really clear. If the river carries a heavy load of sediment—sand, silt, and other small particles—it blocks the sunlight, and the river would be muddy brown. Algae, like all plants, need sunlight to carry on photosynthesis. A green river means the water's clear enough for algae to grow and flourish."

"You just love science, knowing *why* things are the way they are, don't you?" Addie surmised, twisting her ponytail as she rode.

For the first time, Diane was *living* what she had learned in her schoolbooks. She knew she would never be the same again. Experiencing what she had learned firsthand was the only path for her, and she was formulating a plan at that very moment. "I think I want to start my own school, and my students will learn through adventures!" Diane said, looking seriously into Addie's cinnamon eyes.

As the canyon walls grew higher on both sides of the river, Diane suspected they were entering the Inner Gorge of the Grand Canyon. She had read excerpts by John Wesley Powell, the one-armed Civil War Union major who led the first successful expedition down the Green and Colorado Rivers in four wooden riverboats. It took his team of explorers three months to navigate the dangerous river through the entire Grand Canyon.

"It was a most adventurous and courageous journey," Diane began telling the story of the Powell expedition of 1869 as they rode along the river trail. "At one point, three of the explorers were so frightened by the raging rapids in the Colorado that they abandoned the expedition and tried to get out of the canyon on foot, only to never be heard of or seen again," she reported dramatically, swiping the beads of sweat from her upper lip.

"These jagged black cliffs are made of metamorphic rocks named the Vishnu Schist," she keenly began her geology lesson. "They're over a billion years old and were the roots of a tall mountain range that once stood where we are today. See how they're folded? That's our evidence," She nodded and went on, "I just love rocks. They tell us so much about the history of the earth. The Grand Canyon is like a storybook of past times, strange creatures long extinct, and ancient environments."

"So, what caused all the different layers?" Addie asked, really intrigued, the geology bug biting again.

Diane looked out into the pristine wilds that surrounded them and pointed to a cliffside that rose from the river, thousands of feet up, to the rim that showed a perfect profile, or side view, of the Grand Canyon sequence of rocks. "See those horizontal rock layers above the Vishnu Schist?" she asked Addie. "Each of those layers, called a rock formation, were formed in a different environment. The type of rock and the fossils found in them are our clues to the ancient environment in which they were formed. *They* tell the story!"

Addie nodded her head, sincerely interested.

"Sandstones form typically in desert regions or beaches and shallow coastal environments. Shales form in floodplains or deeper coastal waters, and limestones in freshwater lakes or deep oceans. The fossil evidence helps us narrow down the possibilities," she said, glancing up at a small white cloud passing by. "It's kind of like detective work. We hunt for fossil clues."

Addie scrunched her brows, "So, what are fossils?" she asked.

Diane grinned. "Fossils are the impressions of past life preserved in stone. Usually only the hard parts: teeth, bones, wood, or shells become fossils."

"Because...the flesh decays too fast?" Addie surmised tentatively.

"Yes, yes, that's right, Addie. You're becoming a paleontologist now!" Diane said, applauding.

"So, fossils of scorpions or lizards indicate a desert region, whereas fossils of marine snails, clams, and gastropods are only found in the seas. Dinosaur fossils are usually found in floodplain environments," Diane paused, taking a breath.

"Let's be fossil hunters!" Addie said, sitting up tall on Rohan's back, bubbling with excitement.

A small swirling funnel of sandstone dust suddenly crawled down the cliffside, drifted across the trail in front of them, and then dispersed over the river, vanishing as quickly as it appeared.

Holding her scarf over her mouth and nose, Lee yelled out, "That's a dust devil!"

Diane and Addie glanced at each other and shrugged, then Diane continued her afternoon geology lesson. "Geologists can tell us all kinds of things about the earth simply by studying rocks and their fossils along with the other sedimentary features they find in them," she paused, brushing the fine red dust from Mavric's black mane, pondering.

"Remember those checkerboard mesas we saw yesterday? The large, sweeping cross-beds and the crisscrossing layers on the domes are an example of a sedimentary feature, giving us a clue that a desert environment may have once been there. I bet if we had looked carefully over the surface of those sandstone cross-beds, we might have found footprints of lizards or the tail-drag impressions of scorpions on them. Paleontologists call these trace fossils, giving us proof, the evidence, that it was indeed once a desert sand dune," she finished—exhausted, but satisfied.

Studying the rock formations before her, "The oldest rocks are at the bottom...and the youngest ones are on the top," Addie suddenly blurted out, wiggling in her saddle.

"Yes, you've got it!" Diane exclaimed, thrilled to see that Addie was thinking like a true geologist. "The rock layers at the bottom were laid down first, so they're the oldest. Brilliant, Addie!"

Addie beamed.

"Cool beans!" Lee shouted from where she rode in front of them, listening intently to the conversation of the girls behind her.

As the shimmering sun neared the horizon, it cast its evening display of intense yellow light, deepening into an orange haze that filled the canyon. Long shadows stretched from the upper canyon walls into the cooler depths of the Inner Gorge.

Asazi raised his hand, signaling the procession of riders to stop. Up ahead he could see the turquoise-blue water of the Little Colorado River emptying into its mother river.

"We need to find a place to camp," he guided, dismounting.

"There's a spring over here!" Lee yelled back, motioning to the cliff face darkened by water running from between its layers. The seep line was outlined with miniature gardens of green canyon plants.

Dismounting, Addie spied a small black critter with two venomous fuzzy fangs and eight spindly legs scuttling across the trail. It seemed to be following a grasshopper into the bulrushes growing along the base of the spring.

"What's that?" Addie shrieked, gesturing to the oddly angled legs. She hastily jumped back onto Rohan's back.

"That's just a Grand Canyon tarantula," Lee said matter-of-factly. "Although that *is* one of the biggest spiders I've ever seen."

Immediately, Benji jumped off Sa'ami's back. Squatting down by the bulrushes, he rustled through the reeds, intensely searching for the runaway arachnid that measured about four inches from leg tip to leg tip.

Asazi enthusiastically joined the hunt, interested in its prey, the grasshopper. The two adventurers were on their hands and knees, stealthily crawling through the grassy strands, when Benji spotted the giant spider stuck between two thick bulrushes and a small boulder.

As he approached, the tarantula's spindly hind legs began wildly scratching its rather large abdomen, covered in fine reddish-orange hairs. The released irritating hairs floated upward into Benji's nostrils, causing him to scratch his small nose madly, sneezing incessantly.

"That's quite a defense mechanism," Diane chortled, watching the clever tarantula as it finally escaped through the reeds and scurried away, seemingly too distracted to continue its hunt for the elusive grasshopper.

Asazi, however, spied the grasshopper resting on the blade of a reed and successfully pounced on the poor grasshopper just as it was about to jump and take flight. Cupping it into his hands, he tucked it away in his medicine bag after carefully pinching and removing its head and innards.

Noticing the squeamish faces, Asazi offered. "I have learned from the Ute people to take dried grasshoppers, crickets, and cicadas and mix them with berries to make small nutritious fruit cakes." He smacked his lips. "This will do well with the raspberries I collected the other day."

"Yuck!" Diane, Benji, and Addie shouted all at once. Lee turned her head and looked the other way, choking down her disgust.

"I wonder what this pesky flying bug is?" said Benji, curiously shooing away the winged varmint. "Look at its orange wings, funny curly antennae, and those huge, hooked claws."

"Wait, wait, I know that one," Diane said excitedly, reaching for her field journal, quickly flipping the pages. "Here it is," she read her biology notes aloud.

A most interesting predator to the Grand Canyon tarantula is the tarantula hawk, a giant spider wasp with a dark blue, iridescent body and brightly orange-colored wings, with long legs for grappling its victims. The adult female paralyzes an unwitting tarantula with its stinger— the second most painful sting of any insect—and drags the dazed spider back to its nest.

Once there, the female covers the entrance of its burrow, trapping the spider, and then drills a hole into the tarantula's abdomen to lay a single egg. When the egg hatches, the larva feeds on the still-living spider for several weeks— avoiding the spider's vital organs—keeping it alive until the larva turns into an adult wasp.

The giant spider wasp flitted aggressively around Benji's head, unhappy that he had scared its prey away. "Shoo, get away," he swiped at the angry predator.

"I think I'd like to sleep up there tonight," Diane shuddered, angling her head to a large sandstone ledge that jutted out twenty feet or so above the river, hoping to avoid the strange insect life in the Grand Canyon. "The horses will have water from the spring, and the alcove underneath our ledge would be a protected place for them to settle in for the night."

Having made up her mind, she dismounted, unloaded her gear, and made the climb up the cliff. The rest of the trail-worn clan followed her, wearily carrying their bedrolls on their backs as they staggered up the step-like layers, panting in the sweltering heat of the late Arizona afternoon.

"This is perfect," Diane proclaimed heartily, laying out her bedroll so that her feet pointed out to the edge of the ledge and her head lay safely inside the cliff face. "Don't want to roll off that edge in the middle of the night." She chuckled casually as she said it, but she was completely serious. Diane stood on the edge, looking down pensively at the rushing green river below, and frowned slightly. *No, I don't want to roll off into that,* she repeated to herself, sighing and swiping the sweat from her brow. She laid out Benji's bedroll next to hers and against the cliff wall for safety.

Addie, Lee, and Asazi laid out their sleeping blankets on either side of theirs. There was even enough room for Sa'ami. The tired black bear lumbered up the rock layers to stake out his sleeping place by Benji and curled up by the stony wall, gazing down at his little friend crawling on his knees.

"Ouch!" Benji shrieked, still hunting for the tarantula amongst the reeds. He clasped his hand over his ear and began to moan.

Sa'ami immediately stood up on the ledge and rocked anxiously from one front paw to the other, whimpering softly.

Diane and Asazi scurried down the rock steps to see a yellow-striped insect fly away and into its nest in a hole in the ground.

"A yellow jacket!" Diane cried out, "He's horribly allergic to them."

Asazi gently pulled Benji's hand aside and saw that his ear was deeply red and already swelling.

"What's that?" Diane asked. She watched anxiously as Asazi pulled from his medicine bag a small deerskin pouch and began dabbing a dry powder on Benji's lumpy-looking ear.

"Ocotillo root," he said, handing her the pouch. "Go and make some tea with this; it'll help take down the swelling."

Diane dashed off and found Lee already making a fire to boil some water. She came back sometime later with a hot cup of ocotillo tea. She was relieved to see that Benji's ear was already beginning to look quite normal. *I've got to make note of this in my field journal,* she thought, sighing loudly.

Benji sat and sipped the tea. Feeling a little better, he grunted as he slowly clambered up the rock-ledge steps to his bedroll on top. Sa'ami greeted him with a big bear hug and slobbery lick up the side of his face. "Yuck," Benji grumbled, falling exhausted onto his sleeping blanket. Sa'ami curled up on the dusty ledge next to him, and they both began to snooze.

That night, the silvery edge of a crescent moon peeked over the canyon wall shooting a shimmering white moonbeam over the rolling river.

Diane looked at the sleeping blankets all bunched together and frowned. "We better not have a fire tonight." She shrugged with disappointment.

"A spark could ignite trouble," Lee agreed.

"But look at the stars," Addie sighed.

Asazi leaned back against a log and gazed up at the stars—campfires of his ancestors.

The inky-black sky looked as if it were fairy dusted with tiny, brilliant stars in a twinkling celestial dance. It was indeed—*magical.*

Flitting erratically across the glowing moon were numerous dark, flying creatures with thin, leathery black skin draped tightly over their thin finger-like bones, homologous in structure and evolutionary origin to those found in the human arm, but quite different in function. Their fuzzy brown bat bodies noiselessly darted hither and thither over the tamarisk trees, whose dense flower clusters attracted a menagerie of delectable insects.

Shuddering, "They're kinda spooky," Diane whispered, but

she was entranced by their fluttering wings flapping wildly in between the glittering stars. She lay back on her arms folded behind her head, staring up into the starry sky, sighing deeply. *They can eat five thousand insects a night,* she pondered, remembering her teacher describing a night, much like this, she imagined, digging for dinosaurs in the badlands of the West. He was observant and brilliant on a number of subjects—a true naturalist. *Something I'd like to be when I grow up,* she confirmed to herself.

With the canyon air so clear, they could easily make out the Milky Way, which seemed so close they took turns trying to touch it as they lay in their blankets, talking and giggling.

"It looks like the spine from some monstrous sky creature," Addie said, as she reached up one more time to grasp ahold of its wispy tail.

Diane was about to say, *this is the most magnificent night sky I've ever seen,* when all at once, a thunderous clap filled the air, followed by a distant, deep, unearthly grumbling that sounded like a freight train moving through the canyon and headed their way.

"What was that?" Addie shrieked.

Everyone sat straight up from their bedrolls. Even Sa'ami and Niki could feel the tension in the air and cowered on their haunches, anxiously looking about.

Nothing was moving—not the long wiry limbs on the creosote bush or the showy blue flowers of the desert sage, but they could feel the rumbling coming closer, getting louder, and the rocks began to vibrate beneath them. Even the stars seemed to shake slightly, making Diane's stomach feel queasy. She squeezed her eyes shut, then looked away to her brother.

"Hold on, Benji!" she shouted, feeling him suddenly vibrate toward the edge of the ledge. She grabbed ahold of him and held him tight to her as the vibrations grew stronger.

Closer and closer the terrifying sound came until the trembling finally passed through them, as if a powerful locomotive had sailed by the station platform without stopping. Everyone held onto each other as they felt the earth train move through the rocks and then groaned under them, changing its sound as trains do, as it rumbled away.

CRASH! All at once, an outcrop of boulders nearby slid from their perch and tumbled noisily down the cliff, plunging into the sloshing river below. The sound of rocks smashing into rocks and splashing into the water was deafening. More large boulders, precariously balanced all along the canyon walls, teetered and fell to the great powers of the earth. Diane held her hands to her ears as her heart pounded hard in her chest.

"What *was* that?" Addie asked again breathlessly.

"I think that was an earthquake," Diane replied, astonished. "I've never experienced *that* before," she said, exhaling a long, drawn-out breath.

"*Incroyable!*" Lee mumbled, trying to muster up some enthusiasm.

"The Great Mother Earth must be dancing tonight in celebration," Asazi offered.

"Celebrating what?" Diane asked tensely, still grasping tightly onto Benji.

"Tomorrow, we discover the last Secret of the Five Rays of Light. She is happy that our journey is almost over," he said soberly.

A sudden deep sadness came over the clan of adventurers. They had experienced so much together. They were friends for life, and they knew it, but what would happen after tomorrow? They stared raptly into the silent night sky, unable to sleep, pondering what the last few days of their journey would bring.

CHAPTER FORTY

MUD WAR

A chilly morning breeze blew across the Colorado River and swept up the craggy canyon walls, slapping the edge of the woven blanket across Diane's face, waking her abruptly. Startled at first, her eyes wide and blinking, she gazed out at the beautiful scene before her and exhaled, cuddling back into her warm blanket. The gentle sound of the lapping water below their riverside ledge was calming, and the rock face across the river from her was still dimly shaded in expansive morning shadows.

Glancing around, she realized everyone was gone, and she was left alone. Not even their blankets remained. A little time to myself, she sighed, feeling a little lazy. Smiling contently, she leaned her head against her folded arm and watched an emerald-green canyon swallow as it darted over the feathery tamarisk trees lining the river, catching flying insects in its aerial swoops. The sun gleamed off its metallic green back, marked by a shade of deep purple at the base of its neck that shimmered in the morning light as it fluttered along the depths of the Inner Gorge.

The tamarisk tree! I've read about it, and I know I took some notes. She pulled out her field journal and began flipping through the pages.

She read to herself.

Tamarisk trees were brought from Europe and Asia to fight erosion but eventually found their way into the Grand Canyon. They easily adapted to their new environment along the banks of the Colorado River and its tributaries. While their lateral roots spread out one hundred and fifty feet, stabilizing the banks, their long taproots reach a hundred feet down to the water source, stealing life-giving water from the other Grand Canyon tree species like willows and cottonwoods.

Tamarisk trees were aggressively becoming the dominant species in the Grand Canyon's riparian community. Their ability to reach more water had actually lowered the water table, not only affecting the survival of other native plants but wildlife as well, that were dependent on both water and the diversity of vegetation.

A good idea going sideways, she decided, shaking her head, frowning. *We've got to be more mindful of future consequences.* Diane slipped her field journal back into her knapsack and fell back onto her bedroll. Another cool breeze splashed her face, tinged with the unusual fragrances of the earthy canyon. She inhaled the oddly sweet, damp Arizona dirt scented with wild desert plants. *I love that smell*, she mused, snuggling deeper into her blanket.

Diane heard and felt the thud of a large boulder rolling into another boulder under the river's surface. *That one was as big as a house!* she pondered, awestruck, imagining her small suburban home rolling along the bottom of the river. *Water is more powerful than most people realize.*

Diane shifted to her side, propping herself up on an elbow, and looked for an imagined brick chimney or shingled roof to surface. Disappointed, she watched a golden-mantled ground squirrel run down the side of the cliff, stopping on the ledge in front of her, chewing a treasured seed. His lumpy cheeks were filled with foraged booty. He abruptly stopped chewing when he noticed Diane staring at him.

"Go on," she murmured to him in a gentle voice. "It's all right. Eat your breakfast."

"Whee!" Diane heard in the distance, and she sat up suddenly as faint laughter echoed through the morning canyon. Startled, the small reddish-headed squirrel blinked his buff-rimmed eyes and scampered off.

"Whee!" She heard Lee's voice again, followed by Asazi's, then Addie's, and, finally, Benji's squealing with gleeful laughter.

Not wanting to be left out of the fun, Diane hurriedly jumped out of her bedroll, rolling it up tightly, and gathering her things, packed them quickly. Sensing that all the raucous laughter involved water, she decided her simple undergarments would do best. As she lifted her sleeping shirt over her head, a mother mule deer sprang onto the trail directly below her, apparently disturbed by all of the noise up the side canyon.

Diane froze so as not to alarm her, when all of a sudden, twin fawns followed their mother, leaping effortlessly onto the trail to nibble the tender young plants along the moist seep line in the cliff. She held her breath, smothering a giggle, as she watched the spotted young ones play, happily enjoying their luscious meal.

They're so cute.

Awkwardly, she lifted her shirt slowly, just a little at a time, and waited. The mother warily noticed her movement and jerkily lifted her head from her grazing, her ears anxiously twitching, as she paused to stare at her. Each time Diane froze, she dropped her eyes to the ground, trying not to look like a menacing predator, for she remembered that only predators had two eyes in the front of their head.

She enjoyed this game with the mother mule deer until the fawns, sensing their mother's concern, scampered down the trail and turned up an adjacent side canyon out of view. The mother mule deer peeked at Diane one last time and then followed her young ones. The game was sadly over.

Diane quickly took off her sleeping shirt, grabbed her gear, climbed down the rock ledge, and loaded her things onto Mavric's waiting back. She gave him a morning kiss on his nose and dashed down the trail toward the laughter and the bright blue turquoise waters of the Little Colorado River.

What are they doing? She chuckled.

When she skittered around a rock corner on the trail, she saw the most amazing sight. In a natural water slide, completely coated in glimmering white travertine, Lee was floating in front with Asazi, Addie, and Benji all straddling behind her in a line. Each holding onto the other's waists with their legs, they floated down a side channel in the Little Colorado like a toboggan on a giant water slide.

Cascading over mini-rapids, they floated, laughing and splashing, toward her. The small water channel twisted and turned, flowing up over boulders, sliding down into holes, finally dumping the river clan into a deep pool at her feet.

"Come on, Di! Let's do it again!" Benji yelled, waving wildly, obviously having the time of his life.

She gave them each a hand out of the powder-blue pool and

then followed behind on the beaten path—an old game trail that ran alongside the rocky water slide.

"You go before me, sis," Benji directed, beside himself with joy, as they all jumped into the water above the first rapids. Diane locked her legs around Addie's waist and held onto her shoulders while Benji did the same behind her.

"Ready?" shouted Lee, still standing in the water channel, holding the human raft at bay.

"Ready!" they all yelled back in unison.

Lee lifted her legs and held them straight out before her, and the people raft began floating through the channel downstream.

"Whee!" they all screamed, laughing as they slipped over the first small rapid.

"Ouch!" Diane yelled, "I hit my bum on a boulder!" She guffawed in pain.

"Lean back and lift up over the rapids, Di," Benji instructed over the deafening sound of the rushing water.

"Whee!" they all yelled again as they floated over a swell and then slipped into a deep hole. This time, Diane leaned back and lifted up as they flowed through the small rapid, avoiding another painful collision with a submerged boulder.

Swishing and swirling, they turned, laughing as they slid through a narrow channel between huge white-coated boulders. The heavily mineral-laden water made it easy to float, painting everything white in its wake.

"This is so fun!" screamed Diane joyfully.

They slid into the last twisting channel and plunged into the pool at the end, still laughing and splashing. Asazi was the first to climb out and extended his hand to help everyone else.

"Let's do it again," Benji pleaded, pulling on his sister's arm.

Rubbing her sore bum, she slowly shook her head no. "I'd love to," she said, a tad disappointed as well, "but remember what the old ferryman said. We need to make Devil's Corkscrew by early evening so that we can find Indian Gardens before the last ray of light vanishes behind the canyon wall."

Diane knew Benji appreciated the three trips he had already taken that morning before she joined them. He wasn't happy, but he understood. "We tried to wake you, Di," he mumbled, seemingly sensing her disappointment and perhaps feeling a little guilty.

"That's alright," she said and lovingly patted his wet head. "Let's go see what other adventures await us today, okay?"

He smiled and ran to Sa'ami, who was waiting patiently on the game trail in the shade of a rock ledge. The big bear was swaying nervously from one front paw to another, and upon seeing Benji, he thumped the ground hard with both front legs, rocking Niki nearly off of the top of his head. Benji reached him just in time to catch Niki and gave each animal friend a wet hug.

"I wonder what kinds of animals use this game trail," Diane asked Lee as they trudged along, soaking wet, splattering water droplets onto the dusty trail.

"That kind," Asazi said, gesturing to a small herd of bighorn sheep that stood on the sandstone layers of a rock alcove along the trail not far ahead. The light brown, stocky wild sheep, with distinctive white rumps, were most curious about the creatures making all the unusual sounds that echoed off the canyon walls.

Five short-horned mothers, or ewes, with their young ones, stood transfixed, staring at the strange two-legged noisemakers that were approaching. It seemed as if some of the young tan lambs felt the clan's energy as they sprang and bucked, tossing around in circles with aerial acrobatics, while others butted their heads together in playful fun with their tiny young buds for horns.

"They're not afraid of us," Lee offered wisely. "Their predators, like mountain lions, wolves, bobcats, and coyotes, only stalk them from above, usually perched on ledges or boulders ready to pounce. We're below them, so they don't see us as a threat, just a curiosity."

Asazi made sure the horses had plenty of spring water to drink and gave each of them a handful of grainy biscuits as an extra treat.

"Ouch!" Diane whimpered, trying to squirm into her blue jeans.

"Look at the back of your legs," Addie said, wincing. "They're all chafed from riding."

Asazi gave Forjon one more biscuit and sauntered over to the girls. "What's wrong?" he asked, concerned, as Diane turned around, showing him her deeply reddened skin.

He opened his medicine bag and pulled out a container, handing it to Diane. "This is pine sap salve. A gift from the Mother to soothe skin irritations."

"Thank you," Diane said, gratefully accepting the gift. "It smells good, like the forest," she added, sniffing the greasy salve.

"Keep it. Addie and Benji may need it too," he offered, and with that, he mounted Forjon.

The orange morning sun shot an array of glimmering sunbeams across the Colorado River, warming the drenched adventurers as they rode their horses across the Little Colorado. Benji held up Sa'ami's large muzzle as he walked across the shallow turquoise waters at the mouth of the Little

Colorado, making sure the bear wasn't tempted to drink the poisonous water.

The trail continued to climb up along the black metamorphic rock, sometimes touching the lighter sedimentary rock layers above and then descending again to the river's edge. As they traveled the narrow river trail, the dry dust kicked upward from the horses' hooves was held suspended in the air as reddish clouds made up of millions of particles that glittered brilliantly in the sunlight.

By late morning, they descended once again to the river's edge. *Temperatures felt like they're over a hundred degrees,* Diane imagined, feeling the intense heat radiating off the dark rocks.

Asazi signaled for them to stop to give the weary horses and riders a rest and to quench their parched throats.

Wiping the sweat running down the sides of her cheeks, Diane dismounted and led Mavric to an expansive riverbank that looked like a very silty beach. Mavric stopped abruptly and would go no farther. She walked in front of him and pulled on his reins, but he still refused to take another step forward. So, Diane stepped farther onto the brown beach and pulled Mavric's reins with all her might. She leaned back, using her body weight for leverage, when suddenly, her feet slipped out from beneath her.

"Oops!" she cried out as she fell into the thick, viscous mud that looked like her mother's morning coffee with a lot of cream. She was completely coated with it, and her clan broke out in hysterical laughter at the sight of her.

Asazi heroically stepped into the mud to rescue her and—whoosh—slipped, falling face-first, almost on top of her. His face was dripping in gooey mud, giving him the terrifying appearance of a scary mud monster. Steadying his balance, he slowly staggered to stand up, but—whoosh—slipped again and fell this time on his back into an even deeper quagmire of mud.

Diane could hardly stop herself from laughing. Joyful tears ran down her cheeks as she snickered and reached down to help Asazi out from the depths of the mud soup. Covered from head to toe, he took her hand and, with a quick yank, pulled her toward him. They both fell into the muddy pool again, laughing and splashing mud at each other—and at the gawking bystanders.

Benji couldn't resist and ran onto the muddy bank to join in the fun. Standing completely still, he stiffly fell backward, like a tree falling in the forest, into the mud. The resulting splat sent the brown ooze flying in every direction, spraying slimy globs of mud all over Addie and Lee, who were standing on the fringe of the muddy beach, chortling. With that, they both ran and jumped into the mud, starting an all-out mud war.

CHAPTER FORTY~ONE

ELVES CHASM

The horses stood silently on the bank, seemingly astonished, as they watched their human friends playing in the soupy mire. Mavric took a curious step closer but then quickly backed away, tossing his head and nickering with obvious disgust.

Sa'ami paced from side to side along the edge of the muddy bank, somewhat uncertain if the loud screams were only of playful frolic or a strange cry for his protection. Niki chittered on his head, running in circles, befuddled as well.

Laughing, the adventurers emerged from the beach looking like horrifying monsters from a mud planet.

"Look," Asazi said, pointing up the side canyon that fed into the river. The fine-grained sediment deposited by the tributary stream had accumulated over time, forming the muddy beach that shifted, reshaped, and on occasion, completely disappeared with the changing currents.

From the side canyon, the small stream flowed through a deeply cut gulch of sandstone that was heavily striated with thinly bedded rock layers. Reminding Diane again of a squashed layered cake. *I must be getting hungry,* she mused.

"Let's follow the stream up canyon and see where it leads," Asazi suggested. "We may find a watering hole for the horses."

Each mud monster led their hesitant horse friend up the side canyon, which went back a ways and turned abruptly to the west. Sa'ami cautiously sniffed Benji from head to toe to make sure he was all right, then fell in line, following his clan upstream.

To their amazement, the stream led to a stone grotto, a shallow picturesque cave, with an enchanting waterfall that cascaded into a deep, clear pool of emerald-green water. Luscious hanging gardens of delicate green ferns grew on the moist cliff face edging the hidden pool, shaded from the searing noon sun. A fine mist rose up from the water's surface around the fall, created by its tumbling energy.

"This is beautiful," Diane exclaimed, utterly astonished. "It's a secret paradise."

The caked mud was drying on her body, baked by the hot summer sun. She could feel it shrinking on her skin, making tiny mud cracks that were flaking off with her every movement and the strong breeze that gushed forth from the powerful waterfall.

Asazi was already in the pool, briskly swimming toward the flowing cascade. Addie and Benji followed, diving underwater to release them from their bondage of mud. The horses waited until the unearthly mud monsters disappeared and then stepped into the shallow end to quench their thirst and cool their tired legs. Asazi swam right into the sputtering waterfall and disappeared.

Where'd he go? Diane wondered, wading through the aquamarine water.

Just then, Asazi emerged atop a huge travertine boulder

wedged between the two cliff faces, having toppled down from a rock formation above, perhaps millions of years ago. Two other large, roughly elongated boulders—travertine chockstones—had also lodged themselves vertically in this jumbled chasm, balancing precariously upon each other. Over the next millions of years, the persistent and subtle force of water would eventually erode them away as well.

Today, though, as if by the snapping fingers of mischievous elves, the sculpted boulders formed a most magical chasm of luscious green maidenhair ferns with velvety, moss-covered crevices and pristine waterfalls. Red monkey, cardinal flowers, and yellow columbines grew wildly from the steep cliff walls of layered sandstone.

"Look at this," Addie said, pointing to a myriad of tiny rainbows.

Droplets of water dripped regularly from the tips of the delicate ferns, each shining like a brilliant crystal, casting a rainbow of colored light from its prism. Purple, blue, green, red, yellow, and orange sparkles danced on the surface then melted into the depths of the emerald pool.

Asazi stood on the travertine ledge, rocking on his toes and breathing heavily.

He let loose with a fierce war cry and leaped off the mossy boulder, plunging into the cool pool of rainbows. He came up splashing and spluttering.

The clan applauded vigorously as they hurried to take their turns. Diane, closely followed by Benji, Addie, and Lee, looked like a water snake slithering across the pool's surface that magically disappeared into the waterfall.

The heavy spray of water on her head and shoulders felt like a natural massage with a dozen tiny fingers digging deeply into her sore muscles.

"Ah, does this feel good," Diane sighed as Lee swam up next to her, finding a water spout of her own to enjoy the same wonderful sensations. Benji and Addie paddled beyond them, into the dark grotto behind.

Sa'ami sat with Niki on his head at the edge of the green pool, splashing dozens of squiggly tadpoles his large paws had disturbed. Splat...splat...splat, he slapped the water while Niki ran in circles between his ears, chittering away.

"*Allons-y*! Let's go!" Lee sighed, slowly swimming away.

Diane reluctantly gave up the water massage and swam after Lee into the mysterious waterfall, wondering where everyone had disappeared. Just beyond the falling cascade, they found a small opening to a natural rock staircase and slowly ascended the dimly lit spiral corridor.

The walls were damp and clammy from the mist that blew occasionally into the narrow passageway. It was musty smelling and slippery. Diane wrinkled her nose to the wet, earthy smells and touched the dank walls to steady herself. She immediately recoiled.

"Yuck! That feels so slimy and squashy," she said, wiping her wet fingers on her dungarees.

Lee gave her a nudge, and they climbed up, twisting around and around, as if they were going up a staircase in a castle tower. Just then, they heard the muffled giggles of Benji and Addie screaming, followed by a loud KERPLUNK as they hit the water and came up laughing.

"Come on, Di!" echoed off the castle walls.

Finally, Diane and Lee emerged on top of the huge angular boulder where they had seen Asazi just moments before. The bright white sun beat hotly on their faces.

Still snickering, Diane gulped as she peeked over the edge and waved down to Benji and Addie. She was higher than she thought, at least twenty feet or so above the emerald water's surface. Lee hesitantly stood next to Diane atop the ancient boulder—a remnant from another time, another environment.

"Ready to jump?" Diane said excitedly, beaming at Lee, who grimaced and sheepishly stepped back, her fists balled tightly. Shaking her head stiffly, her eyes bugging, Lee shuddered.

"Come on, face the bear!" Diane encouraged, grasping Lee by the hand, and she began counting to three.

Diane stepped forward, tugging on Lee, who finally shrugged her shoulders and nodded her head. "Three!" Diane yelled as they both drew a deep breath and together leaped from the boulder.

"Geronimo!" Lee shrieked shrilly all the way down into the pool below.

Feet-first, they plunged into the deep aquamarine pool, finally dissolving any resistant dried mud that quickly vanished. Bobbing joyfully on the surface, they laughed heartily.

"That was fantastic," Diane declared, now perfectly cleansed of any traces of her mud monster. Lee smiled widely, splashing Diane in the face, clearly pleased with her bravery. She had indeed faced the bear!

Diane breast-stroked toward the edge of the pool. Upon seeing her, Mavric whinnied and surprisingly swam to her, obviously happy to see his friend again in her recognizable human form. His long, powerful legs gracefully kicked through the water, just like a dog paddling, but with much longer strides. She grabbed his long snout in both dripping hands and gave him a soggy kiss on the nose. He vigorously nodded his head up and down, flaring his nostrils in response.

Turning to swim back to the edge of the pool, Diane saw her chance and quickly swam over Mavric's submerged torso and clambered onto his back, straddling him. Lying low across his neck, she held tightly onto Mavric's thick mane.

"Giddy-up!" she shouted, and he leaped effortlessly out of the water and onto the dusty trail. Patting him gently, she praised, "Good boy," and scratched his ears. He responded playfully by shaking wildly, spraying water everywhere.

Benji was sitting lazily with Sa'ami in the shallow end of the pool, watching his big sister's clever antic, giggling. With Asazi's help, he had taken their gear off Mavric's back, giving the horse some time of his own to enjoy a good swim. Benji's eyes brightened with an idea of his own. He stood up and tugging Sa'ami by the ear, led him into the deeper green water.

When his back was submerged, Benji paddled over the bear's floating bristles and, imitating his sister, straddled the giant bear. Wrapping his scrawny arms around his thick neck, Benji signaled Sa'ami to climb out of the pool. With a nudge of his knees, the black bear lumbered easily out of the aquamarine water. Both drenched, Benji sat triumphant on Sa'ami's back, grinning.

Everyone applauded and cheered.

Sopping wet, the rest of the clan mounted their horses and followed the sandstone side canyon back to find the river trail again. They then turned westward along the mighty Colorado to beat the descending sun. Sa'ami and Benji sauntered behind, dripping.

"Time to find Devil's Corkscrew," said Lee tersely, drying quickly in the hot desert air.

"Any idea what it looks like?" Diane asked Asazi as she rode alongside him.

"What does a 'screw' look like?" he asked. "I have never seen one."

Using her hands as she spoke, she described it as an incline that angled upward and went around a pointed piece of thin, cylindrical metal with a flat top on it. He fell silent, pondering, and Diane knew he was trying to translate this curious description into his natural world of experience.

"A switchback," he declared, finally making the connection. "And what exactly is the Devil? I've heard the townspeople speak of it," he asked somberly, tilting his head.

"It's not a what, but a who." And Diane went on to describe the belief in an evil being that ruled over a place of fire and brimstone called hell, where all the bad people went when they died.

"We don't believe in such a place, nor such a being," he said solemnly. "How could an all-powerful Mother Earth and Father Za, God of the Sun, creators of all things on Earth and in heaven, create such a being or such a place? Why would they do this? For what purpose? *All* are their creations and their children. They love all their children unconditionally— that means without judgment.

"Perhaps this place called hell exists only in the anger and remorse in a person's soul. Only man judges each other as good or bad," he continued. "Your parents love you unconditionally regardless of what you do. Why would not our spiritual parents, who love perfectly, not love us the same—*unconditionally and without judgment?*"

"Hmm," murmured Diane, pondering deeply the wisdom of this different way of thinking—a new way, at least, for her. She appreciated the ancient beliefs of Asazi's people, beliefs handed down through generations of Mother Earth's children.

She rode in silence for a while, contemplating his words. This new way of thinking felt good, made sense somehow, she mused, riding along. Trust your feelings and follow them. They will always guide you, Diane reflected on Za-tha's words.

A hot blast of Arizona air swept over Diane. Its intense heat felt like it was burning her nostrils as she inhaled. She wiped the glistening beads of sweat from her nose and upper lip. Shadows began crawling across the lower canyon floor and up the steep rock walls. The hazy yellow sun was even lower in the sky when Asazi stopped abruptly and pointed up into another side canyon.

CHAPTER FORTY-TWO

DEVIL'S CORKSCREW

"There it is!" Asazi said warily, gesturing to the longest, steepest set of switchbacks they had ever seen, rising from the canyon floor and zigzagging through hundreds of feet of colorful rock formations of crimson reds, mottled greens, and muted blues.

"Cool beans," Lee muttered in a dragging drawl. She tugged down hard on the sides of her raccoon-skin cap, firmly setting her jaw with determination, as she pulled on Bentley's reins, turning him southward into the side canyon.

The heat radiating upward from the sun-drenched rocks sank over the cooler river water and produced a cool early evening breeze that now blew gently through the shaded side canyon walls. It drifted across Diane's face, leaving her feeling rejuvenated after the hot afternoon sun. But for only a fleeting moment.

"I can see why they call it Devil's Corkscrew," she murmured, riding up to Lee and Asazi on a hard-breathing Mavric. His neck was sweaty with shimmering dark stripes, cascading downward onto the rocky trail. "If you tried to climb those switchbacks in the heat of the day, you'd most definitely think yourself to be burning in that terrible place."

She chuckled nervously. "The black walls of this Vishnu Schist absorb the sun's heat all day and then fry you as you pass, like a hot dog on a grill." She could almost feel the skin on her arms sizzling in the heat. She rolled down her sleeves to protect them from the intense rays.

There were only a few fading hours of sunlight left to climb the switchbacks and find the secret Indian Gardens. Before they began the arduous ascent, they stopped to water their horses and let them nibble on the tall grasses growing at the mouth of the side canyon.

A few minutes later, nourished and refreshed, they turned from the welcoming breezes of the river up canyon toward a bleak desert environment and the Devil's Corkscrew.

Back and forth they climbed wearily upward on the narrow trail, worn by years of foot travel by the native people that first lived in the canyon hundreds of years before, then by prospectors and their mules, photographers, and the occasional wild game.

"Look at that!" shouted Lee, pointing to an outcrop of rock jutting into the canyon. A huge male bighorn sheep with large curved horns stood majestically on the ledge looking out over the desert canyon. Keeping a wary eye out for predators, like coyotes that lived in packs in the canyons or the solitary mountain lion that denned high up in the rocky walls, the male watched his female and two young ones nibbling the scant desert plants safely beneath him.

Up...up...up...they climbed through the heavy haze of the setting orange sun, along the lightning-bolt-like trail that was gashed into millions of years of earth's history. Diane peered back down the trail they had traveled and could see only a sliver of the emerald-green Colorado River snaking its way between the rugged cliff walls far below. They were nearly to the top.

The horses began breathing heavily. Streaks of sweat poured down their necks as they staggered on the stony trail.

"We'd better walk the rest of the way," Asazi guided, dismounting from Forjon and swiping the sweat from his own forehead. He took a long swig from his waterskin and poured some into his horse's mouth.

Diane and Benji slid off Mavric and watered themselves and their thirsty horse. Feeling almost lightheaded and dizzy, she held her hand to the rock cliff face and could actually feel the heat. Curious, she touched the rock wall and felt her fingertips sizzle. "Ouch!" She recoiled instantly, blowing on her hot fingers. She took Mavric's reins, patting him gently on his snout, and led him up the forever path. Benji trailed behind, leading Sa'ami, who tossed his head, happy to see his little friend.

Upward they trudged for what seemed like an eternity. Finally, they cleared the switchbacks and entered a narrow canyon with high, sculpted walls that looked like large lake-bottom ripples, only vertical. Diane's cheeks were glowing crimson, and she was panting sporadically. Addie's freckles were pulsating pink, and Benji was sweating up a storm, his face bursting with red blotches.

"Ah!" she sighed as she stepped under a rock ledge. It felt so much cooler in the shade, and the clan smiled at each other in relief, mounting their horses once again. Benji rode along on Sa'ami.

"You three look *rode hard and put up wet*," chuckled Lee. Diane, Addie, and Benji looked at each other and began laughing. They were completely worn out and drenched from sweat—quite soggy looking indeed.

"Very funny!" Diane smirked, her heart still pounding in her ears from the tortuous climb.

They followed a small running creek through cool terraced ledges of tan sandstone sculpted with smooth channels and plunge pools that created a cascading bedrock water slide.

"I'd love to slide in that creek," Diane said wistfully.

"Can we?" pleaded Benji, sauntering alongside on Sa-ami.

"It *does* look like fun," she sighed deeply. "But we just don't have the time." She shrugged. "We've got to get to Indian Gardens before the sun sets."

When they finally left the narrows and reached a flat, broad expanse of soft red shales, they were stunned by a majestic view of the vast canyon.

Diane was just beginning her evening geology lesson, "That high white cliff toward the top is a rock formation made of sandstone. See the cross-bedding, Addie? That means a desert was once here. It's below the younger, moldy-looking gray layers of limestone of a deep ocean..." when suddenly her voice trailed off, and she stammered mid-lecture. "B-but the slopes are made of s-softer materials, like...shales," she sighed deeply, her eyes growing as wide as the canyon, as she mumbled on, "that erode into fringing...aprons at the bottom of buttes...monuments...and s-s-spires." She stopped, finally speechless, and just stared at the magnificence of the Grand Canyon before her.

Lee rode by, waving her hand in front of Diane's face. She didn't flinch. Not a muscle. "Diane," Lee said curtly, somewhat alarmed. "Where are you?"

She gasped, waking from her trance. "I never imagined anything could be this beautiful. There are no words to describe..." she drifted off again.

"Hmm, how can you tell the difference between sandstone and shale?" Addie asked, sincerely interested but trying to kick Diane back into her teacher mode.

"By the way they erode and the formations they make," Diane slowly murmured, finally coming around with a shake of her head, "but also by the 'rock-bite test.'"

Addie scrunched her face, looking quizzical. Diane chuckled lightly, then said in her teacher voice once again, "Take a small bite of a suspected sandstone rock, and it'll turn into sandy grit in your teeth. If it turns into a soft mud ball on your tongue, you have shale!"

Addie laughed heartily. "I want to try the rock-bite test at our next stop."

Diane put her forefinger to the rim of her white hat and beamed a radiant smile.

The clan came to a bend in the trail, and then stopped abruptly, taking in another astonishing scene. They could see the distant high walls of the upper canyons and their first expansive view of the South Rim. Intense orange and yellow rays of sunlight cascaded into the canyon, giving it a serene, enchanting glow.

"You can almost feel eternity here," Diane whispered in a peaceful tone. "It feels like what I imagine heaven would be—powerful, majestic, yet peaceful," she continued, almost breathlessly. "Reverent, you know?" She turned to Lee. "Like being in church. You almost feel God's presence here."

All at once, Mavric whinnied in alarm, jerking his head back. His eyes bulged; nostrils flaring, he reared up onto his hind legs, almost throwing Diane from her saddle.

"What in the—" she sputtered. "Whoa!" she panted, frantically clutching onto his neck.

Asazi jumped off his horse and ran back to steady Mavric. As if in slow motion, Diane saw a coiled canyon rattlesnake hidden under a sage bush just off the trail. The rattler leaped into the air, its jaws wide open and its huge poisonous fangs readied to strike Asazi's leg. Without thinking, she whipped her boomerang out from her belt and threw it with all her might directly at its triangularly shaped head.

Thud! The boomerang hit its mark, and the Grand Canyon rattlesnake fell stunned on the trail at Asazi's feet.

"We need to be extra careful now," he said, bent over panting, resting his hands on his knees. "It's almost twilight, and the rattlesnakes are actively hunting their evening meal," Asazi warned. Taking a deep, calming breath, he added, "And thank you!"

"He was going to bite you!" Diane exclaimed, exhilarated at last with her success but feeling sorry for causing the snake pain. She was known to carefully capture a guest spider in her home and release it outside. "I would want to be treated with the same respect if I were visiting its home," she would tell her brother, referring to the spider. Clearly, she was the visitor in the snake's home this evening.

"Probably," Asazi said shakily. "I didn't see it when I rode by. I must have woken it and then frightened it by running toward it. This one wasn't given a chance," he shared as he took a long stick and picked up the limp snake, moving it gently onto a boulder off the trail, "It was too startled and just reacted defensively."

Diane noted the great care he took protecting the life of the snake as he continued, "My people have observed that a rattlesnake will usually first offer a warning with a shake of the rattles on its tail. Then, if the danger persists, it will give a 'bump' with its snout, preserving its venom for hunting its evening meal. It doesn't want to waste it on something it can't eat, like a human. If the harmless bump doesn't ward off the intruder, it will bite, but discharge only some of its venom, again conserving most of its venom for hunting."

That's actually brilliant, Diane reasoned, listening intently.

"The third time it strikes, it releases all its venom. The rattlesnake will have to wait until the next day for its body to make more venom before it can hunt again," Asazi explained soberly.

I have to write that down in my field journal, she decided eagerly. "What happens if it dies?" she questioned, completely mystified.

"It goes to the animal spirit world," he offered. "We believe that animals have spirits, too, and have a special place with Father Sun in the afterlife. The Great Mother Earth gifts the animal's body as nourishment to her other living creatures."

Diane pondered these ideas, adjusting her hat on her head. At once, a dark-hooded peregrine falcon plummeted down from a craggy ledge higher on the canyon wall and flew by the clan with stiffly powerful wingbeats. Its cream-colored underbelly gleamed in contrast to its slate-gray back as it glided, occasionally dipping its upturned wingtips.

Startled by the movement, Diane glanced sideways at the falcon. Its piercing dark eyes were marked with a thick dark line that ran down its cheek to its neck, looking a bit like a dark mustache. Just then, it opened its curved beak rapidly and loudly repeated, "Kak, kak, kak," as it blinked its beady eyes and soared away hurriedly. Diane watched in awe as the widely fanned tail disappeared in the fading light, flying north to deliver its message. She removed her hat and scratched her head, whisking a strand of blonde hair behind her ear as she noticed the faint trail of glittering lights.

Remembering that the peregrine falcon was the fastest flying raptor in the world, she pointed it out to Benji. "It can fly over two hundred miles an hour," she said joyfully.

"Geez, sis," Benji mumbled.

Cautiously, they made their way west into the setting

sun, along an expansive greenish slope that flattened before them and stretched from the south cliff face of a box canyon northward to a plateau that jutted into the middle of the Grand Canyon. Its edge overlooked the Colorado River some thirteen hundred feet below.

"Green's my favorite color," Diane said briskly as they moseyed along the gentle slope of layering green and purply-red siltstone and shale. "Green for the plants of the earth," she said, swiping beads of sweat from her upper lip.

The trail turned south and headed into the large box canyon with high cliff walls on three sides. In front of them, they could see an oasis of cottonwood trees with a thick underbrush of lush grasses and shrubs, offering life-saving shade in this hot, dry environment.

"There's running water ahead," Asazi reported, cocking his head to listen. "That *must* be Indian Gardens. Those cottonwood trees can only grow where there is a good source of nearby water. This garden must be fed by springs that flow year-round," he surmised wisely.

"My people make great use of the cottonwood tree. We use the thick white trunk to make dugout canoes. Our horses like to eat the bark, and my people eat its sweet sprouts and inner bark," he continued, sitting tall on Forjon's bare back. "We even make a bitter medicine tea out of the bark."

Their hearts were light and thrilled that they had safely reached their final destination just in time for the setting of the sun. The trail meandered through the thick riparian woodland and led them under a cool canopy of white-trunked cottonwood trees with their lustrous triangularly shaped leaves.

They dismounted, not sure of what they were supposed to find there, each one prickling a little with apprehension. Every destination had its rewards, but also its surprising challenges.

CHAPTER FORTY-THREE

THE HERMIT'S CACHE

The white patchwork-quilted clouds turned yellow, then pink, in the glow of the sinking sun. Its orb was a brilliant orange, like creamy sherbet in a ruby-red grapefruit haze. The anxious clan stood still and watched, waiting patiently as the clouds parted, revealing the last ray of light to shine onto the canyon floor before them.

Nothing, Diane thought, a tad confused and disappointed. In steely anticipation, they watched as the last ray of light began to narrow...shrinking smaller...almost disappearing behind the western canyon wall. Shaded in the dimming light, Diane exhaled loudly, releasing the tension felt by all.

Just then, an old man wobbled slowly into the sliver of vanishing light. His long, scraggly beard blew in the evening breeze over his tattered, sweat-stained shirt. His holey and strapless, worn boots gave him the appearance of a hermit—and somewhat of a scary one at that.

"Who goes there?" he asked gruffly, waving a crooked cane warily at the clan of adventurers.

"Dino Diane," she said, taking an awkward step back at the

full sight of him. His pants were torn at the knees and shredded at the bottom, held up around his waist by a frayed hemp rope. His faded checkered shirt also bore holes at the elbows, and torn threads were unraveling at his turned-up cuffs. His hat was old and moldy-looking, stained from years of sweat, bent, and tattered at the edges.

Surely there must be a mistake, she whispered to herself.

"Dino Diane?" the old bent-over hermit repeated and sneered. "Sounds like you wrestle dinosaurs." He chuckled to himself.

"I have, sir," she said as she stepped forward, offering her hand in friendship.

"Have what?" he sneered again.

"Well, I've ridden dinosaurs," she clarified, standing her ground with her hand extended.

The old hermit shook his head and pondered, surveying her closely.

She smiled widely, and her friendly smile was infectious. He stepped forward and took her hand with his grimy one.

"Herbie's the name," he said, finally shaking her hand. "At your service, Dino Diane, rider of dinosaurs. You are welcomed to my humble abode." Taking off his mangy hat and sweeping it gallantly before her, he bowed like a true gentleman of old and then saw Benji, still riding atop Sa'ami. As a spasm of fear swept his face, his eyes widened, and he rubbed them roughly in disbelief.

"That's my brother, Benji, and that's Sa'ami, our friend and protector," she said, smothering a chuckle, making proper introductions all around.

"Well," he paused, "you're all welcome to my home to stay the night," he said hoarsely. "It's been a long time since I've had visitors. Your presence is honored and a nice change."

The last ray of light disappeared behind the canyon wall,

cloaking the canyon in a quiet twilight. A gentle, cool breeze blew down the canyon and softly rustled the triangular green leaves of the cottonwoods.

"What do you think?" Lee muttered as she rolled out her sleeping blanket next to Diane's.

"I'm not sure what to think," she responded honestly. "But Za-tha's never been wrong. He's never let us down," she said fervently. "He's *always* been there for us."

"We'll just have to see what the evening brings," Lee finally said, still sounding a bit doubtful.

As the horizon finally faded into a dusky purplish-blue and the first twinkling stars appeared high in the sky, Herbie the hermit went fast to work building a nice bonfire, splitting a log into tinder with an old, worn hand ax.

He then cooked up some hot rabbit stew loaded with vegetables in a big black kettle hung over the fire. Stirring the stew, he added some wild purslane to thicken and make it more nutritious, and then started the conversation.

"So, Dino Diane, tell me how you got your name," he began, "if you don't mind me asking."

Excitedly, she shared their story of the Cave of Ages and showed him the last eggshell fragment she had in her amulet. He tumbled it over between his fingers, eyeing it suspiciously.

Tendrils of steam rose from the kettle, and delicious smells filled the evening air, causing the hungry adventurers' mouths to salivate and tummies to rumble. The hermit chuckled at the chorus of tummy rumblings. With a large ladle, he scooped up some hot stew and poured it onto old tin plates, terribly worn and nicked along the edges. He then offered them each a bent spoon and an ash cake that he had made in the fire while the stew was cooking.

"Mmm, mmm, MMM," Diane sighed, "This is the most delicious stew I've ever tasted," Diane said, grinning in utter ecstasy. "And, what are these little biscuits?" she asked, chewing on one.

"Slow down," the old hermit said, chuckling again. "They're called 'ash cakes,' and I made these with acorn flour mixed with pinyon nuts from atop the rim and some raspberries offered by Asazi here. I add just enough water to make the mixture doughy and roll it into small balls in my hands. I flatten each dough ball like a tortilla and toss them in the hot white ash of my campfire until they're golden. Tasty little morsels, aren't they?" He laughed again, turning serious. "So, what brought you on this journey?" he asked, leaning into the fire, looking genuinely interested.

Diane paused, then started with the story of the saddlebags of gold, meeting Asazi and his grandfather, Za-tha, and the quest to find the Secrets of the Five Rays of Light and true wealth.

"My, my," he said finally, "I'm exhausted just listening to your stories. And you say that the fourth ray of light taught you the secret to joy?" he repeated.

"Yes," she answered, innocently and confidently.

"Would you like to hear my favorite saying regarding that subject?" he asked.

"Yes, of course," she replied briskly.

"Whenever I get worried about someth'n, I always say to myself, *Release, relax, be joyous regardless*," he recited.

"I like that," she said. "May I use your saying, too?" she asked.

"I'd be honored, little lady," he said. Seemingly aware

that everyone had finished their supper, "May I also *show* you someth'n special?" he offered, with a curiously familiar twinkle in his eye.

"Certainly," she responded, a tad befuddled.

The old hermit took a nearby stick and stuck the end of it into the flickering fire. It immediately burst into flames. The pungent odor of the tightly packed juniper bark shreds and yucca fibers wrapped around the end filled the air. The torch lit their way as Herbie led the adventurers up a narrow trail along the base of the west cliff face.

Shuffling along, the procession climbed upward along the rocky wall shaded by the stifling canopy of cottonwood trees. The heat radiating from the solid rock was held captive by the thick, leafy foliage. Beads of sweat formed across Diane's nose and dripped down the sides of her face. She was excited, with a smattering of apprehension, and *hot*. Up...up...they trudged until they cleared the canopy and looked out over the shadowy treetops.

Diane's breath caught in her throat as she gazed out at a most magnificent view of the vast night sky, filled with millions and billions of bright, twinkling stars.

Just then, the moon came out from behind a dense, drifting cloud, obscuring the stars, and all at once, filled the canyon below with glimmering moonlight that lit up the oddly shaped rock formations. It was almost...magical...like a silent cityscape made of shimmering stone buildings.

Only Diane's soft panting filled her ears, along with an occasional swoop of a canyon swallow. A lukewarm breeze brushed her cheeks, melting away any fears, as she looked down at the horses and the glowing, crackling fire below, and sighed.

Before them, the adventurers saw a small, dark opening surrounded by a wall of natural stones purposefully stacked and plastered together with mud and dried grasses. The old hermit finally stopped at the low stone entranceway.

"This was an ancient cache, or storage room, made by the garden people who once lived in this canyon hundreds of years ago. They used it to store their corn and other vegetables, like beans and squash that they grew in their gardens on the canyon floor." The hermit turned and bent low to hobble inside.

As the flames of his torch sputtered under the splintered wooden doorway, it lit up a small golden critter that was crawling on the chiseled stone bricks nearby. It had a long, almost translucent body, supported by eight short spidery legs, and a long, jointed tail that curled up over its head, tipped with a large, bulbous poisonous stinger. It remained completely still on the wall, glowing in the light of the hermit's torch. Two large, scary pincers, like those on a lobster, gave Diane the spine-tingling willies, "What is that creepy thing?" she muttered to Lee, shuddering.

"A scorpion! Stay clear of it," Lee said tensely, brushing Diane safely to the other side of the wall as she ducked under the doorway behind old Herbie.

Diane quickly followed. The rest of her clan skittered to the opposite side, avoiding the deadly arachnid.

Diane turned to make sure Benji got through the doorway safely and froze. In the flickering light, Benji's eyes were bugged wide, his mouth agape, with a startled look of wondrous surprise etched on his face. She followed his stare to the scorpion still glowing on the stone wall. Written on the wall under its translucent body was the name *Estebanico*, scratched lightly into the stony surface. Brother and sister stared at the scrawled letters, then at each other, and smiled broadly.

When they were all finally inside, the hermit held his torch high to shed light into the small stone room. The man-made front and side walls were plastered against the natural cliff face in an alcove with a low stony overhang, making the ceiling. In the corner lay a painted gourd decorated with owl feathers, and leaning against the wall was a long walking staff, or spear, that looked very old. It had an unusual metal blade attached— unlike anything they had ever seen before.

Diane glanced at Lee, questioning. Lee shook her head and shrugged her shoulders. To the right was another small opening in the wall, only big enough to enter by crawling on your hands and knees. The opening was blocked by a large stone door. Flickering on the wall next to it was the carved circular symbol of the Aszanii. A small, dark hole occupied the center. The hermit turned to Asazi and asked, "May I have your Aztec Stone?"

Asazi hesitated for a moment, then reached into his medicine bag and removed the deerskin-wrapped relic. The hermit took the pointed stone and stuck the golden tip into the dark hole of the Aszanii symbol. Herbie closed his eyes and began mouthing silently. At once, the Aztec Stone began to glow brightly, filling the small chamber with a radiant golden light.

Benji tugged on Diane's duster, beaming. The clan's eyes bugged wide when the ancient symbol moved, slowly depressing into the wall, and the stone door...inch by inch... jerkily opened.

The old hermit gestured for the clan to make their way inside. One by one, each stunned adventurer crawled on the dusty stone floor into the darkness. Diane finally stood in the black abyss with Benji by her side. She could feel him shaking with excitement, stilling tugging on her duster. "Stop it!" she whispered, taking his quivering hand in hers and squeezing it gently.

Lee and Addie stood behind Diane, breathing heavily. She sensed that Asazi was nearby. Awkwardly, Herbie made his way through the dark opening, bringing soft light into the space. Before them, the flames of the torch lit up a cavernous room filled with huge dark piles reaching high to the towering ceiling.

CHAPTER FORTY~FOUR

LOST GOLD OF CIBOLA

D iane gasped loudly as the dark cavern magically filled with dozens of lit torches. Their light fell upon piles of sparkling silver nuggets that reached the twenty-foot ceiling, overflowing onto another pile of dusty blue turquoise stones, which towered over a third pile of gold nuggets much like the gold they carried in their saddlebags. Beyond these first treasures were other heaps of nuggets scattered at differing levels throughout the vast cache. Deep in the middle of the room was a gleaming stepped pyramid covered with golden trinkets and precious artifacts from the Aztec civilization.

"The lost gold of Cibola!" Benji whispered, tugging on Diane's duster again.

"You're rich!" she exclaimed in utter disbelief, brushing Benji's hand aside. "But why?" she said imploringly.

"Why what?" the hermit responded, with a gravelly tone in his voice.

Pausing for a moment to gather her thoughts, she said, "Why would you...why would you choose to live...like this...when you could...you could live like a king?" Her words stammered out slowly.

The hermit removed his mangy hat, his grizzled hair shimmering in the torchlight, as he stared at his hat in his wrinkled hands, pondering. "And what would this wealth buy me?" he asked seriously.

"A nice house, fancy clothes, jewelry, and...I don't know," she said, stumbling again, then blurted out, "Being free! At least, that's what my father says: *money buys freedom.*"

"Don't I already live in the most magnificent home of all?" he questioned solemnly. "This beautiful canyon! And what happiness would fancy clothes, jewelry, and trinkets *really* bring me?" he continued, shaking his head. "Am I not *clearly* free?" he proclaimed with a dark glint in his sunken eyes. "Who are you to judge me and the way I live as anything less?" he finally said soberly, squinting, his piercing eyes and words penetrating deeply into her soul like a sword of enlightenment.

"Freedom," said the old hermit, "is when you love and accept yourself just the way you are, and you don't worry about what other people think of you."

Suddenly, it all came together for her. The final secret of the Five Rays of Light.

"Judge not, and that includes not judging yourself." the hermit said, putting her thoughts into words.

Diane *knew* the wisdom of these words. She *felt* their truth deep in her soul, and she realized in that moment, as she gazed out over the lost treasures, that the most important thing in life was the wisdom she had gained from these ancient mysteries. And they made her *feel good—joyful.*

"Love is unconditional," she said earnestly, remembering Asazi's words from that afternoon. "That means that love comes without judgment. I was wrong to judge you," she admitted openly and firmly, "and for that I am sincerely sorry," she finished, lowering her head and falling to the ground to sit cross-legged in front of him. Then, hugging her knees to her chest, she gazed up at him.

All at once, the torchlight flickered and burst into a shower of glittering lights that twirled around in a whirlwind of radiant light swirling from the hermit's feet to the crown of his head. The darkness in the cache was swallowed up in the brilliant light, and for a fleeting moment, Diane thought she saw the roof of the cavern disappear and the starry sky above. For the last time, Za-tha appeared before her, taking the place of the old hermit.

Behind him appeared the young woman wearing the white deerskin dress and her daughter, along with the two young men from the Aszanii village that Diane had met that first eventful night. The short one with bright yellow eyes winked at her. *Messengers!* Diane realized in that moment. *The blinking raptors!* Then she turned to Za-tha, her eyes filled with wonder.

"YOU!" She drew a startled breath, her big green eyes sparkling brightly in the glow of the light that filled the enchanted room, the source of which seemed to emanate from Za-tha himself.

"Greetings," he said, his arms stretched outward in front of him, his palms facing open to her.

Placing his two hands on her head, he said, "You have done well, Diane. You have persevered, shown great courage, and discovered the secrets for all ages, the secrets of true riches, true wealth. Each Secret of the Five Rays of Light has brought you a deeper understanding of the ancient mysteries of life. The first, 'Let *kindness* always be your first impulse.' The second, 'Whatever you *think, see, feel,* and *know*, you will create.' The third, *'Forgiveness* is the way to true *freedom.'* The fourth, *'Appreciation* is the key to *joy.'* And lastly, *'Unconditional love* is free of *judgment.'*

"The great Mother Earth is most pleased," he said solemnly. "When you *live in the moment,* you live in JOY, and you are FREE to be yourself, to express yourself in all the wonderful ways you are YOU. When you live in joy, you are free from the dark feelings of fear, hate, guilt, jealousy, or anger, and only peace remains. For JOY is the greatest feeling of all. To live in JOY is to experience true wealth. So, just BE. Be in JOY!" said Za-tha sagely.

With tears glistening in her eyes, Diane looked soulfully up into Za-tha's uniquely crystal-blue eyes. "To be in joy is to appreciate everything around you," she paused pensively. "I've seen so much beauty since I left my home in Chicago. I thank you, and I promise you, I will share my love for nature with everyone I meet, especially, someday, with my students. I will teach them to appreciate our beautiful earth and care for all of the wild and wonderful animals that live with us," she said heartily. "And I will teach them the Secrets of the Five Rays of Light—*by living them.*"

With that, Za-tha bent down and picked up four turquoise stones from the pile nearest to him. Blowing the dust away, he rubbed them against his deerskin sleeve and placed a shiny light blue stone in each of their amulets. He turned toward Asazi and, reaching into his red shawl, pulled out a Keeper's necklace of a turquoise stone wrapped in golden wire hung with braided black horsehair.

"This is for my grandson, Asazi," Za-tha said, hanging it around his neck. "Today, you have become a true zaman and the official Keeper of the Aztec Secrets. Our Aszanii brothers and sisters are here to bear witness," he glanced sideways at the four villagers. "I am most pleased, my grandson," he said lovingly, putting his hand on his grandson's shoulder.

Asazi beamed the biggest smile Diane had ever seen from

him. He stood tall, his tanned chest high, with his strong chin up, looking deeply into his grandfather's eyes—appreciative and regal. Her tears flowed easily, touched deeply by this beautiful moment.

"Remember these ancient mysteries, Diane," Za-tha said, turning his attention to her again. "They are indeed the secrets to joy in this life and are of far more value than the Aztec treasures before you. The Great Mother Earth and Za, the Sun God, have chosen you to share these ancient mysteries with the world in the hope that Earth's children will awaken and once again honor and appreciate the world that was created for them and care for it, and *all* of its inhabitants. Honor the Great Mother Earth by preserving her pristine forests, clean rivers, and wild animals. Protect them.

"Most of all, remember, when each of us learns to love ourselves, appreciate ourselves, accept ourselves as we are, and see and respect everyone else in the same light, only then can peace prevail upon the land. Teach these things to your students by your living example and one by one, year after year, they will spread like the morning sun shines its light upon the earth, a little more each day, as it turns and passes by the sun."

Za-tha bent down and kissed her on the forehead tenderly. He then turned his attention to Addie. "Animal whisperer, you are well-respected by my people. We invite you to come and live with us. Know that you are welcomed and highly valued in our village," he offered.

Addie didn't hesitate. She had come to adore Asazi and the ways of his people. "I've been secretly hoping for this invitation," she admitted. "Yes, thank you. I would love to live with your people."

"Good. Then when you have reached the end of your journey,

Asazi will bring you home to us," Za-tha concluded.

Asazi and Addie smiled shyly at each other, their eyes twinkling brightly with a spark of love that was finally being revealed.

"Tomorrow, you will follow the trail southward out of the canyon. Then from the rim, head southeast to Flagstaff, and from there south to Vulture City. There you will find the Vulture Mine Assay Office to exchange your gold into whatever you value. Stay out of sight as much as possible, and tell no one of the gold you carry. Know that you are protected, but always make wise choices."

He held out his arms to say goodbye for the last time, and Diane sprang up from the floor and gave him a long, soulful, thankful hug. Her heart was filled with immense gratitude and joy.

"I am always with you," he assured her, lifting her chin with his wrinkled finger, looking warmly into her green eyes. "So be it!" he said finally, and stepping back, vanished with the other villagers, for the last time.

Still smiling, Asazi noticed the old hermit's cowboy hat lying on the ground at the spot where Za-tha had stood. He bent down and picked it up. Brushing the dust off against his deerskin pants, he gently placed it on Addie's head. Diane and Lee glanced at each other and grinned.

Ducking back under the ancient wooden beam, Diane stood on the ledge in front of the stone cache, looking out into the shadowy canyon cloaked in moonlight, feeling at peace. A dark blue light bathed the steep rock walls, spires, and oddly shaped buttes, while a chorus of crickets drifted on the cool breeze that softly swept over her. She watched as Asazi led Addie by the hand down the trail in front of her. Diane, Lee, and Benji followed behind on the moonlit path.

Every now and then, Asazi stopped to pick several long, wide blades of grass growing along the old trail. "Bear grass," he noted out loud, handing them to Addie. "It only grows in areas where people live. A gift from the Mother."

The little procession of adventurers walked back silently to the glow of the roaring campfire. Somehow it had grown brighter and warmer than it was when they had left. It crackled and popped as they approached and settled around its blazing flames. Sa'ami and Niki raised their sleepy eyelids, acknowledging their return.

Asazi sat with the bear grass at his side, twisting it around a young, flexible sprig of willow stripped of its leaves and bark. He bent it into a small circle, six inches in diameter, and began weaving a design into the center with thin split blades of the grass. "My people use this fibrous plant for making baskets. They are an important part of our daily life. Everyone learns how to make baskets in our village. We use baskets for food gathering, cooking, as water containers, to carry and store food, even for sifting seeds—they have many purposes." Diane watched with silent curiosity as his hands worked quickly and artfully with the nimble blades of bear grass.

"You can have my share of the gold," Addie offered, sitting down next to Asazi and the sizzling rocks ringing the flames. "I won't be needing it."

"Are you sure?" Diane replied, surprised and deeply appreciative, as Addie nodded. "Thank you *so* much, Addie. We'll split it equally, of course," she beamed at Addie.

"What are you going to do with yours?" Diane asked Lee as she leaned back against a fallen trunk from a cottonwood tree, huddling between Addie and Lee.

"*Je ne sais pas!*" Lee shrugged. "I don't know! I'm not exactly sure," she murmured, looking up at the star-filled skyscape. "I want to find my papa and bring my mama and my sisters out west here…somewhere. I miss my family so much. I just don't know *where* yet." She shrugged again, taking her coonskin cap off and laying it across the log behind her. "How about you?"

"I've always dreamed of becoming a teacher, but now," Diane paused, "I want to start my own school when I grow up," she replied. "I also want to buy my family a nice home in Tempe when we get there. The Tempe Normal School for teachers is there, just outside Phoenix. I'd like to live close by."

"Won't they be surprised?" chimed in Benji, happily inspecting his new addition to his amulet as he patted the black bear.

Cuddled up next to Benji slept Sa'ami, already snoring. His thick black jowls rippled with every poof of exhaled air. Little Niki slowly crawled down from the top of the bear's head, stretched and yawned, then curled up under his bristly chin, her beady black eyes glinting in the firelight. Everyone watched as her eyelids grew heavy, and she dozed off to sleep again.

"So, Estebanico *did* find the lost seven cities of Cibola and the gold?" Benji finally asked out loud what he had been pondering most of the evening.

Asazi looked deeply into the flames of the campfire. "When word came to us that the Spanish conquistadors conquered the Aztec Empire and stole all of the gold from their temples in Tenochtitlan, my people, the Keepers of the Tlatoani Treasures, moved the gold from the seven cities to its final resting place, here in this secret cache. By the time Estebanico arrived at the Zuni pueblo of Hawikuh, in what is now the territory of New Mexico, the gold was gone, and he found only a quiet adobe village."

"But how are we seeing his name scrawled on the walls in so many places?" Benji pleaded, bewildered.

Sputtering sounds suddenly hissed from the crackling fire. "He discovered the Keepers and followed them through the Aztec Portals," Asazi reported soberly. "He found this secret cache and took what he could. That was his medicine man's gourd and staff you saw in the corner of the small antechamber. He vanished after that, never to return or be heard of again."

"Gee whiz," Benji mumbled. "And we found his saddlebags!"

"Speaking of that," Diane interrupted, finally breaking the mesmerizing spell of the story, "We'd better send a Western Union telegram to Mom and Dad as soon as we get to Flagstaff," Diane reasoned. "I'm sure they're worried sick by now. Mother's such a worrywart," she said, deeply concerned, biting her lower lip. "We'll send another telegram to our grandparents, letting them know to meet us in Vulture City."

"Not to mention, there's probably a posse or two searching the mountains and the abandoned mine for you both as well, contemplating your demise by now," Lee added. "I'm sure they spoke to the store owner and stable blacksmith and found our tracks. Maybe my papa is worried about me, too," she said dolefully.

Sensing Lee's sadness over missing her family, Asazi put the bear grass down by his side and reached into his medicine bag, pulling out some globe mallow roots and a deerskin pouch containing a few small grouse eggs wrapped delicately in cattail fluff. Addie sat down next to him with a cooking pot, a mixing spoon and bowl, a small bundle of sugar, and a water pouch. She was grinning crazily, giving away the surprise.

"What is all that for?" Diane asked.

Lee knew immediately, and smiling broadly, put everyone to work.

Asazi worked on grinding the mallow root into a powder while Benji took the cooking pot and filled it with water, placing it in the campfire to boil. Addie added the sugar and continued to stir the mixture until it became extremely hot and syrupy.

There was excitement in the air, replacing the somberness of the evening, and the sweet aroma from the cooking pot wafted upward, filling the adventurers' souls with delight.

Lee picked up a twig and broke up the end into stiff fibers.

"Diane, take this and use it as a whisk to whip these egg whites into stiff peaks," Lee instructed, handing her a mixing bowl of already separated eggs. She gave Niki the yolks, which she lapped up heartily.

When the liquid became like a syrup and the white peaks were stiff, Lee slowly poured the hot syrup into the egg whites while continuing to whisk.

"Okay, Asazi, it's ready for the mallow root," Lee said crisply.

Asazi added a little water to his mallow-root powder, making a paste, and then added it to the mixture once it cooled down. Lee gleefully whisked the ingredients together until they were well blended.

"That smells scrumptious," Diane declared, her tummy suddenly rumbling again.

Lee hastily poured the mixture into their individual tin cups to let them set and cool for a while. "*Voila!*" she announced, bubbling herself.

"Mmm, mmm, MMM," Diane sighed, shutting her eyes in delectable joy.

She dipped her bent spoon again into the marshmallow, still warmed in the center and burnt on the bottom, having accidentally placed her cup on a hot rock lining the campfire. It was fluffy light, gooey sweet, and she loved the acrid charcoal flavor mixed with the warmed sweet.

Even Benji closed his eyes and sighed an "mmm, mmm" or two, as he used his fingers to pull on the stretchy white substance, plopping it into his mouth. "This is the best treasure of all," he giggled with delight. Licking the sticky marshmallow from his fingers, he leaned back against a log, seemingly content.

White goo lined his lips, and Lee glanced at him and laughed. "I agree wholeheartedly," she said.

Everyone enjoyed the fun treat, especially Lee, who seemed to be feeling a little less homesick.

Asazi and Addie just gazed dreamily at each other, and Asazi picked up the bear grass again.

Satisfied, Diane stared at the glowing embers of the fire, enjoying the smell of burning juniper wood and pondering the fate of Estebanico and the Thorn brothers. Would she ever see them again? The fire sputtered again and burst into flames— orange and red tongues lapped at the warm evening air and then settled mysteriously down.

Life is all about decisions, she reflected. The poor, blundering Thorn brothers had everything. If they had just chosen to go south, back to Durango with their three saddlebags of gold...They just didn't appreciate what they had and wanted more...choices!

Noticing that Diane was deep in thought, Lee asked, "What are you thinking about?"

"Do you think we'll ever see the Thorn brothers again?" she asked, still mystified.

"I don't know," Lee replied slowly, "but they sure were a thorn in my side," she chuckled.

Appreciating Lee's sense of humor, Diane said, "You make me laugh, Lee Planchet!"

Just then, Asazi grunted loudly, holding up his bear grass creation in the firelight.

"What is it?" Diane asked, admiring the unusual designs and crafty workmanship. He had somehow woven horsehair into the center and attached a few ghost beads, colorful stones, and feathers. "It's lovely."

"It's a dreamcatcher," he beamed. "It's a gift for you, to help your dreams come true."

That night, instead of dreaming about a nice home, fancy clothes, and the like, Diane dreamt of crystal-clear emerald waters, red canyon walls, and leading her students down a rocky trail into the depths of the Grand Canyon. She would teach them all about the geology of this magnificent place, along with nature's medicinal and edible plants, wildlife, survival, and the ancient mysteries. She saw her future in her dreams, interwoven like the blades of bear grass, and felt richer in her heart than she had ever imagined.

CHAPTER FORTY-FIVE

THE WOLF YOU FEED

A lone black raven cawed overhead, its morning greeting reverberating off the canyon walls as it soared in large swooping circles in the hazy blue sky among the rippled white and silvery-edged pewter clouds. Another raven joined the first, and they flew in an aerial dance, their wings dipping and touching as they soared and swirled in the cool morning air.

Diane opened her eyes to the splendid beauty surrounding her. The rising sun glimmered upon the west rock wall, illuminating a massive white sandstone cliff chiseled by the same natural forces that had carved the Grand Canyon over six million years earlier. Its arching, large cross-bedded layers formed a sedimentary rock layer about six hundred feet thick, a remnant of the ancient sand dunes that once dominated the area over 270 million years before.

Lying in her warm blanket, feeling especially relaxed this morning, she heard a little scuffle by the smoldering campfire and noticed small elongated footprints in the moist silty ground next to her bedroll. Two small kangaroo rats were fighting over a piece of carrot that must have missed the kettle the night before. Their hind legs and big feet made them look like miniature kangaroos of Australia. One of them wrestled the carrot away from the other and triumphantly hopped away, mimicking their Australian counterparts.

Someday I'd like to explore Australia, she mused. "I want to travel everywhere!" she said out loud.

"I'll travel with you," Lee said, stepping into her fantasizing.

"That's a plan," Diane said delightedly, trying to imagine both of them all grown up, traveling around the world together as best friends.

Asazi came up then, holding Mavric and Bentley's reins. Addie followed behind with Forjon and Rohan.

"It's time to go!" he said somberly.

Diane felt his sadness and proclaimed, "Well, I for one am going to make the most of these last days together and have as much fun as possible." She stood up and posed, her hands on her hips, her feet apart in a firm stance of empowerment.

"Me too!" Lee chimed in, striking the same dynamic pose. Asazi and Addie just laughed and applauded. Benji snorted with giggles. Diane and Lee together took a deep synchronized bow, which made them applaud even more.

Hastily rolling up their sleeping blankets, the dramatic duo tied them to the back of their saddles and mounted their horses. Benji took his sister's hand, and she swung him up behind her onto Mavric's blanketed back, as the ride out might be too strenuous for Sa'ami with Benji's weight on him, too. They had about four miles or so to travel up to the top of the South Rim, and then would venture on to Flagstaff.

It was still chilly in the canyon in the wee morning hours before the sun rose over the eastern face of the mottled limestone which was about 250 million years old, making it the youngest rock formation in the Grand Canyon series.

They rode on a relatively flat trail of soft red sediments atop layers of colorful green and purply shales through sagebrush, yucca, and prickly pear cactus that meandered back into the box canyon. Up ahead, they could see the trail begin its ascent up an enormous pile of rock debris, perfectly positioned where the two canyon walls met.

"Isn't that odd?" Lee said, perplexed. "Look how the east wall is much higher than the west canyon wall. The rock layers don't line up."

"That's an excellent observation," Diane said, somewhat puzzled herself. She turned in her saddle and gazed back down the canyon, toward Indian Gardens. "Look at that," she said, pointing in utter amazement. "Look how this canyon stretches all the way to the other side and up to the North Rim. It must be a fault line, caused by an earthquake—like the one we heard the other night, but *this* earthquake must have been enormous. It cracked all the rock formations down the middle, violently thrusting this east wall upward," she said keenly, using her hands to demonstrate their movement. "When they ground past the rock layers on the other side of the fault, they crushed its edge forming this pile of shattered rocks that we're riding on," she hypothesized. "It's almost unbelievable. I wonder what tremendous forces *inside* the earth could possibly fracture solid rock and cause them to move."

"Pretty powerful, I imagine," Lee murmured in disbelief. "*Incroyable!*"

As they turned the corner of the next switchback, four mule deer abruptly stopped eating their breakfast and looked up quizzically at the adventurers on horseback. Their huge ears stood straight up, just like those on mules—pack animals that were part donkey, part horse. With the arrival of the giant bear, they scampered away, jumping effortlessly over large, rugged boulders up into a side canyon eroded away by the tributary forces of water.

"There must be dozens of waterfalls here in the spring," Diane commented to Lee as they sauntered along the narrow, rocky trail.

"How do you know?" Addie asked, riding up behind them.

"Look at all of those dark streaks on the cliff face," she said. "That's from running water. It must be a beautiful sight to see. I'd like to come back someday in the spring to see it," she added wistfully.

"Do you really think you'll come back?" Addie asked, gently twisting her ponytail. The hermit's old cowboy hat sat back on her head. She looked adorable.

"Yes, absolutely," Diane said confidently, smiling. "I love this canyon, and it's only a few days' ride from Phoenix. Maybe someday they'll build a railroad to the South Rim."

The colors of the canyon walls changed dramatically from the green shales to gray, then to a muted purple of a younger limestone. Climbing higher still through shades of ochre, they passed through endless layers of shales and limestones representing millions of years of time and myriad ancient environments. They rode by a huge boulder, poised precariously on the edge of the trail, balancing on its tip, looked like it could topple over at any moment and go crashing down hundreds of feet to the canyon floor.

"Look at that, Di," Benji said, looking up at the giant boulder. He had been marveling at the talismans in his amulet when the dark shadow blurred his vision. "It's as big as our house!"

As they turned another sharp switchback into a shaded side canyon, they were delighted to find numerous springs pouring water out of the rock wall. The entire cool alcove was covered in shade and thick greenery, and the horses stopped to munch on the green, succulent plants and drink from the small pools at the base of the cliff.

The adventurers jumped off their tired horses and dashed to the cliff wall, each finding their own spring. With their mouths wide open, the clan let the chilly spring water flow into their thirsty throats and all over their faces to cool their heated bodies. Addie took off her red bandana, soaked it in the cool water, and then tied it around her neck, giggling as the water dribbled down her back, chilling and tickling her.

"Hold out your hand," said Diane, with a glint of mischief in her deep green eyes.

Addie looked at her quizzically, then opened her palm. Diane placed two small rocks in her trusting hand. "Bite them— well, take a nibble," she chortled, "and tell me which one is sandstone, and which one is shale, like this." Diane modeled the bite test for her. Addie put a corner of the rock in her mouth and gently bit down on the edge, then moved the crushed pieces around with her tongue.

"It's gritty," she said, spitting it out. "This must be sandstone." She then put the other rock between her teeth and repeated the test. As she swirled the pulverized rock with her tongue, it turned into a soft mud ball and melted away. "Yuck," she said, "that's definitely shale," she said, spitting it out with disgust. Addie drew a long swig of water from her spring and washed out her mouth, pleased with herself all the same.

Refreshed, they mounted their horses and finally made their way out of the canyon and onto the South Rim. Up top, they dismounted and stood at the edge of the rim, looking back at the majestic Grand Canyon for the last time. Tears brimmed in her eyes and ran down Diane's cheeks. Overwhelmed with its beauty, she promised herself she'd come back often to explore the canyon and to remember the magical time she had there with her forever friends.

"Watch me!" Benji shouted enthusiastically to the clan. They gathered around with curious expressions and waited patiently. Benji walked over to the black bear and stood stoically in front of him, with his palm out, facing Sa'ami's moist nose. He rocked slightly on his heels and toes; the fingers of his other hand crossed behind his back. He drew a breath and whistled shrilly. Sa'ami suddenly sat, as if on command, playing along with his little friend. Excitedly, Benji whisked around behind him and fell stiffly onto his huge back, hugging his thick, bristly neck, then whistled again. As Sa'ami raised his powerful hind legs, he lifted Benji from the ground, the boy's scrawny legs dangling on opposite sides, straddling the giant bear's back.

Finally, Benji sat proudly on Sa'ami's back as the black bear paraded around the clan with Benji grinning from ear to ear. Triumphant at last, Benji had devised a surefire way to get on Sa'ami's back without the use of stepping stones, tree branches, or swimming. Once again, the clan applauded and cheered Benji's perseverance and ingenuity.

That day they rode through sagebrush and sweet-smelling ponderosa pines, listening to the loud jeering and gurgling sounds of the blue jays, dropping down in elevation to the stunted juniper and pinyon forests and then again onto the dry, open grasslands dappled in colorful summer wildflowers, buzzing with bees.

"I was thinking about the Thorn brothers and the choices they made," said Diane pensively as Asazi rode up alongside her. "Life really is all about the choices we make, isn't it?" Her soulful green eyes sparkled brightly in the golden Arizona sun.

Asazi pondered her question, then replied solemnly, "Grandfather once shared with me a story he had heard from an old Cherokee chief that was teaching his grandson, just as Za-tha was teaching me...

'A fight is going on inside me,' he said to the boy.
'It is a terrible fight, and it is between two wolves.
'One is evil—he is anger, envy, sorrow, regret, greed, arrogance, self-pity,
guilt, resentment, inferiority, lies, false pride, superiority, self-doubt, and ego.
'The other is good—he is joy, peace, love, hope, serenity, humility, kindness, benevolence, empathy, generosity, truth, compassion, and faith.
'The same fight is going on inside you—and inside every other person, too.'
The grandson thought about it for a minute and then asked his grandfather,
'Which wolf will win?'
The wise old chief simply replied,
'The one you feed.'''

"Hmm," Diane sighed deeply. "So, my thoughts and feelings are the food that feeds my wolf," she paused, reflecting. "Then, I choose for the good wolf to win in me! I choose to watch my thoughts and be in JOY, contagious JOY!"

They rode in silence, both seemingly contemplating the ways of the world and the choices they'd made that brought them to this grand adventure they shared together.

CHAPTER FORTY~SIX

FLAGSTAFF
FAREWELLS

B y early evening, they wandered into the black lava fields of numerous dormant cinder cone volcanoes that dappled the landscape like upside-down licorice ice-cream cones. Here the terrain rose again in elevation as they entered yet another conifer forest at the base of a huge conical-shaped mountain with five towering peaks.

"Those must be the San Francisco Peaks!" Diane shouted briskly. "It's a composite volcano made of five different volcanoes all in one. It's just north of Flagstaff."

"Judging by the direction of the setting sun," Lee said, "we must be along its eastern slope, and Flagstaff should be fairly close."

"I'd like to go into town early tomorrow morning and send a telegram to my grandparents, telling them to meet us in Vulture City," Diane said, sighing deeply. Thoughts of seeing her grandparents warmed her, but saddened her as well. Her amazing journey was about to come to an end, and that meant she was about to say goodbye to her very special friends, not knowing when, *or if*, she'd ever see them again.

At the base of the sleeping volcano, edged by quaking aspens and ponderosa pines, they found an inviting meadow sprinkled with purple lupine flowers and bull thistles that looked like delicate fairy dusters, and made camp.

As they entered the cozy meadow, a herd of wild mustangs galloped across the far end. Their thundering hooves shook the earth beneath the clan's feet. A tawny stallion with a flowing blond mane held his head high, looking powerful and unrestrained. Glancing sideways at the docile clan horses, he led his herd of free-roaming wild horses, descendants from those first brought to the Americas by the conquistadors, across the open field. They disappeared in the conifers as quickly as they appeared, a trail of dirt and grass flying behind them.

"That was magnificent!" Diane said breathlessly. "Did you know that primitive horses were the size of a Labrador retriever and had toes instead of hooves?" She peered at Lee, who was ogling the herd with her mouth opened slightly.

Lee ignored her, lost in a daze.

"They evolved on this continent around 3.5 million years ago and went extinct here around eight to ten thousand years ago. Paleontologists aren't really sure what happened to them. They may have been overhunted by early humans when they arrived later in the Americas, or perhaps, the climate changed turning their grass-covered steppes into unpalatable tundra shrubs," she continued, gently stroking Mavric's neck. "Christopher Columbus and other early Spanish explorers, like Coronado, Soto, and Cortez, reintroduced them to these lands in the 1400s. I just love paleontology. Its science and history, all in one."

Diane looked once again at Lee, who still stood transfixed, staring after the herd of wild horses. Her eyes were glazed, dull and stone-like. Diane could almost see her wagon wheels turning.

Under a star-dusted sky, Diane leaned back into her saddle draped over a fallen tree trunk with her field journal on her lap, eyeing the twinkling lights of the Milky Way's backbone above them.

Our last night together, Diane sighed as she sat with her clan around a crackling and hissing campfire, everyone consumed in their own thoughts. A wisp of fire smoke drifted up from the flames, momentarily obscuring the stars above.

Jotting down a few notes about the bear grass, the dreamcatcher, and wild horses, her thoughts turned to Za-tha and the quest with her clan of adventurers to discover the Secrets of the Five Rays of Light. She began writing:

The Secrets of the Five Rays of Light
1) Let Kindness Always Be Your First Impulse
2) Think It, See It, Feel It, and Know It; You'll Create It
3) Forgiveness is the Way to Freedom
4) Appreciation is the Key to Joy
5) Unconditional Love is Free of Judgment

A sudden night breeze blew over her journal, flipping the pages to her early entry regarding Za-tha's unusual questions, "Are you open? Are you ready?" From a pine branch in the shadows, an owl hooted loudly, breaking the silence. Everyone looked up and saw a great horned owl in the flickering amber firelight. His large golden eyes blinked slowly as he adjusted his talons, gripping the bark.

Diane turned to Asazi, who was admiring the majestic bird of prey. "What do you think Za-tha meant by asking me if I was open and ready?" she asked, perplexed, scrunching her eyebrows.

Asazi looked deeply into her eyes. "Are you open to new ways of thinking about the world and ready to act on your expanded beliefs?" he responded. "Your life will be filled with endless possibilities when you are open to receive all that the world has to offer. Know in your heart that you are worthy."

Diane became silent, contemplating his words.

"That is why you have been chosen by the Mother. You have a pure heart, already filled with joy, and you made the choice to be open to receive her messages. You have shown great courage, and you *are* ready, Diane," he said sagely. "The Mother is most pleased."

He nodded to the tufted-ear owl in the tree, "Have you noticed the birds of prey that have accompanied us on our quest?" he asked, raising an eyebrow. "They are messengers to the Great Mother Earth. When you were faced with dire challenges and needed protection, they let the Mother know, and she was there for you. They reported your safety as well afterward, so her heart could be at peace. Always remember Za-tha's words. The purpose of life is joy, and that high vibration will protect you, just like your white scarf provided a cloak of protection, for evil cannot exist in that energy. Only when life lessons need to be learned can it seemingly prevail, but only for that purpose, so there is always a golden nugget to every experience. This is the secret for all ages."

He paused, pondering. "I am sure they reported more to the Mother, but only she knows the mystery of those messages."

He will be a powerful zaman, she mused. "Thank you, Asazi. You will indeed be a great zaman, just like your grandfather."

Everyone nodded in agreement, and he beamed. Diane added his wise comments to her field journal to remember always.

In the morning twilight, Diane awoke early and saw Lee standing in the meadow with her hands on her hips. She turned to Diane and announced, "I know where I'm going to live. Right here." She pointed firmly to the ground. "I'm going to build a ranch and raise horses here," she said, with a determined look etched upon her face.

It was decided around the morning campfire that Asazi and Addie would remain behind with Benji and Sa'ami while Lee and Diane went into town to send the telegram to her grandparents. Lee had also decided to send telegrams to her mama back home and to her papa in Durango, in case he'd remained there waiting for her.

"We should be back in an hour or two," Lee surmised as they rode to Flagstaff in the chill of the early morning air.

They returned a little while later to find Benji and Sa'ami playing tag, rolling in the soft meadow grasses filled with wildflowers of red Indian paintbrush, owl clover, and white fleabane. Sa'ami was right at home, as this side of the mountain was still very wild and uninhabited by settlers.

Diane and Lee dismounted and walked up to the clan to lay out their plan. They all agreed that it wasn't safe to bring Sa'ami any closer to the townspeople or any settlers they might encounter along the way to Vulture City. So, it would be best for Diane, Lee, and Benji to leave now on the two horses, and only Lee would return with Mavric, while Diane and Benji would head by stagecoach to Phoenix.

Lee was hopeful that Asazi and Addie would stay on for a while to protect Sa'ami and help her build the ranch with her family once her gold was exchanged and deposited in the bank in Vulture.

"We'll stay and help you Lee," Asazi offered, looking to Addie. Everyone nodded solemnly.

"Well then, this is goodbye," Diane murmured, with tears welling up in her eyes and overflowing onto her cheeks.

She gave Addie and Asazi each a big long bear hug and could hardly tear herself away. Her heart felt like it was going to break with the pain of having to say goodbye to her dearest friends. She wiped her tears and walked over to Forjon and Rohan and gave them each a tear-soaked kiss on their soft noses, rubbed their ears for the last time, and patted them gently on their long snouts. They both tossed their heads up and down in understanding and farewell.

Diane then turned to Sa'ami and really began to sob. "I'll miss you so much," she said sadly, her heart truly breaking. "Thank you for taking such good care of us and being such a good friend to my brother." She hugged his bristly neck and kissed his big black nose. Sa'ami looked into her sad, soulful eyes and seemed to understand that this was goodbye.

Then, with huge tears rolling down his face, Benji ran to Sa'ami and jumped on the big old bear's back. He was in shock from the suddenness of the decision and wouldn't let go of his animal friend.

"I promise," Diane said to her brother, trying to comfort him, "once we get settled in Tempe, we'll come back and visit him often."

Reluctantly, Benji let go, kissed Sa'ami on the top of his head, and rubbed his little button nose against Sa'ami's moist one. As they mounted their horses and rode off to Vulture City, Sa'ami held his big paw up in the air as if waving goodbye. An obsidian tear trickled down his muzzle.

CHAPTER FORTY-SEVEN

REUNION IN VULTURE CITY

The ride would have been much longer, hotter, and dustier if it weren't for Asazi and his Aztec Stone. He surprised the travelers with their last ancient portal hidden in the abandoned pueblo at Wupatki. He also shared with them that the Aztec Trail had portals all the way to their ancient capital city of Tenochtitlán in Mexico.

"There's a secret portal in a grand pueblo in the Phoenix Valley along the Salt River," Asazi informed the wind-swept adventurers.

"Then, we can see you again in Phoenix?" Diane cried out, tears of joy welling up in her eyes. She grabbed Asazi and Addie again and gave them both a tight squeeze.

Benji joined them, giving Addie the biggest bear hug he could muster, then, standing as tall as he could, faced Asazi and raised his hands, palms forward, in the Aszanii's traditional sign of greeting and parting. Asazi returned the formal gesture and then bent over to whisper in his ear, "Remember what I said. Everyone's special. It's up to you to find out how."

How strong and grown-up he looks, Diane reflected, beaming at Benji.

They exited the Aztec Portal, leaving the cool pines of Flagstaff behind, and rode instantly into the sizzling summer heat of a vast desert of sagebrush, barrel, and saguaro cacti. *Feels like opening an oven door,* Diane considered, recoiling from the intense heat.

"Whew! It's hot," she muttered, swiping the pouring sweat from her glowing red cheeks. She noticed Benji, too, was drenched from sweat.

"Look how that tall cactus is holding up its arms like it's being robbed by an outlaw!" Benji giggled in his sister's ear as she squeezed his arms that were wrapped around her.

In the searing distance, the desert floor appeared to suddenly melt away like ice and became a shimmering mirror, rippling across the horizon. Tentacles of steam glimmered in the baking sun, rising up to grab at the legs of unsuspecting passersby. Diane squinted her eyes in disbelief.

"I think that's what called a 'mirage,'" Lee said, as Niki suddenly popped from Lee's cap and ran down her arm to sit atop Bentley's neck, panting hard. Lee took off her coonskin cap and fanned it awkwardly across her face, frowning.

"Fanning hot air is not too refreshing, no matter how fast I fan," Lee said, fanning faster.

"Hot is just plain hot. *Incroyable!*"

Finally, they could see wooden buildings nestled on a forsaken plain. Behind them stood a jagged, mountainous range and the prominent Vulture Mountain, which the telegraph clerk in Flagstaff had described to them. Dried tumbleweeds rolled in the hot breeze before them, and somewhere in the gulches nearby, they heard a coyote yip and howl. As they approached the town, a swirling dust devil blocked their path, and they waited impatiently while it slowly whirled past.

Through the drifting desert sands, they could see the wild western town full of cowboys on horseback, prospectors, and working miners walking the dirt streets, kicking up dust as they moseyed along. Mothers shuffled their children into the general store of what seemed to be a prosperous, bustling town. Because strangers came and went frequently, no one particularly noticed the four people standing on the porch of the only watering hole in town, the stagecoach depot outside the Vulture City Saloon.

As soon as they got word of their children's mysterious telegram, and later, of their disappearance in Durango, Diane's parents had come west in a panicked, desperate search for them. There they stood nervously on the wood-planked porch next to her grandparents. Mother was crying in anticipation, dabbing her eyes with her lace handkerchief. They could hardly believe their bulging eyes when their suntanned daughter and son sauntered up on horseback dressed like mangy cowboys, flanked by a peculiar-looking frontier girl wearing a raccoon cap. They were covered in desert dust from head to toe, but their parents, not caring, dashed to them.

Benji clambered off Mavric first and ran into his mother's waiting arms. Diane quickly dismounted, giving the reins to Lee to tie to the hitching post, and turned to give her father a great big hug.

"I'm so glad to see you. I just *knew* you were alright...but it's so good to squeeze you again," he said, choking back tears.

Diane released her father and scuttled to her mother, who

417

was smiling and crying all at once. "Mom, I...am...*so...* sorry," Diane whispered into her ear as she gave her a loving kiss on each cheek and embraced her tightly. "I appreciate you so much, Mom. I'll never be angry and disrespectful again," Diane said softly, her eyes becoming misty as she gently pulled the soggy kerchief out of her mother's hands and dabbed the huge tears from her worried face.

"And I'll work harder at understanding my little girl, who is suddenly...all grown up," her mother said tenderly, her big brown eyes brimming with tears of joy.

Tears now welled up in everybody's eyes as welcoming hugs and relieved pats on the back went all around. Diane turned to Lee with a big grin, her eyes beaming brightly.

"Everyone, I'd like you to meet Lee Planchet, the greatest French trapper in Colorado and my new best friend," she said heartily, making proper introductions. Everyone gave Lee a warm hug, too.

"Oh, and this is her little friend Niki," she said gleefully. On cue, Niki peeked out from the secret compartment in Lee's cap, stood on her hind legs, and lifted her little black paws in greeting.

Her parents and grandparents were astonished at first but then laughed and cheered at the sight.

"Clearly, you have quite a story to tell," said their father calmly with a gleaming twinkle in his eye, shuffling his family toward the music streaming from inside.

The saloon doors creaked as they swung open, allowing everyone to enter. The room was dusty and stuffy hot, smelling of stale beer and sweat. It was early afternoon, so the place was rather empty. A large candle chandelier hung unlit over half a dozen round tables. Oozy piles of smoky, melted wax covered the wood-planked floor beneath it. Every table and windowsill had a darkened kerosene lantern perched upon it, waiting for the evening chaos of rowdy cowboys, thirsty prospectors, and tired miners.

A few cowboys and prospectors leaned up against the polished wooden bar that ran adjacent to the swinging doors, guzzling their drinks, talking in muted tones. A large pair of steer horns were mounted on a plaque above the huge bar mirror, bracketed by kerosene lanterns on either side. Faded black and white images of happy prospectors holding large nuggets of gold from the nearby hills were fastened haphazardly to the smeared reflective surface.

Near the wooden staircase that led to rooms upstairs, a table of raucous cowpokes were playing cards, arguing over the last hand. Diane could only make out a few words through their drunken drawls, but "cheating" was clearly one of them.

A piano player in the corner tried to drown out their yelling by playing a rather loud, off-key version of "Camptown Races." The piano obviously needed tuning. Certainly, the extreme heat and dryness of the desert did it no justice.

It feels like a hundred and ten degrees, Diane thought, swiping the beaded sweat from her nose and upper lip.

Her family found a table nearer the front windows, far away from the noise, and drank cold sarsaparillas while Diane kept an eye on their horses and retold the whole story of their great adventure.

Their eyes bugged, and their mouths gaped open soundlessly through all the incredible stories of the Thorn brothers and the runaway mine cart, dancing Indian spirits, a giant black bear, riding dinosaurs, a zaman that sent them on a quest to discover the Secrets of the Five Rays of Light who turned into a golden eagle and an old hermit...and finally, she told them of the saddlebags of gold.

"Tell them about Asazi and how he turned into a wolf and Addie, who can talk to animals," Benji added excitedly.

And so, she did.

It was a good thing Lee was there to confirm her story by constantly nodding her head up and down in profound agreement. Every now and then, she would soberly add a comment or two, describing an experience from her own point of view.

"Good thing you telegrammed letting us know you were safe and going to Vulture," Father said, "I'd hate to have to explain all this to the posse that was searching for you all. We notified them immediately, so they could call off their search. They scoured the mountains for days. Your papa, too," he said, gesturing to Lee. "They were afraid you went over the edge in the mine when they found the broken danger sign. They'd never believe your tales."

"I'm sorry we worried you so," Diane said, then opened her amulet and poured its contents onto the wooden table. Her parents and grandparents leaned forward to inspect the many talismans, her keepsakes to remember each secret of the Five Rays of Light. Her mother picked up the piece of dinosaur eggshell and turned it over in her fingers.

Lee watched her run her fingers over the peculiar bumps on its surface. "Her new name is Dino Diane!" she chortled, slapping Diane hard on the back.

Diane's grandfather just beamed. He was a quiet man, a strong, hard-muscled carpenter with hazel eyes that twinkled. He was a kind man that said very little but listened attentively.

"And you rode a dinosaur?" Diane's mother murmured in awe, completely bedazzled by her daughter's bravery. Diane nodded her head.

"And Benji saved you from a giant rattlesnake with a

boomerang?" Mother asked again, stupefied.

Father just listened and shook his head in amazement and quiet admiration. "It seems you've found your balance," he said, leaning back in his chair. "It's important to read and learn, but it is equally as important to experience life by living it," he sighed, winking at Diane. "And I'm thrilled to see you two getting along so well, finally."

Just then, Benji pulled the boomerang from Diane's belt and showed it to them. "Mine's in the throat of the giant rattlesnake," he said proudly, showing them his amulet with the rattlesnake painted on it, then dropped his eyes to the table, looking wistful. "And I rode a giant black bear, too!"

Diane caught the sadness in his eyes, "That reminds me," she said, hoisting her knapsack from the floor, rummaging through it on her lap. "Here it is!" she said, as she unwrapped a brand-new boomerang from a red bandana and handed it to Benji. It was designed with black bear paw prints on the tips and several red triangular rattlesnake heads, leading up to a coiled rattlesnake in the middle, matching the one on his amulet. "This is from Lee and Asazi."

Lee grinned. Benji's eyes widened and glistened as he slowly reached out and accepted his treasured gift, holding it up for everyone to see.

"And you have saddlebags full of gold on those horses tied up out there?" her grandmother whispered, leaning into the table so no one else could hear as she avidly swept long strands of black hair salted with gray from her perspiring brow. Her dark eyes gleamed against her wrinkled brown skin.

"Yes, Grandmother, we do!" Diane said, chuckling, her eyes bright and dancing.

"Then what are we doing here?" her father said, pounding his fist on the table as he stood up abruptly. "Let's go!"

He casually escorted his daughter and Lee out the squeaky saloon doors. Everyone else was told to sit and enjoy their refreshments so as not to attract attention. He alone would accompany the girls to the Vulture Mine Assay Office. As he walked out into the intense Arizona sun, he briefly glanced at the bulging saddlebags draped over the horses' backs. They unhitched Mavric and Bentley and walked them nonchalantly down the dirt street toward the Vulture Mine Assay Office.

Sometime later they returned to the saloon with conquering grins.

Diane's mother could hardly believe her daughter's new appearance, confidence, and the dollar amount on the bank slip she handed her. Mother's eyes were as large as tea saucers, and she nearly choked on her lemon meringue pie.

"You've got to try this pie with calf slobbers," Benji said, giggling. "That's cowboy talk for 'meringue.'"

"That's for you and your brother's schooling and future," Mother said proudly, finally clearing her throat.

"And that future includes a new home for all of us," Diane said joyfully. Then, with a big smile, she announced, "When I graduate with my teaching certificate, I'm going to open Dino Diane's Adventure School of Science, where my students will learn through discovery and adventures."

Her father just smiled, knowing, indeed, that she could accomplish anything she set her heart and mind to do.

"What are you going to do with your third?" her father asked Lee.

"I'm going to buy property in Flagstaff and build a ranch to raise horses and take care of abandoned and injured wild critters. I sent wires and telegrams to Mr. Wilcox at the general store and the owner of the stables to pay our accounts in full and then telegrammed my family, letting them know that they have a place to live out west here with me," Lee answered, taking a long swig of sarsaparilla. "Asazi and Addie have agreed to stay on for a while to help me until my family arrives."

"If you need any help from us, just let us know," her father offered kindly. "I suspect we'll be visiting you often," he said, chuckling. "But, seriously," he continued, "President Lincoln signed into law the Homestead Act of 1862, outlining how a young woman and others can homestead, claiming a hundred and sixty acres of government land as their own. I will help you with your application for a federal land grant and advise you on how to be prepared for it. It'll take about five years. You'll be of age by then. That's what I do. Legal things."

As Benji stared at the saloon doors, already missing his best furry friend, he suddenly stood up, interrupting the conversation, and pointed to the depot in front of the saloon. "The stagecoach is here," he said grimly.

Everyone got up from the round table and walked briskly out the swinging doors into the hot desert breeze. As Diane followed her family, a gust of wind blew off her hat and carried it back onto the saloon floor. She turned to retrieve it, and as she bent down, she glimpsed the same beautiful woman from the train sitting alone at the saloon counter, beaming a radiant smile, her hand over her heart, patting it lightly. She seemed to glimmer in a white light with an emerald-green aura that fringed the space around her.

When Diane stood up, the woman had vanished, but the glowing green aura remained. Like a cowboy's lasso, it slowly shrank in size and drifted downward to encircle a piece of parchment with curled edges that lay on the shiny wooden bar where the woman had been. Diane squinted, looking ever so closely, and saw a small glitter of golden light within it. Next to it lay a squiggled length of rough twine dyed red.

She glanced all around the room for the mysterious woman, but she saw only the table of cowboys playing cards in the corner, gulping down Red Eye and foamy beers, taking no heed of her. In a state of wonder, she slowly approached the worn, burnished bar to see a small gold nugget on the parchment with a written message in cursive. The green aura disappeared, and the gold nugget sparkled as she picked it up and held it in the palm of her hand, reading the message:

Dino Diane,
May this last talisman always be a reminder of the
Hermit's Cache. Let it also be a symbol of hope for the
future for the earth and all its children. You have my
permission to use the cache to fund your
science adventures.
But take only deserving students who love nature and
have a sincere desire to make a difference in my world.
Wrap the hemp twine around your little finger and tie it
into a knot. Wear it always!
Anytime you want to send a message to Addie and Asazi,
Tap it against your amulet three times and say,
'Messenger, come forth!' And, I'll send a messenger to
you. My messengers bear witness that you have shown
great faith, courage, and compassion on your journey. I
am most pleased.
Always remember to live in the moment and BE IN JOY!
Love eternal,
M. E.

P.S. When you become a teacher, travel to Hawai'i.
I will let you know when you are needed.

Tears began to well up in Diane's eyes again. As she reached to touch the message, the parchment shattered, like broken glass, into tiny glittering lights that flashed for a mere moment or two and then disappeared, leaving only the piece of red twine with a frayed end lying on the saloon bar. Diane picked up the hemp twine and twisted it around her left little finger, tying it into a "message knot." She squeezed the gold nugget in her hand, then gently dropped it into her amulet, giving it a squeeze, too!

As she walked out through the saloon doors, a beautiful sun was glowing yellow through a break in the afternoon clouds, shedding magnificent five rays of light on the desert landscape. A golden eagle swooped high in the sky, engulfed in its glorious glow. In its talons was a length of red hemp twine with a frayed end. It dipped its wings and winked a piercing eye at Diane as it circled once more and then turned to the north and flew away.

Diane knew in her heart that this was just the first of many messengers to come.

Father helped load her grandparents, mother, and Benji into the musty, snug compartment of the stagecoach. Diane asked the driver if he wouldn't mind if she rode with him up front under the open blue sky.

"Why I'd be honored, little lady," said the rugged, bearded man with big warm eyes that twinkled in his sun-creased face.

Diane turned to Lee and gave her a huge bear hug with tears drizzling down her cheeks. They had become forever friends, and this parting was the most heartbreaking of all.

"As soon as we get settled in the Valley, we'll come back to help you build your ranch," she promised, walking over to Mavric to give him a wet kiss goodbye. He pressed his snout against her lips as she rubbed his ears, as if he sensed the change that was about to come. Bentley came up to her, looking for his goodbye kiss, too. It was a most difficult farewell.

"There's no reason we can't take him with us," Father declared, smiling. "I'm sure you'll need transportation to and from school. Right, Grandpa?"

Grandpa nodded, and Diane's heart leapt with joy.

Lee turned to her and hugged her back. "Cool beans," she mumbled, happy for her friend. "Don't forget, we're going to travel the world together. Remember, Australia."

Diane winked at her with a glint in her eye, "Perhaps Hawaii first," she said with a faint note of mystery.

The best friends hugged one last time, and Diane climbed up next to the driver while Lee tied Mavric's reins onto the back of the stagecoach and stood waving goodbye. Little Niki sleepily crawled out of her compartment and sat on Lee's shoulder, waving her tiny black paw.

"*Au revoir*! Dino Diane, goodbye," Lee shouted out with a sob in her voice as she dabbed away a tear from her cheek with her billowy sleeve tinged red with Grand Canyon dust. "*Au revoir, mon amie!*"

As the driver cracked his whip and shouted gruffly to the team of sweaty horses, "Giddy-up! *Vamos!*" Diane blew a soft kiss to Niki. The stagecoach lurched forward on the dusty trail, heading south to the Valley of the Sun and a new life for Diane and her family.

She looked back over her shoulder and waved one last time, shouting, "AND THE ADVENTURE CONTINUES!"

EPILOGUE

I n a distant rocky gulch, in the shade of a tall, spiny saguaro, a lone coyote howled as the stagecoach rumbled along into the desert sun, slowly sinking toward the horizon. Circling high in the sapphire sky, a turkey buzzard floated motionless on the Sonoran wind as Diane's words drifted up to the eternal blue heavens. Mother Earth listened and smiled.

"She has learned well," said Mother Earth solemnly. "Although she has more horizons to reach in seasons to come, I am most pleased."

"The seeds have been planted," confirmed Father Sun. "Now, let's watch them grow."

That night, all snug in twin beds in their grandparents' home, Diane stared up at the ceiling. "I miss the stars," she whispered, starting to fall asleep.

"Me too," Benji sighed. "It was scary, but it *was* fun. I wish we were back out there, under the stars. I miss Sa'ami," he whimpered softly.

Feeling a tug on her heart, Diane reached under her bed and dragged out her knapsack. Opening a side pocket, she removed something wrapped in tan deerskin. With a sparkle in her eye, she said, "We can see him, Benji, anytime we want."

Sitting up suddenly in bed, rubbing his drooping eyes, "But how?" Benji asked, bewildered, knowing his sister was always filled with surprises.

Diane turned up the lantern in their small room and, unwrapping the deerskin, held up a long, slender object into the light. She raised an arching eyebrow in the same mischievous way she always did when she was struck with a brilliant idea. "With this!" she said, holding a glimmering Aztec Stone.

THE END

FURTHER READING

My wish for you is that you'll be a lifelong adventurer. Experience all you can. Learn all you can. Find something that interests you and become passionate about it. Your life will be forever enriched. Then, share the joy of your passion with others and enrich their lives. To learn more about the beautiful places and topics in this book, you can visit the following sites:

Cibola – The Seven Cities of Gold by Bill Yates
Published on 04 June 2015
https://www.ancient.eu/article/804/cibola---the-seven-cities-of-gold/

Durango – Prehistory and History of the Durango Area
https://durangodowntown.com/durango-prehistory-and-history-of-the-durango-area/

Durango, CO
https://www.durangogov.org/274/History

Facts for Kids: Ute Indians (Utes)
http://www.bigorrin.org/ute_kids.htm#

The History of the Chicago River
https://interactive.wttw.com/chicago-river-tour/history-chicago-river

This Time, Let's Light a Green and Blue Fire
Jun 22, 2019
https://chicago.suntimes.com/2019/6/22/18713423/chicago-river-metropolitan-water-reclamation-district

Cliff Dwellings – Mesa Verde National Park
https://www.nps.gov/meve/learn/historyculture/cliff_dwellings_home.htm

Mesa Verde National Park
https://en.wikipedia.org/wiki/Mesa_Verde_National_Park

Art of the American Southwest
https://en.wikipedia.org/wiki/Art_of_the_American_Southwest

Lost Dutchman State Park – Science
https://azstateparks.com/lost-dutchman/explore/science

Aztec Riches – Where Was the Source of all that Gold?
https://raregoldnuggets.com/?p=5491

How to Pronounce Tlatoani
https://www.youtube.com/watch?v=__ULDONIQ0g

Zuni-Cibola Complex
https://en.wikipedia.org/wiki/Zuni-Cibola_Complex

Circlestone Ruins in Superstition Mountains
https://sites.google.com/site/boglekevin/circlestoneruininthesuperstitionmountain

Hieroglyphic Trail
https://www.americansouthwest.net/arizona/superstition-mountains/hieroglyphic-trail.html

Spanish Inquisition
https://en.wikipedia.org/wiki/Spanish_Inquisition

Pike's Peak Gold Rush
https://en.wikipedia.org/wiki/Fifty-Niner

Dinosaur National Monument
https://www.nps.gov/dino/index.htm

Bryce Canyon National Park Wikipedia
https://en.wikipedia.org/wiki/Bryce_Canyon_National_Park

The Narrows
https://www.nps.gov/zion/planyourvisit/thenarrows.htm

Zion National Park – Geology
https://www.nps.gov/zion/learn/nature/geology.htm
https://en.wikipedia.org/wiki/Zion_National_Park

Angels Landing
https://en.wikipedia.org/wiki/Angels_Landing
https://utah.com/zion-national-park/angels-landing (video)

The Grand Canyon
https://en.wikipedia.org/wiki/Grand_Canyon
https://www.nps.gov/grca/learn/nature/grca-geology.htm

Little Colorado River
https://en.wikipedia.org/wiki/Little_Colorado_River

Elves Chasm
https://www.knowablemagazine.org/article/physical-world/2019/deeper-understanding-grand-canyon

Nature, Culture, and History at Grand Canyon Indian (Indian Gardens)
https://grcahistory.org/sites/rim-to-river-and-inner-canyon-trails/bright-angel-trail/indian-garden/

Wupatki
https://en.wikipedia.org/wiki/Wupatki_National_Monument

Pueblo Grande
https://www.phoenix.gov/parkssite/Documents/PKS_Pueblo_Grande_Museum/DesertFarmers.pdf

Archeological Parks and Prehistoric Native American Indian Ruins of Central Arizona
https://www.ajpl.org/wp/wp-content/uploads/2016/04/Arch-20171114.pdf

Historic Vulture City, AZ
https://www.vultureminetours.com/

Vulture City, AZ
https://en.wikipedia.org/wiki/Vulture_City,_Arizona

AUTHOR BIOGRAPHY

D.J. Kristoff is a world traveler, adventurer, seeker of truth, and award-winning science teacher extraordinaire. The locations in her stories are real. The science and history are real. She earned the nickname Dino Diane while on a dinosaur dig with the Museum of the Rockies at Camposaur in Montana, the excavation site of the real Dr. Alan Grant of Jurassic Park, paleontologist John Horner.

Kristoff has backpacked and rafted the Grand Canyon, scuba-dived the Great Barrier Reef, ridden a camel around the Pyramids of Giza, sailed the Nile, and explored the tombs of the pharaohs. She's trekked the outback of Australia and the tropical rainforests of Hawaii, hiked over flowing volcanic lava, gone on photo safaris in Africa, helicoptered over Victoria Falls, walked with lion cubs in the African bush, ridden elephants in Zambia, cruised the Zambesi River to witness the annual male elephant gathering, and much more.

Currently living in Fort Myers, Florida, DJ Kristoff began her education career teaching eight-grade science in Tempe, Arizona. There she founded and directed the Students for Environmental Awareness Club. She guided as many as 50 adventurous eight graders hiking and backpacking into the deserts and wildernesses of Arizona and Utah, teaching them geology, biology, anthropology, paleontology, and ethnobotany. Now, as a children's author, she inspires middle-grade students to love nature and science with her magical books.

Please share the adventures of Dino Diane, the science, history, and wisdom with your children and grandchildren in the middle-grade versions designed especially for them, **Saddlebags of Gold** and its sequel **The Secrets of the Five Rays of Light.** Sign up to be notified of the launch of the Dino Diane's Adventures Series at

www.DinoDianesAdventures.com

And the adventure continues...

Made in the USA
Middletown, DE
24 June 2021